CRUISE SHIP CRIME MYSTERIES

The Curious Cargo of Bones

PAUL DAVIS MD

Blewitt Pass Publishing

ISBN: 978-0-9885791-0-1(Paperback)

ISBN: 978-0-9885791-3-2 (e-Book)

March 11, 2013

Seattle, WA

This book is dedicated to my Mother who taught me an appreciation for writing at a very early age. Also to my sister and all the friends, co-workers & passengers I worked with on cruise ships over the years.

CHAPTER ONE

Rome
Affairs of the heart

THE LIGHTS GLITTERED in Alan's eyes as the noise washed over him. He hated sitting at the head table, yet he knew that, from time to time, it was part of his required duties. His black Tuxedo still looked trim on him, and he had been told over the years that tuxes made him look 'sharp' in the eyes of the crowd.

Alan Mayhew considered that, even though he had always been more comfortable in slacks and a white shirt unbuttoned at the top – the usual casual-yet-smart attire of a respected crewmember aboard the ship – he actually *liked* dressing up and wearing his official regalia. After all, he was the ship's doctor, Alan Mayhew MD of the Gold Cruise experience, and once in a while he had to sit at the head table and carry the conversation with some of the captain's guests.

It turned out the captain's welcome dinner had, literally, started with a bang. A raft of the on board fireworks had been fired as soon as the cruise liner was safely out of territorial waters, coinciding nicely with the captain's welcome dinner.

Alan was glad to see that everyone enjoyed it equally – it was always a treat to put on a bit of a show for the clientele, and this year the ship's crew had been sensitive enough not to buy any of the thunderous fireworks, sticking to the less invasive whizzing rockets.

Over his many years as a doctor-on-board he had seen quite a few cases of fright and shock as some of the elderly passengers didn't take too kindly to fireworks.

Alan was always on the case when it came to noticing things like that. It was his job after all, and he had come to respect his own careful diligence when it came to noting which events would be hazardous or threatening for the crew.

After the fireworks, the passengers – all two hundred and fifty of them – had started filtering through to the main dining hall that sat high in the centre of this floating city, accompanied by the sounds of Brett Jarulcho, a fairly notable jazz singer who entertained them with his band, as they found their seats.

The main dining hall was decked out like a grand ballroom, reminiscent of the 1920's or 40's eras. Sweeping lines of glittering glass stretched to the impressive chandeliers in the high ceilings, while the walls dripped with heavy red sashes accented with exquisite gold trim.

Each table had artful lamp stands, securely bolted in place, casting pools of light over the many shimmering dresses and dinner jackets that graced the evening's entertainment.

The walls to the rooms were parsimoniously decorated with tropical plants, which owed their luxuriant cascading foliage, descending nearly to the parquet floor, to the care and attention of teams of ship stewards. They always reminded Alan somewhat of that science fiction movie, *The Triffids* as they leered over the guests' tables. Alan suppressed a wry chuckle as his mind indulged in a flight of fancy with the plants suddenly bursting to life in an attempt to eat the passengers.

Tonight it appeared most would not have even noticed, as they were enthralled by the wonder and spectacle of the night, the smooth voice of Jerulcho, and the dazzle of the Gold Cruise experience.

"Spotted your first one yet?" said a voice at his elbow. Alan turned his head to see the round face of the ship's navigator, and second-in-chief command, Officer George Alleyway – smiling as usual – indicating the throng of passengers ahead of them with a conspiratorial wink.

"My first what?" Alan inquired with a raised eyebrow, knowing that George could be referring to any number of things and not really wishing to be drawn into many of them.

"Your first case. The first patient; the unlucky omen, my old boy, of course." George clapped him on the back as he sat in the currently vacant seat beside him.

There was a tradition amongst the crews of many cruise liners that the first injury aboard a vessel was known as the *Albatross*, after the epic poem *The Rhyme of the Ancient Mariner,* and it was often viewed with a degree of superstition even aboard the well-established and modern vessels such as the cruise liners that roamed the high seas.

Alan knew the custom. The first injury would generally be an indication of the voyage to come. If it was a bad one it could cast a doom-laden pall over the whole cruise for the crew.

But Alan, as a physician of long standing, was not a naturally superstitious man. He had spent far too long dealing with all of life's quirky maladies and unexpected events to be that fearful of the unknown. He might have been a dreamer and an idealist, but he was also, above all things, pragmatic when it came to these matters. Besides, he knew that George Alleyway was only trying to spook him on the first day – another fine tradition.

"Did you know, George, that most of the time in my experience the very first injury is usually presented in the first couple of hours of a ship setting sail?" George looked puzzled if not shocked. "Usually seasickness, or knocks and scrapes before people find their sea legs are the first injuries or illnesses that I have to deal with – nothing extraordinary about those." He paused. "Or you get the ones who seemed never to have boarded at all and are simply fearful of their surroundings in the absence of any landmark on the horizon." Alan grinned as he made a *splat* motion of one hand falling onto the table with a dead stop.

"Um...what?" the navigator asked, visibly at a loss to understand what Alan had just described.

"Oh yes, people dropping down right on the gangplank or the archway into the cruise liner. Happens more often than you think; trips, falls, and sudden heart attacks." Alan enjoyed describing the misadventures, watching George's face flush from red to a pale pink.

"In fact," he went on, "you're looking a bit peaky yourself. Are you feeling quite all right?"

George swallowed and wiped his brow. Alan laughed. Now it was his turn to clap his friend on the back.

"Don't worry, George, you can't spook a ship's doctor, we have *seen it all*, believe me."

At that point George realized he was being had and laughed along with the doctor and calm was restored once more. The ship's navigator then began filling the good doctor in on all the gossip while he had been away. Alan listened, taking a sip or two from his glass of red wine.

Alan liked the ship's navigator – these days they were of a very young, earnest sort, fresh out of college with next to no experience, but Alleyway was different. He was a veteran of several cruise liners, and he had made his way around the world many, many times. He assumed he was like himself, another traveling spirit, at home on the waves and always excited about the next port. To look at him, George was a large, somewhat flabby man with that jovial air of the Boston Irish.

"...and so," George concluded his story, "*that* was why the cook came in late every shift. He was asked to leave at the next port."

Alan chuckled and relaxed a bit. Despite all the high pomp

and circumstance it was good to be back on the cruise again – much better than that disastrous holiday he'd just had. He shuddered at the mere thought of it.

He was a strange sort of man, he guessed; he liked working the cruises, and he liked seeing the parade of humanity and humor that was presented to him on a near daily basis.

The band started up again and the singer's voice drifted over the crowd as Jerulcho launched into *Fly Me to the Moon* with its accompanying tinkle of piano and double bass. You could almost see the effect he was having on the crowd from the head table. The whole atmosphere of the night loosened and a hushed calm descended on everybody. *Yes,* Alan Mayhew thought, *being a doctor aboard a cruise liner wasn't so bad after all...*

The ocean going Gold Cruise Liner, the *Ocean Quest* had left the port of Rome earlier that day with its attendant crews and full complement of passengers. Crewmembers who had not been aboard its outward passage had hurried to the port of Rome, catching planes, trains and cabs to get to the docks in time for the debriefs that started every new contract.

There was always an air of excitement when a new Cruise schedule was first underway, even though many of the hands aboard deck had been manning the vessel for months by now.

Cruise ships operated a rotating policy of many of the non-essential staff coming in and out of contract during their never-ceasing journeys circumnavigating the globe. So, it was quite possible for a crewmember to serve a ten-month contract traveling back and forth from the Mediterranean to Florida, and then rejoin the same vessel months later at Mumbai.

There were also and nearly always new crewmembers, especially below deck amongst the stewards, porters, luggage men and the kitchen crews. This created a constant lively air in the community of a cruise liner, a place of brief, passing but intense friendships and seafaring romances, a fact that Alan knew only too well.

Even though the Company frowned upon romances between crew and passengers, which could ultimately get you kicked off a cruise ship by the Staff Captain, romances between crewmembers certainly did exist and, although not encouraged, it was a well-known fact that once at sea *anything* could happen.

In Alan's mind this cruise would probably be no different, there would be brief romances, arguments, friendships forged forever – or at least until the next port – there would be affairs, fights and a few drunken accidents. *That was all a part of the "fun of the ride,"* he mused.

Alan didn't quite understand why normal people went on cruises and immediately seemed to throw away all of their previous values and inhibitions. Quaint, sane-appearing people suddenly seemed to become wild things, debutantes, and "enfant terrible" when they took to the seas. The doc surmised that it was probably ever thus; the Sea has always provided a strange, shifting landscape for all sorts of human dramas to play out, and none quite as odd as the man approaching him now – Captain Halvorsen.

The captain wore his best white and gold uniform for the night, although Alan knew the captain had several, so he could maintain an aura of power throughout his contract on the cruise, and he looked resplendent as he always did. His salt and pepper hair and chiseled jaw line gave him a distinguished, commanding air as he spread his grin across their corner of the table.

"Well, gentlemen, the night is young, everything is ship shape and Bristol fashion, and, might I remind you – *we* are not in our graves yet."

Alan inwardly grimaced, Captain Halvorsen was always like this, ebullient, generous, and a veritable force of nature, difficult to swallow sometimes, but the doc knew that at least half of it was a carefully constructed act. After all, the captain had to be the beating heart of the ship, and command respect and awe from those around him.

"So, what do you say, gentlemen – shall we venture?" he swept a hand down from the head table and out into the ballroom. "You know that it's better to be seen to mingle." He grinned, tipping his captain's cap at the ooh'ing and aah'ing crowds.

And I bet there are a few you want to mingle with. Alan thought with a dry smile, accepting the captain's invitation as he descended to the floor.

Most of the crewmembers hate doing this, the meet-and-greet necessary aboard a cruise liner, but Alan found it positively, and constantly fascinating. There was every type of humanity aboard a cruise liner; it was in fact a microcosm of society at large and provided the best laboratory for study of the human psyche and relationships.

"Ah my." the captain muttered, as his eyes goggled at the site of two elegantly dressed young women. Alan sighed and rolled his eyes, now he appreciated the sight, but sometimes he tried to think with ... *higher* areas of his body.

These two lovely visions were one of the classic types of people that you commonly got aboard a cruise. They were probably members of the ND club (the Newly Divorced), or the *Roos* (the name the crew gave to RW's, or Rich Wives). A Gold Cruise ship like the *Ocean Quest* attracted a lot of different types of people, but among these financially higher echelons of society, there were some definite types of people that you met again and again.

There were the armies of the Golden Oldies, finally enjoying their freedom from work and family, with their stiff-lipped husbands sporting silver hair and being herded by their diminutive wives. There were the *newlyweds,* who floated along in clouds of their own mutual fascination, the ND's who characteristically wore tight and flashy clothes, desperate to regain their dignity, their lives and not least their lust. Some of these are known as 'silverbacks' due to their hair color (not uncommon in 60 year olds) and their penchant for 40-year-old men.

A smaller group were the *lizards* as Alan had come to affectionately name them – middle aged men who either themselves were divorced or who had never managed to marry, and saw the cruise as their chance to capture a rich wife, and to sponge off her money for at least the immediate future.

Although not many on Gold Lines, there were families of bedraggled parents trying to shepherd their brightly colored and riotous offspring, and then, finally there was the *rich wives.*

The two *Roos,* toward which the captain was steering his stride, taking Alan along with him in his wake like a buoy, were stereotypical. They were probably the semi-neglected wives of entrepreneurial businessmen, each a CEO in their respective firm, or perhaps they were the forgotten spouses of successful sportsmen, who went on a cruise with their girlfriends to achieve a little bit of revenge. They were rich and favored, and they knew it.

"Good evening ladies." Captain Halvorsen said, with one of his winning smiles. "I trust you are enjoying yourselves?"

The *Roo's* giggled and made the introductions. The first, Debbie, was a stunning blonde bombshell in her mid-to-late-thirties, a deeply tanned skin owing itself to many, many hard hours of work on the sun bed. She had a subtly hawkish face, with a nose and mouth, which could only have been the result of a several surgical procedures. There was a certain stiffness about the full lips, and a pout which permanently made her look as if she was slightly annoyed, or out of breath.

Tearing one's gaze away from her face, the rest of her left little to the imagination. It was a classic hourglass figure; wrapped with a black, stretch fabric that gathered itself in folds at the hip and the shoulders. Its sheer, shiny cloth, pulled tightly across her abdomen, revealed the slight bulge of her belly, until the eyes rested on the "piece de resistance" – the gigantic *presentation* of her upper body. They were undoubtedly unnatural in origin, and, Alan assumed, quite possibly had cost more than the cruise itself.

Debbie giggled and waved her champagne glass at the pair of them.

"Why hello, Captain. Is this your first mate?"

Unfortunately, her voice sounded like a cat being dragged across glass. Alan's smile froze, noticing that the captain seemed to be immune to aural assault.

"No, my dear ladies, no, this is the good ship's doctor. May I present to you Dr. Alan Mayhew MD, one of the best physicians I have ever had the pleasure to serve with."

"Oh, so you'll be the one to go to if I get a bump?" said the second lady, obviously another *Roo* judging from the gold band that graced her ring finger.

The second lady was similar to the first, but shorter and dark, whereas Debbie was tall and blonde. The vision of her augmented femininity was the almost black, russet hair – obviously straightened for hours before a mirror – underneath which was a pale face with full features. She was about five-foot-three, and Alan's easy six-foot stature dwarfed her. Her ball gown was short, simple and curve hugging, diving low in a V-cut to reveal her own twin assets. She was giggling when Alan realized that his eyes had wandered.

"Maria," she claimed, offering him her hand. Her voice had a slight Spanish or South American lilt, and spoke of hot countries, waxy trees and dusty streets.

"Charmed, my dear, and have you traveled far already?" Alan smoothly continued, being quite accomplished in meeting and greeting the richest of passengers.

"Yes, a little, we are traveling from Spain – to Rome – back to Spain and then obviously to America on this cruise."

Between he and the captain, Alan managed to find out that Debbie and Maria were wives of baseball players in Chicago – they wouldn't say which ones – and were on a round-the-world trip while their erstwhile husbands were lost in an intensive training camp before the baseball season opened again. *A Revenge Trip* - Alan laughed to himself and subtly wondered about the lives of others.

However, Captain Halvorsen seemed entranced, caught at the first gate, the younger part of Alan chimed in somewhere in the back of his mind, and he had to suppress a chortle.

Oh dear captain, a flash of a smile, a hot figure and surgically enhanced breasts and you're caught faster than a fly in a sweetshop. But Alan knew that this was all for fun and would probably not lead to anything – the *Roos* would value their established marriages with their rich sportsmen husbands too much. Enough scandal to keep the media interested, but not enough to risk losing the family fortune.

"I, uh, Captain?" Alan tried to brush in, "Captain, we really should be doing the rounds." The *Roos* grimaced; Debbie's enhanced pout taking on monstrous proportions under the chandelier's unforgiving lights.

"I'm sorry ladies, but we must spread the captain around a little bit – you can't have him all to yourselves all night," Alan joked, noting that the prospect suddenly seemed very appealing to Captain Halvorsen, indeed.

Alan steered the captain away from the honey trap and on to the next round of faces, an elderly couple who were desperate to meet the captain of a cruise liner – the other extreme of the types of passengers aboard.

These two oldies, from Minnesota, had saved all of their lives to enjoy a fabulous cruise, and were now making their dreams come true. Alan always felt a little humbled by these sorts of passengers, and made a special mental note to keep an eye on them, to ensure that they had the most comfortable trip possible.

The faces came and went – a young family, a Las Vegas entrepreneur, more golden oldies, more new divorcée's. After a while Alan's head started to whirl from all the social attention while the captain, it seemed, was just getting into his groove. He indeed was really beginning to enjoy his moment in the limelight, and enjoy the free champagne just as much. As he had always said to Alan in the past – there were, after all, some perks to wearing a uniform on a cruise liner.

Alan found it more difficult to understand someone like Anders Halvorsen than he did the older couples who saved all of their lives for their Gold Line Cruise holidays.

The captain was one of those sorts of people who thrived in the spotlight and loved the chaos of the social whirl, always managing to regain his professional composure by the morning, and attacking his job with the same single-minded dedication. Alan saw Anders as a good captain; nevertheless he didn't understand how he could stand the flatteries, the compliments, the fluttering eyelashes, and the boasting.

Alan himself held a purely watchful eye on the crew and passengers that surrounded him while aboard ship. He was not necessarily a quiet man. His friends and his lovers over the years would attest that he was a very confident man, but he always maintained the role of the reserved people-watcher than he did the center of the action. He just felt more comfortable that way. He could easily befriend anyone he met, but only let a rare few into the inner shell of his emotions.

Captain Halvorsen didn't seem to comprehend this way of being, and as a result didn't really understand the doctor. He thought that Alan should let his hair down more, shouldn't be so reserved, should, as he put it, 'chase some more tail'. Alan hadn't told him about his burgeoning relationship with Tiffany, one of the cruise directors of Gold Line cruises. He thought it was common knowledge, but the captain seemed to regard all shipboard romances as momentary flings.

Secretly, Halvorsen distrusted any romantic involvements on board a cruise, not liking how emotions got in the way of the job. He much preferred to keep it simple, not get too involved, and have one hell of a good time while doing it.

Still, this entire social whirl made Alan's head spin. It was the first big night of the cruise and everyone had the right to let his/her hair down; but the doctor wasn't really feeling it.

Begging his excuses to the jubilant parade led by the captain, he retired to the edge of the hall, to one of the glass elevators that soared up to the open top decks. He knew this was the perfect place to do a bit of star gazing before going to check the infirmary to ensure that everything was ready for the days ahead.

When he got to the traffic-flanked elevator he found it empty, which was unusual. There were almost always a few people making use of it. After all, the cruise liners were *very* busy places. The elevator itself was crowded with the grubby little handprints from the children who found tapping on the glass, at the level they could find amusement in looking out over the drop. Alan smiled and thought of how glad he was that he was not one of the cleaning staff aboard the ship.

As the elevator zoomed up, the doctor realized what was wrong. He was missing someone. He was missing Tiffany, with her sarcastic, cheery, flirtatious humor, her easy way of dealing with people, her no-nonsense approach to those that upset her. And of course, he also longed for the long swoop of her back and beautiful body.

Alan and Tiffany had only met a little while ago, and in a storm of passion their relationship had been cemented on a previous cruise, where her critical thinking had helped him discover the truth behind a curiously unpleasant event. That is *when they weren't holed up in his cabin.* Alan smiled to himself at the memories.

Up on one of the top decks Alan breathed deep and exhaled, finally enjoying his first real moment of pleasure all evening. The glow of the subtle lights interfered only a little with the sky around the *Ocean Quest* as he breathed the Italian and Mediterranean Sea air.

It was peaceful at night traveling the world's oceans. Alan felt like it was one of the best balms for the soul that he had ever experienced. Whatever your hurt or ailment was, whether it was a broken heart, worries about your life or general loneliness, going to the edge of the seas at night, watching the lapping of the dark waters, and the shimmering of the stars above, could refresh the soul.

Alan had been doing this ever since he was a young man. He fondly remembered his father taking him out on night sailing rides in the quiet waters of the sloughs in San Francisco Bay.

Alan remembered when he took his first solo sailing expedition. It was much different than when he had gone with his father. He took his small sea-going yacht way out to the northern parts of San Francisco Bay until he found a secluded cove that seemed to beg him to stay-for-awhile. Embracing the welcomed solitude, he watched the stars and sipped hot cocoa through the night.

The sounds of Brett Jerulcho below still filtered up as he launched into some Perry Como numbers, but they were more distant and competing with the chugging of the engines as the cruise liner frayed its passage through the gorging swell in a slow and measured motion.

The very first night of a new cruise was usually quiet – at least from a behind the scenes point of view. The cruise liner operated only a skeleton crew of those second-mates who either really needed all the hours they could log, or who had lost their draws in the secret poker games that occupied each night aboard the ship.

Even though it was late in the year, it was still a warm night. But someone like Alan, who had traveled the seas enough to be known as a bit of an *'old salt'* could tell the weather was changing.

Oh well, it wouldn't affect them that much since they were heading for the warmer waters of Spain, Malta then across to Tunisia, then Algeria, before the long sea journey to the Canary Islands and the

Bermuda's. Before long they would all be roasting away, sweating, and not enjoying quiet nights out on deck.

But for now, Alan breathed the cool air and enjoyed the solitude, thinking about Tiffany, wondering when he would see her again.

It was then that he heard the sob coming from beyond the side rails of the top deck. To some eyes, the *Ocean Quest was* built like a ziggurat of pristine white-painted metals, glass, steel, and iron. Layers and layers of decks rose to the sky like the ever-decreasing levels of a cake, until it reached the small viewing top deck where Alan was currently standing. It was a tiny space, with traditional wood board floors and a few powerful magnifying telescopes bolted to the guardrails. When you peered over the edge, you could see all the different decks -- the swimming pools, the central space, the ballrooms, and the table tennis courts extending away tens if not hundreds of feet out of sight.

Alan heard the sobbing again. After all, it was carried clear by the still night air. Making sure the sunk-in rail lights didn't illuminate him, Alan crept over to the guardrail, and peered over. He had been a working crewmember of enough cruises to know that there were a number of reasons for a good cry at sea, and not all were helped by a stranger's involvement. Sometimes people need to be given the space to let their feelings out, which can be difficult even on such a large vessel as the Gold Line Cruiser, given that there always seemed to be a bit of a claustrophobic atmosphere as passengers shuttled between the same spaces and events.

In fact, that was one of the reasons Alan knew that cruise directors like Tiffany worked so hard providing entertainment, activities, distractions, and enjoyment for all of their captive audiences. His heart suddenly thumped in his chest as he thought of her. The soft cries below and his own loneliness, made him even more sympathetic to the unknown griever. He leaned over the edge of the rail.

He couldn't quite see, but the sobbing seemed to be coming from the deck straight below him. It was a deck of sun loungers, which were affixed and riveted in place. Unlike the many carry-stacks of sun loungers and cruise equipment that littered the decks of a full-size cruise ship; there were many such places on a ship this size. Really only an extended balcony in between quarters, rooms, and hallways inside the vessel, the space was often used as a sun lounging spot for the quieter souls who preferred a bit of peace and tranquility.

The person below must have known this was an out of the way

place, as that deck along with the very top deck were two of the most remote spots on the entire ship, save some of the more obscure engineering rooms way below deck. Alan could now see a woman sitting right on the edge of one of the loungers, at the far end of the deck.

No light illuminated her, so he could only see her silhouette, which seemed to be proud – a strong straight back with a good posture and shoulder-length hair. The lady was sobbing and dabbing her nose with a tissue.

He was about to hail the woman to ask her if she was all right, when he heard the clanging from the door opening below. Alan lurched up again out of sight. For some reason the familiar sound of the metal door shocked him. If this was a friend, a consoler or a partner, who was he to get involved?

"No." The gruff but whispering voice of a man reached his ears.

"But…" the woman hissed back, the wind snatching at the other words so Alan could not quite make them out.

"We cannot do this," came the reply to the missing assertion, and with a sob suddenly there was the sound of clacking heels and the familiar clang of the metal door once again.

Alan breathed slowly, raising his eyebrows. Well, it wouldn't be the first time he'd unwittingly overheard something he shouldn't. Despite the liberating and exotic atmosphere on board a ship, despite its size, there really were never any secrets on a boat – no matter what size or destination.

Alan Mayhew penciled in this encounter as just another affair of the heart gone horribly wrong, or the excesses of drink and being in a strange, new environment.

The doctor thought no more of it then, not until much, *much* later.

CHAPTER TWO

After Leaving Rome
A physician's eye

THE NEXT DAY STARTED EARLY, with already warm light filtering through the porthole in Alan's cabin. The doctor had forgotten how good it can be, working on a cruise ship, waking up every morning to a fresh scene, to the gentle bobbing of the boat, as long as one forgets some of the irritations of that same job; not enough time to go ashore or explore various ports; the staff captain calling a fire drill in the middle of your rest time or shore leave; the endless officer and department meetings, the games certain nationalities of crew play to try and 'beat the system', among many others.

On this ship, his cabin was a generous one. As the ship's doctor he was lucky to have a larger berth than most of the other crewmembers, with his own en-suite bathroom, except, of course, for the other officers who all had larger cabins. He was very lucky indeed not to have to share a cabin, or have one without a window or porthole. Alan thought of this a little smugly.

Well, I have put in a lot of years of service on boats, and most have been in worse conditions than these. It's probably about time I had a little bit of luxury to myself, he thought, while he took a leisurely shower and then laid his clothes out for the day, looking forward to the new routine.

It was early, very early in fact, but Alan Mayhew was the kind of doctor who liked to make sure he started the job at a run.

Halfway through a contract it can start to become chaotic since you have to start managing invoices of supplies, checking stock and working out from which ports you can obtain the supplies. So Alan had always found that it was best to start a journey as prepared as possible.

Alan had worked on a lot of cruises, and not all of them were as efficient as this one. Sure the crew could get a little wild, and liked to blow off some steam every now and again, but their general philosophy was: work hard, play hard, and Alan could respect that.

As he ran the shaver along his neck, and trimmed the edges of his beard that was starting to show a few spots of grey, he idly wondered just what the day would bring. The first day always brought a few complaints – usually seasickness, some bumps, and lumps as people got used to being on board a ship, but generally nothing too serious. In fact, Alan thought at least George Alleyway had it right; the *Albatross* did indeed characterize the whole cruise – during the first few days you would invariably meet the passengers who would make several appearances throughout the journey. As a ship's doctor he would get to know their history, develop case files for each patient, and by the end of the trip he would know more about a few people than they even knew about themselves.

Alan reflected, in every sense of the words, you were an emergency stand-in doctor. People never want to see the doctor while on their holidays, not the normal passengers anyway, but you would have to be able to provide expert medical advice on a wide range of conditions on the spot, as it were.

As an MD he had to be much more knowledgeable than the average ER doctor or family physician. One had to be able to deal with all of their past chronic illness, passing complaints, emergent situations like heart attacks and strokes, all manner of wounds and injuries, infections: parasitic, viral & bacterial, and even – thankfully rare – terminal illnesses. He didn't know many medical practitioners who had to have quite as broad an area of knowledge as a good ship's doc did.

He put on his clothes, and as he did so, he noticed the outside seascape gently surge, rise, and fall. He was slightly surprised by it. Usually the daytime Mediterranean seas at this time of the year were as calm and gentle as a smooth blanket. Occasionally – very occasionally – you encountered a storm, but the fall crossings were generally very well timed to avoid the changes in the sea winds that raced around the continents of the world.

Mediterranean storms were terrible. He remembered a time when he was caught aboard a cruise in one of these beasts, and a shiver of apprehension ran up his back.

The warm winds stream up off the continent of Africa into the Mediterranean, and sometimes a shift in the northern colder jet streams brings it into contact with bands of lower barometric pressures. Then you get a real humdinger when the hot and the cold and the two different barometric pressures collide, creating an invisible vortex while they fight and compete.

Alan looked out again, wondering whether this time there was a looming storm ahead and decided there probably wasn't. The sky was too clear, and there were too few clouds to worry about an impending storm; the swell was just a bit high, that was all, but it wasn't at all like the last time.

Greece, 1992

They had been moving away from the port for Athens late in the evening when the storm hit. On shore, it had been a glorious, uproarious day and night, as the Mediterranean port nights often were. It was true what people said that there was something in the air down there in the hot countries. Here, everyone definitely let go of all their inhibitions and seemed more passionate, more red-blooded than at the other European and North Atlantic ports.

Some of the passengers had come back on board with a little too much, enthusiasm and good cheer from their time on shore. Even though the trips on land were often planned, and it was possible to sign up for any number of guided tours with the on-board tour manager, many passengers went native trusting their instincts in a strange land touring on their own or falling victim to the plethora of awaiting taxi drivers and would-be tour operators that are always found just outside the ship. The local taxi unions usually have a strong hold on getting a taxi right outside the ship, especially in Greece, Italy, India, and Hong Kong. A walk to the port gate will allow the passenger more opportunity to access a greater variety of tours and taxi drivers, often at a fraction of the cost of the union drivers. The downside, of course, is that the gate can be several kilometers from the ship. In some ports, one is not allowed to walk within the port – too many opportunities to place or remove drugs from containers. Of course, if you sign up for one of the ship sponsored tours, you are guaranteed that the vessel will wait for you, whereas if you 'do it on your own' you may need to race back to the cruise ship before the ship leaves without you.

That night the cruise director had hired a comedian and a traditional Greek Laika band until the next stop. Cruises can often hire lots of little acts to entertain the audience – particularly in the case of newer, idealistic companies – rather than hire just a few big name entertainers throughout the entire cruise. The Greek Laika band was a burly team of flamboyant ruffians, where the cruise director had found them; the doc had never found out and hadn't cared either. They were loud, boisterous, and noisy, and loved the idea of entertaining an entire cruise ship.

As for the comedian, he carried on with some pretty traditional jokes; the one in particular, which Alan remembered almost word for word....

"...It started out innocently enough. I began to think at parties now and then – just to loosen up and be a part of the crowd."

"Inevitably, though, one thought led to another, and soon I was more than just a social thinker."

"I began to think alone – "to relax," I told myself – but I knew it wasn't true. Thinking became more and more important to me, and finally I was thinking all the time. That was when things began to sour at home. One evening I turned off the TV and asked my wife about the meaning of life. She spent that night at her mother's. I began to think on the job. I knew that thinking and employment don't mix, but I couldn't help myself. I began to avoid friends at lunchtime so I could read Thoreau, Muir, Confucius and Kafka. I would return to the office dizzied and confused, asking, "What is it exactly we are doing here?" One day the boss called me in.

"He said, "Listen, I like you, and it hurts me to say this, but your thinking has become a real problem. If you don't stop thinking on the job, you'll have to find another job."

"This gave me a lot to think about.

At that point a roar of laughter interrupted him – Alan smiled at the thought.

When the chuckles and giggles had died down, Sigismund – *yeah that was the guy's name* – went on, "I came home early after my conversation with the boss. "Honey," I confessed, "I've been thinking…"

"I know you've been thinking," she said, "and I want a divorce."

"But, Honey, surely it's not that serious."

"It is serious," she said, lower lip aquiver.

"You think as much as a college professor and college professors don't make any money, so if you keep on thinking, we won't have any money."

"That's a faulty syllogism," I said impatiently.

"She exploded in tears of rage and frustration, but I was in no mood to deal with the emotional drama.

"I'm going to the library," I snarled as I stomped out the door.

"I headed for the library, in the mood for some John Locke. I roared into the parking lot with NPR on the radio and ran up to the big glass doors. They didn't open. The library was closed.

"To this day, I believe that a Higher Power was looking out for me that night. Leaning on the unfeeling glass, whimpering for Emerson, a poster caught my eye, "Friend, is heavy thinking ruining your life?" it asked.

"You probably recognize that line. It comes from the standard Thinkers Anonymous poster. This is why I am what I am today: a recovering thinker.

"I never miss a T.A. meeting. At each meeting we watch a non-educational video; last week it was "Porky's." Then we share experiences about how we avoided thinking since the last meeting. I still have my job, and things are a lot better at home. Life just seemed easier, somehow, as soon as I stopped thinking. I think the road to recovery is nearly complete for me. Today I took the final step... I joined a political Party."

Following another wave of hilarity, Sigismund enchained with the joke about the magician's lesson. In this routine, he pretended to be following a recorded instruction tape on how to do this magic trick where you are given "all the necessary aspects of the trick in the box". When he opened the box there was a green silk scarf and a banana. He started following the instructions but quickly realized that the *banana* was supposed to be a *bandana*.... How do you put a *banana* around your head? Sigismund's antics on stage had provoked a near riot of laughter – Alan had been sure that more than one ladies had needed a change of undies by the end of the evening.

Then Sigismund went into the joke about the magician in the bar on a ship that also had a parrot. Of course the parrot would announce loudly to all the passengers that this or that was in the left hand or up the sleeve and ruin his routine. Then when the ship presumably sank, the parrot and the magician ended up on the same life raft. The parrot then said, "I give up, magician, where did you hide the ship?"

Anyway, by as early as nine o'clock that night the Laika band, complete with the long-necked and electrified Bouzouki, small drums, mandolas, mandolins and a pair of cymbals; were roaring drunk. They had managed to encourage the entire ballroom audience to join in on their song choruses.

It was at that moment the storm hit.

Since leaving Athens, the sky had been getting heavier and darker and Alan had kept on popping his head on deck to see the racing black line of cloud signaling that a large weather front was approaching. Consequently, he had rushed to the infirmary to ensure that the nurse on duty with him that night had been briefed and ready for slips, sprains, and knocks. A good storm usually meant one or two fractured arms, ankles, and occasionally a hip, especially with an older crowd.

Going back to the ballroom, the rain was now drumming the windows heavily, and the ship lurched as the waves met the sky with its own competing forces. There was a loud 'ooh.' as the crowd roared in excitement, in unison with the tinkle of glasses as drinks slid across the tables.

Alan rolled his eyes and groaned. If they weren't careful, he would have quite a few cuts to clean up, as glasses were drunkenly dropped in the unsteady weather, followed by glasses being picked up, or stepped on. For just a split second, his mind played a movie of every imaginable horror story he might be greeted with.

"It's getting worse," a voice near his elbow said.

He turned to see Rick Hammer, an on board navigation engineer. So far on this trip, their paths had crossed only a few times. Rick himself nursed a half-emptied bottle of light lager and gestured to the Laika band.

"That's not Laika, you know." He smiled at Alan and leaned leisurely against the wall. "That is *rebetiko* – it is to Laika what mariachi is to the traditional Mexican troubadours."

Alan had raised his eyebrows, not seeing the significance.

"*Rebetiko* is the underground, rebel music of Greece. It started as a working class folk movement, and sings about drug abuse, living in shantytowns or the criminal life on the streets. A *rebetiko* band can get quite wild, and I am sure that these guys are only really getting started."

Alan looked over and saw that the Laika – no, the *rebetiko* band, he corrected himself – was now standing up and some of them were dancing for the crowd. Each shout was punctuated by a cheer from the audience, and a large gesture from the lead singer to take another drink, which he was also doing with great vigor.

The storm seemed to spur them on, as even this medium-sized cruise liner – still a giant on the waves – rolled in the gathering swell.

"Yep, *rebetiko* will get them going all right." Rick motioned towards the passengers. "I do not envy your job tonight, doctor." He laughed.

"Oh, it's tomorrow morning I dread," Alan admitted to the navigation engineer. "You would be surprised at just how many people come to the infirmary for hangover cures."

Although Alan had some remedies he had learned over the years to help people with hangovers, he went on, "You know, in over four thousand years of human history there has never been a miraculous hangover cure discovered, and of course passengers expect a cruise doctor to be able to pull one out of his magician hat, so they can do the whole thing again the next night."

Rick Hammer laughed, as he and the doctor proceeded to watch the band, while waiting for the worst to happen.

Waters off Rome, 2012

Alan shook himself out of his reverie as he packed his carry bag with all the essential things he would need for the infirmary.

Ah, he thought, *so that was when I first met that Rick Hammer character*. He shuddered to think about what happened later back in 1992, and tried to put the navigation engineer out of his mind for the time being.

He hated to start the cruise with bad feelings, and he had taken this contract especially as a way to relax and get back into the routine of a normal cruise on a vessel, which he knew, was comprised of mostly friends among the crew.

Back then; Rick Hammer had appeared a very resilient, independent young engineer with a fairly robust sense of humor. He was a naturally likeable chap on first appearances, and it wasn't until considerably later that Alan had realized just how much of a dangerous man our dear Rick Hammer actually was.

But cruises were often like that, Alan reflected as he left his cabin. You formed quick and strong friendships, and you often saw the same faces again and again if you were a 'career-man,' or someone who regularly worked on cruise liners.

You could generally split all the crewmembers into two large camps – the career cruisers and the temporaries. The career-men, like Alan were people who kept on returning to work on the cruise vessels, year after year, contract after contract. The sea was their home; it was in their blood. It was their calling. They were a grizzled and a hard-living bunch, people who had mostly seen it all, all the ports of the world, all the different types of people therein, and all that they get up to.

Temporaries, on the other hand, made up the other half of the crew. Temps were mostly younger people from the hospitality or the service sectors who realized that they could make a quick couple of grand by taking an extended contract on a cruise liner. A few months out of their lives, they get the chance to see a few ports, meet a lot of new people, and have enough money for that new car, to put a down-payment on a house, or move to a new city – if they could get past the stringent employment requirements that is.

Alan stepped out of his cabin and walked the corridors that led through to the infirmary. *Yes,* he reflected, *the Ocean Quest was a good ship.*

After a few minutes of quiet deck-time, since there was hardly anyone up and about at this time of the morning, he neared the door that led to the hall to the infirmary at the aft of the ship.

"Doc. Hey, Doc," said a voice from behind him suddenly.

Alan turned, with one hand on the handle to see one of the ship porters hailing him from the other end of the corridor. He was a young man, in his twenties, obviously a fairly healthy young man, but Alan could immediately see that he had a problem with his back, or hips. He had abandoned the mop and bucket he had been using to wash the floors and was hobbling over.

"Hi, Doctor." He took in a breath. "I'm glad I saw you. Can you help me please?"

"Of course, come down to the infirmary, what seems to be the problem?"

The porter winced and looked a little embarrassed. English was certainly not his first language, and Alan assumed that he was a temporary contracted employee picked up on one of the recent journeys.

"It's just – is it true that we don't pay for medical treatment? I work. I work for Gold Cruise?"

Alan smiled. This was a familiar question from the new crew. Yes, it was generally applied across the cruise lines that the crew's medical treatment was free, and while it was abused from time to time, as some of the more unsavory members of the crew tried to wrangle prescription drugs from the infirmary to resell or for family members on shore, Alan did find that the system by and large worked very well at keeping the crew healthy despite their smoking and drinking excesses.

"Of course you are covered, young man. Just joined the company, have you?" He ushered him into the infirmary, where Nurse Watkins was already on hand and ready for the expected onslaught.

"I think you'll learn the ropes before too long. Gold Cruise is a pretty good employer, and we can patch you up and get you back to work. Now, take a seat."

The young porter did so, with a little difficulty as Nurse Watkins started doing the inventory for the day. Alan didn't need to cast an eye over what she was doing – she had worked before with Gold Cruise and Alan had heard some very good things about her.

The young man was named Ernesto, and had been hired in Athens alongside a team of other porters, cleaners, and luggage handlers. They were the typical sorts of temporary workers: hard working, determined, quietly busy, and generally never seen by most of the passengers aboard the cruise.

Sometimes Alan liked to go down and hang out in the crew dining hall below decks, drink in the mixture of languages and hard humor that was always a refreshing change from the glitz and glamour above-decks or some of the games that were constantly being played in the officers' mess.

Alan ran the young Ernesto through the basic range of motion evaluation – physical tasks such as touching his toes, reaching up above his head, seeing how far he can turn his head and torso from one side to the other, side flexion, and the basic neurological testing to make sure no nerve roots were being impinged or vertebral collapse had occurred. The problem was relatively obvious without even the examination, but Alan wanted to ensure the damage was not anything more than a muscular strain. And just to make sure there was no game playing going on, he did some of Waddell's tests, to rule out fictitious behavior.

"So, this looks like a problem with the muscles around your spine that holds your lower back. Does it hurt worse when you turn in a certain direction?"

Ernesto nodded and held his hand up behind the small of his back, near his kidneys.

"Don't worry, young sir, it's a simple sprain, that's all. And you say it happened when you were carrying something in the hold?" Although this type of injury was common on board a cruise liner with many hundreds of tons of food, luggage, and equipment being hauled around at every stop, Alan always liked to ask.

He was passionate about people's health, about nipping problems in the bud, and believed good preventive care was the best defense against future problems. Too many times he had to treat people who had injured themselves during their lives by exposure activities like smoking (asthma & chronic obstructive pulmonary disease) or sports activities like jogging, ski-jumping, football, etc. (arthritis), and were paying for it in later life.

"Yes, it was in the hold, Doctor," Ernesto told him. "I was helping my friend out. He is Stefano who works in the luggage crew. There is this big, big crate that has come in from Athens and no one could move it and it was very late that night, so Stefano asked me to help him move it."

"Ah, I see." Alan sensed a problem. "So, you are not actually a luggage handler yourself?"

"No, Doctor," Ernesto squirmed. "I am just a cleaner. I was only helping my friend out. We didn't want to hold up the loading."

Alan sighed, considered for a second, and then smiled brightly. "Right, well, it does mean that, insurance-wise you are *not* covered if anything else happens to your back. You were doing someone else's job after all, but it is your first time ... so we can probably overlook this one thing."

Alan was a little annoyed that this Stefano or the department manager hadn't stepped in, but he also knew that everyone was pushed for time when at port. It is the busiest time for the crew as they have to unload baggage, load more baggage, food and other supplies, check reports and manifests, do the security checks, and check all the equipment to make sure it is functioning...

He understood why it happened, but if he saw Ernesto again during this Cruise with a similar injury he'll have to have a word with Captain Halvorsen about the department manager down there, and see whether things were as they should be. In Alan's experience, it was the department manager who was where the 'buck stopped. He himself was the manager of the Infirmary, so any problems with his staff of two nurses were his responsibility, and likewise with the other service departments.

"Okay, we'll put some special gel on it, and give you a muscle relaxant and anti-inflammatory for the pain." He turned to his nurse. "Miss Watkins, can you see to that, while I fill out the report?" He smiled at the young woman who was, by all accounts more than happy to help.

He chose wording that indicated that Ernesto had a sprain in his lower back 'because of work duties'... After all, he was at work, and it was because of the lack of correct supervision that he had sustained the injury.

While Alan had no time for time-wasters, he sympathized with those who were honestly trying to help out and do a good job.

There was no need for Ernesto to get into trouble, because of the manager and his friend Stefano.

When he looked up, he saw that Nurse Watkins had already had Ernesto's shirt off and was finishing applying the gel that would help the sore muscles relax. Ernesto smiled shyly at the lovely young nurse, and she returned the smile. He then suddenly blushed furiously and Nurse Watkins turned away, embarrassed.

So, we may have a budding romance here in this very infirmary, Alan thought, and chuckled to himself. Well, it wouldn't be the first time he admitted and pretended to be busy, giving the young pair a moment while the nurse administered to her patient.

Nurse Watkins was a diminutive woman in her mid-twenties with short mousey-brown hair drawn back in a taut ponytail. She wasn't slim, but she wasn't pudgy either, more like a layer of puppy fat that Alan knew looked attractive to some guys. It gave her that innocent, fresh appeal that Alan knew would have Ernesto sizzling in his boots.

"Er, thank you, thank you very much, Doctor. I won't do it again, Stefano can pick up his own luggage," Ernesto stammered.

"Oh, don't thank me, thank the lovely Nurse Watkins here – she's very good at what she does."

Both Ernesto and Nurse Watkins blushed again as they mumbled their pleasantries, and Alan stopped them by handing the cleaner his medications in paper envelopes with all the instructions printed on them. They weren't very strong, and a sufficient quantity for the next week, at which time the muscles should have healed.

"Take one of each twice a day, they'll help but do not cure. The most important bit Ernesto,"—the porter looked worried—"you must rest your back when you can. Take your breaks in your cabin, don't do overtime or extra shifts. Remember to bend your knees and let them do most of the work while your back heals. And do the same after you are healed so you don't injure yourself again. With a bit of common sense and a drop of luck you'll be fine by the weekend."

"Thank you, Doctor, thank you," Ernesto said again and hurried out.

Alan turned to Nurse Watkins, smiling broadly. "So, my dear…?"

"Kelly, Doctor, Kelly Watkins."

"Call me Doc or Alan, whichever you prefer, and I will call you Kelly, How's that? You did a very good job, and I can see that your previous recommendation is rightly deserved. You have a careful and accurate manner, well done."

"Thank you, Doc. I have worked on a couple of cruise contracts before, and enjoy the work."

"Good. We should get on splendidly then. Oh, one thing though..."

Kelly, biting her lip in acute apprehension, winced, waiting to hear what he had to say...

"That young man might need some more of the anti-inflammatory cream tomorrow." Alan put a new roll and tube on the table. "Take these over to his cabin when you get the chance tomorrow. Do it at the end of your shift, and you can leave early."

Alan grinned to himself as he turned to start doing his own preparations in the infirmary. Of course, he couldn't see as his back was turned, but he would have bet a lot of money that the young Kelly Watkins was smiling and blushing at the same time.

*   *   *

A few hours later, and Alan hadn't had much to do. He had checked the supplies and his reports. As was always the case, he had a few passengers on which he needed to keep tabs. He made a note in his notebook, which he carried around with him wherever he went, of those people who would required his attention at regular intervals. This was his 'Red List' as he referred to it mentally. He also put the important meetings and patients in his Blackberry, as he had found it to be a very good 'to do' mechanism.

On a cruise like this there were always a number of people that needed looking after, and a few – hopefully no more than one or two – who would become regulars at his office. He prided himself in knowing each one, who they were, and what their particular complaints were.

He chatted away with Kelly, finding out a bit more about the girl. She was amenable and easy company to work with, efficient and thoughtful – just the kind of colleague he liked best. So much more pleasant than some of the nurses who thought they should be doctors; usually the ones who made the big mistakes because of their big egos; or the ones who wanted to run everything and were so disorganized that they couldn't even complete the nursing duties.

As they were chatting, it become obvious why she had such glowing reviews – a story that Alan had to remember to jot down in his memoirs.

Kelly Watkins had been the nurse to the attending doctor on

this very same vessel, the *Ocean Quest*, on the previous cruise. It was the cruise that Alan himself had *not* been a part of, as he was trying to get a well-earned break on a sailing trip around Alaska and northern Canada. It turned out that the journey had not actually been as restful as he had hoped, and he was very glad to be back on board his 'home ship' after the ordeals that he had been put through.

But for now he was happy for Kelly to tell him her story.

She had finished nursing college with honors, and had worked in a few private medical firms around the State of Michigan for a few years. She had developed her experience and expertise, becoming a key worker in her last post there, and even volunteering as a medical worker at a shelter for the unfortunate people who could be found living on the streets in Detroit, a city that had in itself fallen into bad times because of the downturn of the economy and the auto industry.

After a particularly bad encounter, Kelly decided to take a break from the dreariness of the shelter work and re-organized her life such that it would afford her a change of scenery, literally, which led her to the Gold Line Cruise experience.

"So, I was working at the shelter," she began, "nights, you understand." Her soft voice washed around the room while she refilled cupboards and safe boxes in their shared space.

"And one night there was this character who came in. Old Gregg the staff called him. He had a high, whiny voice and took an unhealthy attraction to any of the female staff. I was apprehensive, as always – who wouldn't be? It was night time, and I was the only nurse there and Old Greg asked to see me."

"You should have had security with you," Alan said immediately. One thing he couldn't stand was violence or intimidation towards women.

"Yeah, well, sometimes it doesn't work out that way in the charity sector." She frowned, and then continued, "He came at me with a knife. I screamed." She paused again, shaking her head. "I managed to get a table in between him and me and shouted for help until the door was broken down by the night receptionist – a bull of a man who grabbed Old Gregg and threw he and his whining voice out of there. I was so relieved, but that was enough for me, at least for the time being. I decided to work on a cruise ship like one of my friends had done a few years before to see some new parts of the world, do some more ... work..."

"*Refined?*" Alan suggested.

"Exactly, more *refined* work. I must be the unluckiest girl alive, because when I signed up for a three month contract I had no idea my first month would be with Doctor Hauffman."

Doctor Hauffman... that name rang a bell, but Alan couldn't put his finger on it. It was a name that he had heard in the cruise line circles – another career man maybe? Someone who one of his old crew colleagues had talked about?

"Doctor Hauffman was the guy who was working this vessel before you. He was a tall, thin Norwegian man, slightly balding, specialized in osteopathy before he came here anyway."

Kelly blushed, but this time Alan could tell it wasn't a pleased blush but a real, gut-wrenching embarrassment sort of blush. She went on with her story. She had then suffered a month from hell, as she was the nurse to one of the most oily, lecherous men she had ever known. While not violent, he was certainly worse than Old Gregg.

"Dr. Hauffman made it his specialty to 'find' his patients before they even presented themselves to the infirmary."

He would attend all the formal dinners, the Captain's Ball and all of the entertainment wearing his Officer's whites. He would slide up and down the bar waiting for the right moment to strike. His victims were always the older, better-heeled sort of women, the newly divorced, or the rich wives for sure, Alan assumed from Kelly's description.

Apparently Dr. Hauffman would violently exclaim in his thick accent that an emergency was at hand. The woman in front of him was in dire risk of doing severe injury to herself unless she immediately attended his infirmary for a – and Alan could only guess what this would mean – a 'check up'.

Dr. Hauffman's story was always the same; he had spotted a small twist in their skeletal structure, in the way they moved or the way they held themselves which would turn into a serious complaint in later life. Alan had to admire Dr. Hauffman's audacity, because the 'physician's eye' was well known among all physicians, but seldom used in order to get women to bed.

Alan Mayhew had always prided himself on his ability to diagnose, but sometimes it was a power that he found difficult to turn off. Being a physician meant that somewhere, some small part of your brain was always scientifically analyzing, making judgment calls, studying the bodies and clinical signs of people around you.

Small symptoms, which others might consider nothing, a lack of breath, an abnormality in how one moves one's back, a flush of blood to the cheek or the color of the whites of someone's eyes, for

Alan could all be indicative of greater problems.

So this Dr. Hauffman was using his medical skills for his own benefit, and as the newest nurse on the ship, Kelly had to remain silent while he plowed his way through the crew and passengers, each time 'diagnosing' a patient and asking them to attend the infirmary for an 'examination'.

"Thankfully, he was rebuffed more times than not." Kelly laughed. "He was not a very good specimen of a man, you know. But with some of them, afterwards, he would tell me that he had managed to seduce a newly divorced passenger. It was always consensual, but still – very creepy."

"That certainly sounds like it." Alan laughed, feeling a mixture of horror and humor at the strange ways of some of his fellow doctors.

"In the end I couldn't stand it – I told Captain Halvorsen about it, and he ended his contract early. I understand it wasn't particularly the seducing that the captain was against."

"No, I bet not. The captain himself has been known to seduce a fair few women in his time." Allan guffawed.

"Clearly." Kelly laughed. "But I gather that him using his position as the ship's doctor was just too much for the captain to take. He was asked to leave just before you got here," she blurted, and they both laughed.

"Although"—Alan pulled a disgusted face—"I think I want to anti-bacterial wash this whole infirmary again now."

"Don't worry, I already did – twice." Kelly exclaimed.

Then she told him about an Italian customs officer that had cut his hand on one of the land tours. It required a lot of *debriding* that Dr. Huffman left to Kelly. Consequently, she had long discussions with this fellow. He told her all about the 'mules' they would spot in line at the Leonardo Da Vinci airport who had swallowed various condoms filled with cocaine or heroin. Apparently prior to getting some high-tech toilets, the officers were required to strain the contents of the bowls with cream-colored strainers. For this reason, he instructed his wife never to purchase a cream colored strainer for their apartment in Rome. Alan had to smile at envisioning the hot Italian fellow arguing the manner in which his wife would clean their toilet – *it must have been some fiery discussion,* he mused.

The time flew by as they enjoyed some laughter while finishing their drug inventory. It was getting near the end of her shift. As the ship's doctor Alan Mayhew was never officially 'off duty', but he tried to keep to regular hours while his was working on the cruise.

As the only MD aboard this ship, Alan was permanently on call, no matter what time of day or night if the case was severe enough. Most times, if it was a minor affair in the middle of the night the shift nurse would see to the treatment, take notes, and then apprise him of the developments that had occurred through the hours of darkness.

But tonight was going to be different. This was the first night and Alan wanted to be the one to do the night shift. He made it a point of always doing the first night shift of every cruise. This often translated into Alan being awake for at least 20 hours before returning to his normal routine. He felt that if he set this example to his staff, and made himself available right at the start of the journey, he would find the rest of the cruise go much easier.

He left early – around five o'clock – to see if he could rustle up a quick bit of food from the officers' mess, and unwind a bit walking on the decks before getting back to work. He stretched, and bid Kelly a good evening.

On board a cruise liner like the *Ocean Quest* there was always something to do, and one thing or another to interest him or reports to complete for the corporate office. Alan could never understand the people who came on cruises and would say they were bored. *There is always something to do.*

While turning his mind to these mundane thoughts, Tiffany burst out at the forefront of his brain to the thunder of his heart pounding. It was a pleasant sort of pain, a melancholy, which he was surprised to feel so deeply.

It's not that Doctor Mayhew was cold-hearted. In fact, he was a very sensitive man indeed, but he had certainly known love and loss in equal measure. He had even lost the great love of his life – Jo Ann. The pain of that loss still ached like a phantom limb.

For a long time he had been consumed by feelings of emptiness, feelings of worthlessness as if there was a great hole ripped through his midriff: a wound that he could diagnose but could not heal.

That was until Tiffany. She had awoken in him a new stirring of life. For the first time in a long time, his heart was open once more, and this new melancholic pain he felt at that moment was not something from which he wished to hide, nor was it something he wanted to ignore or repress in any way. This was definitely not something that made him freeze emotionally. Instead, this melancholy filled him with a sort of *good* hurt – one that promised good things to come, and he wanted the hours, days, and weeks that they spent apart to fly by at warp speed.

Alan was surprised at himself because he had not realized how deeply he was coming to love the woman. Laughing at his silliness, he found that his feet had indeed taken him all the way to the foyer where banks of phones were connected to the ship's satellite communication array. He smiled at the front desk manager, sat down at a booth, pausing for a second to breathe, and then punched her number.

It was easy to use the phones, sometimes easy to use the Internet aboard the ship. Not inexpensive at all which is why the Internet cafes at the ports were filled to the brim with crewmembers trying to connect on Skype or other Internet methods, with their family and friends. At 50-75 cents per minute on board, one's salary could easily disappear in one conversation. Alan just imagined what it must have been like for the sailors of old that would also be away from home for months at a time, long before the Internet or telephones existed – *lonely for sure*. Along with the modern conveniences, he also knew that every communication was logged by the on ship security systems and monitored by the security officer – all outgoing communications made their way to his communications screens.

Alan wasn't aware who the security officer was on this cruise yet, but generally he trusted this arrangement as the SO's were usually chosen from the private sector, ex-intelligence analysts, some of them even from naval intelligence. Many of the security officers were British for some reason, and many of the other security personnel were ex-Gurkas, the elite officers of the Nepalese army. They tended to be levelheaded, calm in emergency situations, and very good at 'sniffing out' troubles. But Alan knew that with the economic downturn, staffing for all kinds of positions onboard ship was changing. The companies were going to the countries with the cheapest labor force, and only selecting those who spoke adequate English plus other languages.

The phone beeped, tried to make a connection, and then timed out. Alan was puzzled – usually communication aboard the ship was even easier than on land as the messages were beamed straight to the satellites that hovered high above the earth. Of course, that was often the issue, if the ship was not in range of the satellite, communications could be unpredictable. Obviously, there was no need to bother with the physical phone lines and cables that were so often disrupted by wind, weather, or lack of maintenance on land, but here on the ship, you had other atmospheric parameters like sun spots to contend with.

He tried again. *Beep... Beep... Beep... Blip.*

Again the phone failed to make a connection. The doctor looked over to the front desk clerk to find the lady busily cleaning her nails, a large frizzy perm piled on her head over thick horn-rimmed glasses.

"Excuse me, ma'am?"

The front desk manager ignored him.

"Hey, ma'am." Alan called louder. This time when the lady didn't respond he stood up and walked over, forcing her to notice him.

Her nametag read 'Maud'. She fixed Alan with an icy glare that sent shivers down his spine.

"Listen here, sir, unless you're Prince Charming and you're about to tell me that my chariot awaits, I am really not interested."

Alan opened his mouth but he was so shocked he could not even articulate words. He couldn't believe the front face of Gold Cruise had just said that.

"Wait a minute, Maud, I happen to be Dr. Mayhew, I am an officer on board this ship."

At this, Maud stopped cleaning her nails, put her file down, and looked at him again in a new light. "Sorry, Doc, but the offer remains on the table. I'm pretty sure I won't be able to help you."

"What? You don't even know what I was going to ask."

"On the contrary, I do. You were about to tell me that the phone lines were down. I was about to tell you that I know. I am sorry but there is nothing I can do, and then you were about to say sorry, and then I would go back to wondering just why on earth all men are creeps."

"I'm sorry; did you say "creeps"? Have I said something to offend you?"

Maud looked at him, sighed, and rolled her eyes, her resistance lessening.

"No. Look, Hon, I know it's not your fault – you're just the closest man at the moment. You might not be a creep but all the rest probably are. I'm sorry about the phones, I've talked to the telecommunication guys and they tell me it's the weather, there's a big storm coming in soon before we hit Athens – it has completely screwed with all of our phone lines. The satellites can't receive or send signals out through the pressure front. They're doing their best trying to realign to a different satellite, but by now I am really getting quite bored with having to explain this to everyone. Happy?"

"Athens did you say?" For a second Alan had a moment of

déjà vu, of storms and crazy *rebetiko* bands.

"That's what I said, sweetheart. Now, is there anything else I can do for you, and by that I mean I don't really want to be doing anything – as my job is pretty redundant at the moment."

Apparently Maud had recovered her composure, and her sense of injustice. Alan wondered just who had riled her up like this.

"No, no, thank you, Maud. And for what it's worth, not all of us XY Chromosomes are jerks. I hope whoever it is who has got up your nose gets his due."

Maud looked at him sharply, as if he was making fun of her. Deciding that he wasn't, she smiled brightly, a broad, toothy smile that reminded Alan of a hungry Tigress.

"Don't worry, Doc, he will."

Leaving the perpetually annoyed desk clerk, Alan chuckled to himself as he made his way out to the front decks. Sometimes being in his position was a blessing in disguise. As a doctor he could sidle away from situations and the personal dramas that sometimes surrounded him on a cruise ship.

Outside, the air was heavy and the wind was indeed picking up. Above them the clouds had formed 'waves' and had dropped much lower in the atmosphere – a sure sign that a storm front was building. From past experience, Alan knew that the storm would probably be at its worst nearest to land – in their case along the coast of Greece. That was where the different thermals from the land mass and the sea would meet and whirl up into the near atmosphere, sucking the weather in towards itself, concentrating the storm, or dissipating it.

Apparently, Alan thought, *Greece just isn't my lucky spot – A Greek Tragedy is about to unfold.*

*   *   *

Later that night, Alan realized just how right he had been when he had given a second thought to the impending storm.

He spent some time pondering as the sky started to darken, and continued to get ominously darker. Across the speaker system came a ship-wide announcement that they would be making Athens docks at some point in the small hours of the morning, which was much later than expected due to the weather.

Instead the passengers would then wake up to a new port, and they would be spending a full day in Athens, before leaving the next morning. Alan whistled from where he stood, watching the computer game consoles whir and blink around him, passing in front of the video arcade and nearing the casino. This meant that their whole schedule was pushed out by a day. Usually this wasn't such a big problem, since the cruise navigators and pilots could correct the vessel's speed to accommodate for an extra day or the loss of a day. Still, it wasn't a good omen for the cruise...

Not that it seemed to matter to the casinos on board the *Ocean Quest*. The entertainment deck housed the casino on the ship, and when you entered it was like walking into an Elmore novel. The lights suddenly blushed red and crimson, the fittings changed to schmooze velvet and brass, and the blinking lights of the machines surrounded you, drawing you in.

As usual, the casino on board had opened – corporate directives insisted on getting it operating almost as soon as they left the port, since it was one of their major sources of income, along with the alcohol sold onboard in the numerous bars and ship's cafes. A bit of history revealed that back in the 1970's when Carnival Cruise line started, they were unable to pay the crew when they got into their first port. Their solution was to empty the slot machines and that gave them enough money to pay the crew and buy some diesel fuel.

The casino guys and gals were all of a certain well-bronzed, pert looking sort in their regulation red and black uniforms. The tall, athletic men were enough to deter the rogues, and to flatter the women. While the smaller, perky gals offered a bit of eye candy. Alan grinned to himself and wondered where the company got them all – the cruise lines must have permanent hiring offices in California, Vegas, Florida, and Rio, advertising for that certain 'professional beach look'.

Up ahead of him one of the guys, a broody-eyed, dark curly haired hunk, which according to his nametag was Frankie, offered him a friendly greeting.

"Hey, Doc, what brings you down here to our little den of iniquity?"

"Good evening, Frankie, just seeing how everything is around the ship. How's it looking down here? Have you heard about the phones?"

"Oi yeah"—Alan grimaced with Frankie's Bronx accent spitting the words — "complete load a crap, huh? But whatcha going to do about it?" He gave him a lopsided grin and shrugged, as if he had seen it all.

"And that's not all, Doc...." He signaled over to the gaming managers' office that was set up on a little balcony over the casino. "Boss has been told we're staying open extra hours tonight, on account of the storm. Keep people busy; keep 'em happy, that's the motto."

"Provide for every need," Alan quoted from the company manual.

"Well, something like that." Frankie laughed. "But not *every* need." He pointed over to the line of blackjack tables where there was, as it was termed in security circles, a 'situation'.

Seated at one of the tables was a well-endowed, magnificent *edifice* of a woman, and Alan recognized her sort immediately and groaned. On every cruise you have women and men like these; loud, obnoxious people who seemed to have only one thing in mind when they go on international cruises. Alan guessed a part of it could have been described as *making themselves known*, but...

This exceptionally tall woman, perhaps in her early forties, wore a black dress that hugged every curve of her body. No – Alan changed his mind – it wasn't exactly hugging, it was more like a team of structural engineers had painted it on. It was a backless dress, with delicate straps climbing snugly over her strong shoulders. One strap was adorned with an unusual arrangement of feathers and beads. Alan was no novice in the art of viewing ladies' dresses, but he couldn't for the life of him see just what was, how should he say it – keeping all of her in. And there certainly was a lot of her to be kept.

Deep in an argument with the table teller, she gestured and turned to fling a gold-adorned hand at the rest of the casino. Alan immediately saw that her hefty hand could possibly block out the light. In fact, her frontage probably had its own gravity well. Her dress extended down to her knees, and her thighs accentuating her height, descended into some of the most sadistic looking stiletto heels – the highest he had ever seen. Even from where he stood Alan could overhear some of the conversation – he cringed.

"What on earth do you mean my credits aren't good here?" the woman demanded, flicking an errant strand of her beehive hair out of her eyes. It was clear that she already had had a few too many to drink, as her voice climbed in to shout at the terrified young female teller.

"Um – it's, I mean you are very welcome here, but there is a note on your account…." She gestured to her walkie-talkie.

"You little gutter rat." the woman snapped, "Do you have any idea who I am?" Poised and ready to do battle this androgynous specimen looked as if she was about to slap the poor young teller across the face.

Alan looked at Frankie with alarm. He seemed not too worried. Suddenly Alan understood why. Emerging behind the woman were two well-bronzed, well-built casino security guards. They drew closer to her in a flanking maneuver.

"Don't worry, Doc," Frankie whispered. "I've seen this thing a hundred times before." He gave the doctor a wolfish grin.

"Sometimes the casino heavies get a bit, uh, *heavy*. Let me see what I can do about it..."

Frankie strode leisurely toward the woman; with Alan following in his wake just to see what this young man could do redress the situation. As the drunken woman berated the teller, Frankie waved off the security and coughed loudly behind her.

"Excuse me, ma'am, what seems to be the problem?"

The enraged being turned on her stiletto heels, wobbled, and her whole demeanor changed in an instant. It was like watching an avalanche, or watching one of those time-warped programs of spring breaking out in the Arctic, Alan thought. Her prodigious chest thrust out, her shoulders flipped back, and one hip poised to the side to take full advantage of her hourglass figure. Her eyes fixed on Frankie with a predatory smile.

"Why... hello, sir. Can you help me? I seem to be having a little problem?"

"Well, you know we aim to please," Frankie countered.

The woman giggled, tittered. "I'm sure. My name is Charlotte, *Lady* Charlotte Hemmingsworth." She extended her hand adorned with gold rings and Frankie took it, brushing his lips over the knuckles.

"A real live Lady, huh? No why doesn't that surprise me?" Frankie murmured, not for one second releasing her from his gaze. "It seems we have a bit of a problem here, but, if you will forgive us, I think I know a way we can work this out... *discretely*..."

Lady Hemmingsworth's eyes widened with delight, as if she couldn't believe what the young man was about to suggest.

Frankie boldly leaned in, whispered in to the Lady's ear, and then stood back. The change in her was incredible; Lady Charlotte was at first glad, then puzzled, and then a slow smile spread across her face once more.

"Why that sounds just delightful, thank you, young man." Charlotte drew herself up to her full height, her beehive appearing to grow taller. "You know, I must recommend you when I get the chance, *some* people can be so *helpful*," she said carefully, casting a catlike look over her shoulder at the young woman, before she gathered her silver clutch purse and stalked off out of the casino.

The security guards visibly relaxed, breathing out a sigh of relief, went back to their posts. The young woman teller also looked relieved and gave a 'praise the heavens' look skyward.

"Do you know what was wrong?"

The teller replied, "Lady Hemmingsworth has had a security call put out about her, *from her husband*. It seems her husband, Lord Hemmingsworth, doesn't want his wife spending all of his money in one night. She is only to have a five thousand dollar limit in the casino," the teller whispered in Alan's ear.

"Five thousand dollars?" Allan blurted, a man who knew his limits with gambling and kept to the $20 per night religiously on the few times a year he would gamble, of course not on board since the crew was never allowed to gamble on board or hangout in the casino. "I know a lot of people who would love to have a five thousand dollar limit."

"Well, she's blown it already. And on the very first night as well," the teller said with some humor, and then went back to her business.

"Yeah, we get them all here," Frankie said.

"What on earth did you say to her?" Alan inquired.

"Oh, nothing much, I just told her that there was a secret game going to happen amongst some of the *top* members of the passengers who held Diamond Plus status with Gold Cruise Line. She seemed to me like a woman who liked prestige and power." He grinned.

"Oh no – who did you say?"

"I sent her to the Diamond Plus club. I told her there was going to be a big game tonight, because the ship is late. I thought the sound of playing with the richest guy on board would appeal to her."

"Oh God." Alan started to chuckle. "And is there such a game?"

"I have no idea. Probably, maybe, who knows?" Frankie shrugged. "Let them deal with *Lady* Charlotte Hemmingsworth, and not get in the way of us poor workers down here." He grinned again and walked off to his bar, whistling a show tune as he did so.

Alan laughed at them all – at the mischievous Frankie, at the Lady Hemmingsworth, and the whole idea of the casino. It was common procedure on board for very difficult customers to be shuttled around in between decks. Even the good doctor had done it a few times, but only if he felt the person *really* deserved it.

Just then the young woman teller suddenly looked up from her table, with a worried face.

"Doctor? Doctor... quick, there's been a message on the ship's telecommunication's network to have you pick up your phone."

Alan immediately picked up the internal cell phone that he carried at all times clipped to his belt. He knew that they weren't real phones, but more just internal radiophones that allowed different departments of the ship to talk to each other. Since it had not rang, and he was pretty sure he had it turned on, he presumed that it had been affected by the growing storm outside. Alan picked up the teller's receiver to hear the message: "All decks and departments. Code Blue, indoors badminton court, Doctor Mayhew to attend immediately."

Alan groaned. There was no such thing as a "Code Blue". It was the same as when the hospital PA system said will 'Doctor Alcomb' attend room number X – Al-comb or *'all come'* – meant that there was an emergency and the doctor was needed immediately.

It was fairly common for such codes to be used every cruise. It didn't help to have the crew gossip about any major accidents, as loose lips always reached the crew in some way or other anyway.

So, with a heavy heart, Alan realized that something was definitely the matter. He got his things together and raced through the darkening storm to indoor badminton court.

CHAPTER THREE

The Mediterranean Big Sea
A case of over-exhaustion?

THE INDOOR BADMINTON COURT, which also doubled as a small gymnasium for table tennis, squash, and netball, was situated in the middle and sides of the front decks, along with the majority of the other standard gymnasium rooms. Usually a lot of the sports activities organized by the cruise director, were held on the front open decks of the *Ocean Quest.*

Alan thought, *after all it was a Gold Line cruise.* People paid and expected the very best, which meant the ability to play their favorite sports even in the horrible weather. The indoor badminton court itself was smaller than the larger gymnasium on the other side of the ship, and was generally used for children's activities.

There were no portholes in this room, lying as it did a little bit below decks, but there were strong sodium lights high up in the ceiling. Already, Alan could hear the faint drumming of the rain as the storm broke around them. *We must be nearing Athens.*

When he got to the door he found Kelly standing in front of it. She nodded to him. Alan's heart sank. They only ever posted someone at the door if what ever was waiting him inside was not to be seen by anyone else but a doctor. Pushing open the heavy door, Alan stepped inside to find one of the men from the security detail standing over the prone form of a man.

The man in question was in his mid to early forties, brown hair, cut in what would have been middle parting, with sharp features that were fairly handsome – Alan thought he looked like an actor.

"Hey, Doc," the security guard said – Vince, according to his nametag. "I don't know what's wrong with him, I checked his pulse, and well, you know the procedure. I'm not the one to call it..."

Vince didn't need to say any more, the pallor of the man's face said it all, as did the faintly bluing lips, and fingers curled slightly into a locked position. The doctor went through the motions anyway, as he had to, and noted down everything that he saw, heard or did not hear with his stethoscope, recorded, and judged.

"This man is dead." Alan pronounced, "at... eight thirty four, September 18th, 2012." He read the time and date from his watch, it was important to say and record those words as it would then provide a time-line of medical events from which he could work.

"He probably died quite a bit earlier; we have burst blood vessels in his conjunctiva (eyes), a flushed face on one side, a muscle spasm that caused that contortion in the facial muscles, and the pronounced paralysis of his fingers. It is too early to tell, but I would hazard a guess that this man had a heart attack."

"Heart attack?" Vince said. "Thank God for that. I thought it was something he ate from our great chef – looking all gruesome like that."

"Oh, that is usual for massive heart ruptures. Almost all the muscles spasm at once, causing this effect." Alan grimaced at the poor man. "Now fetch me a blanket or something, Vince. Let's at least give the poor guy some dignity."

Vince went over to the equipment cupboards where he knew he would find something that would work, while Alan kept on examining the body.

Yes, the poor man was somewhere past forty. A little early, but not unheard of for a heart attack. He was somewhat on the thin side – maybe he worked in an office, at a desk job for most of the year? Nice but not too flashy clothes, probably a well paid desk job, but not one that would allow him to keep in touch with the latest fashions. Last of all... Alan mentally wrote his checklist, no wedding or engagement ring. A man who is probably married to his well paying office job, doesn't get out too much, decides to get out for an extended cruise for the first time in his life....

"Doc?" Vince called out from the equipment cupboard. He was holding an object gingerly, inexpertly open with his fingertips. "Doc, you should probably come see this."

Alan stood up and hurried over. The door to the equipment locker had been left ajar, and, curled up at the foot of the door was a pair of sexy women's pink lacey panties. They seemed barely big enough to hold *anything*, and left little to the imagination. Alan whistled.

"So, I think I know what gave old John Doe the shock of his life," Vince said, breaking a smile that softened his features.

Alan couldn't help but see the slightly funny side of it all. Maybe our retiring, 'doesn't-get-out-too-much' John Doe had indeed been having the time of his life, maybe all *too* much fun.

"Well," Alan said, "Now all we have to do is find out who those belong to."

"What, Cinderella style?" Vince suggested. "I'd help with *that* investigation."

"Perhaps not the best way to go about it." Alan grinned. "We could always put a lost property ad, down at the front desk...?"

Vince chuckled. "What, 'will the owner of one very small touché to fit one found pink knickers please report to the Captain's Office?'"

"You'd probably get plenty of takers on that offer," Alan joked, before looking back to their John Doe. "We should get him moved to the infirmary, and I will need to see Captain Halvorsen and the Staff Captain. We'll conduct a thorough medical examination there, but the security chief probably needs to do something about this gymnasium too."

"Don't worry, Doc, we've got a procedure. We have to call in the local police – for us it will be the Athens police. They'll do a preliminary report, and then there is weeks of legal wrangling as we argue about jurisdiction. But eventually, it will be a case for the authorities, since we are officially in international waters."

"Really? I thought we would have been in Greek waters by now," Alan exclaimed. "What about the cruise?"

"Shouldn't be affected too much, if it is, as you say, a heart attack. People have died on cruises before."

"I know," Alan said meaningfully.

"You just need a few reports by the right people to make a call on the situation – is it safe to proceed, is there an infection, is there a danger to the crew or passengers. That will be my job after I see your report." Vince looked wearily at the doctor and nudged him in the ribs.

"So, who gets the knickers?"

Alan looked down at the bunched up fragment of pink. "Oh, you do, Vince. You can definitely take those down to the security office."

*   *   *

Alan worked well into the small hours of the morning, examining the body of the John Doe, with Kelly assisting him.

"So?" He turned to his co-worker at 3:00 AM. "What do we know and what can we say about this case?"

For a second Kelly considered it, and then listed the particulars. "We've examined his arteries and heart muscles, and yes, he had a massive heart attack. The rupture caused his body to shut down. The heart failing and the lack of blood flow to the brain essentially killed him."

Alan nodded, and gestured for her to continue.

"Through the rest of the examinations we can say that the man had probably had sexual intercourse in the last couple of hours, to do with … er… blood flow and fluids. Age wise, the man was in the prime of his life, mid forties maybe. Based upon the status of his lungs, probably a light smoker, and based upon the initial look at the plaque in the arteries, my guess would be that he was suffering from high serum lipids – with very high cholesterol. Given these risk factors, he had a high probability of having a coronary event."

"Very good diagnosis, Watkins." Alan clapped, seeing that he had ticked off everything that he had written in his report. "One thing you missed though – blood work."

Kelly frowned.

"We've got to mention it, we've tested everything else. His urine levels were quite acidic, a high amount of alcohol in his system, and the same too with his blood. It looks like he was probably quite intoxicated as well, which didn't help matters."

Alan put together his report, and made sure it was sealed in its document envelope with red-glued tape, an onboard technique to ensure that only managers and those in need–to–know positions could open it. He then put it together to take down to Vince in the security offices.

It was then that there was a knock at the door.

"Hey, Doc?" said a familiar voice. It was Captain Halvorsen.

"How's it going? Is that the guy?" He walked in and pointed to the man on the examination table, who thankfully was once again covered up with the white sheet.

"My God, poor bugger – but hey, what a way to go huh? Vince has filled me in on the details and I've got to say, if there was a way I would want to go – it would at least be like that."

Alan shook his head – how characteristic of their adventurous captain.

"So, Doc, no foul play? No secret marks or bruises or whatever else there is in those old detective novels?"

"None that I can find, Captain. Now I am not a pathologist with extensive post mortem expertise, but with the number of autopsies I have had to perform on the ships, I'd say that he died of a heart attack, just like we initially surmised. It's the cause of the heart attack which is up for debate."

"I think the cause is pretty well established, wouldn't you say?" The captain gave Nurse Watkins a wink, who returned his glance with a frown.

"Yes, quite, well...."

Halvorsen was momentarily put off by his lack of effect on members of the fairer sex. "We have the... hum... item in custody, so to speak, but I don't think we have any chance of finding its owner."

"We will just have to keep a look out for a woman who is missing something."

The captain's eyes betrayed the fact that he was biting back a joke, "some *femme fatale* with the Kiss of Death?"

"Well, something like that," Alan agreed. "It would certainly put you off men for a while – having that happen to you while in full swing, as it was."

Even Nurse Watkins was tempted to smile at this comment.

"Yes, well there are more than a few candidates on board. The Mediterranean seems to bring them all out – must be the hot weather, hot seas..."

"Hot storms," Alan interjected.

"Yes, quite. What a rum old time for it to happen, huh? At least we are nearing the port, and we don't have to carry the grisly thing out to sea. We'll be docking soon, as it happens, but we won't be officially letting people off until tomorrow morning. You should see it below decks down there – we have people pulling extra shifts, getting the cargo bays ready with the extra work. Because of the storm, we've managed to get a message through to the port authority and the Athens police will be taking custody of the poor chap, please give them your initial report, and of course, a copy to corporate. They will depend on your report more than they will on the one from Athens."

"And so who is it then?" the nurse asked. The young nurse didn't realize that Vince, as part of security procedure had to check the body and remove identification as soon as he got there, in order to keep the chain of evidence pure.

"Well, now that we can mostly put it down to natural causes, I think it's safe to tell you two," Halvorsen said magnanimously. "He's a European passenger – a Belgian named Gillais Montague. On the ships manifest we have him down as a normal passenger, a single ticket, who preferred first seating, and no extra details. Could be like anyone, I'd say. Probably one of those guys just trying to find some adventure and companionship on a cruise." Alan was forced to agree with that conclusion.

"Okay, my summaries are all in my report. This will have to go to the port authority, the Athens police force, and the company. I'll keep the master copy in here on the ship," said Alan.

"Good show, Doc. Now, how about we stop this ugly business and you get some fresh air and watch the docking. I have to return to the bridge to oversee it."

"Sounds great," Alan agreed – he had never felt more like fresh air in all of his life than he did right now. It had been a long start to the cruise, and they were only at their second port. "You want to come, Kelly? I've already called in Petra. She'll be covering the rest of the morning shift."

"Oh, no thank you, Doc. I'm really tired already and I think I'll just go hit the sack."

"Well, good job today Watkins. I'm glad you're on board."

She smiled, tiredly, and started packing her things. Absentmindedly she reached up, and undid the latch of one of the side portholes that led into the rainy air of the deck. It was a habit that made Alan smile. On shore, in autopsy labs in the hospital, it was common amongst the staff always to leave a sliver of a window open when a new body came in –'so the soul can get out' it was believed. Even though Alan himself was not a superstitious man, he found the unconscious action of his younger aide endearing.

"Oh, and, Kelly," Alan said as he went out through the door, "That young chap from today, what was his name?"

"Ernesto?" she said quickly.

"Yes, that's the one. If the captain is right and they're as busy as hell down there, he'll probably need some more gel about now. Go and see if you can find him." Alan grinned to himself as he kind of… came off duty.

"What was all that about?" the captain asked as they marched up to the Bridge.

"Oh, it's the first full twenty-four hours on board." Alan returned the smile. "The poor girl is probably feeling overwhelmed, tired, and overworked. I'm just prescribing a little medical care for her, that's all."

"What, by giving her more work to do? To go find some below deck guy to work on?"

"*Exactly,*" Alan said as they marched off.

Tonight was a little different, as the *Ocean Quest* was doing its docking procedure, in the middle of a severe storm. They stood in front of the reinforced, plated windows that stood at one end of the bridge, and saw the glittering lights of the ancient city of Athens spread out before them. It covered almost all the coastline ahead and the doctor realized that they must be very close indeed. If it wasn't for this stormy murk they would probably be able to see the individual buildings as well.

All around the rain lashed down at the cruise ship as it neared the lights, passing flashing buoys after flashing buoys that hung in the blackness like space probes. In fact, they were tethered far below to the sea floor with heavy iron chain links and concrete 'plugs', but in this gloom they looked just like little slightly glowing starfish as they marked avenues of approach and distance counters.

Alan felt the ship was moving incredibly slow compared to how it usually approached a port. From way up here they could feel the bobbing motion of the waves even more so, but thankfully, Alan realized, there were no heavy swells. Either they had missed the worst of the storm, or it would come in later in the small hours of the morning. He checked his watch – *My God.* It was already two thirty in the morning. *Where did all the time go?*

The dock ahead grew larger and larger as they crawled forward, and Alan saw the lights of the Pilot and tug boats that would help with the final approach. Pilot boats were employed by most ports across the world as a means to finely tinker and tune a boat's approach or departure from a busy port. It also provided the port with employment for a number of people and, at the prices they charged cruise lines and cargo ships, a lot of income for the port. Some ports had the pilot come aboard several ports before the one intended by the ship. Ostensibly, this was to guide the ships' officers on any potential hazards, but more often than not, it actually just gave the pilot a nice rest and nicer income. Alan imagined in this instance they were especially needed because a lot of boats had come in from the storm and so there was less time and less space for a vessel like the *Ocean Quest* to maneuver.

Instead, it seemed that the cruise liner was going to be helped along to some of the big docking spaces in the industrial shipping end of the port. Cruise liners were often shunted into these spaces if a port authority could not be bothered to deal with them or the preferred spaces nearer to the port gate and town are filled by other bigger ships or ones willing to spend more money to dock there.

It is easier to dock in the industrial area usually, as there are especially wide areas to maneuver, but it makes for a less attractive experience for the passengers, as they wake up to the sight of grey and unwashed dingy hangers, warehouses and depots. In some ports like Mormugao, India, one is greeted with a humongous pile of coal, rusted sheds and warehouses, and a long taxi ride to the fascinating, old Portuguese capital city of Goa.

Alan could see that the captain was livid, since he was very proud of his job and his vessel. Even though he was a player, he was committed to the welfare and experience of his crew.

Save for the muted thunder of the storm, the lights, and glinting black waters sliding past the ship as if they were atop a mountain, which Alan guessed they were, for a brief moment he once again marveled at the technology, and vision that had led to the construction of this edifice in the waves. It was like being aboard a moving castle, a small floating city.

"Amazing, isn't it?" said one man at his side. Alan didn't recognize him, only that he wore the crisp tweed jacket so usual to academics, professionals, and English landowners. For all that stuffy air, he also was a broad-chested man, with a blue collar shirt and sandy-white hair.

"Yes, I was just thinking the exact same thing myself." Alan told himself he should stop analyzing everyone around him – his damn physician's eye.

"Ah, Doc, I'm glad you two have finally met – this is Dr. Seinz. I invited him to see the docking procedure with us." The captain turned to the guest. "Your wife not with you tonight, Dr. Seinz?"

Seinz smiled graciously. "No, I'm afraid not. She's down with a sea-belly I'm sorry to say."

Captain Halvorsen laughed. "Oh, surely not."

"Yes, absolutely, I am afraid she gets it like no one else at the start of every journey. I can be as fit as a fiddle on the roughest seas, but the mere sight of water and she's off to the bathroom."

"Tell her to come by the infirmary tomorrow," Alan suggested. "I have some sea-sickness tablets, which will help. It sounds like she has just got a sensitive inner ear – the tiny bones and chambers inside her eardrum. They are the first to react to changes in motion and pressure, but acclimatize quickly."

"Really? The problem can be solved that easily? The poor lass has been suffering for years," Dr. Seinz said.

"Easily." Alan assured the gentleman. "So, I take it you're

probably not a medical doctor?"

"Heaven's no," Seinz said. "I'm a professor of archaeology, that kind of Doctorate. Although, there was one time I was asked to deliver a baby on board a plane."

"What?" Both Halvorsen and Alan said in unison.

"Yes, I thought so too. I told her that I wasn't that kind of doctor, but the stewardess said that it was better for the passengers if at least *some* kind of doctor was present. And at least I was used to getting my hands dirty." His eyes twinkled and all three suddenly burst out laughing.

"My name is Alan Mayhew MD, doctor on board." Alan extended a hand for the doctor to shake.

Seinz hesitated, and didn't return the gesture. "Sorry, Doctor, but I think we better not shake hands; I've got this graze on my hand that I have been looking after. I don't want to get your hand all covered in anti-bacterial cream."

Alan shrugged. "Believe me, compared to what I have been doing today that would be the least of my concerns. Let's have a look at it."

Dr. Seinz produced the hand, which did indeed have a laceration across the palm of it. It had a sheen of whatever cream that he had been using, but Alan could see immediately why he hadn't kept it bandaged. It was right on the flexor surface of the thumb and would have reduced the maneuverability of his thumb significantly. The surface of the wound looked fairly healed over with the first stage of tissue re-growth, but there was some angry-looking greenish color spreading under some of the main abrasion.

"Doesn't look too bad, but you might have an infection or something creeping in there. Do you want me to have a look at it tomorrow?"

"Well, sure, yes." Seinz seemed a little puzzled, as if he wasn't used to the 'Gold Experience'. "I only thought it was a graze, that's all. It has been hurting a bit more today, but I thought it was healing rather well."

"Absolutely, Dr. Seinz, the wound is healing wonderfully superficially, but some infection or virus must have crept in. Some simple local treatment would be best, and if that doesn't clear it up then a course of cefalosporin antibiotics probably will." Alan suddenly remembered the body that he had in his infirmary. "Although, it would be best if you and Mrs. Seinz didn't come over first thing in the morning." Alan realized that he would have to find a discrete way to transport the body of the late Gillais without it alarming the passengers or crew, and having the Seinz's walk into the middle of that wouldn't be the best way to advertise to the ship that there had been a death.

"How about you drop by later tomorrow, after shore leave, before dinner?"

"Oh yes, that sounds marvelous." Dr. Seinz beamed. "I was hoping to take my wife out and see some of the sights anyway; there are a few monuments that I worked on in my youth which I would love her to see. If we are quick then we might, be able to get back in time for dinner."

"That's the spirit." Alan smiled at the academic enthusiasm. Tomorrow he would probably be engaging half the day with the port authorities, the Greek police, and translators. Having someone die was always such a messy administrative business.

The doctor turned around to see whether he could interest the captain in helping him out tomorrow with the long list of duties, most of them purely bureaucratic. Instead, he almost flinched when he found that the captain had vanished from his side, and was now otherwise engaged.

Standing over to one side of the public viewing area of the bridge, where frequent members of the cruising club are allowed to view the bridge and get a chance to chat with the officers, the captain had been cornered. No, to put it more accurately he had been trapped.

Lady Charlotte Hemmingsworth. The woman was almost as tall as he was in real life, but her impressive retro fifties beehive rose from her head like the monument to some crow-like deity. Her heavy fake eyelashes batted at the captain as she pushed forward her best assets into the captain's wondering gaze.

Halvorsen must have known that he had a real, bona fide lady of aristocratic proportions and measurements on board his vessel.

And he must have also known that the good Lady Hemmingsworth would have a Lord Hemmingsworth around somewhere, who would probably be none too pleased at the captain of a sea-liner getting it on with his wife.

However, whatever the captain did or did not know was completely drowned by the dazzle of the attention that Lady Charlotte was pouring over him like glue. Quite simply put, Captain Anders Halvorsen was caught like a fish on the end of a line.

Wasn't he married too, come to think of it, Alan wondered, but then again, apparently he had a very tempestuous relationship with his wife. Each of them always seemed to threaten to divorce each other every cruise, while neither of them was about to do it any time soon. Unfortunately, this did occur many times with officers and their partners.

Alan had met this sort of married couple before, and thankfully he had never, ever, fallen into that rut. The erstwhile captain and his good wife had probably loved each other very much, possibly still did. But he would have his dalliances on board, and she would perhaps have her revenge with the gardener, or the mechanic, or the local football stud. Alan laughed at the insanity of it. He could never dream of living life like that, but for some their passions ran high, while for Alan they ran deep.

The Lady Charlotte Hemmingsworth was zoning in on her kill and Alan was too horrified and so entranced he could not take his eyes off them. The captain looked like a happily drowning man, a mouse in front of a snake. The Lady joked and thrust her way, punctuating every comment with a stab of her not inconsiderable assets, and the captain was, for all intents and purposes, doomed.

Alan was just about to excuse himself from Doctor Seinz's company and attempt to save the good captain from himself, when someone tugged on his elbow. He turned to see Ralph, the long-term employee with no real status, except for being a trusted 'go-for', smiling broadly.

"It's for you, Doc. You've got a call."

What, another one that did not go to my cell? The doctor turned to see Ralph put the satellite phone down on the bar. "So the phone lines are back on again?" Alan asked.

"Sure are Doc, this close to port I think they've got satellite boosters and things." Ralph gave Alan a conspiratorial wink. "And I don't think you want to keep this one waiting."

Alan didn't. He picked it up and said, "Hello? Dr. Alan Mayhew here."

"Hello, Doctor Alan Mayhew. This is your cruise director speaking. What have you to report?" said the woman's voice at the other end of the line.

"Tiffany?" He almost stammered.

"*Your* cruise director, thank you very much. I haven't been working my butt off the last few months to be able to shuffle my contracts around just so you can call me by my first name." Alan could hear the laughter in her voice, and his heart leapt.

"And what a cute butt it is, Cruise Director," he returned,

trying to keep his voice low but unable to help himself.

"Enough of that, Doctor Mayhew. You know that over familiarity is frowned upon between crewmembers of the Gold Cruise Line Company. If you carry on with that kind of language I'll have to make a complaint to your superiors."

"I guess you are one of my superiors." Alan laughed. "Unless you mean Captain Halvorsen, and he … hum …, he seems trapped between a soft place and a softer place at the moment."

"Oh." He could *hear* her rolling her eyes. "Everything ship shape and normal then?"

"Not quite, not quite… I can't really tell you over the phone, but…"

"Then don't tell me at all, Dr. Mayhew." Her tiny voice laughed. "Speak to me tomorrow, I'm in Athens."

"No way. Really? Well, that *is* a pleasant surprise, especially after the day that I've had."

"Oh, you poor thing, but I won't hear a word of it, you being all overworked on that old ship with all those glamorous ladies everywhere."

"Well, I've already managed to acquire one pair of very sexy pink knickers," he jested.

"What?"

"I'll tell you later, but it's not what you think."

"It had better not be, Doctor Alan Mayhew, or they might have to start looking for a new medic on *very* short notice."

They both laughed and agreed to a time when it would be safe to meet tomorrow. Putting the receiver down after some more outrageous flirting on both their parts, Alan found himself suddenly not caring that it was stormy outside, or that there had been a death on board.

"Good news I take it?" said Ralph, grinning mysteriously.

"After the day I've had, Ralph, I have certainly heard worse." Still grinning, Alan made his farewells and made his way back to his cabin for the few hours left of the night.

CHAPTER FOUR

Athens
Taking out the laundry

AS EXPECTED THE MORNING brought a flurry of activity for the ship's doctor. Alan had awoken to find the view out of his window uninspiring; the grey watery light of the post-storm sky was made even greyer by the steel and concrete warehouses of the shipping sector of Athens port.

But at least he was going to see Tiffany today. He rallied himself as he got out of bed and started to get himself ready for another day.

He wasn't halfway through his morning routine when there was a loud knocking at his door. Still in his bathrobe, he casually opened the door, where a small man with oiled back hair and thick bottle-end glasses perched on a long nose confronted him. The man's head swung around Alan's cabin, like a bird quickly scanning, and then he analyzed Alan as he looked up and down him.

"Dr. Mayhew, I presume?" his thick Grecian accent stuttered out. Alan nodded and opened the door wider to let the diminutive man inside. "Good. I see."

But Alan could see that the man had not been happy at all at finding a semi-naked doctor in the doorway.

"I am Vasili Passos, Detective for the Port Authority of Athens. I am sure you know why I am here, yes? Good. Now, if you don't mind...."

Vasili proceeded to barge past him into Alan's cabin, take a long look at all the available surfaces and chose to perch on a seat by the small writing desk that Alan had by the porthole. The man moved in quick, jerky movements and was obviously very unhappy. The detective proceeded to explain why.

"Dr. Mayhew – Alan Mayhew. This is very early. I have many, many things to do, I am a very busy man, you see, and now I am on a boat looking for a dead body. Your dead body. The dead body that you are to hand over to the authorities for the post mortem." He barked at the doctor as if it was Alan's personal fault that a man had died on the ship, and how could he have ruined the detective's day by bringing a corpse to his port of Athens?

The doctor guessed that the good detective was not the best sailor in the police department by the way he was clutching at his knees in a wobbly manner even though they were tied up along shore; this only confirmed Alan's suspicions.

"Now look at this for me, Doctor. I am woken up from my long sleep with my beautiful wife, and I am told that there is an American cruise ship coming to my port with a body. But this body is of a French or Belgian man, so the French or Belgian authorities will have to be informed, the French Embassy, and since this has happened in international waters, Interpol has to be informed. I, who should be sleeping with my beautiful wife, will have to look after the body until all of these people can have their dabble at the paperwork and the body. I have to get the city coroner down to the police station; I have to get the French diplomat, the representative from Interpol, the American diplomat, and a representative of the cruise line. And everyone wants paperwork, Dr. Mayhew. Paperwork, paperwork, paperwork."

"Huh," Alan ventured, wondering when it would be a good time to ask whether he could go put the rest of his clothes on.

"And then I get another phone call, and do you know who this is from? This is from the Mayor of Athens. It seems that he has been talking to a CEO of your Gold Cruise Line, and the mayor is up for re-election this year, and so he doesn't want a fall out with a drop in the major source of tourist income for his port. So he wants me to comply with your wishes to make this as *discreet* as possible for your passengers.

"Does anyone care if Vasili cares about discreet? I have a job to do, Dr. Mayhew, and now my beautiful wife will not be talking to me today, because I have had to go to work and not take her on our road trip that we had planned. It was going to be beautiful, Dr. Mayhew, a custom open-top Dodge convertible, a classic car. Mrs. Passos loves her classic cars, and when Mrs. Passos is happy then Vasili is happy. Now I will not be having a road trip, no late lunch in a small tavern I know in the hills, and no early siesta in a hotel near the mountains. Not for me, not for Mrs. Passos."

"Uhm, I'm sorry…" Alan ventured again.

"Yes, quite. Now, I believe I have already said that we are to be *discreet*, and so I have a plan."

The irate little man detailed his plan to the doctor, and almost unable to stop himself from laughing, Alan had to beg time to put his clothes on, and instead of doing what he wanted to do and strip off the bathrobe and openly dress himself in front of this quizzical little man, he chose to do so in the en-suite bathroom, a real contortion exercise due to its small space. He quickly gargled with some mouth freshener, spat it out, and returned to find Detective Passos waiting impatiently by the door.

"Ready? Good. We will attack this operation in two ways. First the body."

They set off at a fast pace to the infirmary, Alan hoping that none of the passengers would notice this shady-looking man accompanying the ship's doctor at a frog march. Vasili looked every bit the gum shoe detective he was; wearing an old battered brown trench coat that came down to his knees, the glasses, and his shiny black shoes that squeaked as he walked.

When they got to the infirmary, they found an altogether different scene unfolding before them. Petra Gacek, the other of the two nurses under Alan's supervision, was standing inside the infirmary with her arms protectively held out as she backed towards the body of the over worked Gallais.

In front of her was the large bulk of Vince, the acting ship security officer in chief, dressed unconvincingly in laundry whites. Alan thought he must have had an early wake up call too.

"Never!" Petra Gacek cried. "You will never take my body."

Alan did a double take, wondering what on earth this would sound like to the unknowing onlooker.

"Look, it's only a short journey, and no one will know, Vince tried to placate the frothing woman.

Petra Gacek was not a woman to annoy. In fact, Petra Gacek was not a woman with which you could, in any way, slight or otherwise, express a difference of opinion. She had a famous temper, so much so that some crewmembers would avoid going for their routine physicals just in case they ended up having Petra doing the preparations and blood draws for their physical exams by the doctor.

She was not a small woman either. This large, imposing female with her own thick glasses could cheerfully wolf down any food put in front of her. There was a story going around that, before she had taken up with her physical therapy and nursing training in her native Poland, she had done a stint as an amateur female wrestler, and Alan didn't find any reason to doubt it. He wondered who would be worse off, security officer Vince or Petra, if the confrontation came to blows.

The source of their argument was obvious, and immediately Alan saw the extent of Detective Vasili's plan. Sitting in the corner of the room was a very large trolley. It was one of the laundry trolleys that the crew rotated around the cruise ship every day, changing towels, tablecloths, napkins, and bed linen, putting their contents through the express industrial cleaners and returning them to their rooms the very next day.

"Oh no, you can't," Alan blurted.

"Oh, not you as well," said Vince, turning around to see the detective and the doctor standing in the doorway. "Look, it was the best idea we had on the run as a way of moving the ... body." He grinned and Petra made an exasperated noise and uttered a string of expletives in Polish. At that moment Alan was glad that he had only picked up a handful of words of that lovely language from the crew and passengers, and that he had not had enough time to learn what each of the new utterances that Petra was now using to describe Vasili, Vince, and probably himself, too.

"Yes, Doctor Mayhew," an annoyed Vasili chimed in. "This is my idea and it is an excellent one. Now – off with the body – into the laundry basket."

Petra growled at all of them, but a reproving look from Alan sent her back to her duties as he and Vince manhandled the body of the overworked Gallais into the laundry trolley.

"Now", Vasili said, "Security Officer, accompany me to the cargo decks. I have a special vehicle waiting."

As it turns out, the police authorities of Athens were more used to dealing with things of this nature than they made out. Their 'special vehicle' turned out to be an unmarked white van, inside which was a fully equipped emergency vehicle with medical bench and locked equipment containers.

"After September 11, the whole world changed," Vasili explained to them both as they made their way through the lower decks of the cargo bay. "Now every major city in the west has vehicles like this, this was Interpol's idea. We now have unmarked intelligence units, unmarked interception units, and unmarked emergency vehicles. It is a sad world now." For a brief moment, Vasili sounded uncharacteristically sad.

However, he was correct; since that dreadful time in the early autumn days of 2001, the international scenes had changed, especially in Alan's world. Customs and security checks were so much tighter at the 'red areas' of the planet: and one of them was the cruise ship that globe trotted the oceans.

'Red Areas' as Vince had once told him, were situations or places that were the most at-risk to a sovereign states' working infrastructure. They encompassed what came in and out of a country, the airports and ports, the land bridges, customs, immigration, and the cruise liners. They were all a part of that infrastructure.

Vince had once reliably informed him that he now conducted a full security review before and after every cruise, as well as his yearly four-monthly full review of his cruise operations. Somewhere, deep in the company's head quarters, there was a record both on paper and in electronic format of every time a lock was changed, a door checked, a camera checked, a crew rota assigned and who was working when, where, and what they were supposed to be doing and with whom. Even out on the high seas the world of security had watchful eyes over all of their activities.

The trio raced to the main bay that was already unbolted and released from its fittings, wheeled back, and the large metal runway had already been secured in place that led down to the service docks.

Even this early in the morning, teams of mini loaders were trundling back and forth, bearing crates of food, extra supplies for the journey ahead, luggage for the disembarking and embarking passengers. Not even a few faces turned and looked to see the three men coming down the gangplank, dodging the other crew handlers and luggage men as they pushed their laundry cart ahead of them.

Out into the warm air of September in Greece, the access road was still damp from last night's storm, and sitting alone in a parking bay was the white unmarked Grecian truck. A couple of similarly clothed – plain-clothes Greek policemen – hopped out when they saw their superior officer approaching, and helped unload the laundry cart of its macabre contents.

The officers shared a few words with Vasili, who barked an irritable reply, and from their smirks, Alan could see that perhaps he was not the only one who bore the brunt of Detective Passos bad mornings and his beautiful wife.

"So, now, job done," the detective crowed. "The mayor will be happy, you will be happy, and Interpol will be happy. You have the medical findings?"

Alan handed over a copy of his medical report to the detective.

"Now," Vasili continued, "I would say do not think of leaving town but..." he waved a hand at the *Ocean Quest*. "We know where you are going anyway, we have your manifest, and we have your boarding and departure list.

"I am sure that someone, Interpol, the French or Belgian Embassy, The Americans or someone will be contacting you again. I hope you are good at your job, Dr. Mayhew." He waved the report in the air as he jumped into the back of the unmarked medical truck. "If my coroner is unhappy with the results, then you, of course, know what that means do you not?"

"More paperwork," Alan hazarded.

The truck started to move off, and Detective Vasili of the Athens Port Authority shouted over the din of the engine, "Yes indeed, Dr. Mayhew. Paperwork, paperwork, paperwork." The diminutive detective slammed the back doors of the truck and that was that. Alan breathed a sigh of relief and hoped that he would never have to see the little man again.

"Funny bugger, wasn't he?" Vince said, as they ambled back up the gangplank now with their empty laundry cart.

"You can say that again." Alan wiped a hand over his eyes; realizing it was early and the rest of the passengers were probably only just waking up for breakfast. "But you would be amazed, Vince," he went on, "of all the funny characters I meet in the course of this job, it seems that just about every eccentric and strange people who travels the seas at some point goes on the Gold Cruise experience."

"You don't have to tell me about it," the security chief joked. "I'm the one who has to throw them off the vessel, and clean up the pieces when everything gets out of hand. And *then* there's the crew to deal with as well."

"Why do we do this job again and again, Vince?" Alan asked jestingly as they made their way back through the body of the ship.

"Because of this…." Vince pointed out at the windows around them, the slight bobbing of the vessel, the cries of the gulls that flocked the port of Athens, and the new, fresh air of a different city.

Alan agreed he was quite right. Some people could lead sedentary lives, some could settle down and find satisfaction in the same routines, but for others such a staid life would never fulfill them. There was some spark of the restless soul, the itchy feet, the wanderlust that burned in the heart of every career-man who worked on the high seas, men like Alan and Vince, even the captain.

Alan had never thought about it too much, but in his more fanciful moments he would envisage himself as an international traveler on the earth, another human being who had already circumnavigated the whole globe many times over. The wonder of it all, the different landscapes, climates, environments, and natural world astounded him and continued to do so to this day.

Alan loved all of the different expressions of humanity, the different cultures, traditions, customs, habits, and behaviors, which he encountered during his travels. There was never a dull moment traveling the high seas, and Alan found himself constantly amazed at all the various manifestations of humanity and life that had crossed his path every day of his working career.

Now that he and Vince had parted ways – Vince went off to finish writing up his report of the morning – Alan was left to take the unoccupied cart back to the infirmary, where he would have to have it thoroughly disinfected, scrubbed down, and pressure washed.

Luckily the ships medical departments and the cleaning staff were prepared for most eventualities, and had several highly toxic chemicals that would do the job quickly. He shuddered to think of anyone else finding out what they had just done, and how many of the more well off guests would promptly ask to leave the cruise and have their tickets reimbursed, once they would have found out that one of the carts which carried their bed sheets had also, recently, carried a fresh cadaver.

Walking out onto the forward deck he was in time to see the tides of people starting to emerge from below decks, ready for another day of adventure in a strange and new port.

In front of them were the tour managers – on this line, crewmembers employed by the company to take the passengers on scheduled, guided tours at every stop over along the way. With a sudden pang, Alan remembered the good-natured Michael, who had been a tour manager some years ago. It seemed like he had died just yesterday.

The tour managers were generally gregarious, highly knowledgeable people, who were often well versed in two or three languages, sometimes more, and who had an instinct for controlling and entertaining a crowd. 'Playing to the Back Row' – Michael had referred to this skill an old term from the theatre, which meant being able to project your performance and be entertaining even to the back row of an assembled audience – the mark of a great actor. The managers would always have to hawk their tours to the passengers aboard the cruise, hoping to get enough to fulfill their requirements. Some managers made a lot more money than others, depending upon their own personal style and the mix, along with the broad trends of passenger type on any particular cruise. The tour managers were always battling the rumors of cheaper tours that could be had, right off the ship or the people who had arranged tours on line to meet them in the designated ports from various cruise critics, blogs, and similar on line social media. It was, assuredly, disappointing to the tour managers to see half the ship leave on 'other' tours. Of course, the guaranteed, "we will wait for you," gave people on tours a lot of confidence if they booked with the ship.

Alan remembered, in Dubrovnik, a storm had come up while half the ships' passengers were ashore. The ship had to leave the exposed area, where it was moored several hours before the passengers were meant to get on the tenders and be ferried out to the ship. I am sure watching the ship leave without them was a stomach wrenching experience for all the passengers. The cruise line had left one of their agents at the tender port and had made arrangements for hundreds of people to stay in hotels, in gymnasiums, and the like while the ship scurried out to sea to ride out the storm. Large flat bottomed cruise ships do much better riding out storms at sea than tied up to docks or anchored in narrow ports like Dubrovnik. The next morning it sailed to industrial port miles away and busses were arranged to bring all the passengers back on board.

Alan realized that he envied the passenger's a little. He envied the fresh excitement they must be feeling of having a new, unexplored city laid out before them. Silently, he bid them well, and wondered idly in what state many of them would return. As long as they were back to check in with the front desk manager a few hours before departure, they wouldn't miss the rest of the cruise. Alan had heard a fair number of stories about passengers, who had only just made it back in time, or who had come back in a physical state or situation that the cruise line and most other passengers could only frown upon. Being totally drunk, stoned, disheveled, etc. was not thought to be cool.

He chuckled to himself as he remembered one particular story of a young gentleman who worked for a very important, multi-national Internet company. One of the biggest names there on 'the web'. The cruise at the time had been traveling through the Caribbean stops – a nice, leisurely, cruise that had stopped for a whole couple of days at each port – before making its way on again under the hot calypso sun.

Well, anyway, this young man, a geeky sort of gentleman, obviously more at home with computer software than a social gathering; but blatantly very, very, *very* rich, stopped off for the night on land at a beach hotel, and returned the next day wearing shades and a hangover.

Suspicions were aroused when two days later the young man had not been seen nor heard from by anyone, but several deliveries of food and drinks had been ordered to his first class cabin. The laundry staff and cleaning staff had been refused entry, which sometimes they adhered to, and sometimes they ignored depending upon the passenger. As it turned out, the doctor was asked to 'delicately' approach the situation in case the young man was ill, or in need of attention.

Alan found that the young man was receiving all the attention that he needed from numerous bottles of rum and a fairly large stash of marijuana – obviously not properly screened when he came back on board and the green was highly illegal for any passenger to have – wealthy or not. He agreed to a supervised flushing of the ganga down the toilet and that he would not buy any more.

Much chagrined, the captain agreed to corporate directive and saw to it that the young man was barred from any future expeditions with the Gold Cruise Line Company.

Alan smiled as he remembered that story, and wondered whether he shouldn't start noting all of these incidents down. Maybe he should write a book or publish his memoirs one day.

Petra Gacek scowled at him when he got back from his 'emergency outing'. It seemed that the night shift had not agreed with her, and having to deal with a cadaver first thing on a cruise was not the very best way to start a new contract.

"It is disgusting, that is what it is," the Polish nurse said, when talking about the events of the previous night. "All of it. Disgusting."

Alan couldn't be sure whether she meant the nature of his death, how Gallais was transported, or simply the fact that he was in the mortuary at all.

The rest of that morning was spent sorting out the paperwork for the late departed Gillais Montague. Alan got one phone call from the coroner – just a courtesy call to declare that he had received the body and was performing his own examinations. He thanked the man, who was considerably friendlier man than the detective, and sent the information down to Vince.

Alan looked at his watch. He was desperate to get away on shore, but had, at least, to finish the official paperwork. Sighing, he bowed his head and carried on through midday. Thankfully, there wouldn't be too much business for he and his staff during the day, as most of the passengers had gone ashore – thus minimizing accidents.

However, he did have the multitude of medical examinations that he had to perform every week on the crew to complete the corporate requirement to have all crew examined while on board during their contracts. This avoided the company's expense of having them examined when they were home off contract and getting employees who paid some doc to pass them, even though they did not meet requirements. He selected the top name from the file, and looked over who was the next of the crewmembers to come in.

There had always been some kind of medical examinations for the cruise workers. Any paid professional who worked at sea had to conform to their own company standards, their countries standards, and also the global agreed maritime law for health standards.

As each of these separate statutes was adopted and was synchronized over the years in this modern world of global communications, the number of medical examinations that each crewmember had to face every trip escalated. *The age of health and safety, and particularly liability insurance was now upon us,* Alan wryly thought, and now it was up to him, as the on board doctor to be able to satisfy all these different requirements.

For the crew of the *Ocean Quest*, it meant that on every cruise they would have at least one medical exam, if not more. Alan would spot any ailments as they developed and nip them in the bud before they got any worse.

It was also a good way to stop any contagion, virus, or infection from spreading amongst the crew – as something even as harmless as the common cold can rip through the confined space and shared eating arrangements of a ship like wildfire. Even a vessel like the *Ocean Quest*, with all of its zoned off areas, hand washing stations, washing signs, and all of its very careful safety precautions, which were checked and maintained a thousand times over, was not immune to germs and common viruses.

The next crewmember scheduled to receive a medical was one of the below decks staff. Alan allowed Petra to run through most of the preliminary tests, the body mass index, blood pressure and other vital signs, heart rate, and a simple exercise test. The man passed all of them with flying colors, but exhibited a few cuts and abrasions to his knees and hands where he worked hauling crates and tins for the kitchen crew. Petra inspected all the knocks and grazes, and went on to perform the mandatory drug test.

It turned out that Petra was well known for her drug tests. The company, obviously, had a no drug policy to be used anywhere on board the cruise ship. Most cruise lines used a random computerized program to choose the next person to be tested. This included all officers, entertainers, and anyone else working on the ship. If your number came up often-it was just the luck of the draw. Of course, the security officers could test anyone 'for cause' if they were rowdy or whatever. It was a serious infraction of the rules to use drugs and the crewmember would have their name 'listed' with their homeport authorities and the local police, and the matter taken up by the relevant authorities. A lot of the bigger and better established cruise companies would keep each other appraised of their recently listed employees. Since many of the security chiefs would know each other, or had worked together in some form or another through their careers at sea, it was quite common for a crewmember who had been found taking drugs, or even worse, supplying them to other crewmembers or passengers, to have their name given a black mark in the eyes of other cruise companies. In this way, the community of the sea tried to protect its reputation.

This did not stop many crewmembers imbibing, or at least dallying in soft and hard drugs, particularly those on the lower rungs of the staffing ladder. Temporaries, who were only employed for a short contract, often saw no need to be as stringent with the company guidelines as the career men and women and consequently would see their contract end early, if Petra tested them positive. The captain of a ship could not turn a blind eye and had to enforce the rules.

None of these considerations stopped Nurse Petra. She loved drug tests. She loved watching the patients squirm as she took a blood sample, or ordered them to produce a urine sample. Nurse Petra preferred hair drug tests, since many drugs made their way out of the bloodstream or urine to the body hair in a relatively short space of time, because they represented what the employee had really been taking over the last several months.

She especially took delight in taking the hair from suspicious members of the crew. If there weren't enough hair on the head, she would then turn to body hair. If she was in a truly determined mood, or she had taken a dislike to the person, she would take body hair from places where it was difficult or often forgotten to shave, and was never embarrassed by asking someone to "drop your drawers."

Petra's latest drug test victim was a particular below deck crewmember that had nothing to worry about, as he seemed to have presented a clean bill of health and activity. His name was Ahmed, and he had a family living in Qatar. Alan felt slightly sorry for the young man as he came under the watchful gaze of Petra. This was because of his age and nationality, which increased her suspicions in the post September 11th age.

Ahmed himself had gone through numerous security checks; several renewed ones since 2011, and appeared to be humble and conscientious. Alan remembered to thank him sincerely for coming in – as politeness and respect were key points of importance for Middle Eastern cultures, and surely he had had a tough enough time already, just for coming from an Islamic land such as he did.

Perhaps Alan felt a little sentimental for the young chap, who was trying to make money for his family so he could relocate them to the west. Since the terrorist attacks of September 11, the middle easterners often tried harder to please as they probably felt that they had much more to prove.

"Is there a doctor on board?" said a voice from the doorway, after Ahmed had gone. Petra looked up, frowned, and then went back to her paperwork. When Alan leaned over to see who it was, a sloppy grin spread over his face.

"Cruise director." he declared, and yes, standing there in his archway was Tiffany, *his* perky Canadian, with a long and mysterious smile that matched the gleam in her eyes.

"You two – out." Petra shouted from where she sat, not taking her eyes off her reports. Alan didn't have to be invited twice.

"So, she knows then?" Tiffany said under her breath, as they moved through the ship.

"I think a lot of people do. We weren't exactly discreet last time we were aboard together." He gave her a playful nudge in the elbow.

"I beg your pardon, I was very discreet." She laughed. "It was you who couldn't keep your hands off me."

"And I still can't," he said, quickly taking her hand, spinning her towards him so her body fell firmly against his chest. He looked down into the wide, deep eyes, and planted a long kiss on her full ruby lips.

"Wuh-Wow," the cruise director said after a moment. "It looks like it really does make the heart grow fonder."

"Eh, what does?" Alan's mind was still on that lingering kiss.

"Absence of course, silly."

"Or should that be abstinence?" he quipped back.

"Absolutely," she barked in a mock-domineering tone, which she then followed by giving his butt a sharp, playful slap.

"Whoa there, little lady!" Alan exclaimed, just as, from around the corner, came two elderly passengers.

The woman, barely above five foot and her husband, himself a smaller gentleman, looked like shocked gnomes. They stopped in their tracks with their mouths open as their gaze went from Alan's medical uniform to the woman in the casual clothes.

"Now you've done it," Alan snorted, as he grabbed her hand, and both he and Tiffany walked quickly around the corner before bursting into gales of laughter.

"You know that little piece of gossip will be all over the ship by tomorrow night, don't you, Cruise Director?" Alan said in a mock-angry tone.

Tiffany laughed, answering, "Of course. Why do you think I did it Doctor Mayhew?" He loved it when they 'played professional' as if they were just two work colleagues who had never met each other before. "Over all the bridge tables and the bingo cards, all the women of a certain age will be talking about what cute little patootie you have – as if they aren't already."

"Why, I ought to..." Alan creased his eyebrows. "You might just have to come back to my cabin and see if we can teach you a lesson or two."

"Please," she said, and batted her eyelashes teasingly.

Alan was getting close to doing that right now. Half of his mind was occupied with dragging her back to his luxurious cabin and not getting out of bed for the foreseeable duration, but as ever, Tiffany was the sane one in the partnership.

"But wine and dine me first, Doctor Mayhew. I know this lovely little tavern not too far from the ship here in Athens. We can go there and you can tell me what all this gossip is that you shouldn't be talking about over the phone or on the ship."

"It's a date, but I can't very well go out in my uniform."

"Yes, I see what you mean. I'll meet you down at the front desk reception in five minutes." She smiled sweetly, knowing that right now, as her man was lost in the throes of physical longing, she could get anything she wanted out of him. But, she warned him, "Don't be too long or I might find some handsome young sailor to take me instead."

"Ah, you little..." He laughed and made a gesture to give her a friendly grab on her behind this time, but before he could do that, there was a loud cough from behind them.

They turned to see that, by now; the elderly couple had rounded the corner and was apparently heading in the same direction as they were. Tiffany and Alan exchanged a gaze filled with cheerful duplicity, and then, amidst the giggles, that were threatening to overwhelm them, they both jogged down the corridor.

Making their way slowly on a constitutional walk around the ship, the elderly couple, who hadn't warmed up to the idea of going on shore in Athens, since it looked much too *noisy* for their tastes, stopped again and watched the two love birds scamper off.

"Young people today," the woman said.

"You just can't get the same caliber of staff these days," the gentleman replied.

*   *   *

Within a few minutes Alan had changed his clothes, had briefly scrubbed once again, and with a dash of aftershave, he was off to the main reception front desk. He felt like he was moonlighting from his job, although he knew that Petra would be covering the infirmary while he was ashore. He probably would go in during the night to ensure that nothing needed his attention, unless of course his mind strayed to whatever Tiffany might have in mind.

At the same moment, Tiffany was reading something Maud had written – when she wasn't filing her nail or examining her make-up.

> *1. Men are like Laxatives:*
> *They irritate the crap out of you.*
> *2. Men are like Bananas:*
> *The older they get, the less firm they are.*
> *3. Men are like the Weather:*
> *Nothing can be done to change them.*
> *4. Men are like Blenders:*
> *You need one, but you're not quite sure why.*
> *5. Men are like Chocolate Bars:*
> *Sweet, smooth, & they usually head right for your hips.*
> *6. Men are like Commercials:*
> *You can't believe a word they say.*
> *7. Men are like Department Stores:*
> *Their clothes are always 1/2 off!*
> *8. Men are like Government Bonds:*
> *They take soooooooo long to mature.*

> *9. Men are like Mascara:*
> *They usually run at the first sign of emotion.*
> *10. Men are like Popcorn.*
> *They satisfy you, but only for a little while.*
> *11. Men are like Lava Lamps:*
> *Fun to look at, but not very bright.*
> *12. Men are like Parking Spots:*
> *All the good ones are taken, the rest are*
> *handicapped.*

When Alan emerged from his reverie his feet had sped him to the reception desk, where Maud, the front desk clerk, was happily chatting away with Tiffany. Tiffany handed Maude her piece of paper with a wink, a suppressed giggle, and both looked up at him with guilty expressions on their faces.

"Say what you will, ladies, but I am definitely pleading the fifth," Alan announced as he grinned at both of them.

Maud snorted. "As all of you men do. Remember what I said." She turned to Tiffany, and made a scissoring motion with her fingers, to which Tiffany suddenly burst into renewed squeals of giggles.

"Hey, what is going on here?" Alan asked, slightly worried about the levels of pathological viciousness in their front desk clerk.

"Come on, you, you shouldn't have anything to worry about, but believe me, you'll want to spend a few hours *away* from the ship this afternoon."

"Why?" he asked innocently, looking over his shoulder at Maud who had returned to cleaning her nails, sighing in an air of satisfied contentment.

"Oh, I have no doubt that you will find out soon enough." Tiffany winked at him and they made their way into the city of Athens.

Athens itself is a busy, confusing city for those who have no experience in capitals punctuating the Mediterranean shores. Confined as it is by its geography and landscape, over the years, rather than growing outward, Athens seemed to concentrate its buildings all on top and beside each other. Although a modern city in every respect, Athens still has room for the tiny, winding streets of the ancient world, and the grand monuments, in their protected plazas, dominating the chaos below.

Alan rather enjoyed the excitement, the hustle, and the bustle of one of the most ancient of all cities in the world, and some say the birth of democratic society in the west. The only thing he didn't like was the roads. He couldn't quite fathom the traffic laws, there did not seem to be any.

By a series of lucky encounters and bizarre pedestrian crossings, they managed to navigate their way away from the port and through to one of the smaller, quieter districts that hedged the bay. It seemed to Alan that as soon as the traffic lights turned green *every* car on the roads thought they had a right to go – and there were no traffic lanes at all.

But then again, he mused, that was probably because he didn't live here and he didn't know the subtler laws of the road for the Greek motorist. Still, it was a rather hair-raising experience all the same.

Tiffany seemed to know what she was doing, and where she was going as she led him by the hand to a little street of boutiques, shops and restaurants.

At the end of the street was a small two-tiered car parking lot, where she paid the warden her ticket fee and went and retrieved the hire car that she had for a few days. It was nothing special, but it was a convertible, and so it allowed them the luxury of winching down the roof and enjoying the invigorating drive thanks to the cooler air.

"I am always amazed at how hot it is this time of year in the Med," Tiffany commented as she unwound her ponytail and let her hair play out in the breeze.

Alan agreed, feeling very pampered that he should be in this car with this beautiful young lady, and no less that he wasn't even the one driving. Now, Dr. Alan Mayhew wasn't a traditionalist by any stretch of the imagination – he loved the fact that women were liberated and empowered in this modern age – but he did like the idea of being able to *take a girl out*. Maybe he was old fashioned, but to him it felt quite proper.

"So, tell me all this gossip," she said as they drove out of the port area to a quieter area, until eventually they started seeing the green and sandy colors of the Mediterranean hills peeking out between the urban developments.

Alan filled her in on the sad story of Gillais Montague, the Belgian – Frenchman whom Vince had found dead on his security rounds.

"Oh my God." She was astonished. "A death on board – how did it happen?"

Alan explained the procedure that he and Nurse Kelly had performed, going into some detail, as he knew that Tiffany wasn't squeamish at all.

"So it was natural causes then – a heart attack in a man that young; that is quite unusual."

"Yes, it is rather, isn't it, but not unheard of, the poor sod. But we do, at least have a possible contributing cause."

"Do tell..." Tiffany loved the case-by-case encounters that the doctor went through as a part of his job. It was as if he was a detective or something, recounting a case of CSI in a recent series on TV.

He then proceeded to tell her about the pink panties that they had found, and the evidence that Gillais had recently been having sexual intercourse with someone.

Tiffany burst out laughing. "Oh no...,"she said, still choking back the giggles, "that is awful. The poor girl must be distraught – imagine that happening to you while on a dirty cruise? And you know that she must have been married, obviously."

"Obviously?"

"Of course, or she would have been so upset she would have ran to fetch help, no matter the circumstances. No girl would just *leave* like that unless her being there was something that she had to hide."

"Oh, of course. So, you are saying that there is someone on board who is, kind of *responsible* for the French-Belgian's death?"

Tiffany frowned. "Well, unless it happens again then I'd say no, obviously. If it happens again then you're looking for a Black Widow."

"You mean a lady who, like spiders, kills her suitors after having sex with them?"

"Yes, but I was referring to the pulp movie version. Who was it – Hitchcock? Anyway, you had better watch out, mister." She made a monstrous face and they were both laughing again before Tiffany said, "Aha, we're here."

They had emerged from the city proper into an area high above the cliffs, with small picturesque stone, whitewashed villas all around. She parked next to a large, wooden and stone-built tavern, done in the traditional style with low roofs and a step down to get into the basement bar.

What followed then was a very pleasing tapas meal overlooking the Mediterranean Sea as the sun was high and gulls floated past them down over the gorges and cliffs that led to the ocean. They could make out the smaller Lego brick of the *Ocean Quest* far below them as they ate Panini's with seafood, olives, and bread rolls and guacamole and salad. It was one of the best, freshest meals that

Alan had had in a very long time, and he drank in the moment he had with this beautiful, vivacious lady as they sipped a light beer.

For her part, Tiffany told him of her latest contract which was about to end soon – her journey was heading *out of* the Mediterranean and further to the southern European ports in Spain, southern France, while Alan's was heading *into* the Mediterranean Sea, down to Egypt, and back across to follow, for a little way, the route that Tiffany was taking before launching on its cross-ocean voyage to the Canary Islands, the Bermuda's and to end in Fort Lauderdale. Tiffany would be finishing her cruise weeks ahead of Alan's, and so they began to plan whether they could meet again somewhere else around the world.

"But I will have to catch up with you, you know, you'll be half-way across the Pacific by the time I get to you, probably."

"Not at the rate we're going." Alan laughed, thinking of the bad weather that had allowed both of them to be in the same port at the same time.

"A girl in every port, huh?" She raised her glass.

"Only the good looking girls." He toasted her back as they teased.

"Although, Doctor Mayhew, if you give me the silent treatment like you did last time, I don't think I *will* meet you in my swimsuit on some Caribbean island," Tiffany said as they got up to return to the car and back to the world of work.

"Silent treatment? What do you mean?"

"You haven't phoned me at all for days and days, and you are on a new cruise." The doctor could tell that there was at least some degree of jealousy in Tiffany's renewed teasing remark.

"What do you mean? I tried to call."

"Likely story." She elbowed him in the ribs.

"The phones were down."

"Oh really? Then how come I left messages with you at the front desk?"

Alan was flabbergasted. That was impossible. He thought back through the days. "When did you leave the messages? Was it yesterday – just before or during the storm?"

"Of course, I did – during the storm, you big lug. I was worried about you."

Alan considered for a second. He had tried the phones and they had certainly not been working. He couldn't imagine that Tiffany could be lying to him, but perhaps Maud was – the front desk clerk had seemed in an awful mood yesterday. But that would mean that there was no *outgoing calls* last night and the day before, and yet the satellite relay could indeed accept *incoming calls.*

"I think I know what has happened," he said, thinking about the bothersome Maud. "I am truly sorry, Tiffany, but I think there has been a misunderstanding somewhere."

"Hmm... Well, I'll believe you this time..." She pouted, before breaking into a grin to show that she wasn't really annoyed.

She probably thinks that I am just being a bit 'senior', Alan said to himself, and not wanting to sound as if he was making excuses or making a fool out of himself, he left his explanations at that.

But, his thoughts continued unabated, like a terrier after a rabbit. *It is very, very unusual for a storm to disrupt 'outgoing' calls only. They are all part of a satellite relay – that would have to mean that our transmitter wasn't working properly but our antenna was...*

Being an accomplished seaman, with years of experience sailing both as an employed doctor and as a yachtsman, on sailing boats and on pleasure cruisers, Alan Mayhew knew a thing or two about the technology that was needed for a successful sea-going voyage.

There was something here that didn't quite fit.

CHAPTER FIVE

Athens again
The phone, the trousers, and the cupboard

WHEN THEY ARRIVED BACK at the port, they were just in time to see some of the first tours coming back to the ship. Alan knew it was still early for the tours to be arriving back, but he presumed that they were running several shorter 'city tours' this stop, since they were on a tight time schedule, thanks to the storm.

The weather had turned into a muggy sort of watery day – still warm – and the doctor felt comfortable in his short-sleeved shirt, but it was probably cold by Grecian standards. As they drove, or more like poured through the traffic to the waterside, Alan noticed one gang of twenty-five or so *Ocean Cruise* ship clientele and their tour guide.

This tour guide was a young man named Stefan from the ship staff, a true globetrotter whose accent indicated that he was probably from Norway or Sweden, but who had made his home going from place to place around the world, working on cruise liners, at hotels, as a host in rich ski resorts, cooking in youth hostels, or backpacking. He was a nice, well-mannered thirty-something man who already had that worldly gaze, which Alan saw often amongst other travelers much older than himself.

Right now Stefan was leading his gang of passengers – a mixture of the older members on the cruise – back to the boarding gangway, and it looked for the entire world as if he was a scout leader with a troop of errant charges. Only many of these errant charges had purple rinse hair and monocles. His lanky gait indicated that he was still trying to be enthusiastic and expressive with his wards, but some of the pep had gone out of him somehow.

Alan and Tiffany parked their rental car and they easily caught up with Stefan and the tour.

"Afternoon, ladies, gentlemen." The doctor greeted the passengers warmly, nodding to those that he had the chance to meet. "I trust you are having fun?"

The members of the tour all agreed and were enthusiastic

about their experience: it was one of the things, which always cheered Alan up. Who would want to work in a dull office, where the scenery never changed and almost everyone was miserable and hated their job? Working on a cruise – despite the long hours, the miles of paperwork and forms, and some of the customers that you had to deal with – at least most of the time people were happy to be where they were and enjoying themselves.

One such bubbly passenger was a lady that Alan knew from previous cruises – Babette, the cruise line's unofficial playwright.

Babette was an attractive woman of middling years, who flashed the doctor and Tiffany a large grin. "Doctor Mayhew. Tiffany. Lovely to see you again, I hope you have been practicing the voice lessons I taught you," Babette teased. This was a running joke between the three of them, as for the past several cruises this playwright had been trying to get Alan to act in one of her plays. Tiffany, on the other hand, had graced her stage many times in her role as a cruise director.

Technically, Babette was a passenger, but was such a regular user of the Gold Cruise Line Company that she had become, over time, a welcome feature of the *Ocean Quest*, working alongside the cruise directors to produce onboard plays for the entertainment of the crew and passengers. Her plays had become quite famous amongst the long-term crewmembers, who, on the eve of each performance, found themselves wondering what part they would be asked to perform.

"Well I do enjoy the stage, but I may have to disappoint you this time, Babette." Alan thought about all the paperwork he would have to be consumed with over the unfortunate case of Gillais Montague.

"We'll see about that." Babette laughed. "I'm sure that one of these days we'll get the famous Doctor Mayhew on stage."

Alan chuckled, surprising himself when he found that he was pleasantly embarrassed.

"So, Babette, lovely to see you again," Tiffany said. "Can you give away a trade secret and tell us what your latest play will be about?" Tiffany liked Babette and enjoyed working with her when she had the chance. Babette usually spent the first half of the cruise plotting and writing her scripts, and then closeted herself with the cruise director while they prepared props, decorations, and organized the production of her plays.

"Well, it's a comedy…" Babette said mysteriously. "And I think I can tell you, it will discuss the difficulties of finding an appropriate man, something to which all of us can relate."

Tiffany laughed, nodding in agreement but squeezing Alan's hand affectionately.

The rest of the tour group seemed equally excited about their cruise and about the forthcoming play that Babette had been describing to them.

The same could not be said about Stefan however. Alan and Tiffany could see that he was doing his best, but something had happened to deflate his usually upbeat demeanor. Stefan was a very tall, very thin man who had that lean, compact frame. *Probably a high metabolism,* Alan judged, and wondered if he knew that fact about himself.

He wore his hair short and slightly curly. Most seasoned globetrotters seemed to go this way in the end; either cut it all off and save the hassle of trying to find a barber in a foreign port and try and translate, in a foreign language, the style one wanted. Because of the nature of his current employment, Stefan had chosen to go the short and easily manageable route.

Stefan was one of the key members of the on-board *Trinket Trade*: a halfway serious crew to crew trading system that included favors, work shifts, and easier and harder duties, based on the treasures and trinkets that each one could amass at the various ports.

The Trinket Trade developed on cruise liners, and was probably a natural phenomenon amongst any group of people who spent their time at sea. Alan could detect hints of the pirates of yore, or that of Captain Cook and his famous bag of glass beads.

The trinket trade emerged from the fact that at every port of call at least fifty percent of the crew could not make it onshore since they have to work. Below decks and in private quarters, heated haggling worthy of some of the best underworld black market gangs would take place, while crewmembers swapped their gifts for others, or tried to bid on another crewmember's gifts. Crewmembers who went ashore would generally buy mementos from the ports. Some of them were nice, authentic, and as descriptive of the culture as possible. For example, a traditional Hawaiian grass skirt, a set of the Grecian musical instruments, the hand pipes, an Indian singing bowl, a Moroccan hand-woven wall hanging. Others, however, were merely tokens to suggest which country the crewmember had been visiting; small plastic leaning tower of Pisa, a flag lapel pin of whichever sovereign state, a floppy Mexican hat, a handful of the local currency, saints' pictures and rosaries, carved animals, fridge magnets, etc.

This was all done good-naturedly and generally with good

intentions. Some of the below-decks staff comprised of the luggage carriers, the kitchen staff, the cleaners, and the loaders never got much shore leave but wanted to send trinkets and memento's home as gifts to their families and loved ones.

Sometimes one would meet cleaners who had agreed to work every night shift on the whole cruise, or waiters who habitually served the loudest and most boisterous, obnoxious tables, all as a part of their agreement with another crewmember to trade for a particularly valued treasure.

Alan smiled; as the whole process was fun – the collecting of strange artifacts and even the tacky gifts that every crewmember went home with – was enjoyable to watch.

However, today Stefan seemed despondent. The doctor and Tiffany walked with him at the head of the Tour as they boarded the ship again and asked him why.

"My wallet got stolen, can you believe it?" he said. Alan recognized that those with high metabolisms were usually highly strung emotionally as well. It had probably to do with the stresses and strains that their endocrine and hormonal system went through on an hourly basis.

Stefan continued, "After all the safety talks that I give out to the passengers; we're sitting in a small tavern in a better part of Athens and someone steals my wallet. Made me look a right fool, and I will be lucky to get a large number of tourists to take tours at the next port now. Word will go around that even Stefan, the tour guide, cannot keep his own belongings safe, let alone those of a group of up to forty people."

"Oh, I'm sure it's not as bad as all that," Tiffany mollified him. "You never know – if you fill out a police report you might have it waiting for you a few stops down the line when they recover it and airmail it to you."

Stefan and Alan both smiled at the well-meaning pep-talk, but the doctor agreed with the tour guide when he said: "No, no point really – all that paperwork to fill out? And it was probably stripped of all its value and thrown in a bin anywhere in the city by now."

"Have you phoned the credit card company?" Tiffany inquired, concerned. "You know it's one of the first things that you should do, especially since you are leaving the country in less than twenty four hours."

"No need – thankfully." Stefan smiled, looking on the bright side. "I never carry credit cards with me on shore – too dangerous if you lose them – just proof of identification, international money cheque, and local currency."

"Well, then I'd say that you made an excellent example for your tour," Alan remarked encouragingly.

"Well"—Stefan gave him a lopsided smile—"you live and learn, don't you?"

Having items stolen was an occupational hazard for the international globetrotter. There were many times when Alan himself had been deprived of money, even identification, at the hands of opportunist thieves. It all came with the territory, he often thought pragmatically.

There was, indeed, a certain amount of strength to be found in being penniless and at the mercy of the local authorities in a foreign land. It was through these experiences that Alan had learned just how kind, normal, everyday people throughout the world really were. It was also, he considered, a very good lesson in self-reliance – being able to find your way out of a tight spot and find yourself a way to safer waters.

These thoughts brought him back to his most recent spot of troubles in Alaska, and the very reason, save the beautiful woman at his side, why he was now on this very cruise.

"I never did fill you in on my gossip, did I?" Alan turned to Tiffany. "My recent 'sailing trip', as it was supposed to be, in Alaskan waters."

"I wondered when you were going to bring that up." Tiffany jibed him.

"Gossip?" Stefan said brightly, his current problems forgotten. "Another misadventure at sea?"

"Oh and then some. There have been far too many misadventures at sea for my liking in recent years – I should have known never to go on a "pleasure cruise" with someone I hardly knew."

The trio (and the tour) was now filing in past one of the security men logging back into the ships records electronically by passing their boarding card thru the scanner. It was customary procedure to keep tabs on all the passengers – just in case – and it did happen, some people got lost or were tardy wandering around the port.

"I'll tell you both if you like, but I have to go get dressed in my uniform and report back to nurse Petra fairly soon." Alan laughed – Petra Gacek had a way of trying to control the medical bay if left unattended for too long.

"Some other time, Doctor, I've got to go log the missing wallet

d, Alan learned to sail at a very young age. He started on a
raft, 10' dinghy. Great way to learn. As he grew up, he learned
igger and bigger boats, and in more and more difficult
ents including the south shore of Newfoundland.

y the time he was a teenager, he was sailing in regattas on
cisco Bay, and doing quite well as a racer. He was very much
ith the water, which is essential for a sailor who can always
it.

Vhen he was in graduate school in Southern California, he
w on boats off the coast of Los Angeles. In his residency, he
n sailing the rugged coast of Eastern Canada. He time-shared
6' sailboat with another young physician, and sailed on other
nany adventures in those waters.

Once, while working for one of the cruise ships, Rick
 one of the navigation engineers on board who lived in
sked Alan if he would be interested in joining him on his
during a break between contracts. Alan jumped at the
ty, as he was boat-less during his years as a ship doctor, and
d have been a great opportunity to really see some of the
waters, and nooks and crannies of the State of Alaska that
ot get to see from a cruise ship. Granted, the cruise ships
ake weekly trips from either Seattle or Vancouver up the
ssage to southeast Alaska. They would routinely stop in
, Juneau, and some of the other larger fishing ports along the
l occasionally a few other ports, depending upon the route,
weather, and how the company felt it could make the most

Rick Hammer was a true red-blooded American. Born and
Arizona to a lower middle class family that got by, they were
end Rick to trade school so that he could learn seamanship
 good job on the cruise ships. When he had a break, he would
urn to Arizona and stay with his parents in their mobile
ke so many sailors, he was divorced. Fortunately, he had no
from that marriage. So, as he often said, "I am as free as a
entually this freedom led him to move to Alaska, buy a boat,
he good life'.

Rick lived on the 34' boat when he was in Alaska, summer, or
e was a hearty soul. Even though his home base was Juneau, a
 milder part of Alaska, it was still not the French Riviera.
known for being one of the wettest places in North America.
Vhen Rick described the boat to Alan, expletives flowed. It

with security and I'm famished after that tour.

Bidding their farewells, Tiffany squ
you get back to your room and out of your clot

Smiling, Alan didn't need any encoura

Back in the doctor's cabin, Tiffany
top and stretched while Alan laid out his me
at how at ease she always seemed to be, as if
living room, while she idly looked over his
There was his Rolex watch that had be
Halvorsen some trips before to commemorat
a particularly rowdy night in 2004. There wa
that he had built himself over the course of m
traveled with him everywhere when he was w
hours of painstaking gluing and holding tiny
with tweezers and using a magnifying glass t
was quite proud of that, and had become ;
every time he was on board.

"So, tell me about this Rick then, t
sailing trip in Alaska with," Tiffany called ov
Alan was getting ready.

"Rick Hammer? Ah yes, Mr. Rick Han

Alan was always amazed how simil
clues like the storm in the same port – wor
that first night he had ever met the dangero
only recently that Alan got back in touch
phoned him, out of the blue, when he had hea
the same port as he. This was a usual occurr
men and women of the sea. Friendships and a
out over the whole world, and these globe
catching a flight out to the ends of the conti
with a buddy. Alan always felt like he was a
world' and not one of any particular part of it.

So why had he gone on that God
wondered as he retold his story to Tiffany...

*　　　*　　　*

As the expression goes - the grass i
other side of the fence. On the regimente
watching people in sail boats and other pleasu
their own pace and going where they want to,

As a ch
Melody
to sail
environr

San Fra
at ease
end up i

would c
excelled
a Fisher
boats or

Hamme
Alaska,
sailboat
opportu
this wo
beautifu
one did
would
inside
Ketchik
coast, a
timings
money.

raised i
able to
and get
often r
trailer.
childrer
bird." I
and live

winter.
relative
Juneau

was a wooden boat and according to Rick, who spent most of his free time working on it, "honed to perfection". He did mention that it had all the latest navigation devices, which made sense since that was his profession. He also mentioned that it had all the amenities needed for a comfortable sail, new gas stove, LED lights, solar panels to recharge electronics, a bathroom, shower, etc. Based upon some of the sailboats that Alan had owned or shared, it sounded quite nice with the added touch of being a "relatively new" and "charming wood boat".

During the contract, Rick outlined to Alan some of the potential areas they could go in the time Alan had available. It looked as if they would be visiting portions of Glacier Bay, which the cruise ship was not allowed to enter, giving them much probabilities of seeing bears, whales, bird colonies, and the like. These were all passions of Alan's. Just being able to get away from the regimentation of the ship and leisurely see the wildlife, dropping anchor in picturesque coves, was a welcome dream and anticipated relaxation during the otherwise busy time between contracts, when one had to get everything in one's life in order so that one could go on to the next contract.

Granted, Alan did not know Rick very well. He had had dinner with him and a few of the other engineering officers a few times in the officers' dining room. Usually, they had a different schedule and their conversations were of much different things than medical. As far as extracurricular activities, Alan seldom went to the smoky crew bar to get blotted like many of the staff. First, he did not smoke, and second, his idea of alcohol was a nice quality glass of wine with dinner on occasion. He had not gotten drunk like many of the crew since college fraternity parties. When the engineering officers went ashore, it was often to partake in the 'ladies of the night' or gamble at the onshore casinos, neither, of which were Alan's idea of a good time. He would much rather wander around the local market, have dinner at a café, chat with locals, or go for a swim at some beautiful beach or lovely hotel.

In other words, although Alan 'knew' Rick, he really didn't really 'know' him. Rick ended his contract several weeks before Alan's, and arrangements were made to meet in Juneau when Alan finished his contract in San Diego. Then afterwards, he would fly to Boston to take care of his life.

The planned ten-day's sailing was going to be a real vacation. Alan bought his tickets and several items of sailing gear – sailing boots, warm, fuzzy jackets, etc. – for the trip. Just before Rick left the ship to head up to Alaska, they sat down and had a long chat.

Rick went over the gear, and although he had invited Alan to join him, hinted strongly that Alan should contribute $125 a day to help with food, gas, and the like. Alan did realize that food and gas were expensive in Alaska, and was certainly willing to help even though that was a bit steep.

Alan said, "Sure."

Rick also mentioned that he was glad that there were a few weeks before Alan arrived because he 'had a bit of work to do on the boat'. When Alan inquired as to what these things might be, Rick said, "Oh just some new stuff I want to add to the boat."

*   *   *

"Oh-oh..." Tiffany interrupted him. "I think I can see where this is going, one hundred and twenty five dollars a day?"

"And that is not all, believe me. By the end of it I was well over two thousand dollars out of pocket for which I could have chartered my own boat." Alan cursed, and then laughed wryly at his own stupidity...

*   *   *

The doctor flew through a long series of flights and changeovers to get to Juneau – this should have been an omen for him, but Alan had never been suspicious. By the time he reached Juneau he was just pleased to be there and to be about to start on his private sailing cruise.

It took several tries before Alan was able to get a hold of Rick on his mobile. After a freezing wait at a dockside café, Rick showed up in his battered car, obviously involved in a heated argument with someone on the phone. He signaled to Alan to wait for a second while he stood outside and shouted some more. Even through the glass Alan could make out some of the argument.

"No, I don't care.... What exactly is it worth?" Rick would shout, and wait for the reply. The man's expression would change from glee to thunderous; back to worry before he shook his head and haggled again.

When Rick had finally managed to get a figure he liked, Alan felt that he could leave the café and sauntered over, eager to get going.

"Everything all right, Rick? It's been a hell of a journey so far – and it looks like your day hasn't been going much better."

Rick looked up at him quickly and shook his head. "Oh, just another client of mine; he wants me to do a little job and won't come near the price I want."

"Ah, the trouble of going self-employed." Alan tried to joke with him, but Rick was in a terrible mood. He shrugged his shoulders and they took Alan's stuff over to where Rick's fabulous boat would be moored.

*   *   *

"Well, the sight was a little less than impressive..." Alan admitted to Tiffany. "You'll never guess what was sitting there at the moorings."

She shrugged her creamy shoulders.

"Well we walked past all of these lovely yachts, deep sea sailboats, you know, the whole nine yards of the sailing experience – boats that had been lovingly restored and maintained by professional sailors and fishermen who obviously took pride in what they do..."

"And...? What was it?" Tiffany was excited, barely able to wait for the punch line.

"A plastic dinghy."

"What?" Tiffany frowned.

"There was a blue plastic dingy. He piled my stuff on it, which somehow managed to fit, and proceeded to cast off."

"You weren't going on a sailing trip in a dingy? That's madness."

"Well, you should have seen what Rick was like in the end... But no, not even he was *that* unhinged. He'd moored his boat out past the 'No Make A Wake' sign so he wouldn't have to pay the rental fees for the dock space. You see, he lived in his boat almost all year-round – and had obviously learned all of the little tricks, and places he could go to avoid spending any money."

"That doesn't sound good." Tiffany looked alarmed.

"Well, that is not even the worst of it, not by a long, long shot. It was the worst cruise of my life, I swear. It was almost the *last* cruise of my life as well."

Tiffany's brow's shot up.

"Just wait, you'll see..."

Just at that moment, as Alan was about to launch into the rest of his dreadful story, the on-ship phone rang. The doctor's cabin always had an internal communication phone line, just in case of emergencies.

"Alan? I need some help right now." It was Captain Halvorsen.

"Why, what's the matter?"

"Just come quick – and bring a spare pair of pants with you."

"What?" was all the doctor had time to say before the phone went dead.

"It looks like the captain needs a spare pair of trousers – and quickly." Alan said bemusedly to Tiffany, who promptly burst out laughing.

"Sorry? I don't understand?" Alan said as he gathered his things, threw his whites on, and grabbed his spare medical bag as well, just in case.

"Oh – this I have *got* to see." Tiffany laughed as they both shut the door behind them and raced through the ship.

Thinking that it must be an injury, or perhaps even an embarrassing problem, Alan made a quick time getting to the elite captain's cabin, with a giggling Tiffany behind him…

"What is so funny? This could be a serious case," Alan said with not a little annoyance at Tiffany's uncharacteristic outburst. When they finally arrived he would understand why.

The doctor knocked on the cabin door, and when there was no answer, he knocked a little louder. After a few seconds there was an unlatching sound and a timid voice said, "Doctor? Is that you?"

"Yes, yes, myself and Tiffany. Now open the door, man, and let me see what the emergency is."

"No, I can't – not with Cruise Director Tiffany there," came the muted reply.

"Okay, okay…Tiffany." He turned to his giggling companion. "I'm afraid you will have to sit this one out. Wait out here unless I call."

Tiffany, holding a hand across her mouth, only nodded.

When Alan entered the spacious cabin and closed the door behind him, he found the captain's room in complete disarray, and the captain himself standing in the middle of it, wearing only his dress white shirt, his socks and sock clips, and a pair of large boxer shorts. His strong legs looked pale-in.

"My God, man – what is the problem?"

"It's that little vixen down at the front desk."

"Maud?"

Captain Halvorsen nodded. "She must have found out that I

didn't spend the night in my cabin."

The doctor could immediately think of at least three reasons why he wasn't here last night, and one of them was a certain Lady Hemmingsworth, with whom he had been so captivated the night before.

"Just look at what she's done – I'll have her keel-hauled, I swear."

On the bed, on the chair and on the floor were all the captain's spare dress trousers. And each one had one alteration. They each had the… how could he put it? The *gentleman area* of the trousers cut out, very carefully.

Alan's eyes goggled. "Ah, I see...."

"No, I don't think you do – this is an attack on my person and the office of captaincy aboard this vessel," Halvorsen roared.

"Well, certainly an attack on the office of the captaincy's trousers," Alan hazarded, and Anders scowled at him.

"Yes, quite. Well, it turns out that Maud doesn't like the fact that I haven't told my wife yet that I am going to leave her – nor did she like the attentions that my position thrusts on me by some of the more impressionable female members of the crew."

Captain Halvorsen managed to find a way to retain some of his manly dignity. "I only have my civilian blacks and there's a dress dinner tonight. I'll end up breaking my own regulations."

Alan had to smirk, and shook his head; sometimes the antics of the captain were unbelievable. "Just be thankful, Captain, that you weren't in them at the time."

He gulped. "You're telling me. I have no idea how she got in, but I bet there is a young lady on the security staff who is in cahoots with her."

Alan said nothing but produced his own dress trousers. They would probably be a little small on the captain, but no one would realize. He, as did all of the officers on board, had a spare pair back in his cabin anyway – and this would avoid the embarrassing situation of the captain having to explain to head office, and possibly face disciplinary action, precisely how all of his dress trousers had been ruined. This way the captain could discretely order a replacement through the laundry/uniforms section, and hope that not too much scuttlebutt would ensue.

"Well, no great harm done; after all," Alan suggested as the captain got dressed.

"No, no I suppose I walked into that lion's den myself..."

The good doctor thought it polite not to comment.

"No more shall be said about this, do you understand?" The captain smiled conspiratorially at him.

"Of course, Captain, always happy to be of service in an emergency."

At that, Alan Mayhew thought it was best if he left the captain to gather his own thoughts – and clothes – and left the cabin to find a grinning Tiffany.

"You knew, didn't you?" he whispered. "That was what you and Maud were laughing about when I met you at the front desk?"

She nodded as they started to make their way back, and even Alan found it difficult to suppress a smile. "My word," he said, "the antics that go on in a cruise ship."

"Well…that reminds me." Tiffany suddenly threw him a demanding stare. "You haven't finished your story for me, about risking life and limb with Mr. Navigator Rick Hammer, and I have such a long cruise ahead of me." She walked ahead of him at a quick pace back towards his cabin, and Alan was sure she was doing it so that he could take a look at that delightful wiggle of her pert behind.

"I… hum, yes… but…." The doctor also knew that time was getting on. What, with his story telling and the captain's emergency, his allotted lunch break was surely up by now.

"But? Are you refusing me, Ship Doctor Mayhew?" Tiffany turned and looked at him with a sultry, smoky gaze. "Don't you worry; I have a plan…"

She stopped in the corridor and put one arm out, opening the door immediately to her left. It was a cleaning cupboard.

Alan dove in behind her and the door closed, they were in one of the large cabinet cupboards that were on every deck, housing brooms, mops, soap, hangers, linen and blankets for that deck's allotment of cabins.

It was pitch dark, with only slivers of light piercing the gloom.

He heard Tiffany say, "You don't think I came all this way just to say hello?"

Alan could hear the smile on her voice, its breathy quality as he felt two hands tug at his shirt, pulling him deeper into the shadows.

His lips found hers in perfect synchrony, as if their bodies knew what they were doing even without the gift of sight – not that visions weren't playing through Alan's mind, as if suddenly all his other senses had come alive and were that much sharper for the absence of one.

He smelt her fragrance as she kissed him long and lingeringly, playing her lips against his in the lightest feathering of touches to the full, deep kiss.

He could hear the rustle of their clothes, of the simple cotton summer dress that she had been wearing as his own hands reached behind her to the small of this lovely woman's back...

God, I am a lucky man. Alan thought as one of his hands smoothed over the round orb of a pert bottom, and then, suddenly finding the edge of her dress, he stroked a finger up the inside of her thigh and the sheer stocking that glided under his touch.

"Make love to me, Alan," she breathed into his ear, her voice thick as both her hands came up to bury their fingers through his hair. The movement stretched her form against him and he felt the warmth of her firm belly and abdomen against his own, and the soft pushing of her breasts against his chest.

"Here? Now?" he whispered between kisses, one hand slipping under her dress to caress her bottom as the other slid around to hold her by the hip, trapping her against his own frame. He was sure that she could feel him by now, as his own trousers were getting uncomfortable down there.

She murmured a pleasing little cat noise in the back of her throat and pressed her abdomen harder, rubbing against his trousers...

Bring... bring... bring...bring...

The moment was shattered by a vibration in the pocket of Alan's trousers, startling Tiffany – she jumped back.

"What in hell is that?" she demanded with a giggle.

Bring...bring....

"Oh damn it – it's my pager... It will be the infirmary..." Alan scooped the little black device out of his pocket and yes indeed, there was a call registered from the infirmary.

"I was wondering what on earth a doctor brings to his secret assignations." Tiffany laughed and smoothed down the front of her dress. "You'd better answer it; I don't want you to miss any more emergencies on my account."

Alan cursed his bad luck and coughed, readjusting his clothes as he surreptitiously poked his head out of the linen closet. There was no one in sight.

Damn it, damn it, damn it," he swore under his breath several times as he retrieved his phone and called back the number.

"Doctor? So good of you to answer." It was nurse Petra Gacek, and even through the phone line Alan could swear he could hear an element of glee in her voice.

"Yes, Petra? What is the emergency?"

"No emergency, Doctor, but you are in danger of running late for clinic hours, so I thought that it would be my duty as a professional nurse to inform you of this. Also, Mr. and Mrs. Seinz have called to make their appointment – they will see you tomorrow."

The doctor checked his watch – it was nearing late afternoon, and dinner was probably being prepared even as he spoke, in the galleys below. The rest of the tours would be back or getting back soon. Those passengers, who were staying out late into the evening before their morning departure, would be hurriedly trying to pack in their last few hours of shore leave. All in all, he considered, it was definitely time that he was back at work.

"Thank you for informing me, Petra, well done," he said, without much enthusiasm as he clicked off his phone and turned to see the vision of loveliness, his Tiffany closing the door to their tryst firmly behind them.

"I should be going now too – there are tonight's entertainments on the ship I am working on to be preparing for."

Alan scowled.

"But I will phone you before we set sail – *if* you pick up the phone this time." She playfully jabbed him in the stomach and gave him a peck on the cheek. "Until the next port, Doctor Mayhew?" she inquired.

"I will be expecting you," he replied enthusiastically, and watched her wiggle again as she quick-footed away to the reception and off the *Ocean Quest*.

Turning back to his duties, Alan couldn't believe the rum luck he had been having recently. A disastrous sailing trip in which he could have died with Rick Hammer, a storm in port, a death on board and now this.

At least it wouldn't be too long before they could be together again, he consoled himself, and that thought immediately triggered off another thought about his findings today. Yes, he could indeed always be in contact with her *now* via the ships phones, but what about before; why had the transmitter suddenly failed to work that night? He wondered whether he should bring the issue up with the captain, yet decided that if he saw Vince, or ran into any of the other navigation engineers, he would question them on this little mystery.

CHAPTER SIX

Egyptian Waters
A doctor's life at sea

THAT NIGHT ALAN CHASED up the paperwork of the dead French-Belgian fellow, which task occupied the majority of his time. During the day Petra had dutifully logged a few calls, and Alan was pleased to note that his diagnosis of Gillais' death had proved accurate, and that no further investigation was necessary. What he should do about his missing Cinderella of the pink knickers he had no idea, and hoped that either the situation would make itself clear, or that it would come to a peaceful resolution without his involvement.

He recorded an interview over the phone with the Greek Police authorities, the Belgian authorities and the offices of Interpol – all who seemed happy with his work and were eager to put a close on this most complicated case with dual jurisdictions. Thankfully for his own company, Gold Line, and the American Consulate, he would just have to forward them his reports and notes. If there were any problems, he would be informed when he arrived in Fort Lauderdale. No official was worried, since all of the officers – the Captain, Vince and, of course, himself – were in danger of going anywhere. They might be traveling around the world on a cruise, but they weren't *leaving* and would still be aboard the same ship when it eventually arrived in Fort Lauderdale a few weeks from now.

He was working so much, in fact, that he missed the dress dinner entirely. The doctor was generally forgiven of these sorts of misdemeanors, as it is understood that they keep even odder work hours than the rest of the crew aboard since he is on call twenty-four hours a day.

So it was with a glad heart that he finally sunk back into his bed to sleep in the early hours of the morning the next day, as the *Ocean Quest* was approaching Alexandria...

*   *   *

"Doctor Seinz," Alan greeted the newest patients the very next day, "and this must be Mrs. Seinz. Glad to finally meet you."

Alan had started early, had made sure he was refreshed with an extra dark espresso coffee and had opened up the infirmary with a tired-looking Nurse Watkins in tow.

She seemed well rested after her long break – a whole day off, after encountering her first 'cruise-corpse' the night the storm had hit Athens. Mischievously Alan wondered whether the young Ernesto had anything to do with her yawns and sleepy eyes, but not meaning to pry, left her to her daydreams as the first patients of the day came in.

The Seinz were a lovely couple, Alan thought. Intelligent, articulate, and full of interesting stories. It turned out that they were both professional scholars – Dr. Seinz was an archaeologist and Diane was a microbiologist. They informed Alan that this was one of the few non-working holidays that they had managed to take together in their married years, as the doctor showed his wife all the places and monuments where he had worked during his career.

Alan understood these type of people almost immediately – they were workaholics, and passionate about their work. Obviously good at what they did, they enjoyed being able to talk about it to interested parties.

In the true manner of any workaholic, they had started their holiday straight from the office, so to speak; Dr. Seinz had been working in Rome prior to the cruise, and had decided to meet with his wife in the Italian capital, at the tail end of his latest contract, for their transatlantic cruise. It seemed nothing but the best for the Seinz's.

"So, not four days into the cruise and already two of our clients are injured," joked the doctor.

"Yes, but we both brought our problems with us," Diane remarked. "Him with his hand, and as for me I have had sea sickness ever since I was a child."

"Well, let us start with that then – as it seems to have caused the most bother."

Alan conducted a preliminary physical, which included some stretching, walking and balancing, more to rule out any other health problems that might be effecting Mrs. Seinz, and then went on to use the otoscope with magnifying lens, which allowed him to look inside her ear.

There was no overt signs of infection, a little redness perhaps due to swelling, but absolutely nothing that made him feel concerned. He imagined that Diane's sea-sickness, with its associated symptom of disappearing rapidly, was caused by nothing more than a slightly thinner membrane of the inner eardrum, or perhaps one of the tiny bones in the ear was a little closer to the wall of her ear canal than it should have been. It was just enough that when pressure would build up due to height or motion, she would experience dizziness and nausea, but this would soon clear up as the eardrum's position corrected itself.

He informed Diane of the probable situation. "Well, there is good news and bad news. You can indeed have pinpoint surgery to remove the problem completely, but I wouldn't advise it. The ailment is so minor that, really, the procedure itself has more danger of causing problems to you than the condition. What you need to try to do is lower your blood pressure a little bit, go for a jog every day to regulate this, as long as you have no hip or knee problems, take one of these a day"—Alan produced some anti-nausea medications—"and you should be fine."

Mrs. Seinz seemed overjoyed. "Really? That simple? I never knew all these years."

"Also, you could spend some more time on the open decks," Alan encouraged her as Diane Seinz seemed to be a tough-spirited sort of woman, elegant in her way, but with a practical 'get-to' demeanor that must have helped her in her professional career. To the doctor she didn't seem like a woman who would shirk from a challenge.

"Kill of cure, Dr. Mayhew?" Dr. Seinz joked.

"Exactly. The more time that your body is experiencing these variations in pressure and motion, the more it will learn to adapt and adjust."

"So my unfortunate treatment, it seems, is that my husband should take me on more cruises." Mrs. Seinz laughed, while her husband smiled magnanimously.

"And now for your good self, Dr. Seinz." Alan turned his attention to the abrasions on the doctor's hand.

On his right hand there was a small laceration with an area of erythema (redness) radiating out towards the wrist – he must have caught himself on something – perhaps when he slipped, Alan mused, which resulted in the laceration. The initial wound itself was healing adequately, as he himself had said – but peppered around the laceration was a cellulites and that infection was growing more intense. The reddened patch had deepened in color and had spread, edging out from the regions of the laceration along and underneath otherwise healthy skin.

"Hmm..." Alan didn't like the look of this.

The infection was interfering with the natural healing process of the laceration, causing the tiny perforations in the skin to weep, and remain open. The doctor could see immediately that, while there was an *acute* problem developing, a more serious level of treatment was indicated to stem the infection. He explained what was going on to the non-medical doctor, who looked a little alarmed and rubbed at his wrist distractedly.

"Does it itch? Feel hot?" Alan asked as he examined the hand further. "Aches slightly?"

"Yes, all of those. It did seem to be clearing up rather well, but then the ache and the heat didn't seem to want to go away at all," Dr. Seinz remarked.

"Yes, that is definitely the infection. The itching will be the combination of your healing cells fighting the invading infection, and the heat and the ache is the swelling that the infection is causing under the skin. Tiny blood vessels get squeezed by the expanding flesh, and the small nerve endings are telling you that something is wrong."

"Ah, you make it sound quite dangerous," Seinz tried to joke.

"Infections can be, if left untreated – but there are thankfully many ways to treat them these days. Simple antibiotics should kill an area of infection flat, and there are any number of types of antibiotics we have here on board that I can give you."

Doctor Seinz seemed interested, if not a little worried.

Diane shot a querying glance at Alan. "How about cold treatment, Doctor?" In my laboratory we routinely freeze microbial organisms to put them into a state of torpor, and from there we can treat them. Not that I am suggesting that you freeze my husband's hand – far from it in fact – but would cold compress help?"

The doctor remembered their conversation the preceding night, of course – Dr. Seinz's wife was a microbiologist.

"Yes, Mrs. Seinz, cold treatment can help, but in the case of the human body we only really use it to alleviate symptoms or to kill tissue like a mole with cryotherapy. A cold compress, applied as many times throughout the day as you'd like, would reduce the swelling, contracting the inflamed tissues, and allow the blood vessels to open and carry your own natural antibodies to get into the area and fight the infection more directly. It can be a very good idea in some cases."

"I must say that I feel that I am rather letting my husband down at the moment, with me being ill, and not being able to help, even though infections and micro-organisms are my specialty." Diane seemed embarrassed.

"Two very different branches of science," Alan concluded soothingly. "But I am sure that in your research you have dealt with some of the organisms that affect the human body?"

"Yes, quite a lot in fact. In my laboratory we have done a lot of work on the life cycle of various viruses – and you would not believe the results, Doctor Mayhew – it would make you scared of leaving your house in the morning."

The doctor, who had seen the norovirus contaminate whole ships in a matter of days, could only agree.

"Not that your body would be much better. Do you know how many viruses and other organisms survive on the human body?"

The doctor had to admit that he didn't.

"Millions in all probability, if not more. We carbon-based organic life forms are the perfect breeding ground for them."

"That reminds me," Alan said as he started getting the materials ready to clean Dr. Seinz's wound. "I was watching a program some years ago by the British Naturalist – what is his name – *Atterby?* No, Attenborough, David Attenborough, yes, that's it. He was narrating a program on human life in general, and he made the analogy that, if an alien species were to contact the earth – and by this I mean another life form who had no contact with human beings, and no idea how to communicate with us – if they did a 'life scan', measuring all the species in the planet they would assume that micro-organisms were the dominant species. What's more – if they did that same 'life-scan' on human beings, they would probably think that we are merely hosts for other organisms – we are infested with micro-organisms."

"Precisely, Dr. Mayhew. It is fascinating, isn't it?" Mrs. Seinz remarked enthusiastically. "What goes even further, and is much more interesting is that most complex organisms, humans especially, seem to exist in symbiosis with other microorganisms…"

"Do you mean that we depend upon them for our survival?"

"To some extent, yes. Symbiosis means that two or more creatures exist together, feeding each other while helping each other adapt to dangers, to be better suited to adapt to their environment. You will of course know that we all have worms that live in our guts – that feed off of our food and help us digest?"

Alan grimaced; a disgusting thought but yes, it was true.

"Well the same could be said for every area of our bodies,

where there are tiny microbial forms of life that are eating the – how shall we say – surplus materials, and in turn forming their own environment which fights off other invading micro-organisms."

"So what you two are saying," Dr. Seinz cut in, "is that my own immune makeup just wasn't strong enough to fight off these little buggers?"

"In essence, yes."

Diane pulled a face at her husband. "My poor, weak man, with his substandard microbes," she teased.

"Well, thank you very much. If it is all the same to you, my dear, I would rather trust that the doctor here has got something that will kill the whole lot pretty quick."

Alan laughed. "Well, I should be able to find something."

With these words, he disappeared into his locked cabinets of medicines and treatments. A ship had to carry all manner of medical supplies, and be able to cover at least any kind of general emergency, ailment, or condition while at sea. It was often the case that the medical clinic of any ship was one of the most well-stocked and safest places on board.

Alan returned with a small tub of antibiotics. He then decanted some of the contents into a tiny plastic tub. He wrote in the details on his prescriptions' envelope and stuck it onto the package of pills he had gathered.

"Right, well I have cleaned the wound as best as I am able to at present and Nurse Watkins will again apply a dressing. This time, even though it is uncomfortable and frustrating, try to keep the dressing on as long as you can, and with any luck we should only need to change it once a day. What is equally as important is that you take one of these a day – they are quite a powerful antibiotic, which should kill any infections in your system."

Dr. Seinz seemed immensely pleased with the result, as Alan took him over to the accompanying nurse's station where Kelly was already prepared with gauze bandages and surgical tape.

"So this should do the job? I had rather hoped that I would be able to get out and see some of my old excavations in the next port, you know." Dr. Seinz looked a little apprehensively at the bandages as they were firmly applied to the lower half of his hand and wrist.

Nurse Watkins finished the dressing by securing a cotton bandage wrap in the classic around-the-thumb-and-wrist loop to keep the padding in place.

"Well, with any luck it will certainly aid your healing process –

but I am not sure whether you should go near any dirt or dust just yet."

The Seinz's looked crestfallen.

"Yes, I am afraid to say that it will be no manual labor for you for at least a couple of weeks," Alan joked, thinking they would see the funny side of not being allowed to do 'dirty work' while on board a prestigious cruise ship.

Instead, and rather curiously, the Seinz's looked a bit disheartened, as if they were planning to get dirty.

"Well, the doctor's orders come first," Dr. Seinz said after a moment's pause, "it is just – it *is* Egypt, home of the Pharaohs, one of the oldest civilizations on the planet... It would be a shame not to do a bit of digging if we have the chance..."

Alan was slightly amused at this turn of events. He wasn't precisely sure just how much excavating the archaeologist had in mind doing while he had his one night stop over in Alexandria, but quickly thought of a solution.

"Gloves."

The couple looked up at him blankly.

"Well, Nurse Watkins's dressing should prevent most if not all dust and dirt particles getting to the infected area, but if you find yourself in a situation in which you absolutely have to pick up a trowel, I suggest you take with you some pairs of these and tape shut the top around your wrist." He pulled a handful of the blue surgical gloves from their box, and carefully put them into a paper prescription bag. The ship had ample supply of latex and plastic gloves, and the doc knew from previous experience that they probably had many more than was needed for the trip.

A lot of medical supplies for a ship's infirmary are what could be called 'necessaries' or 'logistical equipment': spare medicine tubes, jars and containers, sterile drapes and syringes, gloves, bandages, and cleaning solutions. Compared to the actual amount of oral and injectable medicines, the logistic equipment easily dwarfed that number by the tenfold.

"Make sure you wear them if you are in danger of coming into contact with any soil. It will restrict movement and the tactile feeling of the hand over all, but it is much better than having a serious infection that can last weeks and months."

"Oh, I thought I had escaped those things when I came on this cruise," Dian Seinz said fervidly. *Obviously*, Alan thought, *Mrs. Seinz must be very used to contamination procedures.*

"I think that should about wrap it up for the both of you,"

Alan finished.

"Thank you very much, Doctor," the other doctor said as they got up to leave, "and a most interesting conversation we have had too. I trust we will see you at the officer's dinner?"

Dr. Seinz was referring to the formal shipboard dinner that happened every week, to which certain select passengers were invited, or for which they had bought tickets. Alan was not surprised that the Seinz's had been invited or had purchased tickets.

"Of course, it will be a pleasure," he replied warmly and realized that he meant it as well. It was quite encouraging to spend a pleasant examination with intelligent and well-spoken people. Very often, the passengers he saw were in a certain amount of distress, and a great majority of his job involved trying to calm them down. Other times it meant dealing with 'crowd control' as he liked to refer to it, when he would be seeing a whole family or attendant partners, all of whom were distressed or otherwise exhibiting high emotion. But then again, seeing the doctor on board a Gold Line cruise – supposedly one of the holidays of a lifetime – wasn't exactly anybody's idea of glamour or fun, for the most part, anyway.

Alan knew, however, that there were a few clients who seemed to perversely enjoy seeing the ship's doctor, and this was something that had nothing to do with him being a man in uniform.

What was making him reflect on this, the surprising nature of patients that he saw every day? Alan's musings had started when Nurse Watkins had informed him who the next patient was going to be...

Mrs. Patricia Jones.

"Scheduled in for a hearing test, Doc," Kelly informed him as she escorted Mrs. Jones in. She was approximately 35 years' old and appeared to be in good general health. She was slim, attractive, with blond hair, and quite active on her feet unlike some of the other passengers who were weighing in at over three hundred pounds and not moving quickly.

Mrs. Jones was wearing normal attire from the neck down. Yet, from the neck up, was a different story. Her traditional floppy straw hat was straddled with two very bright yellow sound-deadening headphones. Dangling around her neck was a fairly efficient appearing carbon and HEPA filter respirators – the type one uses in a factory where workers are potentially exposed to solvents and noxious chemicals. Also, around her neck where the tell tale plastic nose prongs that would accompany oxygen bottles. These prongs extended to their inevitable location in a backpack that was definitely out of character for the high-fashion clothes that she and the rest of the cruisers were wearing.

After getting all the particulars from Mrs. Jones, the doc got down to why Mrs. Jones wanted an audiogram.

"It's that couple next door to me, Doctor. The ones with the very loud voices."

"Loud voices, madam?"

"Yes, of course, my dear man." Mrs. Jones seemed to be regarding the doctor as a bit of a simpleton. "When I came on board I naturally made friends with many people, Doctor Mayhew, and those who are my neighbors even more so – one has to live with them after all, even if it is for a relatively short time. Well, I have even been having dinner with them and they are shouting all the time – the noisiest people I have ever heard."

Mrs. Jones then indicated that she had been forced to listen to some rather loud conversations here on the ship and she was concerned that those individuals had damaged her hearing.

The doctor was fairly astonished, and asked how far away these individuals were when they were speaking, and Mrs. Jones responded that they were at maximum 15 feet away, her zone of comfort around anyone.

Alan smoothly continued, sensing that this was indeed going to be a strange one... "So, have you suffered from any infections in your ears over the years, Mrs. Jones? Or have you had problems with them in the past?"

Mrs. Patricia Jones looked at the doctor, and in all seriousness said, "I was a dog in my previous life and consequently have very sensitive hearing."

It was all Alan could do to keep a straight face.

She went on to describe the fact that throughout her childhood she was forced to listen to individuals who spoke loudly, which obviously affected her ability to do any constructive course in school.

"I see, Mrs. Jones, I see. And what about the respirator? I see that you have filters here?" Alan hoped that his tone came across as one of professional compassion, and not professional disbelief. Half knowing that there was going to be another unusual response; he girded himself for the inevitable smile on his face.

"I am afraid, Doctor Mayhew, that I am also hypersensitive to various smells. You should see what happens to me around fresh paint, or perfume, or any sort of bleach at all." Mrs. Jones gave him a mournful look.

"I see, your reincarnation explains that..." Alan couldn't resist saying, and when Mrs. Jones sent him a sharp look to see if he was mocking her he added "Dogs have very sensitive senses of smell of course," throwing her an innocent smile.

"Yes, perhaps you are right," she added after a moment. The patient indicated that she was highly sensitive to paint, and she was unable to stay in a place that had been painted any more recently than two months for more than 4 minutes without breaking out in a rash. She also indicated that she was highly sensitive to cologne perfume and immediately would have a reaction if she encountered even a whiff.

Not to precipitate any acute episode in Mrs. Jones, Alan neglected to mention that the Medical Center had been painted only last week and that both Kelly and he were both today wearing cologne, granted neither of them bathed in it, but both did enjoy wearing a dab or two of quality scents.

"So, Mrs. Jones, the oxygen tanks as well? We have covered the hearing and the nasal symptoms. Do you have a problem with your breathing as well?"

"It happens when I get excited, Doctor. I am afraid that when I am agitated my oxygen levels simply plummet, and I must replace them in order to be able to calm down."

"I see... Do you have any asthma, or any pulmonary related disease? Perhaps some history of these in the family?"

"No, I don't think so, Doctor," Mrs. Jones replied, and then sat back to bask in the glow of her diagnosis.

It was pretty obvious to the doctor what was at fault; Mrs. Jones was one of these unfortunate individuals who had been taught to believe that she had various hypersensitivities, multiple chemical sensitivities, and a variety of other not very well accepted diagnoses in the medical world. As the medical infirmary did not have a proper audiogram machine or an audio booth, Alan thought quickly of how he was going to cope with the troubling and troubled Mrs. Patricia Jones.

It was often the case on cruise ships that, because it was a paid service, the *patient was always right* – a situation that was not ideal in his mind, and which led to problems of this kind. For the passengers of the Gold Cruise Lines, all of whom had paid quite a lot of money to be able to come on this cruise, there were minimal charges for medical services, minimal was the byword in this, and in many other cases.

Alan had to think of some way to explain to Mrs. Jones that they did not have a proper audiogram on board, and avoid the conclusion that she could raise blue murder until the vessel was turned around and returned to a port that did indeed have an audiogram. Or, on the other hand, another outcome could be that Mrs. Jones would find her way to make an official complaint against the "noisy passengers" – people who the doc was sure were completely unaware of what they might have caused and were more than likely not at all responsible for Mrs. Jones's condition.

Then Alan remembered that one of the laboratory instruments did have some high-pitched and noise frequency analyzer when used in the calculation of various chemical evaluations.

"I have just the thing, Mrs. Jones... A highly specialized device, which will have the problem sorted out immediately." Alan retrieved the instrument and set about to 'examine' Mrs. Jones's external canals, which were perfectly normal. There wasn't even any scarring of the temp membrane.

Alan ran the quasi "hearing test", and reassured the patient that the individuals who had spoken loudly had not damaged her hearing. After a few other words of reassurance, Mrs. Jones left the clinic with all her apparatuses.

"What was that all about?" Kelly asked after *the reincarnated dog* had left. The young nurse had obviously sensed that this patient would present an … *interesting* case, and so decided to leave the main medical centre examination room and do some filing instead.

"You went into hiding on purpose, didn't you?" the doc accused her.

"I'm sorry, but it seemed that nothing less than a fully trained doctor with a uniform would provide her with the 'medical services' she was looking for," Kelly countered wistfully.

"Well, all I can say is that I feel sorry for the fairly normal-looking gentleman that would be her husband," Alan replied, sighing, and going back to his notes to write up the latest encounter for the multitude of records that needed to be kept, even for a trivial matter, such as Mrs. Jones's hearing.

What annoyed him the most about these sorts of patients was that their fictitious ailments generated a lot of paperwork – and this paperwork would follow the patient around from one harassed medical professional to the next, leading to lost time, lost wages, and possibly even misdiagnoses further down the line. Unfortunately, the Mrs. Jones of the world could have been saved from themselves, if a medical practitioner had initially indicated that her problem was psychological-not medical. She could have gotten proper psychiatric counseling instead of trying to prove to the world that she had 'multiple chemical sensitivities' or 'fibromyalgia', etc.

But Alan had seen a lot of these types of patients on cruise lines. He wondered why the Gold Cruise Line Company and cruises in general attracted them.

"Maybe it's me," he said to himself as he considered all the bad omens that had seemed to pursue him since he boarded the *Ocean Quest*.

Alan was not normally superstitious by any stretch of the imagination – but he didn't like the way that the odds were stacking up against him, as first one complication arose, and then another. He hoped to heaven that there wouldn't be another death this side of the Nile, or he would start to wonder if his life was being secretly filmed for a murder mystery.

But at least we will be making the shores of Egypt soon, Alan thought. He always liked Egypt, with its aura of mystery, its fragrances, and smells, and tastes of an ancient land with even older mysteries. Every time he visited, he still got that faint rush of adventure.

CHAPTER SEVEN

Alexandria
Lucky escapes and unlucky coincidences

THE *OCEAN QUEST* HAD PULLED out all the stops to make landfall at Alexandria the very next day. By the time the passengers woke up, once again, there would be a day of shore leave with a morning departure. The tour staff was experiencing one of their busiest schedules during the next twenty-four hour period because of all the tours on offer.

Early the next morning Alan had a chat with their unlucky tour manager, Stefan, over breakfast in the crew's mess. Like him, Stefan had decided to take an early bite below decks with the general staff to prepare for the day. Alan and Kelly had worked on through the previous day, seeing to all of the medical examinations and health checks that were needed before making port.

The doctor had pushed himself a little harder on that previous day, trying his best to clear the decks so he could have a few hours to explore one of his favorite destinations in the world.

"Yes, it always reminds me why I am doing this job," Stefan agreed; all traces of his previous unhappy self having vanished.

Stefan was an essentially optimistic soul, and had the good fortune of being able to use that character trait to his advantage as a tour manager and on many of his travels.

Talking of his change in mood, Alan remarked, "I see nothing will keep you down, huh? Not like some of my patients." The irksome Mrs. Jones came to mind.

Stefan laughed. "Well, I've done all the paperwork regarding the stolen wallet, and now, if all the pax turn up for the tours I will be conducting, then I will be making a profit. One of the reasons I came on this cruise was because it did the Egyptian run." He winked and did the universal finger rubbing gesture for money.

Alan laughed. "Yes, there is that part of it as well for your department. Tell me, who have you got on your tour today? Are the

Seinz's part of your trip?" Alan knew that there were always several tour staff and managers on board, often leading competing tours and running below-decks bets on who could make the most money, taking commissions and tips. Of all the tour managers on board at present, Alan preferred Stefan because of his easy-going, happy-go-lucky nature.

"Yes, they should be – although I think the doctor himself should be leading the tour – I might have to start paying him a commission when we get to the Tomb of the Kings."

"Really?" Alan was intrigued.

"Yes – didn't you know? Dr. Seinz was a big name a decade ago in the continuing excavations around a lot of ancient sites in Egypt. I had to do a lot of research when I took this job, and think of my surprise when I saw his name on my log sheet. I said to myself, 'where have I heard that name before?' He only wrote one of the guides that I was using for my research."

"Wow! You will have to know your stuff then – there may be a test in it."

"Lord, I hope not. I'm worried enough as it is." Stefan chuckled and shook his head. "But he seems a nice sort." He looked up from his cup of tea. "Do you want to come along?"

Alan considered; he did have a few spare hours. "Sure, why not?"

"That's a deal then, but it'll cost you." Stefan grinned.

It was fairly usual for crewmembers to accompany the tours when they could, sometimes as extra chaperones, sometimes as simply tourists. Unlike Alan who enjoyed the opportunity of getting out and seeing the sites and meeting some of the passengers on a non-medical basis, some of the crew absolutely hated this detail as it meant having to herd a whole variety of personalities, get them to the right places at the right times, and try to make sure that everyone was happy and satisfied. It entailed a healthy 'service smile' as some of the previous tour managers had called it. You had to have the ability to have a wide, foolish grin on your face even when the clients were annoying the hell out of you; insects were biting you and the locals were charging fifteen percent extra to help you out.

Stefan was a natural. He recounted to Alan the secret of his success as he tutored the doctor on the basics of being a tour manager.

"Well, you have to have two eyes open, so to speak – one keeping an eye on your group, and the other on the environment. A tour always attracts hawkers and pickpockets, who see a big, plump group of generally westerners as 'easy pickings'. Judge which client is going to cause you the most trouble, assess which one is probably in need of the most help and keep an eye on them. And *smile*." Stefan dazzled him with a set of winning pearly whites.

"How do you do it – be so upbeat all the time while herding the cats?"

Stefan considered for a moment, shrugged. "I guess I just never see much of a reason to be unhappy – I have got one of the best jobs in the world." *He certainly looked content,* Alan thought. "And then there was Brazil as well – that taught me a lot."

"Brazil?"

"Yeah, back before I became a professional cruise staff, as it were, I was a 'professional globetrotter'. Straight after college I would work in whatever job I could get my hands on for six months, then get my money together and go off for another three months around the world, picking up whatever jobs I could. Gradually, as I became better at it I would be able to find more work while traveling and less work in the West. I started looking after cattle in Australia, manning ski resorts in Austria, kitchen staff in Thailand... Those sorts of 'traveling jobs' eventually led me to the cruises."

"So what happened in Brazil?"

"Well, back before all of that, as I said, I was just a sort of backpacker really. I was near the Brazilian rainforest one time and I was waiting for this guide to get back in touch with me since he was supposed to take me out the next day. Well, anyway the next day came and went, then the next and the next and I thought, 'stuff this' – I'm going anyway.

"So I made my way out into the Brazilian rainforest, nothing but my camping equipment, my provisions and a map."

"Wow," Alan said. "That is a pretty brave thing to do."

"Not really, I figured that the local people did it all the time, so why not me?" Stefan went on, "Anyway, so I was out there for about two hours enjoying the bird sounds, thick foliage, etc. before ... they found me – or I found them."

"Who?"

"The local thugs. There were six of them, all dressed in a dirty mix mash of combat gear and all carrying rifles or machine guns."

"Oh no! How did you ever get out alive?"

"Elvis."

"I beg your pardon?"

"Let me explain. So, it turned out that I had stumbled onto

some sort of encampment or something, they had their cook fire and bivouacs there all set up, and I just came walking through the jungle straight into the middle of it as if I was a gift from the Gods." Stefan mimed their surprise, "Hi, I'm Johnny Westerner, I have no friends, no idea where I am, and no idea what I am doing, with a large amount of nice American Dollars on me, and probably able to fetch a very nice ransom if you want – thank you very much." He laughed at his own stupidity.

"My heart plummeted, I was certain that I was going to die, I had no support, and no one knew where I was. My brain ran through all the scenarios and I decided that this was it; this was going to be the worst day of my life, whatever I had left of it."

"So what happened – and what has Elvis got to do with it?"

"Well, the leader jumped up – a big brute of a man – and started screaming in my face in Portuguese slang, then in broken English. He asked me what I was doing and how they were going to kill me and that I had better say my prayers or else. I was petrified, absolutely petrified. One of them pushed me down on my knees and I thought, well, this is *it*. All of my previous stupid actions flashed through my head, all the things I wished I had done, had been better at in school, the things I wished that I had said to my mother before I left...."

"While I was praying for my life they were going through my things... They upended my bag, tore out my clothing, and took my water and food. They were leaving me with nothing, absolutely no evidence that I had ever been there before they executed me."

"They took my watch, my phone, started packing all of my stuff away – and that is when they found it..."

"Found what?"

"My Elvis poster. It was the cover of the last album he ever did, and it was a signed copy, with a black marker of 'My Number one fan, Elvis', over the picture of the King with his hand outstretched. I carried it everywhere – it was my most prized possession."

Stefan elapsed into guffaws of laughter, before sobering himself up to continue. "The one who held it dropped it like he had seen a ghost, and then hurriedly picked it up and held it in his hands like he was holding the Baby Jesus or something. He looked over at me with this deadly serious look on his face, saying – 'is this real?' I nodded; Elvis had given it to my mom more than thirty years ago after a concert.

"So, this guerrilla hushed his hand at the other thugs and told them to stop, that this was serious. He showed them the picture of Elvis and they all went quiet, as if entranced, even beyond the grave, by the power of the King. 'Here,' the leader tossed me my water back and picked me up. 'You go that way. Go that way and never come back, you never saw us, got it.' And that was that. I scrambled and ran in the direction he told me before I came to a village in a little under an hour; and they took me in. The next day, they gave me a ride to the next city. From there I phoned my mom and told her what had happened, and to hook me up with the Embassy."

"Oh my God – they let you go for a signed Elvis poster?"

Stefan nodded. "Absolutely, my friend. The King saved my life. To this day I don't know whether they realized how much it was worth – I mean they had no way to authenticate it, anyone could have scrawled that on the front, it is just that my mom was there thirty years ago and we knew that it was an original.

"Or maybe I just happened to bump into the largest Elvis fans in all of the Brazilian rainforest?" He chuckled again, "I'll never know – but you know what I was thinking all the way on my plane ride home? That I had come *that close*...." He held his thumb and forefinger out just a fraction apart. "Yes, sir, I came *that* close to losing it all, everything, on one random afternoon in one random part of the jungle. What are the odds of me walking directly into their camp? What are the odds of my particular tormentors being fans of Rockabilly Doowop?" Stefan shrugged. "Ever since then I have just counted my blessings, and figured that optimism seems a pretty sensible way to go in this life."

After hearing that incredible story, Alan was forced to agree.

*   *   *

Alexandria itself is a beautiful port, built near the ocean's edge with layers of the city extending up to the ancient stone buildings on the hills. As far as tourist ports go, it is a very pleasant place for cruise ships to anchor. The commercial port is, of course, not the charming brick and mortar of the area they tender into. Even moving into the fall season, the air was humid and hot, and the landscape was a washed mixture of gold and browns as the shrubs battled with desertification. Everywhere Alan looked, he saw the white linen of the locals' clothes – the most sensible in this heat – start to emerge, from the long, flowing Bahia's of the locals, to the burkhas, and when the ship arrived, of course, among the crisp white cotton suits of the tourists.

Stefan proved to be a good guide, as he gathered up his charges, and checked off all of their names on his clipboard before they made their way into the city. It was a city of white walls and narrow streets, date palms, and sudden squares with wells that hadn't been changed for thousands of years.

Admittedly, Alan thought, *I am being led around the more picturesque parts of the Old Quarter,* but still, on the whole he was impressed by how the Egyptian authorities managed to look after their ancient culture square in the middle of their modern one.

The only thing that marred the journey was the presence of Lady Hemmingsworth. The Lady was fully decked out this time in what Alan called 'colonial whites' – white linen trousers, a white shirt with a pair of Rayban sunglasses over her eyes, while the overall ensemble wasn't unusual, the assumed pride that she wore it with, and the obvious fact that the clothes were brand new and were probably never meant to be used for *actual* traveling, gave Alan the impression that it was all an act. He was even vaguely surprised that she had decided to attend wearing a pith helmet, after all, it wasn't meant to be a movie set.

Lady Hemmingsworth seemed to take an instant dislike to the other, smaller, rounder, and generally older passengers, preferring to stick to her natural position as supposedly the one in charge. It meant that she was out there in front with Stefan, asking the guide questions such as whether this was the right route to take, and whether a certain monument would not in fact be better to visit for a pleasurable afternoon.

Alan groaned under his breath. He had seen these types of people many times before while working on cruises, and he generally tried to avoid them, if at all possible. He hated the idea that some people *assumed* that they had rights over others, and who would do everything to show just how they were a better class. It didn't take long for Alan to be proven right, as Lady Hemmingsworth started announcing to the tour manager, to the tour, and to the world in general that, "When I had been to Alexandria before, the climate was dreadfully hot…" Or; "Egypt is such a quaint little place, wouldn't you agree, Stefan?"

Alan smirked. Whether Lady Hemmingsworth had a serious eye on the tour manager or had just picked on him as the one with the most authority, he didn't know, but he was determined to remain incognito at the back with the Seinz's.

"She seems quite forceful, you might say?" Dr. Seinz said with a wry smile.

Alan nodded, but not wishing to say anything negative about a passenger, he decided just to nod politically.

"And has anyone met Lord Hemmingsworth? That is what I would like to know..." Diane Seinz said. "Apparently he just takes his 'state dinners' in their luxury cabin and refuses to come out. Royalty," she tittered.

Alan was amused. You certainly did get passengers like this – some of them reclusive, others merely wishing to enjoy the waves and the feeling of being at sea. However, he did think he had better check with Captain Halvorsen whether a porter should check on Lord Hemmingsworth to see if there was anything wrong from time to time. He made a mental note to mention it later.

"Well, as fun as this is," Doctor Seinz said, watching the charade up front of the tour, "I would hate to disrupt Stefan's tour, but there are a few sites that I did want my wife to see..."

Alan motioned that he would go tell Stefan and, steeling himself for the inevitable confrontation, slipped up to the beleaguered tour manager's side.

"Tour Manager? I believe there are a few sites of interest that some of the party wish to visit – I have heard that the"—he reeled off the long name that Dr. Seinz had mentioned—"is of particular importance."

Stefan blushed and threw his gaze to the Lady Hemmingsworth, "Of course doctor. How would you folks"—he called out to the crowd—"Like to see some *real* history in action?"

The tour responded enthusiastically, all apart from the Lady Hemmingsworth, who had collapsed on a chair of a nearby café and was fanning herself with a brochure.

"I simply cannot go on, Stefan. It is this heat – it is too much. We will have to go back."

Stefan looked alarmed. "I am sure we can stop for a few minutes, Lady Hemmingsworth, how would that sound?" He turned to the rest of the tour, most of who were by now looking rather annoyed, and indicated that they wished to be moving on.

Lady Hemmingsworth let out an almighty groan as if pained and slumped further in her chair. "That's it," she cried out weakly. "I think I might faint."

Alan rushed over to examine her, but as soon as he took her wrist to check the strength of her pulse she screamed and sat bolt upright, swatting him away like a fly.

"What on earth are you doing, man? Stefan? This man is trying to assault me."

"No, this man is the ship's doctor, milady," Stefan replied with a smile. "I think his intentions were to try to assess and treat you."

The Lady's demeanor changed in an instant from that of the aggrieved victim, to one of the pampered patient. She smiled brilliantly at the doctor, and produced her long, smooth wrist for his inspection. Alan wondered, with the captain not available, and Stefan being 'only' a tour guide, if he had become the next target.

"Well; crisis averted," Stefan said cheerfully. "Doctor, will you be so good as to look after the Lady while we carry on? You can catch us up at the site?"

Alan squinted at him, but replied cheerily, "Of course." Yet, he had to admit to himself that Stefan had found a way to remove Lady Hemmingsworth from his tour and ensure a peaceful day.

What followed then was a long, unproductive few hours as he tended to the needs of the Lady. She sat in the small café with her feet up, after having ordered an extra chair to be brought for her flagging muscles; and reclined, her tall beehive hairdo waggling in the heat every time she sipped a mineral water, which she had also especially asked to be brought to her. The restaurant owners, middle aged, respectable Egyptians, fell over themselves trying to please her, and failed at every turn, although she did grace them with a smile when they attempted to serve her.

To the doctor, the Lady oozed conviviality, and Alan's heart sank. She peppered him with requests and flirtatious remarks as she 'recovered', ordering him to check her again, and again for any signs of heat stroke.

After a couple of hours had passed, Alan's temper was starting to flare, since he knew this was a charade – his preliminary investigations hadn't shown any sign of heatstroke whatsoever. He also felt a little annoyed at the Lady's lack of tact, in a country, where most of the female inhabitants wore hijabs and burkhas, Lady Hemmingsworth was reclining in full view, having unbuttoned her colonial whites, to reveal her impressive cleavage to the doctor. When he couldn't stop his errant gaze sliding between the massive orbs, he would look up to find the Lady coolly smiling at him with practiced wickedness.

After this show, it took an even longer time to get the Lady Hemmingsworth back to the *Ocean Quest*, during which time Alan rented a cab (to save her feet) and carried her small satchel up the entrance gangway for her.

When they reached the upper decks, since it became quite obvious that the Lady had ulterior motives, Alan promptly informed her that he had a call to answer on his pager, and then took his mobile phone out of his pocket.

It was a common ruse amongst ship doctors, designed to be able to extricate them from delicate or difficult situations.

Holding the phone close to his ear, Alan carried on with the pretense, "Oh, I see…. Of course an over active thyroid can be a terrible thing…. Yes, we have some medication which can counteract the hormonal imbalance," he said loudly, and, begging his apologies to the Lady Hemmingsworth, he made his exit.

His shore leave ruined, Alan wasn't in a very good mood, and even less when he was called to the clinic to see a returning crewmember outside clinic hours who had 'an urgent situation'. This was a crewmember that had been on leave in Nepal. While in that country, he had been sexually active and had not used a condom. As soon as he got to the infirmary, the security guard explained to Alan what had happened to him.

After arriving in the port of Alexandria to meet the ship, and before he got back aboard, he awoke one morning to find his penis covered with bright orange and purple colored lesions-spots.

Horrified, he immediately went to a local Egyptian medical center. The doctor, never having seen anything like this before, ordered some tests and told the seriously worried crew to return in 36 hours for the results. This was fortunately before the ship arrived in port.

He returned 36 hours on the dot and in his best English the clinic doctor told him, "I've got bad news for you; you've contracted a rare form of VD, sometimes called the Qui strain of syphilis. It originated in Southern China. It's very rare and almost unheard of here in Egypt. We, and the rest of the world, know very little about it."

The crewmember looked a little perplexed and said, "Well, give me a shot or something and fix me up before my ship comes in to port. Please, Doc."

The doctor answered, "I'm sorry, there's no known cure. We're going to have to amputate your penis."

The otherwise typical Nepalese security guard with a quiet demeanor, screamed in horror, "Absolutely not. I want a second opinion…"

The doctor replied, "Well, it's your choice. Go ahead, if you want but surgery is your only option."

In a hurry, he sought out another doctor. One that spoke one of the Asian languages of which he spoke several, figuring that they'd know more about the disease.

He found a Tibetan doctor who practiced near the city's small Chinatown. It was an office up on the third floor of a building that also housed a Thai restaurant, a Chinese insurance company, a Korean chiropractor, a small convenience store run by an Indian Punjabi, a Malaysian Physiotherapist, and a massage parlor that had what looked like it had Egyptian girls trying to pass themselves off as Asian, enticing passersby to come in for a massage.

He went into the crowded waiting room of the Tibetan doc who examined his penis and exclaimed, "Ah, yes, the Qui strain of VD. A very rare disease."

The concerned crewmember looked at his member and said to the doctor, "Yeah, yeah, I already know that, but what can we do? The Egyptian doctor I visited wants to cut off my penis."

The Tibetan doctor shook his head and laughed. "Yes, the Egyptian doctors often want to operate. They make much more money that way and keep their marble floored hospitals full. You need to chant, a number of mantras and the practice of some relaxation exercises."

"Oh, thank God," the crew exclaimed.

Then looking a bit more worried again, he asked, "Are you sure you are going to be able to cure it with this plan?"

"Oh no," said the Tibetan doctor. "It will just give you the peace and quiet you will need during the next two weeks."

"Why two weeks?" asked the crew.

The doctor replied, "That is how long it will take to fall off by itself!"

Obviously, the worried crew came to the medical clinic when he boarded the ship, not mentioning to the receiving officer his little adventures and their current consequences so he could get back aboard.

"Okay," Alan said, after the man had dropped his drawers and climbed on the examining table, "let's have a look at it."

He took one look at the man's penis and had to agree with the Egyptian and Tibetan doctors. "Yes, the Qui strain of syphilis. I am going to give you several infusions of a cephalosporin. I have seen it respond in Northern India when some of the locals go to the ladies of the night in Mumbai. And no, it will not fall off."

After sending the security man back to his duties, enjoining him to come back regularly for his infusions, Alan decided to see if Stefan had returned from the tour. On his way down the elevator, he overheard a conversation between a mother and her teenage-adult daughter. The mother seemed to be concerned that her daughter was having sex.

Upon reaching the reception floor and letting the two ladies out first, Alan, his curiosity aroused, followed them to the deck and continued to listen.

Apparently the mother had consulted the family doctor who had told her that teenagers today were very wilful and any attempt to stop the girl would probably result in rebellion. He then had told her to arrange for her daughter to be put on birth control and until then, talk to her and give her a box of condoms.

His elbows on the railing, feigning to look out at the ocean, Alan couldn't help hearing the last of the mother-daughter conversation.

"You found the box of condoms in your case, did you?" the mother asked.

"Sure did, Mom, but you really don't have to worry about any of that – I'm dating Susan, you know!"

Alan coughed a chuckle away and walked back in the direction of the crew's mess where he found Stefan counting his tips.

"It seems that I have made more today just for getting rid of the Lady Hemmingsworth. I should try this trick again, you know you could come along, we'll have one really difficult passenger, and voilà." Stefan laughed as Alan sulked.

"And that Seinz fellow – he really knows his stuff. He took us to the Precinct of Odetsia, a large, open archaeological dig currently going on right in the centre of Alexandria."

"Really? Sounds fascinating – I am sorry I missed it."

"He seemed to know it quite well, managed to speak to the site manager, and get the tour access onto the actual site. It is situated right in the financial district, so all around modern steel and concrete towers and office building rise out of the streets, around this large square where the archaeologists are currently digging deeper and deeper in stepped layers.

"The site was an old priory, or temple of some kind, and when the Egyptian authorities decided to take down this old building and modernize the area they found all these ruins under the foundations.

"The protection of Royal Antiquities was cited, and now the archaeologists have their dig right in the heart of the city. Dr. Seinz showed us the formation walls of the temple, where the old vaults and catacombs would have been – it was marvelous, I couldn't have wanted anything better for a tour."

Alan sighed. "Just my luck to be stuck with a difficult patient all day. Did the Seinz's enjoy themselves? Dr. Seinz didn't end up doing any digging did he?" he asked, thinking about the doctor's hand.

"Not while I was there, but I'm afraid he might be doing so now. He and his wife got so entranced by the dig they decided to stay a few extra hours and help out the site manager. Apparently he had to go off later that afternoon so they agreed to watch over the dig for him."

"The life of an academic, huh? Never stop working," Alan remarked.

"Not the life for me, I can tell you," Stefan joked. "I like my work, but I also like my breaks."

"Well, I could say the same, but I really have to return to the medical centre and get on with my duties," Alan added ruefully. And to himself: *I really have to phone Tiffany and tell her the latest story.*

This was becoming a habit; Alan smiled at his own love-struck-ness. *Am I in love?* He wondered at it. His habit of phoning Tiffany and recounting to her the latest story of life on board was a way of ordering the stories in his head – fit for a memoir – and before he jotted everything down in his journals. He had half a mind to write a book one day, he would call it 'Adventures at Sea' or more appropriately '*Misadventures* at Sea.'

If the phones decide to work today, that is, he commented to himself. With that thought he detoured past the security chief's office that wasn't so far away, and asked a few questions that had been bothering him for some time.

Vince was almost always in his office. A large African American ex-Naval man, originally from the windy city in the Midwest of America, he was built like the proverbial barn door.

After several tours during the seventies and eighties patrolling the cold war seas, he had retrained and worked up the ranks into Naval Intelligence. It was a fraught time, he sometimes recalled, the 'Cold' War was just as dangerous, threatening, and deadly as any 'Hot' one; particularly for the communications and intelligence men, who routinely had to monitor any radio traffic from many different sources. When he finally retired from active duty, Vince found that he couldn't 'do' civilian life, and found the lure of the sea kept calling him back. That was when he signed up as a trusted security chief for cruise ships.

"Good afternoon, Vince," the doctor called cheerfully into the office, to find a beleaguered hulk of a man sifting through paperwork and reports.

"Ah, Doctor, I am glad you called around, although I hope it's not to tell me that it's time for my medical, is it? Not with that Nurse Petra, at least." The man looked mortified.

"No, no, you're not due for another few weeks yet as I recall. It's more of a social visit really, and to see if you can clear up a little mystery of mine."

"Well, in that case that makes two of us – I have a mystery unfolding here on the desk as well."

"Really? Anything I can help with?"

"Absolutely. It's that man Gillais Montague…"

"What seems to be the matter?"

"Well, the autopsy report has had a query put on it by Interpol."

Alan looked concerned. He was sure that he and Kelly had done the best job to their ability, he had made sure he was one hundred and ten percent accurate, as he knew the legal nightmare this case would be.

"What kind of query?"

"Well, I have been trying to follow the paperwork and it seems, if I am correct, that *your* examinations where followed by the Athenian district coroner, and *his* autopsy proved your findings. It was then passed on to the French and Belgian authorities, with paperwork sent through to Gold Line, American Embassy, and Interpol."

"Yes, that would be the appropriate procedure." Alan couldn't see a problem.

"Well, the autopsy report has been sent through to Interpol, as this is a death in international waters, and they have immediately returned a query on the findings, and asked for the body to be examined again by one of their *own* coroners. I believe that they will probably contact you as well, and ask for your findings from the scene of the incident to when you handed the body over."

"Okay, what appears to be the problem?"

"That is the baffling thing, there *doesn't seem to be any kind of problem* with yours or the coroner's reports, here…have a look"

He handed over the paperwork, already a fat file of faxes and communications and copied letters including all the correspondence to the various relevant authorities.

Alan looked over the papers referring to Interpol's involvement and couldn't find anything of actual scientific relevance.

There was no mention of any mistakes or other findings, or reasons for the inquiry, just that Interpol wanted it done.

"How odd. Maybe this is normal procedure with a case of mixed jurisdictions like this?"

Vince fixed his gaze on Alan for a moment, reclining in his seat. "I don't think so. If there are extenuating factors, the character of the witnesses are under suspicion, or the victim had a dubious past, or the situation is highly questionable then they get involved as a matter of course. But in this case the only ones to go near the body were all trained professionals, and the medical findings are backed up by the opinions of two professionals. I don't understand it, and it means a hell of a lot of paperwork for me."

"Well, it *is* unusual for a man of his age to suffer a heart attack during – how shall we say – certain sexual activities... But all of that was noted in my report."

"Yes, I guess that is it, the strange nature of the case over all, you know; a death on a cruise ship, involving sexual relations." Vince sighed and put the folder back to the top of the file. "I am sure that we are not finished with this one just yet. So, now that I have started to pick your brains on this one – I believe you mentioned that you had something you wanted to ask of me?"

"Yes, I did. Has your department been experiencing telephone failures recently? Problems with the satellite array?"

Vince looked at him very curiously, and for a second Alan caught a glimpse of what lay behind the good-natured exterior of the security officer. Vince may give the impression of being a large, monstrous hulk of a man, but he was in fact a very, very intelligent considerate person. He would have had to be to work for Naval Intelligence for all of those years.

"Why, yes, we did, a few days ago – right around the night of the storm. How very astute of you to notice."

"Well, it was a small thing that my friend mentioned to me. She had been trying to communicate with me for a few days, and had managed to get through to front desk, but I knew that during that same period I was also trying to contact her, and the line was completely dead."

"Yes, that would probably be about right." Vince nodded. "We had disruptions to outgoing ship communications for approximately seven hours."

"Which means the transmitter, doesn't it? Not the dish or the receiver?" Alan quizzed. He knew that there were several components to a ship's communications system, all of which had to be working in perfect sync to be able to receive and send electronic and radio signals.

"Correct, Doctor, we noted that there was a problem just as the storm was coming in, but could do little about it while the weather came down. When we had a chance to go out and have a look, it appeared that some of the transmitter apparatus had been damaged due to the winds."

"Really? What kind of damage?"

"A loose connection. The housing had come loose and some of the cables had been rattled about in there, why do you ask, Doctor?"

Alan could tell that Vince's mind operated fast indeed, but decided to keep his speculations to himself. Maybe it was the natural detective in him, but he thought that it was quite fascinating how one particular piece of technology had been affected by the storm – and *only* one.

"I am not sure at the moment, Vince; it's just that I have this feeling, maybe my sense of paranoia, that there is something here that I don't like. There are a lot of things that have happened recently that all seem quite unfortunate and unexplainable."

Again Vince gave him that hard, measuring look he kept reserved for a particularly tricky situation.

"I think I know what you mean, Doctor. You are, of course, referring to the fact that the very night of the storm, was also the night that our Mr. Montague died, and that our communications were down, but only our outward going communications?"

Alan didn't want to say anything. He didn't want to give his fears credence, so he just nodded.

"I have been wondering the same thing, Doctor, the same thing..." Vince said pensively.

Without either of them having to say it, they both silently considered the possibility that these factors were not all unlucky accidents that happened to occupy the same night. After a long moment the doctor shrugged again as if to say '*I don't know, maybe it's nothing*' and Vince did the same.

However, Alan left the security chief's office with a slightly more troubled heart than he did when he came in. Maybe this was all there was to it – a few unlucky instances in the midst of a storm, maybe. *But*, a little treacherous voice said deep inside his brain, *stopping communications would be a very good tactic if you wanted someone to keep quiet about something or if you didn't want news to get to the mainland. Or*, he thought fancifully, *if you were planning a murder...*

CHAPTER EIGHT

Waters off Malta
Infections

"REALLY? AND DID YOU HAVE TO wear your dress uniform?" Tiffany said over the phone.

"No, good God, no. The company just about managed to fill the number of officers thankfully," Alan replied, lowering his voice, so the other passengers in the adjoining booth couldn't quite hear him. "In the end they enlarged the troop of dancers by enlisting some of the children on board. It was chaos."

Alan was referring to last night's pantomime, which had the whole ship rocking with laughter and a huge turnout. It was one of the big entertainments that the entertainment directors had scheduled, alongside the play.

The entertainment of any cruise is always one of the focal points of the entire trip, together with the shore leave at distant and exciting ports. A lot of money was spent trying to make the entertainment as professional and as interactive as possible, with entertainers being drafted – such as the singer Brett Jarulcho – to perform for the entire cruise, alongside smaller acts who came on board at particular stops and performed for a few nights before continuing their journey with other performances on other cruises.

All together there was a mixture of singers and bands, dance troops, comedians, acrobats, actors, musicians, and stage magicians. On top of this was more entertainment, produced 'in-house' by the crew and the passengers themselves. These included major final trivia quizzes, a ship's version of the Marriage Game, a ship-wide Treasure Hunt, short plays and performances by the kiddies groups that performed under the entertainment director's watchful eye.

Last night, the night that they left the Egyptian waters had been scheduled as a "pantomime night" with participation for everyone who wanted to on the ship – save the necessary staff that would rotate through the night on their essential duties.

The theme of the night had been, not surprisingly, Pharaoh's and the Pyramids, with a short comical story about an explorer who went to discover the tomb of the vengeful Pharaoh Tut, played by George Alleyway, one of the ship's navigation engineer, and is subsequently chased by the risen Pharaoh Tut through Egypt, with a full cast of belly dancers, camels, explorers, and strangely a man in a monkey suit.

Alan couldn't help himself from laughing as he watched his ship colleagues stumble their way through the parts.

However, something disturbed the night's entertainment within just a short few hours of the performance – a 'Code Brown' had been called for the ship.

The aptly named 'Code Brown' – although not a real code used for security measures on ship – is used behind-the-scenes primarily by the medical crew to alert each other, and the department chiefs that there is an outbreak of gastroenteritis usually of the Norovirus type which manifests itself with nausea, vomiting, and diarrhea; synonyms being Delhi Belly, the Bangkok Two Step, Montezuma's Revenge, the Pharaoh's Delight, and the Mexican Stand Off.

Needless to say the doctor was the first to notice its effects, and promptly phoned the appropriate persons of the kitchen staff, the cleaners, etc. and, of course, the captain. Within an hour he was getting a steady trickle of passengers – at least five an hour – appearing at the medical centre with classical signs and symptoms.

A couple of teenage boys decided to take their plight in stride and came in the infirmary singing:

> Wake up in the morning; put your feet on the floor,
> Do the fifty-yard dash to the bathroom door,
> Diarrhea!
> When you're sliding into first,
> And you feel something burst,
> Diarrhea!
> When you're sliding into third,
> And you lay a juicy turd,
> And you feel a floppy turd.
> Diarrhea!
> When you're sliding into home,
> And you feel something foam,
> Diarrhea!
> When you hit and run to first

And you feel you're gonna burst
Diarrhea, diarrhea!
And off you run to second,
You can't wait another second,
Diarrhea, diarrhea!
You make it on to third
And you feel a squishy turd,
Diarrhea, diarrhea!
When you're sitting in the lodge,
And you feel like you've been hit by a Dodge,
Diarrhea! Diarrhea!
When you're sittin' in the grass,
And you feel something slide out your ass,
Diarrhea! Diarrhea!

"Well, gentlemen," Alan said after listening to their tune – twice – suppressing a chuckle or two, "I have to say you've described the symptoms very well. Have you, by any chance, remembered to wash your hands and drink bottled water while you were hopping around Alexandria?"

The older of the two boys looked at his companion inquiringly. "I guess we've all taken a swig at the water fountain in town," he answered ruefully.

"Alright then," Alan said, "you're going to do me a favor and carry bottled water where ever you're going – deal?"

"Yes, sir – no problem," the smaller boy replied promptly, while his friend nodded.

"And I'll give you some medication that will calm your bowels – but please watch what you eat, okay?"

"Okay, Doc, no worries," the two boys said in unison as they each grabbed their bottle of Pepto-Bismol and made their way out of Alan's office.

Unfortunately, it happens far more often on board a cruise ship than anyone would like, and can race through a ship like wildfire, but is a part of a life of sailing, where every few days the passengers and crew are subject to different foods, different levels of water hygiene, all the local germs of a foreign land and of course, difference in the standards of food preparation whenever passengers partake of food on shore. Noroviruses are the reason that the hand washing stations and the constant vigilance to hand washing on ships began. For the most part it is very successful. Unfortunately, one cannot make people wash their hands, only recommend, show, and encourage.

Within that short time Alan and Kelly were nursing young adults and people in their mid-thirties primarily, putting the cause of infection down to eating foods at Alexandrian eating establishments without the appropriate precautions. These were the same demographic who liked to go out on the tours and, as often as possible, 'go native' experiencing some of the natural cuisine that is offered.

Same as for the two boys, Alan wondered how many of them had actually washed their hands before eating the finger-dip type foods, who had used napkins, or if any of them had kept to drinking the advised bottled water.

As it was, only a few members of the crew had caught it by the time of the pantomime, but there were significant enough numbers to cause a few scenes to be cut.

"Don't worry; we'll be right as rain by the time of the play," they had encouraged each other, and went on to give the pantomime a good go anyway.

The doctor had been so busy that he had missed the start of the show, and halfway through he had snuck off using the back of the hall. The entertainment crew had obviously been very busy – on the one side of the stage was a painted cardboard pyramid with a sphinx on the other wall. The hall itself was decorated with vibrant gold and orange streamers and banners. The doctor had surreptitiously spied a seat at the back and had settled down next to the Seinz couple.

"I am surprised," he whispered over the cacophony in front of them, "That you weren't asked to perform."

"I'm sorry?" Doctor Seinz looked confused for a second. "Ah, you mean due to my expertise? Well, I have done a fair bit in Egypt that is true, but really I am a Vatican man."

"The Vatican? That was why you started the cruise in Rome?"

Doctor Seinz nodded. "Yes, I was working there for a few months previously before we signed onto this cruise. I work in the catacombs below the Papal City."

"Really? How intriguing, and grisly – what do you do down there?"

"Catalogue mostly, we have recently opened up a new section of vaults and found that they are all tombs dating back to the early days of the Roman Church, sixth or seventh century probably. Because of my long term tenure working with the Papal Council, I have been invited over the years to come back and lead digs into new sites."

"He doesn't like to brag, but it is a huge honor," Diane chimed in from his side.

"Yes, understandably so. You will have to tell me if you have found anything interesting or startling that could make the basis for the next *Da Vinci Code* best seller on revealing Catholic secrets."

The other doctor laughed. "Oh, I am afraid that I am sworn to secrecy on these matters – quite literally in fact. The Papal Council not only regard their treasures as property, but also as sacred ground – anything under the subsoil is regarded as sanctified ground to the Vatican, due to the age and nature of the Vatican City. I can therefore not reveal anything that I find down there, not even in academic circles, until the Vatican decides to release the information."

"But surely leaks have gotten out before?" Alan pressed, not only because of his love of history but also due to his scent for a good story.

Alan had read that novel about the bloodline of Christ – *The Da Vinci Code*, and had gone to see the film many years previously. Its premise had intrigued him, but he had remained entirely skeptical of its assertions. As a subject for the scientific mind he had found the cross over between religion, faith, and historical facts, fascinating.

"Well of course, sometimes academics publish papers anyway, and they are summarily 'black balled', as it were, from the academic community, let alone their current employers," Doctor Seinz went on to explain. "You see, if an archaeologist went about just reporting whatever they thought, announcing their speculations to the world without regard to their sponsors or the rest of the academic community, they would bring the whole discipline of archaeology into disrepute – a bit like your 'rogue doctors' or 'back street surgeons' in your line of business."

Alan nodded thoughtfully; traveling as he did all over the world, he had met a few of those types of so called medical 'professionals' and had also had to treat the problems that they so often caused for people.

"The academic sciences are essentially self-regulating. If you get a wild card or a rogue in the mix, then generally the publications and journals close ranks and refuse to publish their work, and their Alma Mater – or the establishment in which they teach – distances themselves quite quickly and often terminate their position amongst the staff."

Alan was forced to agree to the sense of this argument, since the maritime community operated a similar policy. If one particular individual was proven to be of unsound character then they would also generally get 'black balled' as the word would spread that this person was dangerous to sail with. This thought naturally led him to his recent Alaskan encounter with a certain Mr. Rick Hammer.

"So a life of crime or indulgence really doesn't pay in the academic world, unless, of course, you have the scoop of the century." Doctor Seinz laughed, and waggled his eyebrows melodramatically.

"Stop giving the doctor ideas." Diane laughed and dug her husband in the ribs, causing him to yelp and jump in his seat.

Alan chuckled. "Well, I suppose that you will have to keep your secrets and I shall keep mine. One thing you must tell me, however, is whether or not you managed to keep that hand clean in your adventures this afternoon. Stefan told me that you disappeared at the first archaeological opportunity."

Doctor Seinz waved the hand with its attendant bulky bandaging concealed under one of the blue plastic gloves.

"This old thing?" he said. "Should all be fine – I managed to keep my hands in my pockets the entire time."

"Good show," Alan said. "Then it should be healing up rather well, with at least twenty four hours uninterrupted rest." He then resumed his viewing of the night's performance.

*   *   *

"And so *what* did Stefan do?" Tiffany asked after Alan had recounted his story.

"Fell over, a *l o t*. Luckily two of your old colleagues, the entertainment girls were there to help him up again."

"Oh I bet. I can think of a few candidates with whom I used to work who would rush to help any young man in distress."

"And you wouldn't help a doctor in distress?" Alan teased the cruise director while they both sat in their respective phone cubicles many, many sea miles from each other.

"Well, it depends on the doctor." Tiffany giggled. "The one on board my ship – well, I wouldn't exactly say that he was very bad or anything, but he does seem to have a way of *trying* with the ladies."

"What's his name?" Alan asked, wondering whether he would know the physician.

"Dr. Hoofer? Something like that, Hauffer?"

"Hauffman?" Alan asked.

"Hauffman. Dr. Hauffman, yes, that's it. He's a creep of a man I can tell you."

Alan remembered Nurse Kelly's earlier story of working this very vessel underneath the lecherous Dr. Hauffman. It seems like the sneaky, old goat had got himself a job on another cruise ship in the Gold Cruise Line Company. Right under their very noses.

"Oh, you'll have to be careful of him. I have it on very good authority that he tries to get it on with every passenger and staff – male and female – as long as they are good looking, without looking back. Be wary if he suddenly declares that you have an imminent medical emergency that you never knew that you had."

"Oh he has pulled that one already – twice. He told me my left vertebra was twisting, and that I would need emergency osteopathy, in his clinic, privately of course, to treat what would later become a very painful condition."

"My God – I hope you saw through it."

"Well, thankfully I have my own private doctor who has examined my vertebrae quite closely." Tiffany giggled, "And he hasn't found anything wrong so far."

"No indeed, you have a beautiful spine."

"Why thank you, I didn't know that you were only interested in me for my skeletal structure."

"Absolutely." Alan could feel himself blushing.

"So, needless to say, this Dr. Hauffman hasn't had any luck with me so far, and I think not with any of the other passengers either. Poor man – he is just so creepy. If he calmed down a bit and went at a slower pace, I am sure he could come over as quite charming. Instead there is just a certain ... oiliness to his whole person."

Alan laughed. "Well, from what I hear yes, then that is the same man indeed. If he becomes a bother, ask your captain to radio in to our ship – know that Captain Halvorsen will not even allow that man on board any vessel he is in charge of."

"Really? Then that *is* something indeed – and I promise that yes, if he becomes a bit too much, then I will make sure our captain speaks to Anders. Apart from that, and the 'Code Brown' and the pantomime, what else have you to report, Doctor Mayhew?"

"There are a few things, but I cannot talk about them over the ship phones." He lowered his voice. "But there is something that I thought about earlier.... Do you remember our unfortunate Mr. Montague?"

"The Black Widow Case?" Tiffany joked.

"Well, hopefully not, but it may turn out that you are more correct than either of us would like."

"Really? The owner of the pink knickers hasn't turned up has she?"

"No, no, nothing like that at all. But there have been some complications, all I can say is one word: Interpol."

"Well, that *is* interesting," Tiffany exclaimed. "Does it seem that Dr. Mayhew, MD on board is once again in the thick of it?"

"I surely hope not, I wanted this to be a quiet cruise."

"Ah yes, I remember you saying, you know, you really are going to have to finish that story for me some time...?"

"I'm waiting too, believe me, I am." Alan was sure he wasn't just talking about his recent horror trip with a certain Mr. Rick Hammer. "But for now I will have to do some more research on our Mr. Montague, and see if there are any complications to the case."

"Well, if there is any way I can help, you know that I'm game," Tiffany added brightly.

"Yes, maybe you can. I am not sure exactly if it would look good in the security logs if I suddenly starting snooping around asking questions about our Mr. Montague... If there is anything that you can find out about his boarding, his ticket, or anything else; it might just be what we need."

"You know me, Alan, I can wheedle information out of a stone if I have to," Tiffany crowed, and Alan realized that it was true. It was probably her straightforward nature and confident attitude.

It had amazed Alan to see Tiffany at work with difficult clients, and in potentially embarrassing situations. She could take charge of a room of disgruntled, impatient, slightly seasick passengers, and within minutes have them feeling at ease and eating out of the palm of her hand. She really should have considered the role of a diplomat. Alan told her so over the phone.

"Moi? A diplomat? Good grief, Alan, what do you think I am – a miracle worker? I'm afraid I am far too honest for that kind of work."

Which was also true, but Alan would argue that she would make a very good diplomat or negotiator if he had enough time. It was something to do with her bright smile and accompanying intelligent eyes. When you were talking to her it was obvious that this remarkable woman was listening to what you were saying and responded with shrewd wit.

Evidently, being as cute as a button helped her to get her way in any situation. Of that he was sure. Alan had seen a few passengers and crewmembers fall entranced by her spell as she would lead a room in a game of Trivia, and he supposed that he himself had, too, fallen under the strange spell of her femininity.

Alan spelled out the name of the Belgian for his colleague, hoping that her straightforward, no nonsense, and above all, approachable manner would gain him some information that he would otherwise not be able to ferret out on board.

"G-I-L-L-A-I-S (that's right, double 'L') M-O-N-T-A-G-U-E, when did he buy his ticket? Are there any notes on his boarding pass? Has he cruised with us before?" Alan tried out a few questions to which, he thought, Tiffany could probably find the answers.

"Right, sure thing, Daddy-O. Agent Tiffany is hot on the case."

Alan chuckled. "Well, I hope you are not too hot – that might be a sign of fever."

"I'll be sure *not* to get checked out by Dr. Hauffman if it is." Tiffany laughed, and sadly reminded him that they had other duties to get back to. As a cruise director she would certainly have her hands full on her own boat, managing the entertainment, seeing to every last details and often dealing with every aspect of the trip from the passengers' point of view.

It was her job to oversee all of the entertainment, make sure they were all going according to plan, prepare for the future activity, organize all of the on-board and on-shore activities, and be ready to help out with any tiny complaint that any passenger had. It was amazing; really, that she even had this amount of free time to speak to him.

Alan had a lot on his mind, as he tried to organize all of the things he had on his plate. The cruise was already halfway to the next stop of Malta, and while he had quite a number of medicals to perform he wanted to make sure he had some free time to wander around Valletta – that beautiful port – which he remembered well from previous trips.

Many years ago, he stayed in Malta for several weeks; visiting many of the picturesque villages and helping out one of the local public health docs administer Hepatitis B vaccine to newborns. On another stay a couple of years ago, he and the lady friend who had become his fiancée – with the demon child – rented a car and revisited the island. Much to Alan's surprise, there were many, many changes of the tourist type. Many of the quaint villages were now tourist enclaves of British and German tourist mega-holiday resorts and condos. Since he was there while the ship he was contracted to at that time, was being repaired in the famous Maltese Ship yards, he had a very central 'hotel room' to venture out from in the rented car.

However, he reminded himself that currently the ship was still operating under a 'Code Brown' and during the day he would nevertheless have to see a number of passengers and crew.

Usually these outbreaks lasted only a few days, but the ship's doctor remembered times when he had spent entire cruises battling wave after wave of infection. However, on an experienced and professional cruise ship like this one, Alan was fairly certain that he could contain the outbreak by ensuring that the staff in the kitchen and those on cleaning duties was kept free of the virus. When he got back to the Medical Centre he sent out an alert to the heads of the relevant departments that he would like anyone feeling unwell to come in immediately, and for them to rigorously stick to their disinfection routine.

These would entail gloves galore, anti-bacterial hand washes after handling any potentially contaminated material, and many repetitive protocols. Minimizing of any material contamination (linens, elevators, railings, walls, tables, chair arms, sheets, laundry or pots, plates and cutlery) so that no cross-contamination could occur, and of course, extra cleaning rotas applied to all the bathrooms, toilets, swimming pools, Jacuzzis and saunas.

Because of Alan's long standing experience, he knew that these last places in particular, the bodies of heated standing water were quite often breeding places for whole ecologies of viruses, and as a result he had decided a long time ago not to indulge in them. Hot tub folliculitis (a skin rash) was all too common from Jacuzzis in any public place-on land or at sea.

He jokingly referred to them to Kelly as the 'Toxic Soup', given that passengers from all over the world, all with their own locally-bred germs, could meet and greet each other in those infested ponds.

"Kelly, would you be so good as to fetch me some samples of the water in the pools?" he asked the young nurse at his side.

She grimaced, herself knowing the nature of his inquiry. "Do I have to?" she said jokingly, to which Alan added a couple more collection test tubes to the pile for her to take.

Testing the facilities, often left to technicians from the engine department, and while not performed by many doctors, was an activity that Alan Mayhew prided himself in doing. It involved taking a plastic syringe of water or other liquid from each place, and bottling it in a test tube to be brought back for analysis. By adding a simple chemical reagent, they would be able to determine how many impurities or organisms were present in the water and from there make calculations as to the 'viral load' of any particular tested item. From there, proper cultures could be made and plated out for more specific identification, especially if the number of patients coming to the clinic was increasing during the Code Brown.

Alan grimaced. Yes, occasionally he had to admit to himself that sometimes there was a lot more to being a ship's doctor than the job description. You had turns at being a counselor, a therapist, a confidant, a physician, a surgeon and a laboratory scientist. Sometimes you even had to be a sleuth to determine the causes of some particular condition.

Alan unpacked the sterilized equipment necessary to test the forthcoming water samples, running the preliminary tests to ensure that the sterilized water would really be pH neutral, and that no foreign contaminant made its way into the equipment.

Aha. Suddenly a thought struck him, while he was setting up the laboratory equipment. He still had the blood work available from Gillais Montague. While he had all the laboratory equipment out and ready to go, he could repeat the tests and see if he had really missed anything at all.

He retrieved the test tubes of blood from the specimens' cabinet, which was a secure lock box type fridge that kept all of the blood samples taken in the course of a cruise, in a stable condition.

Moving over to his laboratory bench he took a tiny amount of poor Mr. Montague's blood sample and added it to another test tube of saline solution. By doing this it meant that the compounds in the blood were spread out and easier to isolate, as well as making the sample go a lot further. This was a pretty primitive testing technique, but better than nothing to being able to get to the basis for Montague's demise. He was sure that he would have to send the samples by special medical delivery to Interpol as soon as they wanted to conduct a thorough second investigation. This was going to be his last best chance to learn something from the samples. While he waited for the blood work to process, he retrieved Mr. Montague's notes and read through his own protocol procedure from a few days ago.

He had conducted all the relevant checks for signs and examined the body carefully. No external marks abrasions or interferences with the body of any kind had shown up. He had taken samples of hair, nail clippings, and blood; tested the blood and tried to determine time of death, as well as onset of necrosis, or the processes of chemical change that started to occur in a body after death.

He had checked the heart muscles and found them to be inflamed – a possible sign of a heart attack, but not a firm diagnostic sign. Again Alan read how he had checked the major arteries of the patient, and the state of arterial clogging. Usually in patients suffering from a heart attack there is often severely clogged arteries, and various enzymatic changes.

While he was reviewing his notes and records, his thoughts drifted to a joke he had heard recently, and smiled inwardly at the recollection.

A mechanic was removing a cylinder-head from the motor of a Harley motorcycle when he spotted a well-known cardiologist in his shop.

The cardiologist was there waiting for the service manager to come and take a look at his bike, when the mechanic shouted across the garage, "Hey, Doc, want to take a look at this?"

The cardiologist, a bit surprised, walked over to where the mechanic was working on the motorcycle.

The mechanic straightened up, wiped his hands on a rag and asked, "So, Doc, look at this engine. I open its heart, took the valves out, repair any damage, and then put them back in, and when I finish, it works just like new. So how come I make $39,675 a year and you get the really big bucks when you and I are doing basically the same work?" The cardiologist paused, smiled and leaned over, then whispered to the mechanic, "Try doing it with the engine running.

Returning to his review, and still more puzzled than ever, Alan could find nothing at all. What, at first, had seemed like a fairly normal heart attack had turned into a case of confusing results.

Sighing, he turned back to the completed blood work and took a sample of that to put forward for chemical analysis.

Taking a dab of the rest he took a small amount to examine under the microscope. He affixed the drop of blood between two glass slides and, as the red dot squished, adjusted the microscope to a high magnification to see if he could determine anything that way.

The red blood cells appeared as big, bloated round balloons with shadings marking the interior cell walls. While this was a little unusual, there was nothing particularly suspicious about it.

And then Alan swore. What was unusual was the high amount of white blood cells present in the sample. A very, very high amount. He wondered why this would be the case. It looked like, if he wasn't mistaken, at the time of his untimely demise, Gillais had been fighting off an infection – quite a severe one in fact.

Another strange phenomenon was the fact that Alan could find no evidence of any virus or bacteria in the sample. He knew that white blood cells were produced by the body to fight off infection, and acted as the body's natural 'defense mechanism'. In a blood sample with this amount of white cells, you would expect there to be some trace of what they were fighting as well.

So, what would cause Gillais's immune system suddenly to over-produce white blood cells, and yet leave the system with no trace? In Alan's mind it appeared most likely to be some kind of virus, such as a severe case of influenza or even worse.

I wonder why Gillais didn't come to the Medical Centre to see me, if he was so unwell. For a second his spirit darkened as he considered that he might have saved this man, if he had been in time to treat him.

But he would have probably still had his secret assignation that night, Alan consoled himself. He was the kind of physician who had the tendency to *care* about his patients.

As a professional doctor with a long career behind him, Alan knew the many problems associated with caring too much and had steeled himself through the years with a hard exterior of pragmatism.

There had been cases of the vulnerable: the elderly, the children, those who were chronically ill, which had been enough to break his soul again and again and again. As a younger man he had even wondered how he could go on in his chosen career, but the answer had been immediate and obvious. Because he was the only one who could help in those situations.

Often, as the only trained professional on a ship, he was the first and the last one to be at the scene of an accident, injury, or distress. He was the one that people turned to for help, whatever he felt, particularly at that exact moment in time, his help was needed.

"Just like our Mr. Montague here," Alan said to the notes and the recordings that he had of the young French-Belgian man. Of course, he had considered the possibility that Gillais Montague had been a villain of some kind, and then dismissed those ideas.

Maybe Gillais Montague had been out of shape and while fighting an infection, his heart had given out unexpectedly. The thought reminded him of something else – the funeral of a friend he had attended years ago.

A young woman, who was at her father's funeral, asked her mother, "Mom, how did Dad die?" Her mom replied, "Heart attack."

"What was he doing?" the daughter asked.

Her mother said, "Well, we were having sex."

This infuriated the daughter, because they were both 80 years old. The daughter said, "You guys are 80 years old! You should have expected something like this. You're way too old to be engaging in this sort of activity!"

The mom replied, "Well, you see, years ago, we realized that at noon every day, the church bells rang. So, we decided to work along to that nice, slow rhythm so that your father wouldn't have a heart attack. It worked for years too. My poor husband… he'd still be alive today if that darned ice cream truck hadn't come along…"

Coming out of his musing once again, Alan wondered whether he was a strange man to others – someone who could listen and hear the messages in another body before the person himself even could.

"Perhaps I am." He smiled wryly, more to himself than to the world in general. "For certain, one Miss Tiffany seems to think so."

Alan picked up the phone and dialed the security chief's office.

"Vince, hello, it's Doctor Mayhew here."

"Ah yes, I saw from your caller ID. What is the problem? Have you got a lead on our last discussion?"

"Perhaps, perhaps. Could you get me the details of the office currently handling the recently deceased Mr. Montague?"

"I can do better than that, Dr. Mayhew. I can patch you straight through. We have a telecommunications router here: sort of a switchboard service that allows us to access the satellite communications network."

"Oh really? That would be excellent, thank you."

Within a few seconds of clicks and beeps, the doctor was redirected through to an automated reply of the Athenian Coroner's Office. He was given the option to speak to someone in Greek or in English, and after a few more minutes of clicks and whirs, he was put through to a friendly sounding receptionist.

"Good day, my name is Dr. Alan Mayhew from the cruise ship the *Ocean Quest*. I believe that your office has been involved in the recent case of a Belgian man named Mr. Gillais Montague?"

"Wait a minute, let me check these details and I will get right back to you, Dr. Mayhew," said the receptionist, and Alan was once again put on hold.

After a few minutes a different voice came on the line, another woman with a deeper, thicker Grecian accent. "Hello, Dr. Mayhew, this is Estasia Koukasis, I am the chief coroner of the Athenian City

Authority – how can I help you?"

"Glad to finally talk to you, Ms. Koukasis. I trust you are well. It regards our friend Mr. Montague…"

"Yes, of course – let me tell you, Doctor, that we are inundated with paperwork at this end, with this authority and that authority requesting information. It seems that your unfortunate case has created quite a stir already."

"For which I am truly sorry. However, there seems to be a further complication that I must heap on your plate."

He proceeded to tell the coroner about his findings; the suspicious presence of the increased number of white blood cells in the blood samples, and the lack of any visible infection.

"Really?" the coroner responded, "I cannot believe I did not notice that. I guess that, without any exterior marks or other symptoms, it must have been easy for me to assume the case at face value. I will recheck the results myself."

"Thank you, Coroner. Could you also check the kidneys and liver?"

"Yes of course – what are you thinking?"

"Since the blood collects impurities from the body – perhaps there are still traces of some compound – probably only extremely small levels or perhaps imbalances in the mineral deposits present in those organs."

The coroner saw the sense to this and agreed to perform the checks and informed him that she would certainly contact him with her results. Alan had a suspicion, that Mr. Montague had been fighting off some sort of infection, that even if it was now gone, had dispersed itself throughout the body. There might still be traces of whatever it was in the liver or the kidneys.

If the case is self-evident, then, normally, there is no need to perform these special tests in a usual death enquiry. In this case, initially it appeared that the victim had died from a heart attack. However, occasionally, Alan found that you could determine if there had been any substances or diseases affecting the person, which could have been the major cause of death, either directly or indirectly.

Within a short while, Kelly came back with the water samples, and they both made sure to sterilize the preparation area before they conducted the tests.

"Oh, you just wouldn't believe it up there," Kelly said.

"What wouldn't I believe?"

"All the people, lounging around semi-naked. I think I caused quite a stir arriving in my nurse's uniform to test the saunas and swimming pool."

Alan tried to keep a straight face. "Really? Why is that?"

"Well, they must have thought I was a party stripper or something."

"Well," Alan crowed. "I am sure that they were disappointed, but it wouldn't be the first time that such a thing has happened on board a cruise ship."

Kelly's face was a perfect, scandalized 'O'. "Really? I thought, you know, with the company guide lines being so clear on the matter..."

"That's true, the company doesn't endorse ... adult entertainment on any of its vessels, but," Alan explained, "that doesn't stop some of the more entrepreneurial type passengers from indulging."

Kelly laughed. "Really? I knew that there are some wild times to be expected on a long cruise, but still, I had never heard of..." she fought for the right words.

"Of the adventurously minded?" Alan suggested.

"Quite. Indeed." Kelly suppressed a laugh.

"Well, let's get these water tests in the processor and as we wait, I'll tell you."

The pair carefully prepared the test tubes, and set them up for their chemical analysis before they relaxed in the doctor's chairs, and Alan continued with his story.

"Well, there have, over the years, been occasions where passengers came on board, not for the benefits of the trip or the companionship of the other passengers and the usual benefits of a cruise holiday. Instead, they come aboard with a more financial reason to travel.

"It turns out, that on one of these occasions that there was a young man from America who, aside from having a prize-winning body – he obviously worked out several times a week – was also quite a proficient dancer.

"It didn't take long for the other ladies to notice his figure, as he pounded the decks on his morning jogs, or was in the gym every night before dinner. The crew thought nothing more about it – another alpha male on a cruise ship out to show off his achievements."

"And there are a few of those on board at the moment," Kelly remarked. Alan was forced to agree.

"Well, the crew noticed that every night or every few nights, he would be dancing with a different lady. We all thought what a lucky man. It was obvious he was built like Hercules and had the gift of the gab to boot."

"So how did you find out about his other career?" Kelly asked.

"Well, the staff started to get a little suspicious when we saw him with a lot of different types of women – the young, the more mature, the thin, and the plump. But all of them were what we would call *monied*.

"Now, we are a non-discriminatory organization, and it is not for us to judge the tastes of any particular passenger for that matter, so we all thought nothing of it, just the rather greedy proclivities of a hormonal young man."

"So...?" Kelly urged him on.

"It was a poor young cleaner – not unlike your Ernesto who discovered the true nature of the arrangement."

"He's not my Ernesto," Kelly burst out, her cheeks turning deep crimson.

Alan smoothed over her embarrassment and carried on. "So, this young guy was on his rounds one day – changing the bed linen, mopping the floors, cleaning the en-suite bathrooms, changing the towels and all the other things he was doing. He came to one room on his rota and he found the door ajar, and from it some music emanating.

"Obviously he knocked, but there was no answer. After that he must have decided well, it's his job and the passengers will have to like it or lump it so he coughed and called out as he popped his head around the door…"

"What did he see? Oh my God, I don't know if I want to know."

The doctor grinned. "What he saw I believe was etched on his memory for the rest of his life. We were lucky to escape the whole episode with no more than a minor fright – I thought he might have to undergo psychotherapy by the way he told me the next day."

"What was it? What was it?"

"Apparently this gym-rat-come-dancer – I can't remember his name – was in this ladies room, and he had his CD player set up with some external speakers – this was before the days of the iPod. And there he was, gyrating and wiggling with all his clothes off to the seated form of a woman old enough to be *my* mother, let alone his."

"Oh no. Scrub your eyes," Kelly shouted, elapsing into giggles.

"Precisely." Alan laughed, remembering the white face of the poor cleaner as he had brought him a stiff whiskey in the crew bar that night. "So we had to figure out what to do – do we tell the captain? They were all consenting adults after all, but didn't this constitute harassment or pole dancing or…? It might have only be a matter of time before he brought the whole reputation of the cruise line under a black cloud, or he himself took a step too far and someone complained."

"What did you do?" Kelly was holding her sides to stop herself from laughing.

"In the end we didn't tell the captain, but myself and a few select others who shall remain unnamed for the sake of posterity, managed to see to it that he kept a more low profile and stop this activity…"

Kelly raised her eyebrows.

"First, we had one of the rather good looking male dancers – the one all the female dancers wanted doing the lifts for them since he was so strong – go to his room and ask for a lap dance. Since we knew the sexual orientation of the dancer, we also knew that one thing would led to another and that they would get it on. We asked the dancer to be a bit rough in his activity, which he was more than willing to oblige with. He indicated that certain parts of the lap dancer's anatomy were going to be 'a bit sore' for several days. We also had a few straight members of the kitchen staff, all burly men; go to his room one a day for the next few days asking for lap dances. After being made 'sore' the first night, he apparently refused the other financial offers that were given to him. After a few days, he was refusing offers from crew and passengers, both male and female. I believe he had a very enjoyable cruise after he got over his embarrassment, and got on with enjoying the more acceptable activities that the cruise ship had to offer."

Kelly couldn't stop tittering. "Oh, the alpha man."

"Yes indeed, now let us get back to see about these results…."

The results from the Jacuzzis, the plunge pool and the swimming pool came back just as Alan had suspected. The results weren't dangerous in any way, but there was some viral count present, enough to encourage a virus to proliferate, especially if the person had already been exposed frequently throughout the day to the same virus, and did not observe the needed habit of washing their hands.

Alan immediately picked up the phone and informed the captain, who in turn informed the cleaning crew to close the offending bodies of water and do an emergency scrub of all the areas tested with strong disinfectant. It would put swimming off the activities list, but tomorrow they should be docking in Malta anyway – that beautiful Mediterranean island, its shores endowed of crystal blue, warm waters in which to swim.

Alan always preferred swimming in the natural seas anyway, and before he got on to the next medical examination, he wondered whether he should retrieve his swimming suit from his luggage for tomorrow.

CHAPTER NINE

Valletta
Blessings in disguise!

LUCKILY, THE *OCEAN QUEST* docked in the more convenient cruise port in Malta the very next morning. This was a fact that pleased Dr. Mayhew immensely as he stood on the front deck, watching the famous walled city of Valletta come closer and closer.

It was the doctor had to agree, a striking sight. Valletta itself was a walled citadel, rivaling even the Vatican City for its grandeur, and UNESCO, the body governing the planet's most ancient and awe-inspiring antiquities, had declared it a World Heritage Site.

It appears to the viewer as the fantastical image of what a citadel should be – flush with the coast and leading right down to the water's edge. In some places, the high walls and catchments of the ancient stone gleamed in the strong sunlight as behind it rows and ranks of stone towers, cathedrals, churches, and houses rose high to the emerging central castle.

It is absolutely perfect, Alan thought, and not for the first time, from where he stood alongside other passengers who had come to see the approach.

"Well," he murmured to himself, "perfect if it wasn't for the gulls," just as another 'present' from one of the birds splattered inches from his shoe.

The flock had begun circling when they had crested the headland and made for Valletta port, and now, numbering in hundreds, they were becoming quite a menace. Their huge white and grey bodies dive-bombed the waters around the slowly motoring cruise ship, spiraling around its high central decks in what seemed to Alan to be a very determined effort to repaint the ship to their liking.

Already he had narrowly avoided a few such 'presents' himself, and had watched as a crowd of screaming children who had not been able to avoid direct hits not once, not twice, but three times.

Three turned out to be the lucky charm as now they were running around the front deck in horrid abandon, shouting that they were 'dodging' the aerial guano.

Alan thought that all they were doing was royally frustrating their parents and the other cruise members, but he decided it polite to say nothing, and let their tired-looking parents hurry after them, looking very much like shepherds chasing after anxious, skittish sheep.

"It is supposed to be considered lucky, you know," said a voice from his elbow. Alan turned around to see an older woman, who must have been in her sixties, barely taller than five foot, if that, standing there. He considered that her diminished stature was probably due to quite a severe case of bone density loss, which does affect many women in later years. He thought kindly that she must be in agony most of the time since her condition was often accompanied by compression fractures of the spine.

However, the older woman didn't seem to be letting any of this stop her. She wore her large, bright lilac sun hat with a matching dress.

She was standing as forward as she could be to the front of the deck, although the railings and barriers meant that they were far away from the actual edge of the ship; breathing the fresh, warm air in great draughts and grinning as if she enjoyed every minute of it.

"Lucky?" Alan said with a smile. "I always thought that was just a story that parents told their children, so they wouldn't get so upset when they got... evacuated on by a bird."

The old lady cackled – a truly dirty laugh – somehow betraying the fact that she had led a full and rich life. "Well, it's lucky for the person saying it, since *they* are not the ones who have been hit."

"Quite true," Alan said, again trying to sidestep another swoop of the winged devils.

"So, you're the ship's doc then?" the older woman remarked.

"Yes, yes I am, ma'am."

"Elsie Rottersgate, pleased to meet you, I would say that I was a Mrs. Elsie Rottersgate, but that pleasure has come and gone, then come and then definitely gone again," she informed him in the way that elderly people do.

Alan reflected that quite often people of a more 'golden' character seemed to have no shame, and didn't give a care anymore of how other people viewed them, *and quite right too*, the doctor agreed. *When I am older and have paid my dues in this life, I do not expect to be very particular about most things as when I was young.*

"Yes, young man," Elsie continued. Alan couldn't stop himself feeling a little pleased to hear himself being called 'young man'. "Yes I have been married two times; once to a very nice man of good parentage and a good job, only for him to run off with the hired help. I didn't miss that one at all." She snickered. "And the last time to a rascal of a man who drank too much and was very handy at cards. And you know what? *He* was much more fun and was the love of my life." She beamed at him, idly fingering the locket around her neck, which, Alan assumed, must contain a picture or some memento of her lost (last) husband.

"I am truly sorry to hear of your loss," he felt compelled to say. "Although it is very refreshing to hear someone speak so honestly."

"No, you wouldn't be sorry at all if you had known my last husband. He was a cantankerous, jealous old sod who nevertheless doted on me. He'd have had you on your bottom for being so impertinent as to sidle up to an unattended lady on the deck of a ship and engage her in flattery." She cackled again.

"Well, in that case I am *not* sure that I would have liked to meet him, but I would have probably liked to try his luck at cards." Alan laughed with her, warming to Elsie Rottersgate quickly. "I have been known to be quite good at poker myself, in my student days. I am not a gambler, and I have always set my limits. But being out on the open seas for most of my life all I can say is that I've had my share of hours to learn a trick or two in card games."

"Well, young doctor, we shall have to see about that. You have a date – if you don't mind being seen in the company of an old biddy like me?" Elsie winked at him, and underneath it all Alan could see with his physician's eye that although the old woman might be a bit of a rogue, she was, in fact, essentially a good person, who had loved well and still felt the keen loss of her troublesome husband.

"It would be my pleasure, Mrs. Rottersgate."

"Oh stop that fawning – call me Elsie, and what shall I call you, Doc?"

"Doc will do, but I prefer Alan. Are you going to see the fabulous walled city yourself later? I might come down and see some of the sights if I get some time off."

"Of course. I will be taking the tour with that Stefan chap, although he looks too smiley for my liking. I prefer my men with a bit more salt in their blood." she snickered. Then, wishing him a good day, she daintily walked off to prepare for her shore leave. She managed to avoid being 'deposited' on by the encircling fiends of the sky, as if the very thought of incurring her sharp wit frightened even them off.

Alan chuckled to himself – yes, you certainly did meet some

characters on the cruises, and he was sure that if he ever got around to writing down his memoirs, they would be sure to amuse. Not the least of which was Lord and Lady Hemmingsworth.

Not much had been seen of either of them since Egypt and the 'Code Brown' incident had been declared. It seemed as if they had managed to quarantine themselves off from the lesser 'oik's', and the crew, and were being brought their 'state dinners' in the privacy of their suite. They were also being provided with entertainment, since some of the singers and performers had been asked to attend their large stateroom for the previous two nights. *Nothing but the best for royalty,* Alan thought.

It seemed, from all accounts, that the very thought of being struck down by such an embarrassing ailment as the one that had effected about forty percent of the other passengers simply wasn't to be endured publicly by people of their standards – it *wasn't British.*

Alan was forced to smile to himself – those blighters and their stiff upper lip. It was true that every middle class or better British person he had ever met did have a certain air about them that exuded class and prestige. Then Alan chuckled at the thought of the disgraceful way that Lady Hemmingsworth was throwing herself at the other crewmembers. *Well, perhaps not all the British were a chip off the upper crust,* he mused.

What brought this to mind was Lady Hemmingsworth's triumphant arrival on the deck. This time she wore a pale pastel blue version of her 'colonial whites'. She had managed to corral a number of porters to accompany her, carrying her 'hand luggage' – a travel briefcase 'trolley', a sun shade and a spare hat. Alan was once again, amazed at her audacity.

The Lady's beehive bobbed its way towards them, and the crowd of the other passenger's parted like a wave before it. Alan thought she was like her own vessel at sea, leaving a wake behind her, and throwing everyone affected by her into the turmoil of her passage.

The 'trolley' was, at least as far as the doctor could see, anything but. It was as if it was the latest evolution in trolley technology and owed nothing of its design, save its handles, to those ancient, rattling wire things that had been its natural predecessors. Instead, the *thing* was brightly colored; bulging at the seams monstrosity of velour and plastic, with stream lined, air-friendly grab rails that could extend from it in a variety of ways to enhance its carrying 'experience'.

Not that these factors helped the experience of the poor porter who was helping her, as he was ordered to adjust and readjust the thing as if it were a complicated racecar. The poor man had been left alone to carry the hats and the sunshade as well, and he seemed to be struggling with every step he took.

As much as he really didn't want to, Alan decided to offer his help, more for the young man's benefit than anything else.

"Milady," The doctor called out, walking forward with his best physician's smile. "I see you are well prepared for the day's activities. Can I advise, as the attending doctor on this vessel that you minimize your luggage somewhat?"

"Minimize? What on earth are you talking about, Doctor?" Lady Hemmingsworth seemed genuinely bemused.

"Well, given your delicate constitution"—he knew that this phrase would go down well. It always did with a certain type of clients; the ones with more money and time on their hands to consider their constitution, for starters—"and given your recent upset at the heat in Alexandria, I would advise taking less luggage, but much more water, and the sun parasol, of course."

"Yes of course." Lady Hemmingsworth smiled at him, and folded a pale-gloved hand over his arm. "You are *so* good to me, Doctor, always trying to look after me." Her smile widened a little so that her teeth shone for a brief second too long, and her hand gave his arm an affectionate squeeze.

The porter looked from one to the other, and Alan could see the man trying not to be sick where he stood.

"You there?" the Lady said over her shoulder at him. "Be so good as to go and fetch me some water will you? And take these back down to my chambers on your way, I am sure that the doctor here will look after me, but do be careful when you enter this time – three knocks remember, three knocks. Lord Hemmingsworth does so hate being disturbed."

The young man scowled, then gave the doctor a cheery nod as if to say, "she's all yours now, and good riddance." To which Alan threw him a strained, thin-lipped smile.

Ye Gods! He hadn't actually meant for this to happen. Alan was sure that if he had to spend another day escorting the Lady Hemmingsworth, he would scream -- actually, physically scream.

But, he considered his professional training as a doctor and as a senior officer of this vessel. The Lord and Lady could easily get him fired and bring the whole Gold Cruise Line Company into a bit of trouble with all of the power and prestige that they had amassed over the years. He had seen it happen before. People's whole careers ruined, all over an ill-timed comment or a case of 'brushing up people the wrong way'.

"So tell me, Lady Hemmingsworth," he smoothly continued, enfolding her gloved hand on his arm, taking her arm as if she were his date at the school prom. He started leading her to the railing, walking sedately as if he were merely the attentive escort.

"Anything, Doctor." The Lady again flashed him one of her predatory smiles.

"Tell me, how is Lord Hemmingsworth faring on our little voyage? Is he enjoying himself? I do not think I have even had the pleasure of meeting him once on deck."

The Lady gave a small, displeased look in the down turn of her smile and sighed as if much hurt. "Oh Lord Hemmingsworth is fine, absolutely fine I can tell you. He seems to come on these cruises just to sit in his stateroom and read, or look at charts and recount his memoirs to a tape recorder. A tape recorder I tell you. As if we couldn't have someone come in and interview us both about our adventurous lives, but no, he insists on recording audiotapes all by himself as he sits there organizing his papers, his maps and his thoughts. It truly is one of the most boring things for a girl to have to witness." She put on a melodramatic air as if she had suffered long from this complaint. Although Lady Hemmingsworth was certainly no spring chicken, Alan imagined that Lord Hemmingsworth was probably a few years older than his wife, and that he had married a young, wealthy, and very attractive wife.

Lady Hemmingsworth now many years after that happy occasion was a woman in the 'later epoch' of her life, but to whom obviously the words 'aging', 'time' and 'gracefully' just did not apply.

With his trained medical eye, the doctor could easily tell, that she had probably been the recipient of several acts of reconstructive cosmetic surgery given the skin on her face had a smooth, taut appearance, around a pear sort of look. Her figure while not thin was certainly very well proportioned. Sculpted by a good plastic surgeon, Alan surmised.

Alan made understanding noises as he moved them closer to the front railings. His eyes kept darting around to see if there was any other worthy man who he could palm the Lady off on, and one who would not later cause a scandal.

"So tell me milady, would Lord Hemmingsworth take an interest in visiting the old walled city of Valletta? I could send someone to personally invite him?"

Her look flashed in annoyance at the doctor who was, on all account in her mind, supposed to be her committed suitor.

"No I do not think you understand me. How on earth did you get through medical school? Lord Hemmingsworth is not interested in *activities* or *trips* at all. He told me just last night that if he were indeed interested in such things then he would charter a private jet to take him. In any case, you should know that he has been to Valletta many times – he was asked to attend the diplomatic teams that bestowed the World Heritage Status, and formally attend a celebratory dinner here every year. It is infuriating, you know, the business of being one of us." She pronounced the last sentence with heavy emphasis.

"One of us?" Alan wondered for a second.

"Oh, my dear man, you really are having troubles today aren't you?" The Lady chuckled cruelly to herself. Alan presumed she was thinking that he had fallen in the throes of admiration of her station in life. "One of the Royalty, of course."

"Of course." Alan successfully stopped himself guffawing.

"Yes, we have to deal with the media, the incessant photographers, the journalists, and the requests for our time – the endless dinners we have to go to and speeches. It's interminable, I can tell you."

Damn, Alan thought, as a sea gull's 'present' narrowly missed the Lady. He wished it had had a better aim, and then wondered idly if the bird would take an interest in her monolithic hair. It certainly looked like it could house at least two sea birds in there along with a passing albatross.

The Lady prattled on about all the formal functions and dinners that she had attended in her time, without any sign of concern or grace as to the recipients – usually charities who were immensely pleased to have a lesser known royal attend their celebratory function. The doctor kept watch on the seagulls and tried carefully to maneuver the Lady so she would be positioned in the direct firing line.

Unfortunately, this tactic proved unsuccessful, when the cruise ship sounded its horns as it arrived in the safe docking waters of Valletta port. There was always a loud cheer from the passengers when this happened, and for a second, all the attendants on this mighty floating city felt a part of something bigger.

Alan loved this sensation of family that you acquired on a sailing vessel. For brief snatches of time you feel like you are a part of a bigger unit, a living breathing entity known collectively as 'the ship' –

as if it were something bigger and more conscious than the individual passengers, staff and crew.

He knew that it was a far more common feeling on smaller vessels, where your actions directly affected your crewmates, and they had to trust your decisions and vice versa amidst the hazardous challenges of a life at sea.

He reflected that maybe it was a throwback to when all ships had salt stains on their sails and barnacles crusting their keels. For a second all the crew could imagine what it would be like to be truly, terribly free with no master save the winds and tides.

Not that his last sailing expedition had been *anything* like that at all, he reflected, as Lady Hemmingsworth seemed content on his arm to chatter away. She was a walking commentary it seemed, and had so little regard for her fellow man and cared little if there was any response from him; just merely that she had an audience. However, a much-practiced social politician, the doctor managed to 'ooh,' 'hmm', and 'I see' at the appropriate moments while his brain drifted into memories...

*   *   *

Alan remembered that he had been recounting the story to Tiffany just a few days previously, and mentally retraced his steps to where he had left off...

Alan had started his sailing trip with the navigation engineer Rick Hammer, having boarded at the Alaskan port of Auke Bay.

When he was introduced to the vessel, Alan was most surprised at its state of repair and he was to spend the next number of days sorting thru its state of almost complete disarray. He knew the old adage that 'The cobbler's children always go unshod' and so thought no more of it – at least for the moment.

It was often the case that trained mechanics, trained engineers and accredited builders always had 'pet projects,' which were in a state of half–completion, as their work life took up a lot of their time. Their private interests became more specialized ways for them to investigate the bits of their craft that they enjoyed. In this manner Alan had found many sailors who were building their own small boats, or racing car drivers, enhancing a fanciful prototype engine.

However, what he hadn't expected was to ask to live aboard a vessel that didn't even have such basic essentials, such as a bowsprit, grab rails along the decking, radar, or lifelines.

"Er..." he had ventured, "is this thing safe?"

"Safe?" Rick had laughed. "I have been sailing this beauty for five years and lived in these waters for longer," he had explained, such as the old sea salt he so desperately wanted to be and showed the doctor to his berth.

The V-shaped berth built for the two-person vessel was spacious enough, but unfortunately it was currently occupied by the remnants of Rick's recent escapades. His accumulated charts, maps, and the bits of wires and receivers that he was tinkering with were sprawled across it along with his large array of wood working tools, which he used somewhat frequently to carve this or that – achieving no great result, as far as Alan could see.

Rick apologized and asked if Alan wouldn't mind taking the narrow galley couch – a decision the doctor later regretted as the cramped confines played havoc with his back. But still Alan did not complain as at last, he kept telling himself, he was really sailing again.

An accomplished sailor, Alan Mayhew had won several trophies at Regattas in his time, and he had spent many of his summer holidays on boats and racing vessels around the coasts of America. There was no question at all – the salt was in his blood, and his comrades and loved ones made a point of telling him so. Unfortunately, at the present time he found himself boat-less. He was simply spending too much of his time working on the cruises, such that having his own boat with mooring seemed like a waste to the doctor. Why keep a boat, if for months and months, sometimes the better part of a year or at times longer, you can't use it? 'You have to get wet on the hull' as the older sea dogs would say, which was a truism that Alan had found to work every time.

This was one of the reasons he had taken Rick up on his offer of a sailing trip around the Alaskan coastline. Rick had appeared to him a *constant* sailor, a man who was also in love with sailing and the sea: and someone who would rarely 'let his hull go dry.'

Little did he know, he thought wryly, just how much of an adventure it would become, and that it would start that very night as they traveled to their first destination, Blue Mouse Cove?

Blue Mouse was a tiny rocky cove that was a good spot to hide out from the weather and storms of the open waters. As the night descended, Alan was increasingly glad that they had found it, for no sooner had they dropped anchor a heavy sea fog rolled in. Sea fog is an eerie, whimsical sort of thing, Alan mused.

The witness of a heavy sea fog is presented by a slow

advancing wall of shifting white that moves far quicker than it appears, rapidly engulfing any vessel in a dome of muted, washed-out colors. Since it is generally a low phenomenon, if you are lucky, it will break over your head, affording you glimpses of the stars above, and creating the sensation that you are alone on a tiny island of solitude amidst the night.

Fog is also a constantly changing vision, as the texture of the fog transforms itself continuously, from soft, pale, grey tones to darker more menacing greys; all the while infinite droplets of water vapor shift and eddy on minuscule air currents.

The doctor had no problem believing the stories of those sailors from earlier times who went mad from the spectacle, as the shifting, incomprehensible form suggests shapes, contours, figures and visions of sea creatures, mermaids, and the like.

Alan shivered in his skin, as he thought of just how easy it was to become disoriented. Visual spatial disorientation is a known entity in fog. It is not just visual cues that get distorted either. Sounds bounce off various surfaces, including the water droplets themselves, and distort the sounds that are around the sailor.

Far off sounds – the lapping of the waves against a wharf, the mournful cries of roosting birds are suddenly thrown closer by unknown shifts in the fog; while the close-up sounds of the water against the boat, mute and dull one's own voice, seemingly coming from somewhere far away in the waves. It is truly, a very dangerous experience, and Alan was glad that they had stopped for the night.

"Didn't I tell you that I knew these waters?" Rick laughed as they shared a spiced cup of cocoa and both meditated on the mysteries of the wild seas. "I have been traveling up and down this route for years – I could do it blindfolded," he had assured his companion.

Alan considered whether or not he actually *liked* Rick Hammer. He was one of those loud, rough, and ready roguish types, who was the sort of friend that you *wanted* to have at certain times. He seemed to remind the people around him of the wilder youths they might once have had, and the adventures that they could still have. He seemed to promise adventure and mystery.

Nevertheless Alan hoped that his words were true, because it proved that they might just as well be sailing blindfolded as soon as Alan realized that they had no GPS system, no electronic speed detector, no depth sounder, no radar; not even a satellite phone.

"Don't worry," Rick would tell him. "I have got a host of installations to do on this boat, a little bit of work that I hope to do –

all my own navigation equipment will be there."

Alan remembered the piles of transmitters, receivers and other bizarre-looking pieces of equipment that he had seen on the V-berth.

"As soon as we get a chance, Doc, I'll be settling in and doing them – we'll have a good long day or so, once we get going." Alan wasn't really mollified. "But until then, Doc, relax and enjoy the ride."

This was what Alan tried to do, or at least wanted to do if his inquisitive mind did not start enquiring about the rest of the equipment on board their shared space.

The next day they sailed against the hard current around the coast of Chichagof Island – a rocky outcropping where sea birds roost over the winter. Today, the current was high and strong, and they decided it was better to continue rather than go around the longer and narrower passages. Rick decided that they would ride crosscurrent around the coastline.

It proved to be a fearsome time, but one that was well within the talents of two experienced sailors such as Rick and Alan. The whole day they were in a constant state of alert as they shifted the course, the direction, the luff of the sails. Alan calculated that if the current overpowered them, then they could easily be dashed against the island rocks and the wooden boat would be broken up into matchsticks. He kept his eye on the sails as they had to be manually tightened – there weren't even any winches to make the job easier – giving the whole venture what Rick called 'the authentic experience'. Alan was beginning to think it was just adding up to a bloody dangerous experience. They had sailed on, aiming for Reid Inlet as their next overnight stop. At least Alan got the chance to see lots of whales at Adolphus Point – a truly magnificent spectacle. The vision of the whales kept Alan going through that long, hard day sailing – constantly tweaking and adjusting the sails.

Seeing these massive gentle beasts in their natural habitat had always been one of the life-changing encounters that he had experienced as a sailor. He recalled the time he had had the chance to see them many years ago as a young man from the seat of a single man kayak.

It was their *size* that had affected him so much, their brute strength, obvious intelligence and their noticeable gentleness. Alan wasn't a believer that whales could communicate with you, or could understand their human counterparts any more than he could understand them, yet, as he gazed into the large dish-shaped eye of a passing mountainous shadow rippling underneath the boat, he was given pause to wonder.

He was always amazed when he saw whales. A life at sea can become a very 'wild' experience. It can seem like a totally inhospitable environment, where prolonged exposure to the elements can kill you, and where hypothermia from exposure is a reality for many. The pounding, driving rains combined with the screaming, ruthless winds can make the whole sea voyage a truly physiologically miserable one.

But then the whales would arrive. Here were beasts larger than houses, bigger then trains that could joyfully break water in an explosion of passion and movement. The doctor would feel humbled that even in these wild, inhospitable places, life had found its niche, and flourished.

Later that night, after anchoring at Reid Inlet, all of these thoughts echoed through Alan's mind, while he examined the life preservers. There was no life ring to throw, and only one, twenty-year-old life preserver, which was far too small for him to even attempt to wear. He idly wondered if it was reserved for the women that Rick would invite on to his ship for a 'little cruise', which the navigation engineer had been boasting about during their trip...

Disgusted with the obvious lack of attention to safety, the doctor pondered whether the trip had been a good idea. But he had paid money and at least he had gotten out to see the wild once again. Soon his eyes became heavy, drifting off to the gentle slapping of the waves against the hull, and sleep overcame him.

*   *   *

"Doctor? Are you even listening to me?" Lady Hemmingsworth's voice abruptly shook Alan out of one nightmare into another. It turned out that in his musings he had once again failed to get the Lady splattered from on high by the accompanying parade of seagulls, a fact he rued sorely. Instead, he had received a rather large 'lucky present' himself right on his shoulder.

"Doctor Mayhew. This really is disgraceful." The Lady retrieved her arm and pulled herself back in horror from the offending deposit from the natural world. It was clear to the doctor that Lady Hemmingsworth would definitely not be one to go sailing around the frozen waters of Alaska.

"I am so sorry, ma'am." The doctor was delighted. "I am afraid I shall have to go and see what I can do about this. I do hope you have someone to accompany you on your trip ashore?"

Lady Hemmingsworth was horrified that a person so recently *made dirty* would enquire after her well-being, and she haughtily replied as she backed away from him, "Yes, there is a rather nice businessman from Omaha who wishes to dine with me and his lordship. I shall have him take me out for the day and see if he is really not quite the bore he pretends to be."

With these admonishing words, Alan found himself excused from his nursemaid duties. And with a delighted skip to his step he left to go and change his shirt, and get on with his day without having to deal with the melodramas of the over-active Lady Hemmingsworth.

Suddenly the thought struck him – it turns out that being 'blessed' by a seagull really *was* a lucky omen.

CHAPTER TEN

Valletta
Rogues and cards

THE VISIT OF VALLETTA HAD been truly remarkable, the doctor had to agree. At least, it had certainly been remarkable for Frankie, one of the table staff for the on board casino. He was still nursing a bandage to his head and grinning ruefully from where the small group sat, below decks in Frankie's cabin.

"I would have got him, you know," Frankie said, his cool, hunky good looks marred by the bruise that was forming on his jaw line.

"Don't be a dolt," Elsie Rottersgate said from where she was perched on a chair around the cramped table. The older woman still had the lilac hat with her, but this time it was seated beside her on the floor.

The trio considered the day's remarkable events, and, one by one each of them started giggling.

"I personally think that I had the jump on him," Frankie said disdainfully to the other two.

"Well perhaps at first, but it seemed that he definitely had the jump on you in the end," Alan remarked, keeping an eye on his hand of cards. He was holding two threes, a four and a five of the same suit and a king, and he was wondering just what he could make them believe he had.

They had started playing almost as soon as they had returned from the security office where they had informed Vince, had made the appropriate statements, had filled out the reports and had foregone dinner in favor of a quiet game in Frankie's cabin.

Besides which, Alan wanted to spend a few hours checking up on whether Frankie really was all right, and wasn't suffering from a latent concussion. Seeing that the rakish gambling attendant had won the first two hands, Alan thought there would probably be little to worry about.

"It's just what he was doing that I don't understand," Alan

remarked. "I mean, attempting to steal some purses and bags, right in front of the church? What was the guy thinking?"

"Oh I've met some rogues like that in my time – poor desperate men who see an opportunity and take it – no matter where they are."

"Hey, hey, he did wait for us to walk out of the place and then hit us coming out of the alley; there was obviously *some* forethought," Frankie protested. Alan thought that perhaps his pride was a little more wounded than his head.

"Well, I guess he didn't expect to have the two amateur 'have-a-go-heroes' on his tail, did he?" Elsie cackled at them both. "Men! It's as if they think anything can be solved by running around shouting."

"Well, it seemed the chivalrous thing to do..." Alan butted in. "After all, Diane was quite taken aback by the whole affair."

"Yes, yes, I am sure it was for a woman's honor you two raced off, not the glory at all." She fixed them both with a beady eye and promptly laid down a Royal Flush. Elsie had been doing that a lot recently. Alan wasn't sure what cards Frankie was still holding, and while he was no card counter himself, he was starting to wonder whether the old lady was cheating.

Elsie smiled benevolently at them both as she scraped up her winnings – one plastic green dealer's visor from Frankie, a Maldives key ring from Alan, and an assortment of small change. Frankie had insisted; if they were going to risk bending the rule by allowing a passenger into the crew's quarters to play cards with them, even one as friendly as Elsie Rottersgate, they had to play by the Treasure Trinket Cards Rules, which meant nothing bigger than a coin would be allowed as a bet, and if any one wished, they could place one of their personal belongings or memento's from their voyage and argue what it was worth.

It was Frankie's own personal rule that he only played Treasure Trinket Cards in his own room and when he was off duty, or so he claimed, although Alan had heard of an underground poker league that was currently fleecing half the crew of their earnings. That way he could keep control of his losses and earnings and not end up on a cruise owing money rather than making it.

Earlier that day the trio had been assisting on one of the tours in a haphazard way while visiting some of the ancient sites of Valletta. It was packed of renaissance, baroque, late medieval architecture and history, history, and more history. The citadel fortress had been one of the strongholds of the Knights Hospitaller, or the Knights Templar as they were more commonly known, during the years of the crusades that had raged across this Mediterranean region. The place had grown so powerful that it had become a viable target for the armies of the western nations, and even the Papal city. Its might still showed in strong walls and many hundreds of thousands of pounds worth of rare artifacts adorning every museum and vault.

Alan hadn't really been sure just what Frankie had been doing there other than being an escort on one of the tours. He didn't seem the type to go on site tours, nor had he done so previously. The doctor suspected that it had to do with the large amount of treasure trinkets that Valletta would offer – little mementos – such as ornamental tea towels, plaster of Paris statuaries, framed prints and little seals of the Knights Templar that he could later trade with the below decks crew for favors or cash. Frankie seemed to be an enterprising kind of young man.

They had been traveling for the better part of the day, had stopped at a restaurant with an outside eating area where they had spent a couple of noisy hours, ordering tidbits and dishes of food to put their taste buds to the test. In the afternoon they had gone on a tour of a variety of chapels, churches and museums.

The trio had naturally fallen into conversation as Alan kept up his promise of a 'date' with the dirty-laughing Elsie, and Frankie had dawdled behind the rest of the tour, poking his head into every boutique and gift shop they had encountered. It seemed a natural progression for Alan to invite the casino staff member to join them since he was by now well aware of Elsie's love for rogues and devilishly handsome young men.

All in all, it had been a delightful day, or at least it would have been if they hadn't interrupted the attacker and then been forced to return home to the *Ocean Quest*. Alan had felt perfectly at ease in the company of the elderly Elsie Rottersgate – instead of Lady Hemmingsworth – and had assailed her with jokes and stories of their encounter as the trio walked the narrow streets of the Citadel.

"See, I told you bird poop was lucky," Elsie had noted just before Frankie had said, "Wait a minute – what's going on?"

Startled, Alan had looked up to see Frankie pointing directly in front of them in an alley where Diane Seinz was struggling with an assailant, both holding one end of her handbag.

"Hey! You!" Alan had shouted menacingly.

"Go," Frankie had said, running to the aid of the distressed woman, with Alan hot on his heels.

No sooner had they given chase, the man had abandoned the struggle, letting go of the bag. He had turned and had run full tilt into the back alleys of the city. Alan could see that he was a fairly big man, even under his baggy clothes, and grey 'hoody' that he had pulled over his head.

Since Frankie seemed more than adept at this sort of game, Alan had stopped the chase to help the shaken Diane to her feet, and just as he did, he had heard a cry.

Frankie had tripped over the uneven cobblestones and had taken a bad fall hitting his head against the nearby wall. Rolling and cursing, he stopped, realizing that the chase was up and lay where he had fallen.

With a quick apology to Diane, Alan rushed to his friend's assistance, bidding him to lie still while he checked his vision, making the angry young crewmember track his fingers to check for blurriness of vision, and checking his neck for any wounds around on his head.

Fortunately it appeared he was fine for the most part, and he had sustained no serious damage at all, save some superficial abrasions on his forehead. Alan had helped him to his feet, and had brought the hobbling Frankie over to Mrs. Seinz so she could at least meet her rescuer.

"I'm sorry I couldn't catch him, ma'am," Frankie informed her dutifully, to which Diane muttered that it was no problem at all – she was probably still in a state of shock at the whole encounter.

As smoothly as if she had picked up a thousand accident victims and injured parties, Elsie took Mrs. Seinz's arm and led her away to sit down for a nice cup of tea while they waited for the tour to regroup and for Mr. Seinz to reappear from the nearby museum.

"Oh my God," he exclaimed, "What has happened?" as he rushed to his wife's side.

"A young villain tried to assault her, and where were you, might I ask?" Elsie fixed him with a stern gaze.

"I was… I was … at the museum," the man said helplessly, looking sheepishly from his wife to Elsie. And before Elsie could throw any more nasty remarks at the aggrieved couple, Alan decided to step in and describe what had happened, including that nothing had been stolen and the role that Frankie had played in all of it.

When he had finished his description of the events, Dr. Seinz said very gravely, "Well, I think I owe you a deep debt of gratitude, young sir, how can I ever repay you?"

"Oh, you can put a healthy tip with my name on it at the bar,"

Frankie had suggested jokingly. *Back to his same old self in no time,* Alan thought, "I think I might need it tonight, the way this head is beginning to throb."

"Right – that's it," Alan had interjected. "You are okay to walk, yes?"

Frankie nodded.

"Then you are coming back with me to the Medical Centre where I know I can treat you." Alan smoothly took charge of the crisis as he said to the tour in general. "Will someone phone for the Maltese constabulary to attend to any of the legal matters? We will see to it that everyone is treated and safe and then they can begin their investigation"

"Oh, no need," Diane said quickly, wearily. "Nothing was stolen, and if Frankie here doesn't mind, we will leave him that healthy tip." She dug an elbow into her husband's side. "And well, I really cannot be bothered holding up the cruise or spending my last few hours of shore time sitting around filling in police reports. No police charges are to be pressed."

"What? Really?" Elsie stuttered. "But this young man has been hurt, and they might have him on the things that they have everywhere these days, you know, the CCTV cameras."

"No, really, but thank you, Mrs. Rottersgate, for all of your help. But no, I really do insist."

Alan noted that she looked up for support to her husband, and Dr. Seinz affectionately squeezed her shoulder.

"If you want it this way, darling," he said. Mrs. Seinz nodded.

"Well then," Alan said slowly, seeing her reasoning but not really agreeing with her final decision. He knew that quite often after an accident or a criminal event where there was a victim, the affected parties often displayed classic forms of emotional avoidance, where they no longer want to talk about the issue, deal with it effectively, or think about it in any way. They just wanted to move on and get on with their lives. "I suggest we get our little party here back to the ship anyway, and I will be able to see that there is no more serious damage done."

Once back on board, the doctor had been forced to call in the report to Vince, who kept a log of all such events on a cruise, in case there was a legal, health or even an insurance issue emerging later on.

He had then examined the patients in the Medical Centre.

Nurse Gacek had thrown them a stern and reproachful glance, muttering under her breath at the state in which the crew and passengers had returned to 'her' infirmary; before Alan had announced that she could proceed to washing and sterilizing the surgical instruments if she was annoyed at the clutter. He felt that he had to put his foot down every now and again with some of his more 'difficult' staff.

Examining Frankie once more, he had discovered that there were no fractures or sprains to either the bones of his hand or his skull, merely a bad contusion that would, in all probability, give him a crushing headache for the rest of the day. He had cleaned up the wound, applied some antiseptic liquid to the area and had applied a large dressing to it, advising him to come and see him in the morning as well – just to make sure.

"You have had a lucky escape young man," he had told the heroic avenger. "You could easily have sustained a lot more serious damage other than a laceration and some abrasions."

"Oh, I don't think I was the one with the lucky escape – that was the other guy." Frankie had chortled before taking the non-narcotic painkillers – enough to numb the sharp edge of the pain – and leaving Alan to examine Diane.

"And now, Mrs. Seinz; let me have a look at you."

Despite her protests, Alan managed to convince the lady to undergo a few simple tests. This was more to ensure that she felt cared for, and that she wasn't in shock.

"A little shaken up," he diagnosed with a smile, "but no permanent harm done." After that, he had sent them on their way to report the whole event to Vince before he had returned to sitting at his desk to assess the whole event.

As he drifted back into the moment, he reminded himself that *it could have been much worse*. He was once more in the present at the card game held below deck in Frankie's chambers. *We are lucky the assailant wasn't carrying a weapon of some kind.*

"You seem lost in thought over there, Doc?" Elsie interrupted him. "Are you worried that you are about to be beaten by a woman old enough to be your mother and an injured man who can hardly see straight?"

Alan laughed good-humoredly. "No, I am afraid it seems that you have both beaten me already." He laid his cards down and his compatriots tried not to snicker at his misfortune.

"Well, it's between you and me now young man, and don't think I am about to go easy on you just because you're injured," Elsie announced.

"How about because I was very noble today?" Frankie said. He had already lost half the trinkets that he had been scavenging for his own entrepreneurial efforts amongst the crew.

"Oh, well, that only means that I won't *humiliate* you only, beat you." Elsie beamed, and, true to her word, she proceeded to do just that.

"That's it. That's it." Frankie laughed. "Both of you – out of my cabin at once. I can't have word get out that I was beaten by a gloriously mature passenger and the ship's MD."

"Who are you calling gloriously mature?" Alan retorted, and they all fell into howls of laughter – on Frankie's part, that was slightly painful laughter.

"No, I won't be beaten again, and I need my beauty sleep unlike the rest of you… go on, enough adventure for one day."

They bid their goodbyes, still smiling at the remarkable events, and Alan accompanied Elsie Rottersgate to her cabin, using a back route. He was well aware that passengers were not officially supposed to be in the crew portions of the ship, so he had to get Elsie out swiftly and quietly.

It was already well past twelve, and the doctor knew he would be hearing from Nurse Petra in a few hours from now.

"Well, what a nice young man," Elsie remarked. "Thank you very much for our 'date', Doctor. It has indeed proved to be exciting." She laughed as she packed away her trinket winnings.

"I would say let's do it again, but I really don't think that my heart can take the pace of life around you, so I won't say it." Which was an assertion that Alan Mayhew didn't believe for a minute, seeing in the mature woman, a vitality that few a third of her age could match.

"But I tell you one thing about today, that Seinz couple are on rocky waters, believe you me."

"I'm sorry? What do you mean?"

"Rocky waters, Doctor. A woman of my age with all of my previous husbands can tell the signs. There is definitely something strained about their marriage."

"Really? Every time I have spoken to them they seem to be a couple still very much in love," Alan replied, considering Elsie's assertion. "And Dr. Seinz cannot be blamed for not being there at the precise moment something as random as a mugging that no one could predict would occur."

"Oh really?" Elsie again affixed him with her sharp eye. "It's not that he wasn't there to race after the mugger like our Frankie was, it was that he wasn't accompanying his wife in a strange, foreign city. He was more interested in the local museum."

"Oh, I see, well he is an archaeologist..."

"That as it may be, but he is either a good archaeologist and a bad husband, or a man who has other matters on his mind than a long romantic cruise with his wife," Elsie concluded as they reached her cabin. As she unlocked the door, she added, "Hold it right there, Doc... I've got something that you might appreciate reading."

While she went in and rummaged through the desk drawer, Alan asked, "What is it?"

"It's just a little summary that I think will serve you in future." With another of her cackle laughs, Elsie handed him a folded sheet of paper, bid the doctor a good night, and said that she hoped she *wouldn't be* seeing any more of him in his professional capacity before closing the door. Alan could hear her disgraceful cackle even behind the heavy waterproof doors as he made his way to his own berth, and hopefully a few hours of rest before he was called back on duty.

Maybe the lady is right, he thought as he tumbled into bed. He lay down and unfolded the sheet of paper...and began reading.

Let's say a guy named Fred is attracted to a woman named Martha. He asks her out to a movie; she accepts; they have a pretty good time. A few nights later he asks her out to dinner, and again they enjoy themselves. They continue to see each other regularly, and after a while neither one of them is seeing anybody else.

And then, one evening when they're driving home, a thought occurs to Martha, and, without really thinking, she says it aloud: "Do you realize that, as of tonight, we've been seeing each other for exactly six months?"

And then, there is silence in the car.

To Martha, it seems like a very loud silence. She thinks to herself: I wonder if it bothers him that I said that. Maybe he's been feeling confined by our relationship; maybe he thinks I'm trying to push him into some kind of obligation that he doesn't want, or isn't sure of.

And Fred is thinking: Gosh. Six months.

And Martha is thinking: But, hey, I'm not so sure I want this kind of relationship either. Sometimes I wish I had a little more space, so I'd have time to think about whether I really want us to keep going the way we are, moving steadily towards, I mean, where are we going? Are we just going to keep seeing each other at this level of intimacy? Are we heading toward marriage? Toward children? Toward a lifetime together? Am I ready for that level of commitment? Do I really even know this person?

And Fred is thinking: ...so that means it was...let's see...February when we started going out, which was right after I had the car at the dealer's, which means...lemme check the odometer...Whoa! I am way overdue for an oil change here.

And Martha is thinking: He's upset. I can see it on his face. Maybe I'm reading this completely wrong. Maybe he wants more from our relationship, more intimacy, more commitment; maybe he has sensed - even before I sensed it - that I was feeling some reservations. Yes, I bet that's it. That's why he's so reluctant to say anything about his own feelings. He's afraid of being rejected.

And Fred is thinking: And I'm gonna have them look at the transmission again. I don't care what those morons say, it's still not shifting right. And they better not try to blame it on the cold weather this time. What cold weather? It's 87 degrees out, and this thing is shifting like a garbage truck, and

I paid those incompetent thieves $600.

And Martha is thinking: He's angry. And I don't blame him. I'd be angry, too. I feel so guilty, putting him through this, but I can't help the way I feel. I'm just not sure.

And Fred is thinking: They'll probably say it's only a 90-day warranty...scum balls.

And Martha is thinking: Maybe I'm just too idealistic, waiting for a knight to come riding up on his white horse, when I'm sitting right next to a perfectly good person, a person I enjoy being with, a person I truly do care about, a person who seems to truly care about me. A person who is in pain because of my self-centered, schoolgirl romantic fantasy.

And Fred is thinking: Warranty? They want a warranty? I'll give them a warranty. I'll take their warranty and stick it right up there...

"Fred," Martha says aloud.

"What?" says Fred, startled.

"Please don't torture yourself like this," she says, her eyes beginning to brim with tears. "Maybe I should never have...oh dear, I feel so..."(She breaks down, sobbing.)

"What?" says Fred.

"I'm such a fool," Martha sobs. "I mean, I know there's no knight. I really know that. It's silly. There's no knight, and there's no horse."

"There's no horse?" says Fred.

"You think I'm a fool, don't you?" Martha says.

"No!" says Fred, glad to finally know the correct answer.

"It's just that...it's that I...I need some time," Martha says. (There is a 15-second pause while Fred, thinking as fast as he can, tries to come up with a safe response.

Finally he comes up with one that he thinks might work.) "Yes," he says. (Martha, deeply moved, touches his hand.)

"Oh, Fred, do you really feel that way?" she says.

"What way?" says Fred.

"That way about time," says Martha.

"Oh," says Fred. "Yes." (Martha turns to face him and gazes deeply into his eyes, causing him to become very nervous about what she might say next, especially if it involves a horse. At last she speaks.)

"Thank you, Fred," she says.

"Thank you," says Fred.

Then he takes her home, and she lies on her bed, a conflicted, tortured soul, and weeps until dawn, whereas when Fred gets back to his place, he opens a bag of Doritos, turns on the TV, and immediately becomes deeply involved in a rerun of a college basketball game between two South Dakota junior colleges that he has never heard of. A tiny voice in the far recesses of his mind tells him that something major was going on back there in the car, but he is pretty sure there is no way he would ever understand what, and so he figures it's better if he doesn't think about it.

The next day Martha will call her closest friend, or perhaps two of them, and they will talk about this situation for six straight hours. In painstaking detail, they will analyze everything she said and everything he said, going over it time and time again, exploring every word, expression, and gesture for nuances of meaning, considering every possible ramification.

They will continue to discuss this subject, off and on, for weeks, maybe months, never reaching any definite conclusions, but never getting bored with it either.

Meanwhile, Fred, while playing racquetball one day with a mutual friend of his and Martha's, will pause just before serving, frown, and say: "Norm, did Martha ever own a horse?"

And that's the difference between men and women.

With a smile on his face, Alan then closed his eyes and instantly fell asleep.

CHAPTER ELEVEN

Algerian Waters
A case of more infections

BRRING. BRRING. BRRING.

It felt as if he had barely put his head on the pillow and Alan was once again awoken by the strident ringing of the in-ship telephone. Luckily the doctor had not been drinking the night before with Frankie and Elsie. After all, he was fairly used to this sort of wake-up call. It didn't mean that he enjoyed it though.

"Doctor. You've got a call coming through from Athens, a Ms. Koukasis?" Vince practically hollered over the line.

My God, Alan thought, *does this man ever sleep?*

"Thank you, Vince, pass it through."

"Sure thing," he replied gruffly.

There was a moment of clicks and whirs before the heavily accented voice of Chief Coroner Koukasis greeted him in the dark hours of the morning.

"Dr. Mayhew, I just got off the phone with Interpol who are *very* interested in your guesswork."

"Aha, I see." Alan was still struggling with the whole concept of 'awake'.

"Well, I was talking to them because, in line with your recent findings, I have to change my report: I have found a discrepancy in the autopsy."

"Go on..?" Alan started to become concerned.

"I performed an examination on Mr. Montague's kidneys and liver, and I have made quite a startling discovery. There was, as you suspected, a buildup of the white blood cells – a massive buildup I might add – in the liver, and in the kidneys I have discovered the compound which might be responsible."

"Really? Not an infection with bacteria?"

"No, not at all – it is a toxin, a slight toxin, but a powerful one nonetheless."

"This… this is incredible. What is the compound?"

"The toxin is found in tiny amounts in the common Foxglove plant. It is called *Digitalis*, and acts as a stimulant for the body's nervous and cardiovascular system."

"Ah yes – *Digitalis* was used by ancient herbalists for people with sluggish 'humors'." Alan remembered distinctly from his distant college days. He was still constantly amazed by the history of modern medicine, how centuries and centuries of experimentation, of trial and error (sometimes disastrous error) had led to the library of the herbal uses of plants and common minerals, which had then, in turn, been codified, synthesized as to their 'active' compounds and turned into the medicines of today.

Alan reminded himself that most of our medicines are made in laboratories and do not need to be gathered in certain seasons of the year, and kept in very specific drying conditions. It was quite common for patients and herbalists to die from their own research back then if they made even small errors in collection, etc.

"Yes, precisely, Dr. Mayhew. You may know that Digitalis is a very fast acting drug. From the moment of consumption, it will only take a few minutes for the patient to feel its effects. You may also be aware that the chemical compound leaves the system very quickly, it is metabolized by the body and comes out quite naturally in sweat and urine."

"Yes, that is what made it such a dangerous medicine, because it hit the body quickly, and couldn't adequately be controlled or directed over a longer period."

"Yes, Dr. Mayhew," said Dr. Koukasis. "I cannot be sure where this Digitalis came from – as I say, it is a common herbal compound found in the family of plants sharing the same genus, and there was a tiny amount of the compound left in his liver and kidney. The liver must have started to degrade after the moment of death, so it didn't have the time to metabolize the last of the chemical."

"Well done for detecting it, but tell me, Coroner, surely the young man must have taken a massive dose for it to cause a heart attack?"

"Truly massive, yes. He probably couldn't have eaten enough of the actual plant without feeling the effects and being sick, unless he was forced to, or—"

"Or it was a chemically synthesized version," Alan blurted out. "But that can only mean one thing."

"Yes, Doctor, only one thing; you have a murder on your hands."

"Hum… this is indeed worrisome news, Doctor. But first, we will need to rule out any other source of the toxin on board this ship, or that might have already left it."

"Yes, indeed. I have already informed Interpol of my results. And I trust that they will be contacting the captain of your vessel shortly."

"Thank you, Chief Coroner, thank you very much for bringing this to my attention."

"Merely professional courtesy, Dr. Mayhew, and good luck."

Yes, Alan thought as he put the phone down, *I am going to need it.* As he swung his legs out of bed, he knew the first thing he had to do was speak to Vince. He glanced at his watch. It was 4:40 in the morning, not long before the start of his shift. He phoned to arrange an emergency meeting with the security chief in his office while he got himself ready to go to work.

The thought made him shiver, as he looked out over the darkened waters outside his porthole. *We might indeed have a murderer aboard the ship, and the only piece of evidence we have is a few particles of the Digitalis compound, and a pair of ladies pink knickers...*

*   *   *

"So, what are you telling me, Doctor?" Vince, the mountain of a man, said from across his desk.

Alan had arrived at Vince's office just a few minutes earlier, to the disturbing sight of the ship's security chief ironing his whites.

"I know the laundry crew will do it for me, but they never seem to get the creases right, so I always do it over," Vince had confided in him as the doctor stood amidst the hustle and bustle of his office.

The security office shared space with the telecommunications office and was always a hive of activity on this cruise liner. On the *Ocean Quest* this fact was made more acute by the presence of a couple of video-audio analyzers and a security man who manned the desks. Generally their jobs comprised of checking messages and waiting for reports to come in, but they constantly had the steady flow of telecommunications and surveillance video traffic to filter.

All of the communications on board the ship were monitored, as a matter of course. If a passenger or crewmember used the phone, then there would be computer banks waiting to hear certain 'keywords'. A human operative wasn't even necessary unless these keywords were triggered. Emails and Internet access was monitored in the same way.

The ship ran its own Wi-Fi router, for which all passengers and crew had an access code if they had brought along their Wi-Fi-enabled devices and paid for Internet access time. In this way, the security offices kept tabs on anything potentially threatening that could occur on the ship.

The last way in which the security office operated was, of course, the stewarding of the passengers. From their banks of video cameras they monitored almost the entire vessel, and made hourly updates in their logs as to potentially dangerous situations, which was usually a drunken passenger or a child being too reckless on the decks. If the situation warranted, they could dispatch an officer down to the appropriate area to have a hands-on intervention.

However, all of the potential alarms were relatively rare, and the security officers generally spent their time shepherding people who were 'overly enthusiastic' from a night's adventure back to their cabins, or if need be, the nearest bathroom facility. Generally, there wasn't any sort of need for security intervention, although Vince always had a couple of his staff on ready duty to patrol the vessel, especially to turn up and 'make an appearance' at the end of a long night's entertainment at certain locations on the ship.

"Usually, the most work we have is at boarding and departure times," Vince had once confided in the doctor. "There are any numbers of lost children, lost luggage. You name it, if a passenger can hold it, they can lose it. It is our job to keep an eye out on any of the articles, including people, and return them to their rightful companions."

It was, Alan reflected, quite a 'safe' job for a retired professional like Vince, who had seen more than his fair share of the 'sharp end' of security.

"But it's always interesting, see?" Vince had said. "You always have lots of different factors to consider – which of the passengers or crew is involved, what might go wrong, what actually did go wrong, how can we fix it?"

Yes, while the security career had never really warmed Doctor Mayhew's blood, he definitely could see the interest in studying and understanding people, and the nature of a conundrum, and trying to find ways to think ahead of an impending problem.

This was one of the reasons that he had gone to Vince first, not the captain, as would be protocol. The developments mentioned by the Athenian chief coroner had been alarming, if not downright intimidating.

Vince set aside his iron, and examined the problem presenting itself to them. "So, we have a possible poisoning, using a rare toxic substance, with presumably limited access, and a limited amount of people who will know about it and how to use it."

The doctor nodded.

"Although, that doesn't mean too much to us at the moment."

Alan asked why.

"You see, from where we are standing we do not know the passengers' provenance or background. They aren't required to write down on their ticket registration what criminal records they have, or whether they are an expert in rare toxins." Vince shrugged. "But, there are ways of narrowing down the field."

Images of Vince going door-to-door, or in this case, cabin-to-cabin, his huge bulk squeezing through each door as he went on questioning the passengers, filled the doctor's mind and made him grin briefly.

"So, what do you start with?" Alan was interested in the security chief's investigative method, even though he knew that soon, they would have to involve the captain and staff captain in the whole situation.

"Well, the obvious." Vince flashed him a wolfish grin. "What is that Sherlock Holmes' quote? *"When you have eliminated the impossible, whatever remains, however improbable, must be the truth"*."

"What does that mean in regards to our poor Gillais Montague?"

"Well we start with the obvious questions; who was he seen with? What will his cabin tell us? And then move on to more obvious questions – are there any *Digitalis* traders on board? Is there anyone who is also an herbalist? Anyone blacklisted or who has aroused suspicion on other cruise ships? We generally find with any sort of crime, petty theft usually, that there will be some sort of suspicion around the perpetrator."

"But not so with this case," Alan said.

"No, perhaps not." Vince sighed. "Can I rely on your help when I need it?"

"Absolutely," the doctor replied readily, already a few lines of inquiry bubbling away in his mind.

"It might be handy for you to take a look at the victim's room. I don't mind admitting that I am completely out of my depth here with this *Digitalis* stuff. You might be able to spot a few things that I have missed," said Vince.

Alan agreed, and realized that he was in danger of being late, yet again, to reach his own infirmary. He thanked Vince for the interview and beat a hasty path through the ship.

It was no surprise that he found Nurse Gacek in a bad mood. Apparently she had had a bad graveyard shift already, given that she had been lumbered with a trio of children vomiting all night, and had had to change her nurse blues twice.

"Why anyone wants that many children is a mystery," Petra declared, as she finished mopping the floor again.

When Alan entered, the wafting smell of medical-grade disinfectant filled his nostrils. "Um, perhaps they want a large family?" he ventured, only to be met by Petra's blistering curses in Polish. He was thankful that he hadn't had the opportunity to sit down and learn the language.

"It is not right, as soon as one stopped; the other one started, and on it went for a full hour until all three were empty." Petra shook her head.

"I hope you gave them some Pepto-Bismol?" Alan enquired, donning his long medical coat on and preparing his table to overview the events of the night.

"Yes, of course. I did everything except zip them all in a plastic bubble and paint 'diseased' on the front of it."

The doctor thought that if they did indeed have such a device then Nurse Petra, in all probability, would be the one to use it. He gave up trying to mollify her since it seemed to be an unreachable goal, and after another hour of her berating errant parents for letting their passions lead to that many children, the doctor decided that she probably had had a difficult enough night and sent her off duty, knowing that Kelly Watkins would be coming in very soon for the early morning to afternoon shift.

With a moment of rare quiet, Alan considered everything that had happened already that day, listening as he did to the distant hum of the engines that the discerning ear could just barely hear, in these moments of medical center quiet.

Yet he knew that the mighty city at sea would not be truly quiet; already there would be the laundry crew beginning to turn on their vast Laundromat machines and industrial dryers. The ever irritable Francine, the head chef, would be bustling into her kitchen, ready to start the day by baking some fresh bread. Out on the engine decks and on the bridge there would be crewmembers quietly checking the motors and the electronic read outs, doing their constant triangulations and signals to the next radio buoy, checking course, speed, and power.

The cruise ship itself was never truly asleep, apart from maybe the few nights when it would be sitting in dry dock while it went through its yearly maintenance overhaul. Even then, the doctor recalled, the great beast would always have an around-the-clock crew of workers checking its hidden veins of circuitry and mechanisms before it set sail again.

Alan grew whimsical. If it were a living beast it would have a yearly migration cycle of constant movement and constant activity, feeding on new places and new passengers before depositing them at either end of the world, before roving again and again, stopping for but a few days here and there. He was amazed at the thing's resilience, and the things which man creates.

He shook himself out of his reverie to consider his clues.

One. A dead French-Belgian. Quiet, office-worker seemed to not get out too much and not to have made a big impact on the other passengers or crew.

Two. A pair of a lady's pink knickers, probably from a distraught attached or even married woman, who may or may not be the culprit.

Three. Digitalis, a drug synthesized from a plant compound.

How on earth could he put these things together? Where could he start? Alan knew that Mr. Montague's room might offer up some more clues, because linking all of these elements would prove nigh impossible to confirm, unless they were to conduct a ship-wide search, effectively quarantining the entire crew and passengers, and not letting anyone on or off the vessel for a few days.

"That is," he murmured to himself, "if the captain would agree to it."

"Good morning, Doctor. Have I caught you at a bad moment?"

Alan looked up to see Kelly Watkins, ready in her blues at the door and waiting to start her shift. *Ye Gods she is eager.* The doctor grinned to himself. *She still has a whole forty minutes before the very earliest in which she had to be here.*

"Um, would you mind if you..." Kelly looked around the hallway, then stepped daintily inside and pulled the side of her nurse blue smock trousers down.

"Ugh, I don't think that will be quite necessary, Nurse

Watkins..." Alan said as he stared at the slightly rounded cone of smooth white thigh. He gulped. He was flattered of course, but had never actually seriously considered his nurses in that way.

"I really don't think…" he began, before Kelly cut him off.

"It's just that it's driving me mad. I've been lying there half the night tossing and turning and I thought, bugger this; I'm going to get something done about it."

"About what?" Alan asked, befuddled.

"But maybe you're right"—she pulled the thigh away—"maybe we shouldn't treat each other… unprofessional and all that? I'll have to get Nurse Petra to see to me after my shift."

Horrible images swam around his mind before he could stop them … before Alan could finally put two and two together.

"You have some kind of musculoskeletal problem or dermatitis?"

Kelly looked at him in disbelief, and then nodded, as if her superior was a little slow on the uptake this morning. "Yes, it's this rash that just won't go away." She blushed.

"Um, right. I see." Alan had seen many cases of unfriendly and unwanted rashes, infections and other irritations of the skin, especially being a doctor on routes to many foreign ports with diseases one only saw in the tropical medicine textbooks. He promptly shoved aside his personal embarrassment and switched over to his professional 'Doctor Mayhew' persona.

"Right, let's have a look at you then – up on the examining table please."

Kelly gratefully obliged, shrugging off her smock trousers and lay back.

What appeared at first to be no more than a generous volume of white thigh was, in fact, an area of mildly inflamed skin above her knee and edging to her lateral thigh. A patina of tiny raised red dots – each barely bigger than a pin's prick scattered across the area. On closer examination Alan could see that her incessant scratching had caused tiny, minor blood vessels under the skin to burst, creating small red lines, each no more than a few millimeters in length.

"Ah, I see. Do you suffer from eczema, Kelly? Or Psoriasis?"

"Not that I have ever had before, no." Kelly sounded alarmed.

"Any history of it in the family?"

"Not that I can recall, no. Nothing more than chapped skin in cold winters, that kind of thing."

"Hmm, I see..." Alan said again. "Well, we'll put some Vitamin

E oil or some Neem oil on it, and if that doesn't work, we'll move over to a steroid cream. It looks to me to be contact dermatitis."

"Contact dermatitis? That means that I am allergic to something, doesn't it? I wonder what it could be."

"Yes, probably your soap or the laundry liquids used in your clothes. Have you changed your soaps, shampoos or moisturizers recently?"

"No, I don't think so – not changed the brands anyway."

"Well, it could almost be anything, but my money would be on the laundry liquids used. Often when they change the type of liquids to a different one, a new brand, you can have a few cases of contact dermatitis for those people with sensitive skin. If that is the case then the oil should sort it out. Otherwise, it could even be, as you know, something you have eaten, and unfortunately your body is merely presenting the symptoms down there."

Kelly blushed furiously. "Oh. How long will it take to get rid of it? I was supposed to be meeting Ernesto in the crew's mess for dinner tonight."

There was a moment of silence as both medical professionals minds clicked onto the same idea at the same time.

"Oh no," Kelly burst out, "You don't think..."

"No, no, it is virtually impossible to be allergic to another human being," said Alan.

Kelly slipped off the examining table and trotted to the locker where the spare sets of uniforms were kept. On her way she grabbed a small bottle of the Vitamin E oil, which she immediately started applying liberally to her whole leg. She opted not to use the Neem oil, as it has a most pungent odor that would make her unpleasant to the person sitting next to her. *Maybe some of that at bedtime,* she thought. The doctor could see that she was mortified, and wanted to change her clothes into the new uniform as soon as possible, so he turned his back out of professional courtesy and chuckled under his breath. *Who else, in their line of work, sees a semi-naked nurse rubbing oil onto her legs in the middle of one's workplace?*

"But you really should have a look at your young man, just in case," Alan ventured. "You can do a professional skin check and a dermatological review."

"In case of what?" came the sulky reply from behind him.

"Well, in case it's *his* shampoo or moisturizer or aftershave that you might be allergic to."

"Yes, Doctor," Kelly agreed, and added, "All decent, now we

can get on with work."

Alan had to force down his smile, as he realized that he was about to spend the next few hours with another nurse in a particularly bad mood. Despite the humor of the situation, Alan did feel sorry for the poor girl, who was obviously quite smitten with her young man and was still in that fumbling, awkward, shy stage of her romance with him.

Which reminds me, he thought, making made a mental note; *I will have to see how my other infected patients are doing, Mr. Seinz and the recently attacked Mrs. Seinz.*

However, for now he had work to do. He sighed, picked up the folder with the list of medical annual exams that he had to perform today and opened it.

CHAPTER TWELVE

Algerian Waters
More on the mysterious case of Mr. Montague

"AND SO YOU SEE, UNLESS we have a mysterious grower of Foxgloves and Hollyhocks on board, we are at a bit of an impasse," Alan informed Tiffany, who was shortly about to finish her cruise of Spain. Not liking to talk in the open foyer of the *Ocean Quest*, Alan had taken his laptop to his cabin, and he had secured a video conferencing connection with his beautiful partner.

Despite it being state of the art, the arrangement was really rather frustrating – Tiffany's picture would fade in and out of focus occasionally and halt for a few seconds, while her voice carried on at almost live speed.

Alan assumed that his image was exhibiting the same stop-start transmission for her at the other end, and only wondered whether all this amount of technology impeded things rather than helped them.

"My word, the plot thickens, Doctor Mayhew." Tiffany laughed; her face caught for a second in a wide mouth chuckled and hung in space while the rest of her speech carried on. For an idle second Alan thought it was very unfortunate that the camera would freeze at the moments when you looked least at your best, and wondered whether it was designed that way.

"Well," Tiffany continued, "I do have some more information for the case, something very interesting indeed." Her face grew serious.

"You mean more about Montague?"

Tiffany nodded and lowered herself nearer to her own laptop so she could whisper into the microphone.

"I was asking around, doing my usual thing of making some polite investigations and something cropped up over one of the officers' dinners."

Alan nodded, knowing that it was customary for the captain to have formal dinners on a cruise, while giving him an opportunity to invite certain passengers and impress them with the glitzy side of cruise life. The only problem being that some passengers won or were awarded a dinner with the captain as a part of the many deals that the cruise line or the travel agent offered.

On the whole, Alan, who was occasionally expected to attend the captain's formal dinners as a senior officer on board, had some very pleasant evenings with some very memorable characters, but sometimes you got some obnoxious types who tried to laud their perceived power with the captain. Yes, Alan could remember quite a few embarrassing situations at formal dinners.

"Well, we were entertaining a family at Captain Forster's dinner. A very nice young family had won their place as part of their package with the cruise company," Tiffany said.

Alan nodded.

"Which, I guess is why I was brought along, to describe the many entertainments that we would have on board. Anyway, we got to the end of the dinner and Captain Forster asked for the chocolates and desserts to be brought out. It was a rather relaxed affair and the Captain had been gregarious and expansive," Tiffany went on.

"And if that is the Captain Forster that I have run into during my years on board, he is a big fan of his chocolates, isn't he?" Alan grinned at the recollection. He was glad that Tiffany was crewing on this particular captain's ship. He had worked one small cruise with Captain Forster some years previously, and he seemed to recall a portly man whom the chef had to chase out of his kitchen in the small hours of the morning, as he was regularly found 'refueling' – as he would put it – on some of the cakes and truffles and delicacies that the Chef was preparing for the day ahead.

Tiffany smiled. "Yes, he is indeed. Never travel without a captain, a navigator and a perfectionist, as he likes to say.

"Well, it was the end of the evening and the family was getting tired, so they made their farewells and left for their cabins, leaving me, the captain, our chief navigator and the ship's purser to the last of the chocolates, and that is when things got interesting."

Tiffany paused to remember. "We were chatting about previous journeys and crews that we had been a part of and I mentioned to the captain that I was trying to remember the name of a passenger that had been stuck in my memory – a Mr. Montague..."

"Oh, well done," Alan exclaimed, thinking that he would never have thought of that.

Tiffany bowed at the compliment. "Well at first it fell on deaf ears, no one had ever heard of a Mr. Montague, but the ship's purser looked very deep in thought for a moment, and then said that he remembered something a few cruises back that had something to do with a Montague. The name had stuck in his brain and he was struggling to remember why.

"Of course, this is a long shot, but I asked him what *his* Montague was like and it all came flooding back. The purser had remembered a bookish, thin studious sort of French-Belgian whom he had been interviewed a number of years previously."

"Interviewed?" Alan queried, obviously puzzled.

"Yes, exactly." Tiffany's image became animated, causing it to stop and start again. "It turns out that our ship's purser remembered him because he had been suddenly surprised, when one day a passenger had come to his office unannounced and had asked for an interview. Of course, he had replied that he was happy to have a chat with the man if there was anything that was bothering him or that he wanted to know. Can you ever guess what this Mr. Montague then revealed?"

Alan shrugged in complete confusion.

"That he was an undercover agent, working for Interpol."

"What?" Tiffany was right, Alan could never have guessed.

"Yes," she said excitedly. "Apparently this Mr. Montague was tasked with international cruise travel, he would attend as a passenger on a number of the cruises and"—she chose her next words very carefully—"conduct his investigations."

"Investigations?" Alan was even more puzzled now. "Investigations into what?"

"Well, apparently our Mr. Montague told our ship's purser that there was a constant line of study on all international transport; ever since, you know, September 11th. It seems there is a whole array of things that Interpol is looking into, including smuggling, narcotics, and border security etc., all on cruise ships."

Alan knew that border security had become one of the top priorities for international security, and the safety regulations affecting cruise ships had tripled as every item of luggage and passenger had to be checked and rechecked by a dozen different authorities. This was particularly true of the crew.

"So, apparently now they have a constant team of 'roving investigators'," Tiffany continued, "who go aboard cruise liners as passengers, and get paid to see how thoroughly they are checked, what the security issues are like on each ship, how easy it is to sneak into the engine room – that kind of thing."

A veil of sternness draped over Alan's face. He had heard of this kind of thing happening on board the cruise lines, but had never directly experienced it himself. Of course he had dealt with undercover passengers before, usually agents from the insurance companies or the cruise company itself sent out to report back on the experience of being a passenger aboard one of their cruises.

"Of course we can't be sure that this is the same Montague. The purser couldn't remember the first name, but it does sound a little suspicious doesn't it?"

"Yes, quite," Alan agreed. "Two thin, bookish sorts of French-speaking Belgians named Montague? It can't be a coincidence."

"No, I thought not either. So, the question is, what was he doing on board the *Ocean Quest*?"

"I don't know," Alan answered, "although it would explain Interpol's interest in the case, if he was in fact one of their undercover officers. Why haven't they revealed themselves to the captain? Why have they kept the chief coroner, and not to mention myself in the dark?"

Tiffany nodded. "Someone should get in touch with them – see what we are dealing with."

"Yes, you're quite right. Fax your information over to Vince here and we'll see what we can come up with. I think I am going to be invited to examine his cabin for the security report as well, so I am sure that we will find out some more then."

"It must be something big, whatever it is – very hush-hush." Tiffany looked curious. "International criminals? Smugglers? The drug trade? Maybe he was even on the trail of someone in the terrorism business."

Alan could tell that Tiffany was enjoying the speculation. "We won't know at the moment, but this kind of thing is not unknown." He went on to tell her that sometimes, although very rarely, criminals used the cruise liners as a means of changing their identity and keeping a low profile across a number of countries. By constantly moving between different authorities and sovereign states, there was always a ream of paperwork that followed every crewmember and cruise ship, and it could, feasibly, be easy to lose someone between the numerous *cracks* in the paperwork.

"You know, for some reason this is reminding me of some of the things that went on with our Mr. Hammer," Alan mused.

"Your appalling holiday adventure?" Tiffany said.

"Yes, after that experience I did wonder just how far Rick was connected to the criminal underground."

"Really? What gave you that impression?" Tiffany looked astonished.

Alan nodded, and proceeded to fill her in on the details of his life threatening journey with Mr. Rick Hammer.

*   *   *

Lampugh Glacier, Alaska

The duo were starting the boat for the day, a little ritual that the doctor was becoming somewhat accustomed to. It required one person to climb into the engine compartment and crank the wheel while another had to turn on the gas to the engine and adjust the throttle. Climbing into the engine compartment became Alan's job as Rick would race in between standing over him in the cold weather and 'listening' to the engine before racing to the cockpit and adjusting the throttle.

"It requires exactly the right timing," Rick shouted over to the half-submerged legs of the doctor as he cranked and cranked and cranked.

Alan himself, however, was reminded of every troublesome lawn mower, chainsaw, and hedge trimmer that he had the displeasure of dealing with in the past. He wasn't surprised at this wooden boat either. He had owned a few 'character-full' boats in his time and had met many more engineers who each had a certain sort of psychic sense with their mechanical counterparts.

Or at least they claimed, anyway. Alan grinned to himself when they finally got the engine going.

The rest of the day was spent seeing the glaciers around the tip of Alaska, a truly impressive sight as mountainous walls of ice rose out of the sea, holding onto their rocky cliffs like possessions. The sheer power and force contained within those walls were unfathomable to him. Once they saw a thousand tons of rock and compacted ice cascade into the sea with such formidable strength that they stared in awe for several minutes at the glacier's demise.

This was a constant occurrence around the edges of the glaciers. Alan knew they were really the meeting points of titanic forces, slow forces like pressure, wave temperature and erosion that initiated these gigantic, spontaneous, and impressive effects.

Alan reflected that if one wished to see the might of the sea then one should go to the edges of the glaciers. Here the mother ocean presents itself in all of its forms, and drives them together leading to chaotic results. Sprays and shots of steam erupt from the ocean waves as the ice collapses in waterfalls, while the 'heavy' water of the icy seas itself, which takes on a viscous quality, tries to freeze and is prevented from doing so. Also, of course, one should not miss seeing the mountains of the glaciers themselves – as if the sea had envied the land and had sculpted its own mountains, cliffs, gorges and plains of pure rock-white, stained blue and yellow ice sheets.

All of these experiences would have been enough to make the trip spectacular for Alan. He was a man in love with the sea, in all of its many forms, except for that of his host.

Through the journey Rick had been making a number of radio and mobile calls when they had reception, and would disappear below decks to do so. For a while Alan was curious, and then would forget about it as he overtook the running of the boat from his navigator. Occasionally, he would overhear heated arguments, timings, schedules, as Rick would argue that such and such a time was too early, or too late, or was impossible.

They were spending longer than intended out by the glaciers, because after one of these prolonged and aggravated conversations, Rick emerged from below deck to tell the doctor that they would be taking a day out to rest.

Alan had been surprised, since there were still a number of places left to visit on the trip, and he was eager to fill up his holiday with as much of this beautiful landscape as possible. He considered this delay, and then decided that at least it would give him time to write up his notes and memoirs, and maybe work a little bit on putting his thoughts into order.

Alan was a keen writer and note-taker. One of the pleasures of a life at sea was the time that it gave you to think, and if you were that way inclined, to write. He believed there was some kind of special relationship between the sea and the imagination, which allowed you the time to meditate on your experiences.

So Alan took joyously to his time away from the business of keeping the boat running and set up his laptop below deck. Above deck, Rick was once again on the phone, apparently arranging a meeting with someone.

"No, it's too late – the time has got to be now, you see? When else am I ever going to get this opportunity?"

Whoever was on the other end apparently didn't like the idea, but Rick had seemed to have convinced him (or her) in the end.

"Having problems?" Alan called out cheerfully as he went to see whether Rick wanted a hot cocoa before he settled down to his writing.

Rick glowered at him. "Oh, it's just Milena – my girlfriend. We were deciding when would be a good time to meet up."

"Ah, the affairs of the heart...." Alan sighed, clapping Rick on the shoulder.

"Yeah, something like that, look"—Rick's whole tone changed in an instant—"I am going to spend today doing some of the installation work on the vessel, and I am going to need your help, can you do that?"

"I'm sorry. I thought I would use this chance to do some work on my book today?"

Rick gave him a wolfish smile, and for a second Alan had a shiver of doubt about the young man. "No can do, Doctor, not unless you don't want this boat to be moving again in the future." He laughed at Alan's uncomfortable look, trying to make it a joke.

"Look, I'm sorry, Doc, but we have got to do these repairs; we'll get some time to ourselves in the next few days, I promise."

The first job to do was to change the oil in the engine, which he had to do 'while the engine was hot'. Rick also told the doctor that this would be the perfect day for him to sort out all of his new instruments, while Alan could act as a lookout for any crags and swells while he was busy.

Alan was frustrated and annoyed, but knew the importance of some of these procedures, and if it made the yacht easier and safer, then, he was, of course, in favor of it. So what followed was a long, frustrating morning and afternoon as Alan sat in the freezing cold on the vessel's deck, looking out at the frozen seas, the silence occasionally interrupted by the curses and mumblings that were heard throughout the ship from wherever Rick was.

Alan started to get more and more annoyed as the afternoon wore on, and in particular when Rick had gone quiet for over an hour below deck. He called out to him, but there was no answer, and then he considered his options.

Deciding that at this time there was no real danger to the vessel, he went to check on the errant navigation engineer, to find him deep in concentration on the V-berth, surrounded by piles of wires and what seemed to be radio equipment.

"What are you doing?" Alan asked. His understanding was

that Rick was supposed to be doing 'essential repairs' today.

"Oh, just trying to figure something out," he replied, none too pleased about being disturbed.

"Oh, is the oil change done?" Alan was beginning to lose his patience.

Rick nodded cheerily, "Yup, you don't have to look out any more, I'll take over and take us on to Tarr Inlet and Margerie Glacier."

"Right," Alan said, wondering just what on earth he had signed up for...

*   *   *

"It sounds like a terrible trip," Tiffany sympathized, back on the video camera of the *Ocean Quest*.

"Yes, what made me think about it was what you were suggesting about Interpol and the criminal networks that sometimes try to utilize the cruise liners' network.

"Why? What makes you think of that?" Tiffany enquired.

"It was just the strange behavior that Rick exhibited. While I was there I imagined that he was constantly arguing with his girlfriend Milena, but remembering it now, it seems a little more than that."

"What do you mean?" Tiffany seemed concerned.

"Well, it was dates and times, all schedules of when he would be arriving somewhere, and when a certain thing should *happen*."

"What do you think that he was organizing?"

"I don't know, but, when I count the days, it seems that Rick wanted to keep us out at sea for an extra few days, delay our trip somewhat, and it was only at the end, when I demanded to go back to shore that he got really, really angry."

Tiffany looked alarmed.

"Yes, you will not believe it when I tell you, but I may have to save that installment for our next time on line."

Tiffany pouted, and Alan thought it looked incredibly cute as it was captured on the web camera.

"Oh yes, I have more things to do before I can get the chance to relax. I need to speak to Vince, see what he thinks of the latest on our Mr. Montague."

Tiffany looked cross, and annoyed that she wouldn't get the rest of the story. She looked so adorable that Alan couldn't resist telling her just one more snippet.

"Well, one last installment then. I have been thinking about our Rick Hammer ever since I managed to escape from his boat. If I had known the story of his previous employment I would never have taken that voyage, it turns out that Rick Hammer had been fired with cause, from his previous cruise.

"We all knew that Rick was having some personality clashes with various officers and a failed romance with one of the gals in the spa department. It wasn't until I was on the boat with Rick that I discovered that he had actually been fired from the company. He apparently had been blacklisted for 'inappropriate behavior with female crew and disorganized actions with usual and ordinary work duties as a navigator'. This was a bit of a surprise. As I said, I really did not know him with a capital 'K'."

"Oh, my word!" Tiffany looked aghast.

"Yes, indeed. Rick told me that night after I had been keeping watch, sitting in the bay for the entire day. He then decided to try and make it up to me, since I had not been able to write all day, and brought out some beers while we did some stargazing. He made it sound as if everyone else was at fault, of course. Yet after I heard that, I was sure that I wanted to end the trip as soon as possible."

Tiffany nodded sagely. "Yes, you can't sail with someone so unpredictable, not in those waters and in such close quarters."

"No indeed – not in *any* waters." Alan exhaled a rueful sigh. "But I was foolish, I should have checked up on him before I agreed to go on the trip."

"Yes, you should have," Tiffany scolded him. "But enough of such things – I have a quiz that I should prepare for, and I am sure that a busy ship's doctor has many things on his plate…."

Alan nodded. Preparing for Tunis was the first thing that he should be involved in; along with making sure that the infirmary was well stocked. It was his job to check the list for any of the things that they needed to re-provision with at the port.

"Well, keep me updated on the progress of the mystery," Tiffany said, "and I shall be finishing my cruise in a few days... We have the big bash tonight, and then our final port the day after tomorrow."

"Really? Sounds great!" Alan was happy for her – Tiffany deserved a break. "So, what are you doing once you have finished this contract, Ms. Tiffany, Cruise Director?"

The lady at the other end of the line smiled coyly. "Well we shall have to see, won't we?"

With a grin and a fake screen smooch to the camera the cruise director signed off, leaving Doctor Alan Mayhew with a foolish smile on his face, and wondering where the adventure would take him next....

CHAPTER THIRTEEN

Tunis
Room changes

"SO WHAT DO YOU PROPOSE to do about it?" the lady said, peering over her large sunglasses.

"Well, I could have some of the maintenance crew come over and have a look at it for you?" Alan said somewhat helplessly.

"But what about my blood pressure?"

He sighed and pretended to scan his notes again. Sitting in front of him was Mrs. Patricia Jones. Once again, the hypersensitive hypochondriac was in his infirmary, making complaints of an elusive nature. The *Ocean Quest* had docked in Tunis, the capital of the Governate of Tunisia, and many of the passengers had already disembarked. All save Mrs. Patricia Jones and her faithful husband, who had rang in a huff and a puff demanding that his wife be seen this very morning.

It seemed that Mrs. Jones was having problems with her heart, and setting aside his skepticism, the doc had rushed to her aid, performing the necessary tests that would indicate an arrhythmia or other possible heart defect. He took this sort of complaint in any woman of middle years very seriously indeed, and was only too happy to run through the whole series of tests.

"It keeps on feeling like I am about to faint, and I have this terrible pain in the center of my chest," Mrs. Jones complained from her seat while the doctor examined her.

He listened to her heart, but found it to be operating within normal parameters. He then took her blood pressure, to which Mrs. Jones excitedly announced that this was the right action to take, but her blood pressure was also within the acceptable reading.

"You must have got it wrong, man, do the BP again, or get the nice young nurse to do it if you can't," Mrs. Jones said. "You see if feels like I might burst, I can feel my heart thumping around my body as if I were... were an *oil* refinery."

"Hmm, I see," Alan answered politely while seeing nothing at all. In either case, he checked her again, slower this time, and again nothing.

"Right well, let us see if there is a problem in your ears Mrs. Jones. Sometimes with an ear infection the tissue around the blood vessels can become inflamed, creating an amplifying effect on the pumping of the blood from your heart."

"Yes, that must be it, Doctor. Did I not tell you that I had problems with my ears before?"

"Indeed you did, Mrs. Jones. Now, just tilt your head ever so slightly – yes, there, that's it..."

Alan used his otoscope to examine the ear canal of the 'afflicted woman' for the second time in a week. Again, there was no sign of any problem.

"So, tell me exactly how this condition relates to your cabin, Mrs. Jones?"

"It's the bangs, of course," Mrs. Jones said, visibly exasperated. "I don't know if I am situated just over the engines, the rudders or something else, but all I can hear all night long are the bangs and fizzes and pops of some machinery underneath me. I have very, very sensitive ears as you know, and I believe all of this stimulation, all night and all day long is triggering in me a heart seizure of some kind. Where are those infernal engines? Are you sure the wheels or the spokes or something aren't right under my cabin?"

"Uh, unfortunately we are not a paddle steamer, Mrs. Jones, and since we aren't"—Alan tried not to laugh—"the engines are in fact at the back, quite far removed from the passengers' cabins."

However this did not placate his patient one bit. If at all possible, it made her worse.

"Well then, it must be some sort of electrical fault or something similar, or the heating system or something – and I am sure that if nothing is done about it, the defect shall get worse and worse and we shall all be blown to smithereens."

"Oh I am sure not, Mrs. Jones, that is *very* unlikely." Alan tried to act magnanimous, as if by his good cheer alone he could shake her sense of impending doom and disaster, whether medical or mechanical. "But I will surely make a note of it, and ask for an inspection crew to be sent out immediately. If you were planning to leave the ship today to see the historic port city of Tunis then we could probably have a team in to your room and report back what we find before you get back."

"What, an inspection crew going through my cabin, with all of mine and my husband's things there?"

"They *are* very well trained ma'am – and if these 'noises' are somehow affecting your nervous system..." Alan's voice trailed off in a desperate effort to refrain from exploding in loud laughter. He was truly amused by what was in front of him.

"Is that the best that this cruise can offer me?" Mrs. Jones demanded. "Here I am a paying customer who may just drop dead from all the noxious sounds and chemicals about me, and all you can offer me is a team of workmen to come around and paw through all of my things?" The lady was furious, obviously, and there was little that the doctor could suggest. If he wasn't very careful Mrs. Jones could start making complaints about him, about the captain, or the cruise line. With very little actual medical evidence either way for any of her supposed conditions, it seemed that it would end up being her words versus theirs in court. Moreover, something, which Doctor Mayhew knew very well, was that *the customer is always right.* The cruise line would probably settle out of court if it came to that, to avoid any embarrassing, bad publicity.

"How about this, Mrs. Jones, I will have a word with the captain of this vessel to see if we can get you moved – seeing that it is a *medical* emergency?"

Mrs. Jones beamed.

Alan picked up the phone, and waited a few seconds while it rang.

"Hello, Doctor? What is it, man? Is it about this Belgian bloke, because if it is – ah – ouch... I really cannot talk at the moment – but I will er... let me see...?" Captain Halvorsen sounded very busy, and Alan dreaded thinking about what he was doing at that very moment.

"No, Captain, it appears that we have a medical emergency on board ship..."

"Oh God, not another bloody one, because if you have found another body in the gym or the squash courts or on the bloody Ping-Pong tables or wherever – I don't want to know. Do you know exactly how much paperwork I am – uh – going through right now?"

"Inch by Inch?" Alan suggested, who didn't think for a second that the captain was going through each piece of paperwork alone, but rather delegating the important bits to various officer-level crewmembers on board the ship.

"Yes, exactly... but tell me what kind of emergency?"

"A very important one, *very* important case sir, a passenger needs to be moved immediately."

"Moved where? Dam it – to a hospital? Where?"

"Another room, Captain, if we can move the patient and husband to another room, maybe one up on the fore decks then I am sure that we can keep the situation under control. There's more space in those cabins I believe."

Mrs. Jones looked like the cat that had not only eaten the cream, but had gone to the dairy farm and had cleared them of all their stocks of cow-based derivatives as well. It was well known, that the cabins up in the fore decks, were all first class cabins, which would mean upgrading Mrs. Jones and her husband effectively for the rest of the journey.

"A room transfer, huh? Who is she, Doc – a young hottie you are trying to impress? I thought that you had your eyes on that lady who worked with us last time – Tiffany was it?"

"No, I am afraid not, sir, this is a medical emergency. Will it be all right if I inform the ship's purser?"

"Well, we are not running at capacity any more – we've had a cancellation and a couple of people were only going part way on the cruise, so I don't see why not. Medical emergency did you say, Doctor, sheesh – anything serious?"

"Absolutely not, sir, I will send my report over for you to have a *personal* appraisal of the situation, I know how you take an interest in each and every passenger's welfare, sir."

"Um, yes, of course I do, of course – just what is going on down there, Doc? Anything I should be screaming about and running to the lifeboats?"

"No, not at all, sir, thank you, sir." And with these words, Alan smiled and put the phone down, thankful that the Jones' had not actually been able to hear any of Captain Halvorsen's responses.

"Well, it seems that we are in luck, Mrs. and Mr. Jones." He clapped his hands together. "The captain has taken a particular interest in your concern and has ordered that you be upgraded to first class immediately. Mrs. Jones, I believe that the new room, which is far away from the old one, will not have the same effect on your hearing as the old one. The fore decks are far removed from the engines and are engineered to a much higher standard."

"Well, I guess that will have to do, won't it, dear?" she said to her much harassed husband, who smiled helplessly as if to say "well I have no idea?"

"By the time that you have come back from your outing today

in Tunis, I promise that we will have prepared your room up in the fore decks and if you just mention to the front desk what is happening, then they can provide you with the porters and luggage handlers necessary to move your belongings."

"That will be quite adequate, thank you, Doctor, although I do hope that I get the chance to thank the captain in person. I am sure that he will want to see the poor soul he has saved."

"I am sure, Mrs. Jones."

"Yes, I had a bad feeling about that room you know – from the very first moment I set eyes on it – you know when you can just tell that there is something wrong? I don't know what it is in me – it must be my nautical family – I had a nautical uncle, didn't I, my dear?" She turned to get reinforcement from her husband. He nodded. "Yes," Mrs. Jones continued, "a very nautical uncle – the salt water runs in the blood, as it were."

"I thought I could sense a kindred spirit about you as soon as I first met you," the Doc declared genially. "Now, if you will excuse me I really have to get back to some very urgent work, but it will be with the satisfaction to know that you'll be on the mend now." He layered the treacle thick into his words, and he saw the husband roll his eyes as he escorted the still thankful Mrs. Jones out of the infirmary. When he was absolutely sure that they had moved into the body of the vessel and that he could not be heard, he opened the door to their tiny stockroom, so his voice would be muted, and yelled into it.

"Yes, Doctor?" Nurse Watkins looked up from her station, trying not to laugh. "You do know, don't you, that this is the most prolonged method that I have ever seen anyone use to try and connive a room upgrade."

Returning from his screaming fit in the stockroom, Alan merely sat down at his desk and announced, "You know that the only thing that makes me annoyed is the maintenance checks that will have to be performed now. I am sure that there is nothing wrong with her cabin, but, still, it is our duty to verify that nothing is amiss in that room. Imagine if something was wrong and we didn't diagnose it? But in this case I am sure it is just a simple instance of over sensitivity for a room upgrade."

*   *   *

The historic city of Tunis spread out before the *Ocean Quest* like a blanket. One of the most protected ports in the whole ancient world, Tunis lies in the crook of a long arm of land, at the head of a semi-circular bay. Above its coastal plains rise the towers of glass and steel of the modern buildings, while; nestled at their feet, the winding alleyways and market places of the ancient world still thrive as they did thousands of years ago.

Tunis is famed as a grand meeting place between all of the ancient empires, and was once the site of ancient Carthage, before Carthage had been the victim of rampages and sacking. It is proud of its heritage, and, although Tunisia is not a big state, it manages to earn a large amount of its revenue from the tourist trade.

None of this had even entered Alan's mind for the last while. However, as he sat looking over the balcony at the port of Tunis, he wished he could once more get off the ship and explore the hidden wonders of this remarkable city.

Tunis was renowned amongst the trinket traders aboard the cruise as *the* place to get some bargains, and some even came back with bits of old sculpted marble, claiming to be even from the much besieged walls of ancient Carthage itself.

No, today the good doctor had to stay aboard and nurse a growing headache, given that the lack of sleep was beginning to catch up with him, and Vince would need to take him to examine Mr. Montague's cabin.

He sighed, as he watched the last tender take off to port carrying all that was left of the passengers, except for a notable few, and then turned to his taskmaster, Vince. "Okay, let's get this over and done with."

The latter grinned. "What do you expect to find – a field of that special plant? Or another body or something?"

Alan shrugged, "Absolutely no idea. But I do hope not. Is it still sealed?"

Vince nodded. It was customary when, on those very rare occasions, there was a 'dearly departed' on board, the door would be sealed with a master lock and a 'do not disturb' sign placed on the door of the cabin. That way any curious passengers or crew would either think that the occupant was out, occupied elsewhere, or that there was some maintenance work going on in the cabin. It was Vince who always did this as a matter of course on his vessels.

"It gives everyone time to cool down and think," he explained, as they made their way to the deck which contained Gillais Montague's sealed room. "Also, it is a mark of respect for the deceased, and keeps everything in order for when the insurance, the lawyers, and health people once they get involved."

Alan nodded at the wise decision as they arrived. "So, did you receive Tiffany's fax?"

Vince nodded and waggled his eyebrows mysteriously. "Yup, and I have been on the phone since then. It looks like our man Montague was indeed an undercover officer working for Interpol. I have managed to get that out of them so far, but no one will tell me anything else. They say that they will be sending an investigator to look at his body, and then one to interview the staff and crew of the *Ocean Quest*.

"They want a full release of all documents, which we could contest, as we were technically in international waters, but the company always complies with these sorts of cases. Until then, we are to try to learn what we can, conduct our own low-key fact-finding sort of mission, and report our findings back to them. Because we are traveling rapidly to many ports, and if Interpol put a stop order on an entire cruise ship, it would probably mean 248 otherwise influential and innocent passengers suing somebody, and you and I know who that would be. The powers-that-be have convinced Interpol to let the *Ocean Quest* continue its voyage, as long as we liaise with them and share our findings."

"They must think, if there is any foul play, that the killer is long gone by now – maybe that very second night when the radios went down."

The security chief nodded. "I agree, it makes sense to me, too much time has passed now for any evidence to be considered conclusive."

"You mean the, uh, lady's garment?"

Vince's head bobbed up and down again. "Yes, we have those – but what do they tell us, really? That Gillais had sex with someone? We don't even know if that someone had anything to do with his death, or this *Digitalis* stuff."

"Yes, of course, *Sherlock*, and therein lies the first clue – the *Digitalis*."

"Which is why we have you here, *Dr. Watson*. Now, before we go in, I want you to indicate anything, anything at all, that seems to you out of place."

"Also"—he ticked off the things on his hand—"I want you to indicate anything which could have delivered, contained or hid a dose of this stuff powerful enough to kill a man. I mean, funny colored liquids, packets of dried herbs, prepared food, any sort of thing that could have contained this stuff or the means by which it got into his system, and how it could have gotten there. I don't want me or any of my men suddenly falling over, but I want to know just what I need to send off to the lab for testing, and hopefully that will give us the method of application as well."

"And the method will reveal whether it was a murder or not," Alan concluded for him.

"Exactly, Doc, if we find it hidden in his sock or something, then we can be pretty sure that it's something that was prepared before he even came on board. If he just has a gigantic bouquet of the stuff on his bed, then we have to consider the possibility that it was an accident, misadventure, or even a bleeding suicide."

With a look of amazement, Alan could see that there was an awful lot to this investigative procedure, and before the door was opened he took a few deep breaths.

Internally, he focused and concentrated on the one thing that he knew would help him – the scientific aspects of his physician's training. It was in that reserved place inside his soul, where everything around him would become a series of causes, symptoms and possible effects – etiologies, objective symptoms, and clinical effects.

For years after losing Jo Ann, he took comfort in his complete emotional detachment, and in his separation from the messy world of feeling and friendship. He thought that perhaps he was even robotic to some degree, as he coolly assessed everything around him – the chances for an accident, the negative or positive effects in terms of long term health.

But with the arrival of Tiffany, something had made him reject that aspect of the shell of professionalism, to enjoy his life more, and peel away the mask of the scientific doctor. Now, he felt like he was *losing* something as he carefully concentrated, and tried to see the world in black and white, logical terms – and nothing else. Today however, there was an opportunity to integrate both the scientific laboratory based medicine with the second sense medicine one gets when one has worked with humans, relating doctor to patient for many years. That was the side of medicine that they really do not teach you in medical school – how to have a pretty good idea about a diagnosis, the reasons behind it, and a probable outcome to many situations. This tends to apply not only to the medical situations, but also to personal relationships as well. One builds up a wall so that it cannot be penetrated. Maybe with Tiffany and being able to use his 'second sense', he could get a second lease on life.

Vince, for his part, had been blessed with a good genetic predisposition and it seemed he had the good sense to make use of that advantage, and work on his musculature throughout his career. What stood beside the doctor (as he resided in his assessing mind), was a man who was physically strong, with well-proportioned deltoids and upper arms, still good, strong legs, but who was nevertheless just past the peak of physical prowess. Years of work on ships, many with some of the world's finest Chefs who used the same fattening base food for the crew as they did for the elegant restaurants for the passengers, had taken their toll on Vince's corporal aptitude. Viewed from the side, the security chief was now endowed of a round, moon shaped, abdomen. His exercise with weights and running on the treadmill in the crew gym was the only thing that saved him. Not smoking cigarettes also helped. *He must have been a striking figure when he was much younger*, Alan reflected. He, as many of the 'experienced' officers did, learned to wear your uniforms in larger and more comfortable sizes.

The security chief leaned forward, and the doctor noticed various evidences of old injuries, probably wrestling, martial arts, or boxing, and opened the door to the dead man's cabin.

*   *   *

Gillais Montague was, characteristically, a tidy man. His cabin was arranged neatly with the bed against the wall under the large porthole, a small bedside desk, with a cabinet built into the wall. Any mementos of a personal nature were either scant or entirely nonexistent, a very unusual feature for a cruise passenger.

Vince walked into the room, and swung a cursory look around. "Well, it certainly seems that he wasn't making a home of it."

Alan had to agree. It was obvious to anyone entering that Montague must have been a crewmember or an employee of some kind. Alan knew that everyone personalized their cabins in some way, be it with a small piece of art, a trinket, or a picture from home – and the longer the cruise the more personalization becomes apparent. It was one of those features of passengers, he mused, that they felt the need to 'nest' and to make their cabin their place of safety in a strange environment.

But Gillais hadn't done this. He must have had no connection to this space, and you only have no connection to a space if you either are not staying long, or you have much more important things on your mind...

"We should look for a notebook, or a laptop," Alan suggested. "I think Gillais used this space to work in as much as sleep, so to him it was just another office."

Vince nodded.

"Now he was undercover, so I bet he didn't want to be disturbed by the cleaning staff while he was working," Alan went on. Long years on board a cruise ship had led him to a similar conclusion; sometimes you don't want the cleaners disturbing your work, moving things around, changing the routine that you have created, and so there were a few places that you can scurry away your projects without the cleaners getting interested.

The doctor reached up to above the metal cabinet, and felt around on the dusty ledge that cleaners sometimes forgot to clean during a cruise.

Something firm hit his hand, "Aha." He reached around, grabbed the edge of it and pulled backwards.

Falling into Alan's grip was a small, black leather-bound notebook, with a Biro pen slotted into the binding. He handed it gingerly to Vince, who was wearing his blue plastic evidence gloves.

"Good work, Doctor." Vince grinned as he leafed through the notebook. "I should bring you in on my petty theft cases – you have the mind of a detective."

"Or a master criminal," Alan returned with a chuckle, while going back to examination of the room. "No, there was nothing here, only a tidy, made bed, and cleaned out bedside drawer." He paused for a moment, his gaze fixed on the bed. "Does this bed look a little too tidy to you?"

"What do you mean, Doc?"

"Well, the whole room is so tidy – it's almost as if he didn't use this room before his death?"

Vince raised his eyebrows. "Like maybe he was using someone else's?"

Alan nodded, and returned his attention to the question of the *Digitalis*. There really wasn't any sign of a carrier for it. He motioned to Vince that he wanted to look in the en-suite bathroom, and Vince followed him as he flipped through the notebook.

The small closet bathroom was a different story. Here, there was a towel on the floor, a selection of cosmetics on the little glass shelf under the mirror, a toothbrush in its holder, and, more importantly, a wine glass in the sink.

"Well, now we are cooking with gas," Vince said. "If there are glasses, then surely, somewhere there should be a bottle...." He bent down and had a look under the sink, by the small toilet, and even in the bath. "Nothing for it." He opened the toilet. Indeed, floating in the bowl was a small square of waxy paper; the kind you get as a gift tag on a present.

"Or a wine label," Alan blurted, "the sort that you can write a message on."

"Who wants to do the honors?" Vince nudged Alan in the ribs, "go on, Doc. You're used to icky stuff."

"Ah, does this count as overtime hours?" Alan countered; grinning at the security chief's reluctance.

"Yeah, I guess this is a part of my job..." Vince said as he gingerly fished out the paper and slapped it onto the glass shelf.

There was indeed some writing on it, a fine, swirling hand had written in blue on the wax gift label 'tor something-something nig-t,"

"tor nigett?" Vince mused at the blurred writing.

"Tourniquet?" hazarded the Doc.

"Torn Icky?"

Alan shot a curious glance in Vince's direction. "Why would someone give someone else a bottle or wine for their 'Torn Icky'?"

Vince shrugged. "I dunno – an apology?"

Alan sighed. "What if that 't' at the front is actually a crossed 'f – that would be 'for'."

"Ah, yes, I see," Vince said, a frown crossing his brow.

Alan could see that while Vince had a very sharp mind, he was a bit rusty when it came to word games. He guessed that the security chief didn't have much call to decode letter puzzles any more, while he on the other hand, always had a stab at the local newspaper's crosswords when he had the chance.

"That makes it 'For' something-something Nit..."

"For Your Nits? Well, I can understand being a bit down about having those creepy little buggers, but a bottle of wine? This Gillais must have been quite ... hum ... quite a perfectionist." He threw a meaningful look around the room.

"Tonight," the doctor suggested.

"What? No, Doc, we are nowhere near cracking this case, unless you really are as good as everyone says you are."

"No Vince, 'tonight' – *for tonight*. The gift tag is a promise for a rendezvous, probably exactly before we found the poor man later that night. What we have here, Vince is a gift of romantic intent."

Vince chuckled. "Ho-Ho. So we are dealing with a gift of a romantic nature you say? Now all we need to do is find our Cinderella who enjoys pink knickers and a nice bottle of white."

"It doesn't really narrow the field does it?" Alan agreed, considering the number of romances that were probably blossoming aboard the cruise at the moment.

"No, not really."

"And he was in a hurry; he must have taken the bottle with him."

"How do you know that?"

"Well, our Gillais here was having a glass of wine in front of his bathroom mirror, presumably while he was sprucing up, looking forward to his nightly adventures, 'getting in the mood', as it were. The bottle isn't here, so, I presume whoever was his assignation left the wine with him to enjoy over the evening, and Gillais saved it to take with him to share with her?" This was all guesswork on Alan's part

"Which also supports the idea that this was a *secret* assignation, that the woman couldn't meet our Gillais, and stay with him directly to enjoy a bottle of wine."

"Do you think another man then? A lover? Husband?" Alan tapped his chin in puzzlement.

"Something not quite right, at least," the security chief said.

"Right, well we'll have to test this glass to see if there are any traces of the chemical, and, if there are, then his lady friend must have been the culprit, doctoring the bottle to... what? Get Gillais off her back?"

Vince nodded thoughtfully. "Just what I was thinking. This Cinderella we are looking for is starting to look like a much more dangerous lady then we had first anticipated. We might not be looking for a distraught woman at all, but a very calculating murderess."

"And there was no bottle at the scene, I mean in the gymnasium," Alan added.

"Yes, exactly. Either Mr. Montague was greedy and finished off the bottle himself on the way to the gymnasium, dumping it in a bin en route, or he brought it with him and it was taken away from the scene, which makes our *lady of the night* the only suspected party."

"Well, we'll know in an hour or so if we find any of the toxins, otherwise, I cannot really see any other method of transmission."

"Yeah, it's the only real lead we've got, apart from this notebook." He flicked it open and showed the doctor a series of jottings written in a small, cramped hand. There were lists of numbers with dash marks in between them.

"What are they – phone numbers? Bank accounts?"

Vince shook his head. "I have no idea, but we have access to a financial database that we can check out to see if these numbers correspond to anything. I personally believe that it will have some relevance for Interpol – maybe case numbers, an internal numbering system that they use? Especially these last ones..."

Vince flipped the pages to the last one used, just a few pages in, and here the numbers changed dramatically, letters were included at the start of each one.

R1030, 1115, 2200
A1300
V1600
T1330
B1530
C---?
B---?

"Something about these numbers looks familiar," Alan said, peering down at them. "They remind me of when I worked as a ship's doctor for industrial ships. Just like with cruise ships we kept very detailed records, of every work hour and every incident, and this format – a letter followed by the numerals – looks almost like some sort of shift rota."

"Twenty-four hour numerals," Vince exclaimed. "Yes, I know what you mean – they look like some sort of job or letter for classification, followed by a time."

"But there's no date," Alan noted. "All of these couldn't be in the same day because the times go all over the place, look here this 'V' is at two o'clock in the twenty four hour clock while then next one 'T' is at one thirty in the afternoon; they must be spread across different days. But how did Mr. Montague know which day for which time?"

"There must be a clue in these letters. Could they be people's names, people who can only be reached at these times?" Vince suggested. "And these last, 'B' and 'C' are unknown – even Gillais did not know himself, which is why he wrote the question marks."

"Still no dates however.... No, there is something that is very"—Alan tapped the side of his head—"very reminiscent about them. I am sure I have seen them before. Let me see; R, A, V, T, B, C,

B... and all of the times, apart from the very first at 'R', are during the day. Have you noticed that?"

Vince nodded. "Yes, almost as if the night times are out of bounds in between these letters. Why would that be? Why would Gillais be meeting these people *only* in the daytime and what would keep him so busy at night in between?"

Inspiration crept into the doctor's brain. "A Cruise Ship." He clapped his hands. "Gillais is on a cruise ship, and he cannot do whatever he was doing at night because there are a lot of people around, he would be spotted, but during the day, on most of the Mediterranean legs of this journey we make stops at ports all along the coasts – which means..."

"That these aren't people's names any more, but that they are *places*. R – Rome, where we started, and there are a number of times here because they could refer to days *before* the start of the cruise..."

Vince continued with the list, "Athens, Valletta, Tunis, Barcelona, Canary Islands, Bermuda... These are times to do something during the day at each of these ports."

They looked at each other.

"Meet up with his Cinderella?" Alan suggested.

The security chief nodded. "Yeah, it looks that way, like Mr. Gillais; even though he was undercover, investigating something on board the *Ocean Quest*, he had arranged some secret meetings with his Cinderella during the day at every stop on the cruise."

"Before he met his untimely end," Alan uttered, grimacing.

"Yes, indeed, perhaps his Cinder's didn't really want his affections." Vince seemed to have shaken the cobwebs out of his head now. "But at least we do know one thing – that this was a well-planned out excursion, and Gillais had planned his romance to the last detail."

Alan agreed, surveying the dead man's room once more. Yes, that sounded about right, a very particular man who was very accurate and very precise, probably committed to his job, who had planned his affair with the same precision as the one he exhibited throughout the rest of his life. But if he was a happy man in a situation that was working, why was he poisoned with such a rare and unusual toxin? A jealous husband? A crossed lover? He told the security chief this, who shrugged the thoughts dismissively.

"I do not like the fact that Gillais was an Interpol agent. That is too significant a fact."

Once again Alan had to agree, as they made their way out of the dead man's room, locking the door behind them.

"So, Doc, you get that wine glass tested for the *Digitalis,* I'll get onto Interpol about these numbers and tell them what we have found so far. Good work all round I'd say."

CHAPTER FOURTEEN

In Spanish Waters
The case of a cleaner's hands, and his girlfriend's legs...

THE FESTIVE AIR WAS ALREADY taking over the deck as the cruise liner steamed towards the ocean port of Barcelona, in Spain. Doctor Mayhew pounded the deck on one of his morning runs in the fresh, early air, encountering few passengers apart from the absolutely committed sun seekers, who were setting up their lounge chairs early.

Alan liked to fast walk in the early morning, as early as possible, but so often he never got the chance these days, especially on this, most troublesome of cruises.

He had found through the years that speed walking eased the mind and the body almost as well as a good yoga class, and both acted as a good balm to any troubles, stresses, or worries. While he concentrated on his strides and his breathing, his mind burbled away, throwing up random thoughts and memories in what he was told was 'lateral thinking.' That process of free association when your conscious mind is not a hundred percent concentrating on the task ahead, and instead all the *other* parts of your mind – the subconscious – get to work, linking images and events and facts and feelings together in new ways to reveal hidden connections.

He often found that he would come up with the solution to a pressing work problem after some good exercise, in a similar fashion to waking up with an answer on the tip of his tongue to something that had been troubling him the night before or after doing a good restful meditation.

The previous night, the ship had seen the arrival of the passengers back from the city of Tunis, bearing with them all manners of gifts, oddities and trinkets. The Seinz's particularly had asked for the luggage men to come out and help them stow a few large crates of 'finds'. They had assured the doctor when they saw him that evening that the archeological trinkets were of good quality.

Alan's legs pumped in a steady, constant rhythm, while he thought about how well-composed and resilient the Seinz's were.

Despite Elsie Rottersgate's premonitions, the Seinz's were once again like two birds in love, as they fussed around their luggage, personally overseeing it being stowed and secured away with the utmost care.

"What kind of trinkets have you got there then?" Alan had asked when he next saw them.

"Ceramics," Dr. Seinz replied. "A lovely set of post-Carthaginian vases, nothing too fancy, but it will add very nicely to one's personal collection."

Alan had been impressed. "So do all archeologists have a personal collection of artifacts?" he enquired. "Every archeologist's house must be an Aladdin's Cave of treasures."

Seinz threw him a conspiratorial chuckle. "Well, most have some little thing or other I assume. Of course, we are not allowed to take any actual finds away. They have to be catalogued and handed over to the relevant authorities, the Office of Antiquities, etc., but there are always small things that each site releases being considered of 'no major archaeological consequence'."

"You should see the amount of arrow heads he has," Diane Seinz put in. "hundreds of the little things that look like little more than pebbles to my eyes."

Her husband laughed. "Yes, well, they are quite small I guess. But remarkable things. Kids often find them and call them 'elf bolts' or 'snake stones'. I am afraid I have quite fallen in love with the rather useless things."

Alan envied them, even that small slice of history. He himself had a dozen or so Roman coins bought in one of those historic museums found throughout Italy and then there was the find he made in Irian Jaya. When he was just a young doctor doing some volunteer work in the rural areas of this island state of Indonesia, he came upon the area museum in Jayapura. They were apparently closing down the museum that was filled with carvings, canoes, paddles, adornments that had once belonged to the original inhabitants.

When the passengers had returned from Tunis, the ship had been rapidly transformed into a hive of activity for crew and passengers alike, as the treasures from the market-port filtered back onto the ship. More than he had even imagined, the cruise ship resembled one of those antique merchant traders, or better yet, a pirate ship. The cruise liner traveled the same ancient and well-trodden sea paths that civilizations had been traveling for hundreds and thousands of years and, at each port of call, would fill its coffers with the local goods and valuables. However, on board a cruise liner like the *Ocean*

Quest, it became an event of admirable, frenetic activity as the trinket Trade intensified, underground games of chance played and bets taken for each item.

Maybe that was the reason for which Alan couldn't see many staff members on deck. He thought of all the smoky little rooms where drinking games were played for a particularly lovely piece of art, or a rare book, knock-off Gucci purse or a fake Tommy Hilfiger watch or some cheap electronic equipment.

The cruise company and the captain himself mostly forgave these minor questionable behaviors. Care was taken to ensure that the 'looting' didn't get out of hand. All in all, it was done with good intent in mind, as some of the crew on board who didn't get much shore leave, tried to bargain for that special memento or present for their loved ones back home.

Alan himself had been woken up in the early hours of the morning – or was it the late hours of the night – by the friendly face of Frankie, still sporting a bruise.

"Nice watches, Doc. Some very nice pieces here at some rather affordable prices thanks to the Euro." He presented a range of Rolex style watches all in metallic gold and silver glint, looking as if they had once been designed for astronauts.

"Seeing as you helped me out with my head, Doc, I thought you could get first dibs before, you know, I do my rounds below decks."

Alan looked them over and thought briefly about the collection of different brands of knock-offs he already had. He really did not need one more but these were very good quality and appeared to be more the type that "fell off the back of the truck", rather than some of the more typical Chinese junk look-alike watches. Naturally, he had a number of the fake ones, as he was someone who spent his entire life 'between customs' zones'. These were probably quite good quality, all the rest would probably break after a month or two; and of course there was no guarantee with any of them. It was also a well-known fact among crewmembers, that one did not take these watches into a recognized jeweler for repair. Doing so, risked having the jeweler confiscate or hammer the knock-off to smithereens, in accordance with the legitimate company's instructions. In other words, if it was broken, you tossed it.

"Thank you, Frankie'. I think I'll do this one"—Alan picked the best one of the lot—"thank you very much, and I wish you the best of luck with the rest of your sales and your trades."

Frankie looked like a cat that had just caught a mouse. "Right-

O, I have to make a delivery to a few people, and one of them is someone we *both* know." He tipped the doctor a wink and went on his way, whistling the well-known Rolling Stones song "Sympathy."

Alan chuckled to himself, and went back to bed.

Why was he thinking about these things? Alan suddenly shook himself out of his reverie as his footsteps pounded along the upper decks. Up here there was hardly anyone around. Most people were probably just waking up, and deciding when to go down for a cooked breakfast.

Times.

The thought struck him in a flash. 'Ah yes, times! Times and rendezvous...' His mind was still bubbling away on the question of the times and ports that were held in Gillais's notebook. They were all times during the late morning or the afternoon, when the *Ocean Quest* was docked, and either Gillais himself, or at least most of the rest of the passenger's and some of the crew would be on shore leave.

Alan knew from personal experience that it could be quite a tricky thing to arrange meetings on a cruise ship, at different ports. Over the years, he had agreed to meet friends at various ports, but if even the slightest problem cropped up, then it was always difficult to rearrange, as each party had to find local transport, and the nearest public telephone or Internet café.

Yes, if Gillais had agreed on some rendezvous with his mysterious Cinderella, then they would probably both had to have the details of where they were going to meet in their heads, as if they knew each port very well.

"And that-" he said as he huffed to himself, "would mean that he and his Cinderella were both experienced travelers."

The doctor was so excited about this tiny clue that he almost forgot where his feet were taking him. So lost in his running and his thoughts, with a start he realized that he had come to the edge of the access to the restricted deck.

"Oh damn," he cursed under his breath as he started to make a tight U-Turn and fast walk back the way he came.

The restricted deck was for passengers only, absolutely no crew allowed unless it was a medical emergency or a security issue. There was a very particular reason for this, and that was because the restricted deck was also a sunbathing deck. A nudist sunbathing deck.

"Oh, I see!" said a chirruping voice.

There in front of him were the bouncing forms of Jen-Tina, a name that Tiffany had coined for them. They were two cruise staff that worked helping out the cruise directors with their entertainment. Officially they were designated as hospitality staff, and would be tasked with a number of duties and roles according to the ship's necessity. In this way, the doctor had seen them working as dancers, with children's groups, the pantomime, and even as trainee guides on the guided tours that took place in every port.

They were both young and smooth skinned, full of every possible joy of life that their twenty-something years allowed. Jenny winked mischievously, as his face turned a deep crimson red.

"Going to take a naughty sunbathe, Doc?" Jenny enquired.

"On the restricted deck, huh? Nice and early before anyone notices?" Tina laughed.

"Well I don't see any towels, do you, Tina? Looks like the doc here was just going to cast off to the wind." Jenny put a hand over her mouth to stop herself from laughing.

"Oh shush! You wench, you'll upset the poor man," Tina blurted, just before the doctor burst out laughing.

Realizing that there was nothing that could be said to salvage the matter, Alan sighed, stretched out his legs and returned to his walking at a faster speed, merely throwing them a "morning ladies," as he did so. He knew that this little encounter would be all around the ship before dinner, but he wasn't worried too much, everyone knew what the Jen-Tina duo was like; everyone expected salacious gossip from them.

"As long as I am not hauled before the captain over dinner tonight, it'll be all right." Alan chuckled to himself, and then chuckled some more at his own embarrassment. In fact, he found himself laughing all the way back to the showers. He didn't know what was worse, the thought that the other crewmembers would think that he was sneaking onto the restricted deck to be – how should he put it – a bit more at one with nature, or the sight of the ship's doctor running along the upper decks giggling away to himself.

*   *   *

Yes, Alan thought, as he put his whites back on after a very refreshing shower, *there certainly is a festive air about the ship today.*

Maybe it was all that hot-blooded Spanish air that the cruise liner was sailing into. Last night he had seen the entertainment crew unpacking the flamenco dance dresses, and he was sure that he had seen someone with a pair of mariachis.

Wait a minute – aren't the mariachis Mexican? Alan wondered. He decided that he would ask Tiffany when he next got the chance. Sometimes he knew that the prop department was hard pushed to find all the appropriate equipment, and were forced to use regional costumes and instruments from wildly different places.

For now, however, the doctor was back to work in the Medical Centre, and was once more seeing to the latest ongoing rounds of medical cases.

He had a few medicals to perform, some straightforward investigations for the corporate office regarding the crews overall health, a range of medical physical tests. Everyone seemed fine, and apart from a few hangovers and one higher than usual blood alcohol content, Alan was confident that apart from the one death, the crew on this cruise would get off pretty light.

Of the passengers he saw, he examined and treated one earache, a bad case of having eaten way too many rich foods resulting in an esophagitis, one passenger who 'forgot' her thyroid medicine, an elderly woman having trouble with her knees. She had brought her own medication and Alan looked through what her personal physician had prescribed, finding it to be quite heavy handed, as Alan did not believe in using strong narcotics especially for chronic pain issues.

Alan actually liked treating the elderly passengers on board. They were invariably people who had saved up their money for a few years to be able to go on a cruise, or who had led successful work lives, enough so that their retirement package afforded them the opportunity to go on cruises in their Golden Years.

To this particular older passenger, he advised long soaks in the hot tubs on board the ship, and tried to encourage her to try swimming to help strengthen the muscles supporting the joints.

Alan tried to encourage all of these patients to take what gentle exercise they could, regulate their diet, and improve their general health so they could stave off their need for painkillers. Unfortunately, it was seldom the case that patients had the time to be able to do these treatments, or already had years of extensive painkiller abuse, encouraged by irresponsible doctors.

He bid the elderly lady a warm farewell and saw her out of the door before sitting heavily down on his swivel chair again.

"Oh, it would break your heart if you let it," he announced to the clinic and the world in general.

"Doctor, actually… now that you have a moment?" Kelly looked up apologetically from her nurse's station. She was one of these people who would often have an apologetic look on her face. It seemed to be one of the permanent modes in which she was grounded.

"Yes, what can I help you with?" He smiled at her. "Unless of course you are going to suddenly start removing your clothes again, in which case, really, I must protest… it is not for the daylight hours!"

Kelly blushed at his joke. "No, I promise I won't surprise you again like I did before, but, hum, it is again of quite a delicate nature…"

"What do you mean?" There was a tiny, distant part of the doctor that thought for a dim second: *Am I being sexually harassed by a nurse half my age?*

In the end, it turned out that wasn't the case at all. "No, it's Ernesto. You see, I know you said that it was impossible to be allergic to someone but I am very concerned…"

"Oh, your rash again?" Alan put on a brave, loud voice.

"Well, not quite, Doc. It's Ernesto. He has these awful welts on his hands, I think they are from some of the detergents that the cleaners used, and he seems to have come up in some sort of reaction to it. I was wondering whether that would be what was causing my contact dermatitis?"

"Yes, indeed, it definitely could be. I did forget that Ernesto worked in the cleaning services. Is he free now? If so by all means bring him in. Tell him that I want to do a spot medical check if need be." Alan was a little concerned, because welts could indeed be an allergic reaction, or more likely to be chemical burns, if the source was the industrial detergents that the cleaning staff often use.

Alan knew that the service sectors often used chemicals and products, which are only licensed to their sorts of business, and are not available for public use. This highly restricted form of sale meant that the chemicals companies could produce more and more quite concentrated products, which you were to handle only with certain types of thick gloves. In some cases, there was a need for other personal protective clothing and respirator equipment. These products were easily capable of burning the skin if left to interact with water or oxygen, or if a glove was ripped. Alan had seen some truly appalling cases, similar to industrial accidents. For the sake of the young man, the beau of his staff nurse, he wanted to get Ernesto in to the infirmary quickly.

"Thank you, Doc, thank you!" Kelly flashed him a grateful smile and went to make a phone call.

Within ten minutes Ernesto emerged from the depths of the ship once again, just as he had the very first day that Alan had met him.

"Greetings, Ernesto," Alan said, after he spotted an awkward moment because Kelly and Ernesto didn't know how to greet each other 'above decks.' Alan smoothly interjected his 'friendly doctor persona' to cover up their ungainliness. "Good to see you again. How is your back, and how has your cruise been so far?"

The young man smiled nervously and bobbed his head to say 'so-so'.

"It is my hands you see." He gestured with his gloved hands. "They are throbbing like a pie in an oven."

Alan almost broke into loud laughter – he had never heard that expression before. Otherwise, it seemed, the young man was having a very good trip indeed, as he kept glancing at Kelly.

"Yes, my back is fine now. You have healed me very well," Ernesto said with a twinge of admiration in his voice. "But now, as they say, it is one thing after another." He glanced at his hands.

"Ok, let's see the damage," Alan told him, bringing him over to the examination table. "Kelly, would you be so good as to prepare a saline wash and get some betadine ready?"

Alan automatically rattled off what he would need, assuming that he would have to wash the burns, and dress them with a material, which still allowed the wound to breathe.

When Ernesto winced, taking off his gloves, Alan saw the welts, but they weren't like any chemical burn he had ever seen.

What peppered the backs of his knuckles were patches of inflamed red skin that looked 'angry' and puffy. They seemed to all centered around small abrasions of the skin, which appeared to have been infected.

"Ah. Let's first take some cultures and then mix that betadine with some anti-bacterial soap," Alan said to Kelly.

"Oh!" She couldn't stop herself from taking a worried step towards her man. "Is it serious?"

"No, it really shouldn't be, with the correct treatment anyway. We can clean these up and see to it that we can fight off any infection."

"It's an infection?" Kelly asked.

"Yes, certainly appears to be. This erythema is the skin reacting to fight off whatever has caused the infection in the first place."

Ernesto looked alarmed.

"No, don't worry young man. This is actually not a bad case of an infected wound like some that we see, and cure."

At that, Ernesto visibly relaxed. You could see that he was a very trusting fellow. Alan thought that that quality of his was probably what Kelly saw in him.

While the doctor cleaned and washed both hands completely with the anti-bacterial sterile wash, he considered the only rather strange facet to this whole condition: the raised red dots that were present on Kelly's legs.

"Tell me, Ernesto, when did you first notice a problem here?"

Ernesto thought about it, speaking as he did so and working his way backwards through the symptoms. He had known that something was wrong when the tiny spots had started to 'feel hot' and 'burn' constantly. He hadn't even noticed the spots until after he had felt his hand tingle, as if he had very localized pins and needles under the skin.

After that he had noticed little raised red dots, which he had assumed were just the wear and tear of working as a cleaner, doing a lot of manual labor, heavy lifting and bashing his hands about on the ship. After that, 'the red burns' had started to appear, and, he thought that they would naturally go away if he just washed his hands. He did that yesterday, this morning, and the day before – to no avail.

Alan nodded before he began explaining, "What we need to do is threefold, but do not worry as it is all very run-of-the-mill and straightforward." Alan ticked off the items on his hand. "1. We need to keep your hands clean to prevent any spreading on your skin, and to keep these little wounds clear of any new secondary infection. 2. We also need to treat these wounds with simple bandages and a topical medicine Ms. Watkins will give you. And 3, last of all, we need to give your body the power to knock the infection from your system. To do this, you will take some antibiotics and, to keep your body healthy, I will give you a diet. Also, I want you to sleep well, and keep active by walking."

He reached over for the bottle of pills and started measuring out a small number into a fresh plastic click-safe canister.

"These are a standard course of antibiotics, and they should generally knock out anything that you do not want in your system. They might make your stomach a little queasy for a few days, so remember to eat only what is on the diet and drink lots of water. The chef can get you some of these foods if they are not on the crew's regular menu."

He turned and wrote the details onto the prescription bottle. "We have a couple of other stronger courses of antibiotics, but I don't like using them unless we absolutely have to. I want you back in here twice a day for dressing changes, and if things feel worse, contact nurse Watkins right away, understand?"

Ernesto nodded.

"Quite right, no need to suffer and be in pain while you do your job. I could write you a permission to be excused from duties for a couple of days if you would like?"

Ernesto shook his head vigorously, obviously against the idea. Alan could tell that he was a young man who valued hard work, valued putting the hours in and getting the wages out, and he admired that.

"I will write your supervisor a note so he can find you some alternative work that allows you to keep your dressing on, keep them clean and most importantly, wear protective gloves over the whole hand. That should make sure that you are able to continue with some work."

"Thank you, Doctor, thank you very much," Ernesto burst out enthusiastically.

"And as for you, young lady"—Alan turned to Kelly—"Make sure you wash that rash on your legs with anti-bacterial soap, every morning and every night. Because nothing has broken the skin – you mustn't scratch it. I'll give you some antihistamines to take orally, just to make sure you don't scratch."

Kelly thanked him and he indicated that she could bandage up Ernesto, just as she had done when they first met, while he went and washed his hands again.

There was something annoying him about this. It wasn't Ernesto or Kelly; after all, he was quite fond of the both of them and found their burgeoning romance sweet to watch. No, it was about the lesions.

Infections are regular and usual things that one sees in life, and they are often just a case of one's immune system not being able to deal with one of the many bugs that surround us all the time. You can make the situation better or worse by cleanliness, or not working in service jobs where you have to deal with a lot of muck and dust and dirt.

In fact, if Diane Seinz was right we are mostly made up of viruses, Alan reminded himself, so it wasn't even the fact that he was treating an infection. It was the fact that the infection had had a contact effect on Kelly, even if it was 'second hand', so to speak.

Not many infections are that strong or that unique. Alan understood the principles of microbiology, although he realized he could always ask Diane if he needed help. Basically what he was seeing was either very strong virus/bacteria, or one that was *relatively* rare. Viruses all belong to broad families, like the influenza bug, and it is by identifying these families that one's own immune system learns to build a resistance that fight them off. The doctor reasoned that is why we aren't falling over ill every time we open our front door.

For a virus to affect another person that strongly so quickly without any wounds for it to enter the bloodstream meant that Kelly probably had little immunity to it, which meant that it was either a relatively new strain of something, or it was a very strong version of something.

The doctor knew that cruise ships could become hot houses for all manner of bugs and coughs, the nature of being on a confined space, with limited facilities and then exposing oneself to strange and new landscapes every few days encouraged this. He wondered for a moment whether he was seeing a new strain of a particularly nasty little bug on board his ship.

If so, he would have to inform the captain as a matter of course. And in the very, very worst case scenario ask every one – crew first of all, and then all of the passengers – to take an antibiotic. That would be the absolute last resort and is a nightmarish possibility for a ship's doctor, because it means that you have to try and quickly develop what is called 'herd immunity'.

'Herd immunity' means that there is enough resistance to any particular disease or illness or bug that it cannot spread very far in a group of people because most other people have the antibodies to fight it off.

For Doctor Mayhew to mimic herd-immunity and distribute antibiotics to large groups of the crew and passengers, it would not only be a publicity disaster for the Gold Cruise Line Company; it would also mean that the illness was out of the doctor's control, and that it had become a serious threat to safety aboard the ship.

Alan breathed, realizing just how crazy and terrible that sounded, when all he had was one infected man's hands and some slight discomfort in the nurse's legs.

"Yep," Alan murmured to himself, "You couldn't have made this case stranger if you had tried!"

CHAPTER FIFTEEN

Barcelona
Of prunes and fireworks

"SO, WHAT YOU ARE TELLING me, Doc, is that we have one possible murder case on board, one infectious outbreak, and one of our nurses has a mysterious rash?" Captain Halvorsen waved his martini glass at the ship's doctor.

The cruise party had been invited to the Costa San Bartemou resort on the very tip of Barcelona, from where they had a beautiful view over the sea. One could dimly make out the white shadow of the *Ocean Quest* in the distance. As part of the cruise package, were deals available to various hotels at the overnight stays, and discounted tickets for a number of local attractions; all depending upon what cruise package the passenger had signed up for. Here at the Costa San Bartemou (or 'Saint Bartholomew's Coast') those lucky passengers who had purchased the Super Gold Elite package were invited to stay overnight, and spend their evening at the luxurious resort, enjoy a wine tasting of some of Spain's finest wines, watch a flamenco performance, a local Spanish folk band, use of the heated pool, the gym, an elegant dinner, and a fireworks display at midnight.

About eighty passengers qualified for this extravaganza, and they were the sorts of wealthy souls who indulged in every added benefit that their holiday would allow.

Fortunately for Alan, a number of the officers had also been invited by the cruise company, on the proviso that they wear their officers' uniform and conduct themselves as perfect representatives of the cruise company. Not surprisingly, most of the officers on board had chosen to come – especially to the wine tasting that had started their on shore trip.

Alan usually looked forward to these things, but tonight Alan had mixed feelings as he dressed himself in his very best uniform with its gold buttons down his broad chest and the medical caduceus on the lapel. His mind was abuzz with the case of the French-Belgian and the pink knickers, and the possible infection that had shown up in the young Ernesto, so he couldn't quite relax enough to enjoy himself. After a few long hours of listening to the band and watching the skirts of the dancers flying, he had sought out Captain Halvorsen to tell him of his fears.

"Yes, Captain, that seems to be about the sum or it, sir," he concluded.

"Right." The captain nodded. Despite the fact that he could come across as a hardened party animal, Captain Anders Halvorsen was, Alan had to admit, a very capable officer. He 'played hard', as he liked to put it, because he also 'worked hard,' and his decisive mind could quickly see through to the core of a problem. The captain probably bored easily, Alan thought with a nod, that he was definitely one of those '*Type A*' personalities that needed a conundrum and some drama in front of him. If left to his own devices, on a long or a particularly dull cruise, he would probably just as quickly unintentionally make the drama for himself.

Now was a particular case in point; the captain had given a thank you speech to the Costa San Bart's management crew, who had also turned out in their official uniforms at the reception; and had managed to pepper it with more than enough tact and witticism to make both crew, staff and passengers feel at home, proud, and a part of one big, happy family.

After that role, of course, when the captain had little to do other than the 'meet and greet', as he put it, so he had quickly decided to perform his own wine tasting of all of the house specials, knowing, of course, that the ship was in port for the night, and therefore his expert advice would not be absolutely needed. After some small tumblers of all the very best wines, he was now onto the martinis and spirits, not that it showed in his demeanor – this man knew how to drink and conserve his noble bearing. Of course, an alcohol breath test would certainly have been positive, but no one was going to call for that tonight.

"I'll be damned if any cruise of mine gets a bad press because of a piffling murder and a bug," Halvorsen declared, instantly returning to the intense and dedicated captain that he was, despite the fact that the effect was entirely worn down by the slight slur to his speech, which only a trained doctor would have detected.

"We'll double the health and safety detail, double cleaning shifts for all below decks staff, and instead of using the large ballroom for dinner we'll alternate each night between the large and the smaller dining rooms for the grand dinners. That should allow enough time to clean, prepare the areas and encourage the passengers to use the facilities on the other decks."

Alan nodded, it was a sound plan, he knew that if you constantly used one space and one set of amenities through the course of a long cruise, then no matter how many cleaning staff you use, there is still the buildup of bacteria and germs. By forcing the passengers to explore the other sections of the ship it helps lower the overall threat.

"And then," the captain continued, "there is always the Prunish Gambit."

"Oh – uh, yes I see what you did there, sir, very funny."

Alan suddenly realized what the captain was suggesting.

"Well, back on my last cruise the doctor called it the Prunic Wars, which is probably more apt, but, in some way it sounds a bit marshal and I never like to think of using the khazi in a military way..."

"Perhaps a little too combative, sir?" Alan questioned with a smirk.

"Exactly, a man never wants to think that he is about to go to war when he wants to use the Little Room."

Alan laughed, he couldn't help it. It was a common procedure for the ship's doctor to be involved in the *regulation* of the ship's health, particularly at the start of any cruise. Over the years he had found that by asking that prunes and figs be added to the ship's cuisine on a regular basis, it kept everyone much more *relaxed. One simple way of doing this was to have room service add prune juice to all trays and, in the dining rooms, to have the wait-staff bring a glass to all passengers, as a special entree to breakfast.*

In this case, what the captain was referring to was the benefit of cleansing the systems of all the passengers and crew, to effectively detox, thus helping them to fight off a potentially dangerous infection.

"A prunic incursion," the Alan suggested.

"The battle of the prune," the captain replied, smiling at the thought. They both snickered like schoolboys. If only Tiffany could hear him now, Alan thought. She would be mortified by the way he carried on with the captain.

"Of course, this is only a very minor threat at the moment you understand," Alan went on. "We only have a few cases amongst the crew, but it was quite interesting, and it kept my mind worrying about it overnight."

"Well, good show that you told me about it." The captain tipped his hat at the doctor. "I am jolly glad we have that brain of yours with us on this cruise. This situation with the Belgian chap would be a bugger if I were dealing with it alone. So what's the preliminary verdict, Doc?"

"Unsure," Alan quickly replied. He was very aware of the risks involved in making too many grand claims without being able to substantiate them. Besides, he didn't want to endanger Vince's investigation, or his own for that matter, by letting it be known that there may or may not be a murderess out there on board the ship!

"Good show, good show; playing your cards close to your chest I see. I have heard that about you, Doctor." Anders told him. "For now, all we can do is wait on what Vince has heard back from Interpol and see where we go from there."

"Precisely, Captain, your vision, as ever, is cut glass, sir."

"Cut glass, which is unhappily unfilled." He gestured to his drink. "Another?"

Alan shook his head vigorously. "No, no, not for me – I still have to plan my prunic invasion." He laughed, not willing to tell the captain that, at the moment, he didn't really feel like 'letting go' or 'having a wild night', least of all tonight. He knew Captain Anders thought that his ship's doctor was a little too buttoned up, a little too restrained, but it was just one of those things about Alan that made him who he was. It wasn't that he didn't let his hair down or enjoy himself when the time came, but at the moment he still could feel the cogs of his mind whirring away at the problems on board the cruise, and he didn't want to disturb them while they did.

With a "too bad" the captain bid him a good night and poured himself into the crowd, immediately being snatched into an animated discussion by two *Roo's* who escorted him to the outdoor bar. Alan sighed happily to himself – how the captain did it he had no idea.

At that point, a mustachioed waiter informed the assembled guests that the fireworks would be starting very shortly, if the party cared to advance to the balcony area of the resort. Not wanting to miss this spectacle, Alan fell in behind a mixed group of married couples all in their dinner jackets and evening dresses. The doctor assumed they were mostly wealthy business people comparing cruises and luxury expeditions on which they had traveled.

He tried to eaves drop

"Oh yes, the Maldives is quite a beautiful place, but a little... now I don't mean to be rude, but a little 2000's wouldn't you say, dear?" one lady queried. Her husband looked a little strained as if, no, he didn't understand at all but smiled and agreed all the same. The whole party was in their fifties, and looked to be the sort of 'serial cruisers' that the doctor had so often seen while working.

Then he heard two girls exchanging what sounded like a joke. He slowed the pace to follow them closely without being too obvious – but he wanted to hear this…

The first girl said, "He said to me, I don't know why you wear a bra; you've got nothing to put in it. I said to him, you wear pants don't you?"

The second one intoned with, "He said to me, shall we try swapping positions tonight? I said to him, that's a good idea – you stand by the stove and sink while I sit on the sofa and do nothing but fart."

"Alright! Now, what was the next one?" the first young woman asked.

"Oh, Alice… you know."

"Oh, yes, yes… here goes it," Alice said. "He said to me, what have you been doing with all the grocery money I gave you? I said to him, turn sideways and look in the mirror!" She looked at her friend. "Okay, your turn, Yvette."

Laughing away, Yvette went on, "He said to me, why don't women blink during foreplay? I said to him, they don't have time."

By this time Alan was to the point of bursting in loud laughter, but tried to keep his mouth in check – he wanted to hear the rest.

"He said to me, how many men does it take to change a roll of toilet paper? I said to him, I don't know; it has never happened."

"He said to me, why is it difficult to find women who are sensitive, caring and good-looking? I said to him, they already have boyfriends."

"He said to me, what do you call a woman who knows where her husband is every night? I said to him, a widow."

"He said to me, why are married women heavier than single women? I said to him, single women come home, see what's in the fridge and go to bed. Married women come home, see what's in bed and go to the fridge."

With the last of this whimsical recital, both Alice and Yvette burst out in happy laughter, hurrying ahead of the group and leaving Alan to his own chuckles.

Their steps led them through the courtyard of the resort over a small stone bridge, with the path ahead lit with soft, evening garden lights. Shrubs, rocks and collapsing pillars had been strategically placed for maximum effect. Oblivious of the work that had gone into creating mood, the party navigated their way to the far end of the front gardens which merged with the steps that led up to a standalone balcony comprised of interesting broad stone arch railings accented with the shadows of creeping ivy. From here the balcony extended all the way around to the main resort houses, forming a long curve that all of their hundred-strong party could easily filter into.

"Doctor. How the devil are you?" said a familiar voice from behind him. He turned to see the friendly, red-faced George Alleyway, the ship's chief navigator huffing up to him on the steps to the balcony. "I'm afraid that I haven't had the chance to see you for weeks now, why haven't you been at the officers' mess?"

Alan thought about it for a second. Between being busy dealing with the deceased Belgian, the sudden Code Brown and the infected nurse, he really had not had any spare time, but he didn't want to reveal that to the Chief Navigator. It wasn't that he didn't trust him; it was just that some information, Vince had assured him, had to be kept within the very tight circle of the security chief, the captain, and the doctor.

"I'm afraid I have been treating the sick and the weary, George, I've been out there doing the good work," he lied. Yet, he was sure that his statement could – broadly – refer to a dead man as being either very sick, or at least very, very weary.

"Well, now," George chuckled. "It has been quite boring up in the top deck without your stories, you know. You will have to come over and tell us some more from your memoirs."

Alan was pleased, but embarrassed. "Thank you, George, but I am sure that your own stories are far more enlivening than mine."

George shook his head. "Well I don't know about that, we chief navigators don't get out too much from our computer screens and radars you know, we don't get to feel the air, so to speak."

"So to speak what?" Alan didn't get the hint.

"A little birdie told me that you were caught feeling liberated, Doctor."

"I'm sorry?" He wondered for a moment whether the man was referring to his linen closet liaison with Tiffany that hadn't even been a liaison.

"Now I don't mind what anyone else does, you know, every man to his own is all I can say, but really, you should probably try to keep it to your own cabin..." Alan could see that George was on the brink of being rendered helpless with laughter.

"Just what on earth are you talking about, man?" Alan demanded of him.

"Just"—George wiped away a tear, controlling himself—"your proclivities for certain restricted areas of the ship."

Jen-Tina! Alan could have cursed. He knew that he couldn't trust those two to keep a prime piece of non-existent speculation to themselves. "No really, it's not what you think," he began, but George cut him off with a laugh and pointed his finger out over the descending cliffs and waters.

Phizz... went the first rocket, from hidden installations somewhere on the gentle cliff side that rolled downwards to the waves.

Bang! It exploded in a large starburst of silver-white over the waters and the resort, far over their heads. The illumination lit their party up for a second simultaneously as the explosion quieted their little chat rather abruptly.

Rocket after rocket shot up into the skies, bursting into spectacular reds and greens and orange colors. The lights cartwheeled and spun as Catherine Wheels were added to the mix in a highly choreographed display of power and force.

The lights flared bright in his eyes and Alan was instantly reminded of every New Year's celebration that he had ever been to. Slightly blinded the doctor turned his gaze to the crowd of faces as they oohed and aahh'd at the spectacle. Like strobe lights they would be illuminated for a fraction of an instant and caught in freeze-frame motion.

Bang!

The laughing faces in the crowd were people the doctor had seen in corridors, on tennis courts, sunbathing on the decks, and so on.

Fooosh!

The captain grinning as he pointed at the lights to a team of giggling girls.

Schnapp!

At the steps that led back to the garden, there was an altercation behind the crowd, involving two resort waiters and another couple of men in dark suits. They stood out from the crowd as the only people who were not facing the light display overhead. Alan wondered idly who they were – other resort goers?

"No.." he murmured to himself, since his understanding was that for tonight, the resort had been booked especially for the cruise line.

However, there was obviously some confusion. The waiters

repeatedly seemed to point back along the garden path to the two men while they, in turn, gestured towards the cruise party. Alan decided to wander over to see if he could help, just in case they were passengers that he had not recognized and did indeed belong to their party.

He approached, ducking the out flung hands that pointed up at each passing rocket, and avoided the elbows of pretty women, ultimately reaching the two arguing waiters.

"What seems to be the problem chaps?" he enquired.

"These men claim that they are a part of your group, but their names are not on the guest list," one of the waiters said indignantly, gesturing with his clipboard at the duo.

The two men in question wore dark suits, short hair, and one had a tiny goatee. *Well, they certainly looked the part of elite Gold Cruise passengers*, Alan thought, as he asked them for their names.

"Mr. Keriakis and Mr. Rutherford," the one with the goatee said irritably, neither names rang any bells, so Alan suggested that he could call the ship on his communicator and check their names against the ships log to verify their Elite Gold status.

The men looked annoyed, shaking their heads as if they had given up. The one with the goatee – the Doctor took him to be Mr. Keriakis – fixed him with an unhappy scowl and said, "I'll make sure I file a complaint about this to the cruise line." With that, without waiting for Alan to check with the ship, he took his companion and stalked off, back the way they had come through the garden, and to the entrance of the resort.

"I'm sorry, guys." Alan spread his hands out to the waiters, who looked equally as annoyed at the disgruntled passengers as the doctor did. "I know it's not your fault. We'll get this cleared up with the ship's rota when we get a chance."

They agreed, quite happy that someone else accepted that it was not their problem, and they sauntered back to serve passengers at the bar.

Curious, Alan sighed, wondering whether Maud at the front desk had made a mistake, and how they could iron it out without getting a formal complaint filed against the *Ocean Quest*.

He wrote it off as another confusing incident best left to those that handled the ship's bureaucracy, and went back to enjoying what was left of his night.

After the fireworks the party was again escorted to the wide outdoor area outside the front of the resort where a large samba band started up, playing some lively music for the passengers to take to the dance floor-patio with their chosen partners.

Almost everyone seemed a little tipsy from what Alan saw, and it appeared everyone managed to find a dance partner. The captain was like a 'hot commodity', as he was the one most often asked to dance by the female passengers.

Jenny, of the Jen-Tina's duo, was next with the fullest dance card, which, of course, was no surprise considering her generous anatomical gifts. Jenny was asked to shake her little red colored ruffle dress with a number of mature and middle aged wealthy businessmen and entrepreneurs. She accepted all of the invites, and flirted with each of them outrageously as she gyrated and schmoozed her way through practically all of the available men from the cruise.

Alan smirked at the pleasant image of a happy crew and cruise, wondering just how many disastrous misadventures were going to occur tonight in the hot Spanish night air. He then decided to book his taxi back to the port and spend the night in his own cabin aboard ship. After all, he was sure that there would still be administrative medical center preparations to get ready prior to tomorrow's departure. He needed to take care of these before he could put his weary head down and grab some sleep.

The Costa San Bart had a number of taxi companies available, and in ten minutes they had a taxi waiting for him. Later he learned that some of the companies were on permanent call to the luxury resort, with their only job being to meet the guests travel needs.

En route down into Barcelona itself, the doctor was not surprised to see the city at its liveliest in the warm fall air. Little pubs and restaurants spilled their patrons out onto the streets, and partygoers were dancing to the live bands that played on the cobbles.

As he approached the docks, it got busier with the constant stream of fishmongers and fishermen traffic encumbering the piers. The night trawlers came and went and the vans for the early morning market stalls were loaded up, and boxes of the catches were put on ice.

In most ports around the world, the night is just as busy as the day, because this is when the industrial aspects of the services take over. The night is a good time to load and unload cargo, to pack a transport ship or to refuel before the day shift workers start off to sea to gather more fish or other cargo.

Alan had been through numerous ports; most of the major ones in the world, and many of the smaller ones. By now he knew them quite well, seeing them as an extension of the families of sea vessels that form a never sleeping, constant network of industry that spanned the entire globe.

He paid the taxi driver, thanked him for the journey, and wished him a good night before walking to the port entry area, where he found a couple of the immigration and customs officials who were patrolling the central port areas, usually 24/7. He showed them his various papers and crew card, explained his job on the ship in Spanish, chatted a bit, went through the security screening and went his way. They wished him a happy voyage. He then went through the ship's *own* set of security detail, with officers assigned to the guarding of the entranceway.

By the time Alan was through all of the pharmaceutical checks, the papers, and the questions from the company's headquarters, he was utterly exhausted.

While walking the corridors of his own vessel, he felt a little more at home, as if some distant part of his feet could feel the slight pitch and roll of the hull far underneath him. He knew that it was impossible that he could feel the waves this far up on a stabilized vessel sitting at dockside, but he liked to imagine that there was some difference in his gait and in the feel of his feet as they hit the deck.

He decided first to change out of his formal officer's uniform, so headed for his cabin. It was quite a long walk, but one that was invigorating after his one glass of wine at the resort.

When he finally got there, he found his cabin door slightly ajar. Something about it spooked him, and he immediately slowed his step, easing himself forward to the sliver of light that emerged from the crack of his door...

Holding his breath, he heard the sound of movement as someone busied himself or herself around his cabin.

He exhaled a breath, wondering what he should do; should he call Vince? Run to the next cabin? The thought of appearing like a scared rabbit on his own ship before his very own cabin suddenly filled him with indignant anger as he boldly pushed open the cabin door to confront the intruder.

"Ship's Doctor Mayhew, I presume?" said a voice.

Alan was brought up short by the sight that confronted him.

"What... what are you doing here?" he blurted, confounded.

"Aren't you pleased to see me?" the intruder queried, smoothly pulling off first one glove, and then the other in a well-rehearsed manner. Alan was very attentive as he absorbed the rounded bell of her hips, her narrow waist and the pert way that her breasts pushed out against her blouse.

"Good evening, Cruise Director Tiffany!" Alan uttered, his annoyance and utmost surprise still showing on his face.

"Good evening, Ship's Doctor Mayhew!" she replied, before they both burst out laughing, and then he swept her into a passionate embrace.

CHAPTER SIXTEEN

The Open Seas, the African Coast
Welcome and unwelcome reminders

"YOU SHOULD HAVE SEEN your face last night!" Tiffany giggled as she walked back into the room with her hair down, wearing a blouse that softly flowed down to land just past her hips. Alan was mesmerized with what he saw, drinking in her sensual body.

Alan looked up from the bed, "I thought you were an angel that had descended from heaven to protect my room."

"Well, if you like"—she threw his trousers at him as he fought to untangle himself. She sat down on the bed, showing off her very pretty, smooth thigh—"I told you that my cruise was finishing…" She poked him playfully in the chest. "And that it was finishing in Spain. I thought that you would take the hint."

"What hint?" Alan replied, feeling more and more like a dunderhead. He knew he wasn't an oaf, at least in the eyes of his previous liaisons and girlfriends, but when it came to women – truthfully the fairer sex still largely remained a mystery to him. Suddenly he thought of Elsie's description of the difference between men and women and smiled to himself.

"Never mind, Doctor. It was that you were supposed to search Barcelona high and low for me and I was to be found here, ready and waiting, as it were." She gave him a sly look.

"Well, I have had quite a bit on my plate, what with a possible murder and a possible ship-wide infection…." Alan tired at the thought of the incredible amounts he still had to do. It felt like he was a mouse trying to move a mountain.

"Never mind, Doc," she teased. "I have managed to secure a short contract on the *Ocean Quest*, at least until the end of the cruise at Fort Lauderdale. Assistant Cruise Director"—she grimaced—"I'll be helping out your boys here to finish off the entertainment on this side of the journey, it's not much but it works out rather nicely for everyone concerned doesn't it?"

Alan grinned. "Very nice indeed, *very* nice!"

"And, I wasn't expecting any more employment until next time I ship out, so, this gig is a bonus for me. I'm still waiting on my check to clear from my last cruise considering that they didn't do like most of the cruise lines and hand you a wad of cash as you disembark and sign off."

"My, aren't you the wealthy one? You could have booked yourself in as a passenger in that case."

"What, and have to be treated by the ship's doctor when I was not able to spend my entire time on board with him, since 'he had to work'? Yuck!" She stuck her tongue out. Alan was instantly distracted. "No, I like to work. It gives me something to do and be busy while I put away the hours." She laughed again and jumped out of the way as he made a move to grab her. "And, I start work in twenty minutes, so none of that please, sir!" She pushed his hands away playfully. "Besides which, I still haven't heard the end of your story of what has been going on, on this ship."

"Quite right you are," Alan said, realizing just how late last night's activities had made him. "And yes, I do still owe you a story from the last time, and how I managed to escape with my life?"

"And why did you think this Mr. Hammer was a crook?"

"Yes indeed. All will become clear – don't you worry. Shall we have a midday stroll around the top deck when we are both supposed to have lunch breaks? I can fill you in on the latest of that trip and the current status here on the *Ocean Quest*. You will probably wish that you hadn't chosen to set sail with us this time."

"Is this your Black Widow case?"

"Ah yes, I had forgotten that you called it that – well yes, as a matter of fact, but I am afraid that it seems to be getting a little more serious than that." Alan proceeded to tell her all about finding the notebook and the mysterious meetings in the various ports in Gillais Montague's room.

"Who do you think it was? His 'handler'? Does Interpol even have handlers?"

"You mean senior officers who meet with them and advise them on their case?"

"Yes, or it could be secretive meetings with this mysterious lady friend?"

"The one who sent him wine…." Alan's mind raced as he talked through the conundrum with someone else and especially someone as lovely as Tiffany.

"Well, perhaps, although it sounds to me that seeing the

results of the toxicology screen on the wine glass will be your first stop. If it *is* poisoned, then it looks like this woman really didn't want all of these secret meetings and attention – hence the Black Widow hypothesis." Tiffany smiled at her own smarts.

"Maybe, maybe," Alan chimed in, all the while wishing that the case could be solved that easily, that Tiffany was wrong and he didn't have a murderess on board his ship, or as they say in Spanish, 'uxoricida'.

"Well, Doctor Mayhew"—she walked forward, swaying her hips languidly as she did so—"You tell me all about it in a few hours. I have got to teach a bunch of kids how to play with each other in a civilized manner." Turning around, she laid her hands on his broad chest and gave him a peck on the cheek. "And tonight you can introduce me to this Elsie Rottersgate who is stealing your affections from me."

Alan laughed. "I think you two will get on like a house on fire – Done."

*   *   *

That morning in the infirmary, Alan spent half of his time initiating Operation Prune, as he liked to think of it, making the appropriate phone calls to Francine, the chef, for there was to be a fig pudding and prunes added to any dessert or sauce that the kitchen staff could manage.

He then personally reviewed the disinfection cleaning program, identifying the most at risk areas for anti-bacterial treatments. It wasn't until he was nearly at the end of his shift that he looked up from his paperwork to find Nurse Petra Gacek standing with her arms crossed, looking down at him.

"Yes?" was all he said.

"Medical exam, Alleyway," she said in her clipped tone.

He could see that she was annoyed this morning. He knew that it was because he had been deep in the paperwork side of the job, while she had dealt with the minor cases of sickness and bumps that had come in sporadically. Alan grinned to himself as he got up from his seat to greet the old rogue at the door, knowing that if the tables were turned, Petra would absolutely hate all of the paperwork with a passion.

"Aha! We have you at last!" Alan said to his old friend, indicating a seat.

George looked a sight of over excess as he nursed what was probably a very nice hangover. Alan also knew that the chief navigator was never fond of the medicals that happened according to corporate schedule, but had learned to attend them stoically, much as a ship does a fierce storm.

"Be kind, Doctor," were George's first words while the doctor fetched him an Alka-Seltzer and began his round of questions.

George was an overweight, over-indulgent man, who managed to scrape through the medical mainly because of good genetic background and his token efforts in the gym. Keeping his job had more to do with his exemplary record as a chief navigator with the company. Alan knew that he was an asset to any ship on which he sailed, but couldn't help teasing him a little bit about his health.

"I know, I know, Doc – it just seems that I am just so busy with my ship's duties. Being a navigator, let alone an officer, is very hard work."

Alan agreed, the workload for his officer's pay grade was substantial, and the responsibility was high. If there were any problems in the department then it was the chief who would be facing the firing line, definitely lose his job, and possibly face criminal prosecution.

This reminder of the fact spurred the doctor to ask, "Tell me, George, do you remember Rick? Rick Hammer? The navigation engineer a few cruises back?"

"An off-and-on kind of a fellow, yes. The ladies loved him," George mused. "He would sign on for one contract and then we wouldn't see him for several, and then maybe we'd see him again. Yes, I remember him quite well – it's funny that you asked me that."

"Really?" Alan was taken aback. "Why is that?"

"Because he was in contact with us not so long ago, just before this cruise started actually. He asked if he could have his old job back, but of course, we refused given his earlier conduct."

"Really?" Alan said again. "I'd be interested to hear what that 'conduct' was. You see, I had the most unfortunate time of my life crewing with him on his sailboat in Alaska, just before this cruise. He swore to me that he would never work for Gold Cruise Line Company again." Alan shivered at the recollection of the sudden, unpredictable vehemence, which this particular conversation had inspired in the navigator.

"Well, he seemed desperate when he talked to me; he was pale to his boots, as we used to say."

"You saw him recently?" Alan wondered aloud.

"Oh yes! He was in Rome just before you came on board. I am surprised that you didn't bump into him."

Alan opened and closed his mouth several times. Suddenly cogs had started grinding in his brain. It could be nothing, but it was the unpredictable nature of this man whom Alan had informally and unofficially diagnosed as having a latent psychiatric illness, which made him feel uncomfortable. Thinking back to that experience made him shiver, and returned to being a doctor to shake the memories out of his mind, for now.

*   *   *

Young Bay, Alaska

The unpredictable nature of Rick Hammer became apparent on the sixth day of their twelve-day voyage, as they were heading into Young Bay where we were supposed to anchor before the long six-day voyage ahead.

Rick had been busy all morning, hardly paying any mind to the sailing and captaincy of his vessel. He seemed happy to let Alan do all of the work navigating and sailing in the bitter cold, rainy weather. The cockpit's cramped conditions added to the string of disappointments, as the engineer announced that he still 'had work to do' on the boat, and promptly disappeared below decks. After a few hours of clanging and banging, Rick re-emerged with bundles of equipment that he had been rewiring and reworking.

"What are you going to do with all of that?" Alan asked, since none of it appeared to be for the sailboat he was on.

To which Rick had mysteriously replied, "Just some repairs for a patron of mine." With no further explanation, he then took over the helm and set about turning the boat around to head back into Auke Bay.

It was a hard sail; no time to go below and prepare dinner. When they finally arrived, Rick insisted on anchoring the boat way out in the harbor to avoid the mooring fees.

"But you're more than welcome to take the dinghy into the harbor and get something to eat," Rick had said, seemingly nonplussed.

Famished by now, the doctor had just about enough of the engineer's irritable attitude, mysterious tasks and his sudden changes to their schedule. He quickly offered to pay the forty dollars mooring fees for them both, at which prospect the navigator instantly agreed.

Motoring into the Auke Bay visitors' docks, the weather was cold and miserable, and once again Alan did most of the work. Eventually, after trying again and again to get a hold of the Harbor Master on the ship to shore radio, Alan secured their mooring assignment.

Now, more than a little annoyed, Alan went ashore. All he could find was a greasy spoon café to get a long overdue meal, or what passed as such.

As he was sitting there over his wilted lettuce salad, deep fried mushrooms, and chips, Alan had a small brainstorm. He did not *have* to continue with this trip at all. Granted, he had paid a lot of money in advance, but he was indeed having a miserable time. He decided to make some phone calls. He changed his air ticket, and secured a flight from the nearest airport, at no small cost to himself, booked a car rental and the following night in a local hotel. He was definitely done – he had had enough.

Alan was not one to play the suffering fool willingly. With the thought of spending another six days on board the hazardous Alaskan seas with Rick, he decided it was best for everyone's sanity to cancel the trip early.

Feeling much better, he made his way back for his final night on board the boat. He found Rick gone along with the equipment that he had been working on. Alan decided to do some quick packing with what was left of the evening and settled down for the night.

"Ahoy the ship," came a loud, carousing call, waking Alan up from his slumber.

He looked over at the clock, it was three thirty in the morning and a very intoxicated Rick had just weaved his way on board after spending, it would seem, a raucous night with whomever. After a few mumbled words, he collapsed into the V-Berth, surrounded by his woodworking tools, various bits of the radar equipment that had still not been installed and his charts. He slept sounder than Alan obviously could.

At first light the next day, as the watery, cold-laden light filtered down over the ship, Rick awoke and suddenly announced that there were going to be some changes on board his ship over the next week.

"Milena, my girlfriend, wants to come aboard and be with me. You're gonna have to move your things, make way a bit," Rick decreed, before Alan even had the chance to really wake up.

"Rick, that's not a problem at all – I've decided upon some changes as well, and have changed my plans. I am afraid I will have to cancel the rest of the trip, which gives you the whole boat to yourself and your Milena," Alan replied.

"What?" Rick turned on him, looming. "What do you mean; you've changed your plans?' You are going to give me 1000 dollars cash for the cancellation!"

"What?" The doctor was baffled. "I've already paid you upfront all the expenses for the whole trip, as you requested, what on earth is the 1000 dollars for?"

"No, Doc, I mean it" and at that the so called navigation engineer let out some expletives, turned and started gathering up Alan's things that were not packed in the suitcase: his computer, his cell phone and his other valuables. "You pay me that 1000 dollars cash now, or I swear I am going to throw all of these overboard!"

Alan was taken aback by another sudden change in Rick's mood and his instant uncontrolled outburst of anger. What surprised him even more was the fact that Rick grabbed the computer and other valuables, and threw them up into the cockpit. With this completed, he proceeded to cast off the boat, starting up the engine and motoring off into the bay, taking Alan with him – against his will (generally known as kidnapping).

"I won't have you mess up my plans, Doc, and I've got a lot of plans that you don't need to know about," was all he said, threateningly, as Alan tried to reason with him.

After a few minutes the doctor gave up, deciding that being held hostage was far worse than being down on some mere thing like money! He thought about what he could do if he refused to pay him the money – he would almost certainly lose his valuables to the sea, perhaps he might even be cast off in a dinghy and left to find his own way back to the coast! The other issue was the guns and knives that Alan had seen in among the other 'stuff' that were aboard the boat and which he saw Rick clean on a daily basis.

Alan decided to consent to the ransom without protesting any further, emptying out the contents of his wallet and offering that to mollify the unhinged Rick.

This offering seemed to do the trick, even though it was only three quarters of the ransom. Fortunately, Alan had gone to an ATM the night before to get dollars to pay for the hotel, taxi, meals, etc., that would not take credit cards, as Rick curled the ship around in a wide arc and headed back for the dock, barely stopping as Alan tossed his readily available possessions onto the pier as carefully as he could and leapt for safety. He knew that he had left a lot of his stuff still to pack out there on his couch-bed berth, but at that time was only grateful that he had managed to escape with both life and limb all in one piece!

*   *   *

"Oh my word! Really? Held to ransom against your will?" Tiffany's worried face looked at him from where they stood on deck, overlooking the broad expanse of seas that surrounded them on all sides.

Alan nodded; glad to be out here with the Assistant Cruise Director, and not stuck in the Medical Center. After George Alleyway's medical and a few other minor cases, lunchtime had rolled around, and he had decided to take a half-an-hour out to 'parade the decks' with Tiffany – as they had arranged that morning

"You are lucky you made it out of there alive!" Tiffany blurted, for an instant clutching his hand fiercely.

"Yes, I believe I probably am!" Alan replied. "The only thing that is still nagging at me – is why on earth Rick showed up in Rome, just before the beginning of this cruise."

"Did he know you would be aboard?"

Alan nodded. "Absolutely. I told him my travel plans while we were on his boat, but he swore that he would never work with the Gold Cruise Line Company again. Perhaps it is just my apprehension, or the fact that he is probably a dangerous psychotic, but there is something about it that smells rotten." Alan didn't mention his fears; on the very night that they had left Rome the radio equipment had been 'broken', and that possibly, someone had tampered with it. The thought filled him with dread as to what else might have gone on.

"My dear, I think I have to make a call to someone, will I see you later?"

"I wouldn't miss it for the world," Tiffany replied warm-heartedly as they parted ways.

Tiffany was fairly used to the sudden comings and goings of the doctor, who obviously was a very busy member of the ship's crew. Coupled with this fact was the nature of their relationship: that while it wasn't disallowed for two cruise members to be romantically involved, it was regarded as poor taste to flaunt a budding relationship in front of the passengers.

The views of the ocean spread out before the cruise director as she considered her relationship with the ship's doctor, and all the furtive goings-on aboard the *Ocean Quest*. The answers to which were as mysterious as the waves ahead.

CHAPTER SEVENTEEN

The Canary Islands
Expectations

"VINCE? HI, IT'S THE DOCTOR here. I have a few questions to pick your brains over."

"Oh some more?" the security chief good-naturedly replied. "Well I'll meet them with some of my own. Have you found any sign of the *Digitalis* toxin used to kill Mr. Montague?"

Alan had just picked up the printout from the toxicology screen, and looked over the results of various chemical tests through which he had run the wine glass. It was already late afternoon. Alan stood in the Medical Center taking advantage of the little free time he had, and now that Nurse Gacek had gone off; the only time when he was alone in the clinic.

"I am afraid to say that yes, there are signs of the toxin here, Vince. It looks like whomever delivered that bottle of wine to Gillais also managed to lace the bottle with the toxin."

"Easy enough to do, Doc. It could have been poured over the cork, or a syringe could have been used to insert it straight into the wine. It is, as I feared, we had, or have, a poisoner on board." The security chief's tone was deadly serious.

"Well, that is not the only thing I have to mention, Vince. Can you tell me, when we were back in Rome, on the night before the murder, were there any unaccounted men seen on board, not regular crew?"

"What do you mean, Doc, intruders?"

Alan considered, not willing to announce his speculations that someone had tampered with the radios on board. And yet he knew of one very capable and possibly criminal he now learned, had been in Rome at the time. "Yes, I think so – or just anything suspicious – last minute workmen, repairmen, etcetera, just before we left the city?"

Alan heard the shuffle of papers and the distant clicking of Vince hitting a keyboard at the other end of the line. "I can't see anything obvious here in the security logs, Doc, but I do have something similar at our last port."

"Really? In Barcelona?"

"Yes, we had a couple of men trying to come on board, claiming to be passengers. Luckily Maud down at the front desk had turned them away and called security. By the time my team got down there the men had already gone."

Memories of that Spanish night and the two men who had tried to gate crash the resort came flooding back, "A Mr. Keriakis, and, a what was it – Ruthersfoot? Rutherford?" Alan enquired.

"Keriakis? Did you say Keriakis?" Vince sounded astounded.

"Yes, that is how they introduced themselves to me." Alan then explained his encounter with the men at the Costa Saint Bart's, and how they had demanded that they be let into the passengers' party.

"Well that *is* intriguing, because I have a clue here linking a Mr. Keriakis with our late Belgian!"

The doctor was all ears.

"I sent the details of that notebook over to Interpol, who has admitted that Gillais Montague was one of theirs – an undercover agent." He paused. "Anyway, it turns out that those numbers at the start of the notebook. Before the meeting times are indeed bank accounts and one of those bank accounts are for a firm called 'Secure Holdings PLC' – based in Switzerland I believe. I did some searching of my own amongst some of my old naval contacts, and it turns out that Secure Holdings PLC is owned by a Mr. Keriakis!"

"Really, then that means that there was a strong connection between the French-Belgian and those two men trying to gain access to the cruise ship, doesn't it?"

"Yes, they could have been trying to meet up perhaps? Maybe these men were the meetings that Gillais had scheduled at every port stop?"

Alan agreed. It was probably too coincidental to be false. "Although, you do realize, Vince, that now we have an even greater problem."

"Which is?"

"That if these men were meeting Gillais *outside* of the ship, then who killed him while at sea *on the ship*?"

"Ah, so we are back to our black widow hypothesis."

"Quite. We need to find out what our Mr. Montague was meeting these men for. They could even have been helping him out with his investigations for Interpol."

"Yes, I had thought of that," Vince replied. "Getting any

information out of Interpol is pretty much like getting blood from a stone, but I will keep trying."

Alan put down the phone and felt a rush of excitement; they were close to understanding the puzzle. He wondered whether there was anything he could do to find out about this Mr. Keriakis, what sort of man he was and what he was up to. But again he was running out of time, as he had still to review the latest logs from the new cleaning regime that he had implemented.

With a heavy sigh, he sat down at his station once again and started looking over the reports. He wanted to get the ship running as smooth and as well as possible before they reached the Canary Islands tomorrow, which he knew would bring with it a whole new set of dilemmas.

*   *   *

Alan knew that this part of any cruise was always full of fun and frolics. It was the very picture of the international cruise: long sandy beaches with waving palm trees, and crystal blue waters. It seldom was exactly the same as the postcard version in the brochures, but the passengers and crew alike always enjoyed it.

He also knew that usually a lot people could get quite badly sunburned in this section of the cruise, some even requiring significant interventions. It was also a good region of the world to have to call a 'Code Brown' as the passengers who ate ashore often did not take precautions in only eating cooked or properly washed foods.

Even the air seemed to change as they made their way around the coast of Africa to the collection of islands known as the Canaries, which is actually an autonomous community belonging to the country of Spain. Here the seas could get wild and windy, but for now there was only a gentle westward breeze. From here, the *Ocean Quest* would be making the Atlantic sea crossing to Bermuda, and ultimately Fort Lauderdale – they were certainly moving into the hottest part of their trip.

Not that this part of the cruise didn't come with its own problems, of course. Alan knew that with relaxed attitudes also came more drinking, more partying and more upset stomachs.

Tonight they would dock, and in the morning they would release the passengers for their shore leave.

That evening Alan found himself knocking on Tiffany's cabin door, standing dressed in his officer's formal tuxedo with the black piping down the trouser legs. As preplanned, he asked her to accompany him to that evening's entertainment.

"So, is it one of Babette's creations tonight?" Tiffany asked as they descended gracefully to the main theater. Tiffany was referring to the author of the play, the middle aged Babette, who was a regular passenger aboard the *Ocean Quest*, so much so, that she had, in fact, stepped in to perform the non-denominational services on board the ship's chapel more than a few times.

Babette was looking shy, but glamorous tonight as she sat in the very front row with the captain. She was wearing a black dress studded with sequins. Alan and Tiffany both admitted that they liked Babette, who they had come to know over the course of several cruises. She was a short, not terribly athletic woman, with a generous and a warm-hearted laugh, just as long as the jokes didn't conflict with her quite religious and conservative background. She was always the lady.

Spotting their 'other' date for the night, one Elsie Rottersgate, the duo squeezed themselves in beside the elderly woman. She had on her lap, a pile of crochet that she was working through while waiting for the performance to begin. Who knows how long she had been there.

"Oh, I heard that you had a visitor," she declared, lifting a teasing gaze to the doctor, and waiting for Tiffany to be seated. "Now I am very pleased to meet you, young lady, but I must warn you that this young man of yours is really, truly, quite terrible at cards."

"Good!" Tiffany laughed. "That way he can end this cruise richer than when he came on it."

Alan was pleased that the two ladies instantly had hit it off, so much so that they were busy chattering about men and their foolish ways. Alan turned to see the curtains move then pulled aside to a swirl of recorded Indian sitar music....

*   *   *

ACT I

PAPA: (*Papa is sitting at the head of the table*) Where is everybody? (*Maid comes thru left door – looks and exits quickly*) I see you – where is my dinner?

MAMA: You are early dear (*sits at other end of table*). Tonight we have your favorite dish – wild rice and . . .

PAPA: If you want to make me really happy my daughter would be here at the table. Why can't she be prompt? Her five sisters were always here when they were supposed to be here.

MAMA: She is younger – almost another generation.

PAPA: Girls today see too many American movies. I tell you. . (*Daughter enters*)

GITA: Sorry I'm late.

PAPA: What were you doing that you forgot to be prompt to even respect your father? Your mother expects you to be at meals on time.

GITA: Yes Papa. (*Maid enters with food and stands by Papa's chair*).

PAPA: Make sure this doesn't happen again.

PAPA: Say it.

GITA: Yes Papa it will not happen again. (*Under breath*) Unless I can't help it.

PAPA: I will say no more about it. Do you have something to add?

MAMA: (*Shakes head no*)

PAPA: (*To Mama*) Speak up woman. (*To maid who has put a portion on Papa's plate.*) Keep putting more on my dish, keep doing it until I tell you to stop.

MAMA: Motion to stop. (*Maid gets confused and drops some food on the floor)*

MAMA: Never mind. Just put down the dish and then go and get something to clean up that mess.

PAPA: Before wives stopped serving men, there were never these problems – then the women saw to it that men had ample to eat. Yes, then women could eat with other women and talk with their mouths full. Now it is men and women together and it's nothing but a mess (*pointing to the spilled food).*

MAMA: Would you like me to wait on you dear?

PAPA: You know that isn't what I meant. I am a modern man and you woman are an emancipated Indian female (*starts to eat).*

GITA: (*Coughs*) (*Maid enters, serves mother, goes to Gita*)

GITA: Nothing for me. Thank you.

PAPA: That is not the food she dropped on the floor.

GITA: Yes, I know that.

PAPA: Then eat.

GITA: Excuse me Papa, but I am not hungry.

PAPA: Do you have a fever?

GITA: No Papa.

PAPA: What is wrong?

GITA: Nothing.

PAPA: You say nothing, but you won't eat. You look like you are going to cry any moment. Then what is the trouble?

GITA: Excuse me please (*runs away crying, exits left).*

PAPA: (*Takes a bite of food, then slams his fork on his plate*). There you see your daughter has spoiled my dinner. (*Maid takes dishes out*). It doesn't seem to disturb you that your baby girl won't eat, bursts into tears for no reason (*exit to door for no reason, then comes back to table*) Is there a reason for her actions?

MAMA: You know what it is.

PAPA: If I knew I wouldn't ask you. (*Eats– his plate is still on the table*)

MAMA: She has graduated from college.

PAPA: That couldn't make her unhappy.

MAMA: Each of her five sisters was married right after graduation and now that she has graduated, she isn't married.

PAPA: She just took her final exams a few weeks ago.

MAMA: When her sisters reached the same age, they were married.

PAPA: Yes, Yes I remember you told me that it was my duty to find them all suitable men. Fortunately, I had the money for excellent dowries.

MAMA: You do still have enough money for another good dowry, don't you?

PAPA: Of course, no trouble there. Gita being our last child, I thought we might keep her home for a while.

MAMA: That wouldn't be fair to her.

PAPA: Why not? What could a young husband give her that I couldn't do for her?

MAMA: (*Looks at Papa. He looks at her. Then he gets the point.*)

PAPA: Yes, yes – don't worry. Tomorrow I will talk to the marriage broker. I think a rich merchant would blend in with our family. Or maybe a high officer in the army. That might be a good change from so many merchant son-in-laws.

MAMA: Don't you think a high officer might be too old for Gita?

PAPA: Nonsense woman, an older man would be better established. I personally think someone in the diplomatic corps would give her an interesting life and I would be proud to say, "This is my is my son-in-law." Yes, yes the wife of the ambassador to say Ireland – yes, oh yes – Gita would like to become an ambassador's wife, right?

MAMA: Why don't you ask her?

PAPA: Woman, you mean to say your daughter wouldn't want an ambassador for a husband? Wait. I'll prove that you are wrong *(mumbles, rings bell for maid – maid enters)* Tell Gita that I wish to see her right away. *(Maid exits)* Now woman, I don't want you to answer for her. She is capable of speaking for herself. *(Gita stands at the door.)*

GITA: Papa you wanted to see me?

PAPA: Yes, yes – I want to talk to you about a serious matter. Come sit down here. It's time we thought about getting you married. Your papa has ample dowry for you so that you can marry most any man. What do you say about that?

GITA: Whatever you say Papa.

PAPA: *(Looks at wife)* That's my girl. *(To wife)* See what did I tell you?

MAMA: Your father is going to contact a marriage broker.

GITA: *(Runs and hugs Papa))* Thank you Papa dear.

PAPA: That's my girl, my baby daughter. In fact, I'll call the broker now – the one I used for your sisters and tell him what I want.

MAMA: *(Whispers to Gita)* You must tell Papa what kind of a man you want.

PAPA: Why are the two of you always whispering behind my back?

GITA: The only kind of man I want is a doctor of medicine.

PAPA: Have you a rare disease or is there something you're not telling me about?

GITA: No, no – I just think most doctors are very compassionate, intelligent and understanding people.

PAPA: There is more to a man than that. The man must be honest, reliable, generous, willing to talk things over with his wife and come from a good family. Yes, yes a good family instills basic principles.

MAMA: How true. I agree with you Papa.

GITA: He can have all of those things and be a doctor of medicine.

PAPA: (*Clears his throat.*) If you need me, I'll be in the study where I'll be phoning the marriage broker (*said as he exits left*).

MAMA: Papa is thinking of an ambassador.

GITA: Why? I wouldn't like that. I'd be in some foreign country and I'd rarely get to see you or my sisters and their families.

MAMA: You must tell Papa how you feel.

GITA: Ever since I was a little girl I dreamed of being a doctor's wife.

MAMA: Dreams don't always come true.

GITA: Not in your generation, but now women are getting more of what they want.

MAMA: A man's profession is very important but his character and his ambitions also count.

PAPA: (*Enters*) The marriage counselor says that he has an ambassador. He is a widower, 60 years old and is the Indian ambassador to a small country in Africa.

GITA: Papa, he is a lot older than you. What else does he have?

PAPA: A college professor, 47, teaches anthropology at some small private college here in Southern India.

GITA: Still too old. He sounds dull – yuk!

PAPA: What do you want?

GITA: A doctor of medicine that's young, and oh yes, he should be taller than me.

PAPA: You want a doctor of medicine? I asked the broker and he says that he never gets doctors.

MAMA: Why not?

PAPA: He suggested that if I want a doctor in my family, I should look into my Rotary Club, my golf club and ask my social friends. Well, young lady, I can tell you right now that in my clubs and among my friends – there are no doctors, not even sons of doctors.

GITA: Then I will stay an old maid.

PAPA: Good. You can take care of your mother in her old age.

GITA: *(Starts to cry.)*

PAPA: *(To wife)* Do something – help your daughter.

MAMA: *(Starts to sniffle)*

PAPA: Stop crying both of you. Crying will not solve anything. Let us discuss logically what we can do to find a doctor.

MAMA: *(Still sniffling)* I could find an unmarried plastic surgeon and have him take out my fat.

PAPA: I wouldn't permit it. *(Sees look on mama's face – he stops)* I wouldn't permit it. If he were already a practicing surgeon – he would probably be married. What else?

GITA: You could advertise.

PAPA: What would I say? "Wealthy father has a smart college graduate daughter who wants a physician husband?

MAMA: I already tried an ad for someone and all the response I got was what is our cast and if the girl was fair-skinned. Anyway, the mothers that answered came from very small villages. Probably if any were in the medical profession, they would be barefoot doctors without a degree or anything. Just think they probably don't even have indoor plumbing. (*both women cry even louder*)

PAPA: Never mind. I won't tell you about anything until I have worked it all out.

GITA: You are the best father in the entire world. Papa, as long as Mama and I know this much, please keep telling us everything so we can be behind you the whole way.

PAPA: (*Both women put their arms around Papa*) How can I think with two such dear women so close? I'll tell you what I will do. Tomorrow night at dinnertime I will tell you my plan. Don't either one of you say anything or ask one question before dinner. Now both of you leave me alone while I try to work on the plans of what to do. (*Gita kisses him on the head and exits left*)

MAMA: You aren't going to do anything dangerous, are you?

PAPA: You know me; I always plan everything very carefully before I make any moves. When I have decided I stick with it to the very end. Yes, yes – forever. (*Mama brings the tea and brings him sugar. She adds sugar to his cup and stirs it for Papa.*)

MAMA: The chai is very sweet – just how you like it.

PAPA: You always fix my tea just right for me. You are a good woman and an all right wife. (*Mama pats him on the shoulder, exits left*)

(*Papa sips the chai and takes a paper out of his pocket. He draws and mumbles*)

PAPA: 1. Objective doctor. 2. Question: Where are doctors found? 3. Answer: Hospitals. 4. Which is the best hospital in Southern India? 5. A teaching hospital is supposed to be one of the very best.

MUSIC. LIGHTS DOWN AND UP QUICKLY ON APRON OF STAGE.

PAPA: (*enters elevator, looks at tag on man in white: "Raja". Papa can't quite read tag*) Are you a doctor?

RAJA (*Nods*) Yes.

PAPA: Family Practices? (*Raja nods*) That means you'll go to a little town or to Bombay?

RAJA: I haven't decided yet.

PAPA: You have a choice?

(*White-coated man enters. He smiles and nods at Raja*)

WHITE-COATED MAN: Get any sleep? I haven't. I'm afraid of going to sleep on my feet. (*Everybody gives feeling that elevator is moving*)

PAPA: Any of you not married? (*White-coated man looks at Raja, turns and looks at Papa*) I mean are either of you interested in a big dowry, a pretty, slim girl that is a college graduate? You'd be getting a good wife.

RAJA: I'm not interested now.

PAPA: All I ask is that you think about it. (*The white coat and Raja get out of elevator, shaking their heads and laughing*)

PAPA: (*Calls after them*) I'll be back (*mumbles*) at this moment those young men don't like my style. After all, I am a salesman. I can sell everybody anything. Those men are India's brain tank. They will keep thinking about it. (*Looks at watch*) That is exactly what I want them to do – to laugh, to talk, and to think about that big dowry. Every man has a price. I'll find theirs or his.

MUSIC. LIGHTS DOWN AND UP ON PAPA'S DINING ROOM.

MAMA: (*Is fussing with flowers on table – Gita is walking, pacing, and talking*)

GITA: What is Papa doing?

MAMA: I'm sure that he is doing something good for you. *(Enter Papa. Both women turn and look eagerly at Papa)*

PAPA: *(Sits)* Let us have dinner first. *(Mama rings bell. Maid appears)*

MAMA: You may serve dinner now.

GITA: I can't wait. Please, what about the doctors? What did they say?

PAPA: *(Smiles)* I am in perfect health.

GITA: For that I am grateful to the gods but you know what I mean. *(Maid appears with food)*

PAPA: Dinner first. I am hungry. I wish to eat my dinner now.

GITA: Your wonderful plan, Papa, please tell us all about it.

PAPA: It is a good one even if I say so myself. I will lay the entire plan before you. Put more on my plate. Do you think me a bird that eats only one seed?

MAMA: You are a wonderful man. Unlike other husbands and fathers you share your plans with us. Eat well. *(Maid piles food on the plate)*

PAPA: *(Eats then pushes dish away)* All right, I'll tell you this much. I spent the day at the hospital. Now I will eat my food. *(Maid goes to Mama. She shakes her hand no. Maid goes to Gita. She shakes her head no. Both women stare at Papa.)* Have you already eaten before I came home? Then give the ladies chai and I'll have my usual.

GITA: No, we waited for you to come home. I am not hungry now. Are you finished eating Papa?

PAPA: *(Pats his stomach)* So what is it you want?

GITA: You left us when you were in the hospital.

PAPA: Yes, yes – I was at the hospital.

MAMA: You have a plan.

PAPA: (*Smiles, stands, walks*) Yes, I put the first part into action.

MAMA: We know. It was very good. What did you do?

PAPA: I thought to myself, where do doctors go in the hospital and I answered myself that they go to surgery, but I can't go there. Where else do doctors go? They eat, so I looked in the cafeteria. You wouldn't believe it – so many fathers sitting there talking and trying their best (*laughs*). I saw one little man buying tea for a man in white.

GITA: That's not you. What did you think to do?

PAPA: Don't interrupt. It's very rude.

MAMA: Papa has a plan

PAPA: Right. Number 1. I was to go to the hospital. My number 2 plan is very clever. I said to myself I figured those young doctors ride the elevator. So I rode the elevator.

GITA: To where?

PAPA: Elevators usually go up and down. So I went up and down.

MAMA: (*Rings bell, maid appears*) The chai is getting cold. (*The maid exits left*)

GITA: (*Bends toward Mama, whispers*) How many years is his plan going to take? (*Papa chuckling*)

MAMA: (*Whispering*) I don't know. At least he's on an elevator.

PAPA: I rode up. No one. I rode down. No one. Then, yes, yes some white coats got on the elevator. Doctors wear white coats.

GITA: You talked to them?

PAPA: I asked them who is interested in marrying a pretty college graduate with a big dowry.

MAMA: See, Papa's plan worked. There must have been many, many men that responded favorably.

PAPA: Frankly, none.

GITA: (*Sniffling, kind of crying*)

MAMA: What did you do?

PAPA: Same thing, kept riding the elevator down and up. Finding a man is like riding an elevator. Sometimes you go up and sometimes you go down. (*Sighs*) Yes, yes.

GITA: No one?

PAPA: Not really. Wait.

MAMA: Surely there was one?

GITA: Stop riding the elevator.

GITA: (*Mumbles*) That's what you always say about everything. Wait. (*Out loud*) I have no one. (*Exits left crying*) No one. No one at all.

MAMA: How does it really look?

PAPA: There is one that isn't married. I'll work on him. Oh, don't look so sad. The elevator is always running. There are many men with white coats. Just wait. 'Can not exactly read a man's mind but he responded and that gives me an opening. It is through that little opening – that place that I will get in – and I'll have him. You'll see. Now can we talk about something else?

MAMA: What would you like to talk about?

PAPA: Me. For a change.

MAMA: Do you have a headache? (*Papa nods yes*) (*Mama goes to Papa and rubs his neck and shoulders.*)

LIGHTS DIM OUT, MUSIC, LIGHTS UP IN ELEVATOR.

PAPA: Hold the elevator. (*Moves away from a very dirty patient. Looks at white coats*) Anybody single? (*Dirty patient raises hand*) Do you need a large dowry? (*Dirty patient raises two hands*) Pretty college graduate. Young, marriageable age. (*White coats exit*)

RAJA: (*Looks at dirty patient trying to touch Papa. Laughs, shakes head Indian way.*) Yes, no. Don't ask, I'm not interested (*pause*) yet.

PAPA: Did I hear you correctly? You said yet.

RAJA: Don't get your hopes up.

PAPA: We are almost relatives. Yes, yes. At least friends. Everyday we share one elevator and ride it up and down.

RAJA: Sorry, that it is always down for you.

PAPA: The elevator goes up and when it's going up, I'll always be on the UP elevator. You too could be going UP in the world.

RAJA: It depends on what your values are. I am a very modern sophisticated man. I do not want an arranged marriage.

PAPA: I agree with you. That is why I am just inviting you to come to my house for dinner.

RAJA: To meet your darling daughter?

PAPA: I thought only for a fine and delicious dinner. After the cafeteria food – I imagine you might enjoy a different kind of meal.

RAJA: I'll think about it.

PAPA: I wouldn't think too long. Please hold the door for me. I'll go now but I'll be back and we can talk some more. By the way, what time do you come on duty? And at what time do you get off duty?

RAJA: (*Laughs*) I'm not going to tell you that.

MUSIC. LIGHTS OUT. LIGHTS UP ON PAPA'S HOUSE.

PAPA: I'm home.

MAMA: (*to maid*) You may serve dinner now.

PAPA: What's for dinner?

MAMA: One of your favorites.

PAPA: Where is Gita?

GITA: I'm here Papa. Anything new about the man in white? (*Maid is serving*)

PAPA. After dinner.

GITA: (*Mumbles*) That's what you always say to control.

PAPA: (*Laughs*) Yes, yes I saw the little man, Sagur, in the cafeteria. He's still buying tea for all of the doctors.

GITA: Has he found anyone?

PAPA: I have not heard anything about it. I certainly would have heard if he has caught the mouse even if the mouse were nibbling. (*To wife*) Woman, have you heard anything among your female friends?

MAMA: The women aren't talking. However, his wife is bragging that her daughter may become engaged in the very near future.

PAPA: To whom?

MAMA: All I know is that he is handsome, young, and very well-educated.

PAPA: That could be anyone. Find out his name and what department he's in. Nothing to worry about. (*Mumbles*) It could be the anthropologist.

MAMA: No. That woman will tell only what she wants everybody to know.

PAPA: She's a mother with a child. She will brag – you just lead her on a bit.

GITA: Papa, you are the best barterer in India.

PAPA: That is saying something. (*Pushing plate away*) Just some more chai. (*Laughs*) As you can see, I do not have tea at the hospital like some people I know. But yes, yesterday it felt like I was most successful in my project. The young man told me that he was a modern, sophisticated man and did not want an arranged marriage.

GITA: Sorry Papa. Now you might have to look somewhere else.

PAPA: That's the trouble with your generation. You give up too soon.

GITA: He just told you that he didn't want an arranged marriage.

PAPA: When I'm after something I never take no for an answer. Listen carefully to this. I invited him to just come over for dinner.

MAMA: Did he agree to that?

PAPA: Not exactly. Not at the moment.

MAMA: I must know ahead of time when he's coming so I can have the cook prepare something special.

PAPA: Yes, yes. I always tell you.

MAMA: Thank you. You are a good husband and father.

PAPA: The best husband and father. See, I already have that young man thinking about coming to dinner.

GITA: How long do you suppose it will take him to think about it?

PAPA: Will you stop being so impatient? In business every deal has its own character and takes its own sweet time. I have planted the seed. Now it must take root and I shall water it and nourish it and it will grow. Then we shall see.

MAMA: Are you encouraged?

PAPA: Yes I am.

MAMA: Then I too am encouraged. I was thinking soon there will be a holiday and that would be a perfect time for him to be our guest for dinner.

PAPA: We'll see.

GITA: When are you going to ride the elevator again?

PAPA: It's my life. I ride the elevator every day.

MAMA: Then you will ask him tomorrow to come?

PAPA: We will see.

GITA: You'll do it, Papa. You will carry it off.

LIGHTS DIM AND OUT. UP ON ELEVATOR.

PAPA: (*Is in the elevator*)

RAJA: (*Steps into elevator*) It's you again.

PAPA: Have you been thinking about your future? How long has it been since you have had an elegant dinner?

RAJA: Not since I entered medical school. Now all I do is study, take exams and treat patients.

PAPA: You do know that one our most important religious holidays is next week. I would like to have you at my house for the finest dinner of your life. This is my address. My card. (*Hands him a card*). I will send my car for you.

RAJA: That won't be necessary. I can get there by public transportation. What time did you say I should be there for dinner?

PAPA: Whatever time you get off duty? Then we'll have that special dinner ready for you. (*Papa gets out of elevator*).

LIGHTS OUT AND UP ON HOUSE.

PAPA: Where is everybody?

MAMA: Gita is bathing. The cook and the maids are busy in the kitchen.

PAPA: Good. Good.

MAMA: I am having a maid go to the store for one little item the grocer forgot to send us. I want everything to be just perfect.

PAPA: Don't let there be any accidents or problems with the staff.

MAMA: Only the serving maid tore her apron and when she gets back from the store, she will mend it. Please don't look at the table yet. I will personally set it, but first I must go and see how everything is progressing in the kitchen. (*Mama exits, stage left*)

PAPA: I will take a short swim. (*Exits left, whistling*)

MAID: (*Enters, mumbles*) I feel naked without my apron. (*Doorbell, maid crosses to door, right*). Good evening sir.

RAJA: (*He has a small bunch of flowers in his hand*) I am Dr. Raja.

MAID: Doctor? We didn't call for a doctor. Nobody is sick here. (*Maid tries to hide part of her body where she usually wears her apron*)

RAJA: They are expecting me for dinner.

MAID: Just sit down any place (*crosses to UC door*).

RAJA: Aren't you going to announce me?

MAID: I have to go to the grocery store. Just wait. (*She exits UC*)

MAMA: (*Enters, starts to set table*) (*Enters maid*) What took you so long?

MAID: I sneaked around. I didn't want anyone to see me without my apron. Ma'am, do you want me to set the table?

MAMA: No, I'll do it. Go mend your apron.

MAID: Yes, ma'am. (*Picks up flowers Raja brought, exits left*)

PAPA: (*Enters left*) I always feel better after a swim.

MAMA: That's good dear.

PAPA: Where's Gita?

MAMA: (*Giggles*) I guess she is still getting ready.

GITA: (*Enters*) Shouldn't Raja be here by now?

MAMA: (*Looks at watch*) Yes, he should have been here quite some time ago. But everyone always comes later and later to social functions.

PAPA: We'll hold dinner. Go tell them in the kitchen to keep the food warm. (*Mama exits left*)

GITA: He's late (*paces*). That isn't a good sign. Papa, what do you think about calling him?

PAPA: At the hospital?

GITA: That is where he hangs out.

PAPA: I'll give him a little more time. I would like some chai before he gets here.

GITA: I'll get it for you. (*Exits left*)

PAPA: (*Looks to see if anyone can see him. Phones.*) Please I would like to talk to Dr. Raja (*voice trails off*) (*Loudly*) He left the hospital hours ago? Did he say when he would be back? No, no message. I'll call him again. (*Paces*) How could he be so rude? What shall I do now? Yes, yes I'll see him in the elevator. I will tell him, angry like, that we waited for you last night. No, it's better if I say something like this, very sweetly, "Did you have a nice evening? Why the hell didn't you call if you didn't plan on coming?" (*Mama enters*)

MAMA: What should we do? Dinner will be overcooked.

PAPA: Then let us eat now.

MAMA: Now? What about our guest? (*Gita enters with flowers*)

MAMA: Where did you get those pretty flowers?

GITA: The maid found them on the dining room table.

MAMA: Who brought them? Did you buy them PAPA?

PAPA: Not me. I never give flowers (*Maid enters*). Where did these flowers come from?

MAID: The kitchen.

PAPA: Before that?

MAID: The dining room table.

PAPA: Before that? Could it be from a garden? Who left them on the table?

MAID: Uh. Oh.

MAMA: She's thinking.

MAID: The young man.

GITA: Who?

MAID: The one that came before madam sent me to the store for the things.

PAPA: That's it. Why didn't you tell me?

MAMA: You were swimming and I am never to disturb you when you read, talk on the phone or swim.

PAPA: Now what do I say to him?

MAMA: You'll think of something to say.

PAPA: (*Looks hard at her*) You women are no help. Just plan on repeating this dinner another night.

GITA: (*Says as she exits*) This is just the right way to start a romance.

MAMA: I'm sorry.

PAPA: (*To white coats in elevator*) Excuse me.

RAJA: Hold the door. I'm getting off.

PAPA: (*Pushes elevator button. Everyone jerks about. Says to Raja*) Wait. It's not what you think.

RAJA: I am thinking all of this came from the mind of a very sick person.

PAPA: True. You were about an hour early, the maid tore her apron and so she was upset. So, that is why she didn't tell anyone that you were here. All she could think about was that darn apron.

RAJA: (*Whispers*) Kindly lower your voice. I am embarrassed.

PAPA: So am I.

RAJA: (*In a low voice*) I know nothing about a maid. (*whispers*) It was your (*sarcastically*) beautiful daughter that opened the door.

PAPA: No, that is wrong.

RAJA: (*Pushes elevator button. Elevator stops. Everyone is thrown around. Everyone gives them both a dirty look and they exit.*)

RAJA: (*To white coats*) I'm sorry. (*To Papa*) I'm getting off here. I'm also off with you and any member of your family. I am through with all of you.

PAPA: (*Puts himself between Raja and door*) One minute please. My daughter never answers the door. Only the maids do that.

RAJA: (*Looks at Papa hard*)

PAPA: I am telling you the truth. If it is not so may I go to my grave with my parents' curses on my head.

RAJA: You are certain it was the maid that I saw?

PAPA: My daughter is about so tall and very slender, while the maid (*Puffs up his cheeks*) is very well-fed. (*Draws a picture with his hands. Laughs*)

RAJA: I guess that was the maid. She was obese. Yes (*nods*), I should have called you. What must you think of me?

PAPA: Let us forget all that. Just put all that behind us and we shall start fresh. Now, when can you have dinner for us?

RAJA: I'll call you.

PAPA: Not good enough (*Presses button on elevator*). We are going up and down on the elevator until we settle a time, please.

RAJA: Not this weekend. I'm on duty.

PAPA: When are you off?

RAJA: The weekend after next.

PAPA: That would be a Saturday. Say 7:00 pm. Is that a good time for you?

RAJA: (*Looking at little book*) That looks clear to me. I'll be there at 7 o'clock.

PAPA: Don't worry about that. My car and driver will pick you up at 6:15 pm.

RAJA: The car won't be necessary.

PAPA: I insist. You just come and be sure to be hungry.

RAJA: You did say that I had to come only one time and then you'd leave me alone, right?

PAPA: (*Laughs*) This is your floor.

RAJA: You know?

PAPA: You've gone down and up often enough.

RAJA: Enough for me to know that now we are going up together maybe. Just for a short time. Life is just like an elevator – it has its ups and downs. (*Sighs*) You talked me into it. Good bye, Sir.

PAPA: I never say good-bye. (*Waves, door starts to close. Papa presses button, mumbles*) The bird is in the trap (*sighs*). I hate elevators. (*Elevator jerks*) Why is this elevator stopping between floors? (*Yells*) Hello out there. I'm trapped in this darn elevator. (*Hysterically pounding and screaming*) Someone let me out. Come here and get me out of this damn elevator.

BLACK OUT. LIGHTS UP. MUSIC. DINING ROOM.

MAMA: (*Is looking out of window up stage*) Where can Papa be?

GITA: Papa probably left the office late and got tied up in traffic. You know how that can be.

MAMA: He's probably riding that elevator up-and-down. You know how stubborn he can be.

GITA: The worst. But I still love him. Do you think there is any chance for Raja and me?

MAMA: First I must meet him before I can make any judgment. Then, it's what Papa says.

GITA: What about Raja and me? Don't we have a say?

MAMA: You have said enough. You told your father that you wanted a doctor and he, the dear man, is trying to please you and make you happy. So the final word will be up to Papa.

GITA: I am not marrying Papa and Papa isn't marrying the man I marry, so the last word will be up to me.

MAMA: Don't let Papa hear you say that.

GITA: You can bet if I don't like Raja, I'll let Papa know about it. Of course, in a nice way.

MAMA: What would your poor father do?

GITA: Probably ride the elevator at the hospital.

MAMA: I think not. Papa is almost at the end of his rope. (*Sound of key in door. Both women run to the door*) May the gods bless him. My heavens he looks like he has been in an accident or a fight.

GITA: (*At door*) Poor Papa. What is wrong?

PAPA: (*Leans on Mama*) Woman, you can know what I've been through. I was riding the elevator. (*Women are taking Papa to sit down*)

MAMA: Up and down. (*Papa gives Mama a dirty look*).

PAPA: When the elevator got stuck between floors. Everyone went into a panic and fought.

GITA: Oh, Papa dear. (*Throws arms around Papa*)

PAPA: No it wasn't like that. I was the only one in the elevator.

MAMA: Do you often ride the elevator by yourself?

PAPA: (*Gives Mama a dirty look*) No woman (*To Gita*) Yes, yes I stayed very calm through the entire ordeal. I pushed the emergency button but it didn't work. People had been pushing the emergency one to just get themselves off the elevator. Now when I needed that button – it didn't work. Nothing at all happened. So I waited and waited. After an eternity, I called out (*Mama rings bell*) that someone was stuck in the elevator. The gods were looking favorably on me or I wouldn't be here now. (*Mama is helping Papa off with his coat. Maid appears*) Just imagine . . . (*to daughter*) I could still be in there.

MAMA: (*To maid*) Bring a clean shirt and some slightly warm water in a basin. We'll also need some towels. (*Maid exits*)

GITA: Should I call the doctor?

PAPA: No, no doctor. To go on with what happened, after an eternity of time, a janitor answered me. He said that it was after hours for the handyman and that all the tinkerers were gone. That meant that I would be trapped until morning. I asked the man if there was any other way. He suggested that I could climb out of the elevator – that he was willing to lower a rope to me from the floor above. This rope, he said, could be tied around me. (*Maid brings things and exits*) First I hesitated, but as the hours drew on, I thought that the elevator could give way and you both know what that would mean. So I went ahead with the rope plan.

MAMA: You poor darling.

GITA: So that's how you got all dirty, mussed and banged up. What happened with Raja?

PAPA: The rope swung me against this wall and that wall – over and over again.

GITA: I'm glad that you didn't have a fight with Raja.

PAPA: Of course not. But, you do know that if I had fought him, I would have won.

MAMA: Of course, dear. You are a strong man.

GITA: You did talk to Raja, didn't you?

PAPA: (*Snickers*) He came very early. He thought that the maid was you.

GITA: That is no excuse for leaving.

PAPA: Wouldn't you? He thought that I was misrepresenting you.

GITA: That's for sure. Now I know I have to see him.

PAPA: You will. He's coming for dinner.

MAMA: I must know when.

PAPA: The week after next. I'm sending the car for him. This time I'm not taking any chances.

GITA: What is the guarantee on getting him into the car?

MAMA: (*Mama rings bell for maid. Maid enters*) You may serve dinner now.

PAPA: Both of you eat your dinner. I'm going to bed.

GITA: I'm so sorry for you Papa.

MAMA: I wish I could undo the dreadful experience you had.

PAPA: (*At door*) Be sure the serving maid knows what to as and what to do when Raja comes here.

MAMA: I'll take care of it. (*Papa exits*) Now, let's talk about what kind of wedding you want.

GITA: Not yet. I may not want this man.

MAMA: Papa will not ride any more elevators.

GITAA: Then he will just have to think of other ways to meet my doctor husband.

MAMA: I must go now and fix a plate of food for PAPA. He'll probably eat in bed – after he calls his sisters and their families to tell them about his narrow escape.

GITA: If you want me to, I'll bring the food up to Papa.

MAMA: You may as well start to get used to taking care of a man.

GITA: You'd do better to train my husband how to take care of me.

MAMA: (*Sighs*) I heard that there are many who refuse to travel from the country this way. But they would all be at your wedding.

GITA: You are afraid of feeding everyone that comes this way. Don't be worried; I know that the poor come and go at the wedding feast and that everyone is fed. But you, you will manage beautifully.

MAMA: Yes, we will treat them right.

LIGHTS OFF ON STAGE. MUSIC UP. LIGHTS UP IN AUDIENCE.

• INTERMISSION *

The crowd roared with laughter as the lights dimmed and Alan turned to his accompanying 'dates' to find Tiffany wiping tears from her eyes.

"She gets better every time I see a play of hers!" Tiffany said. "I really must thank her, will you excuse me?" The cruise director got up and scooted down the aisles of seats to kneel beside Babette's chair.

"You've got a good one there, you know!" Elsie waved a crochet hook at the doctor. "Now don't go spoiling it for her."

"Of course, I wouldn't think of it." The doctor smiled warmly at Elsie, who was only teasing him after all.

When Tiffany came back she was still giggling to herself, and, promising to catch up with Elsie Ruttersgate the next day, but she definitely did *not* promise to give her the answers to the upcoming Trivia Quiz. Alan and Tiffany shuffled out with a number of the other passengers.

"Thank you for this evening's entertainment, it was lovely." The cruise director sneaked a kiss on his cheek. "Same again tomorrow night?"

"You bet. I wouldn't miss it for the world." The doctor assured her, feeling on top of the world at the moment. "But right now I need to get back to the infirmary and check how Nurse Watkins is doing; she will just be starting her night shift, I believe."

Tiffany pouted. "Well, I guess I should get an early night for a change too; ready to hit the beach volleyball tomorrow." She winked at him and made her way through the decks to her cabin, still smiling from the play.

Alan watched her leave for a long time, eating up the sight of her and feeling truly content for the first time in this long, stressful journey.

The contentment was shattered when he arrived in the infirmary to find Nurse Watkins flustered by a new patient.

The man was a burly individual, with large hands and a broad neck, wearing the uniform of one of the below deck staff, Kelly was cleaning one of his feet and looked up with a worried glance as the doctor walked in.

"What seems to be the matter, nurse?" He hurried over, peeling off his tuxedo jacket and sliding on some blue exam gloves.

"Infection, Doctor." was all that she said. There, spreading over the man's foot was the puffy red swelling surrounded by tiny raised dots. What appeared to be the same infection that both Ernesto and Kelly had acquired. In this man however, it was made worse by a purpling bruise that spread from the man's ankle to the top of his foot.

"I see." Alan swung into his professional physician's mode easily, calling for some providone, iodine, saline, and some dressing material.

"When did you first notice this?" Alan asked the man; eager to relax the worried look he wore across his face.

"Not quite sure Doc, I dropped some luggage on it a couple of days ago as we were re-shifting the hull for extra provisions. It hurt like hell for a couple of days, but I just thought that was the bruise, and then all these red dots came up."

"You appear to have an infection – you probably got it when you hurt your foot unless you have been doing any unusual activities on shore?" The doctor hummed and aahh'd as he looked at it from all angles. "It's not serious yet – a simple course of antibiotics should cure it, as long as you keep it clean."

"Thank you, Doc." The man was obviously relieved.

"Do you know where you could have picked the infection up? What were you moving around?" Alan was curious. So far the infection had only affected the 'below decks' staff, Ernesto the cleaner, his girlfriend Kelly and now this porter.

The man looked mystified. "There's a lot of luggage down there, Doc. I was shifting some of the heavier suitcases and crates down there when I dropped what I was moving."

The doctor looked serious. "Could you locate which luggage or crate you had dropped?" He didn't say it but he was beginning to think that he could possibly isolate the source of the infection and retrace the steps or path it took to come aboard the ship.

"Well, I could probably show you whereabouts I was working, but I couldn't really tell you exactly which one it was."

"That would be great. What time do you start your shift in the morning?"

The man threw a quizzical gaze at the doctor. "I start at seven o'clock."

"Okay, let's meet outside the crew's mess at a quarter to

seven?"

The porter nodded, before muttering his thanks to Kelly while gingerly putting his boot on over the bandaging and hobbling off.

"I'm glad I showed up when I did," Alan said, beaming at Kelly. "We might be able to find the cause of these infections, and stop whatever it is, before it starts to do anyone any real harm. And, will you let me know right away if you see any more rashes like this one?"

"Sure, Doc, I'll page you as soon as someone else comes in...."

CHAPTER EIGHTEEN

Spanish Waters
The crate and the volleyball

THE NEXT DAY HAD INDEED been one of sun and frivolity as Tiffany had arranged an impromptu volleyball tournament on the private beach near their mooring spot. Unfortunately Alan had been stuck aboard the vessel and unable to attend as he tried to track down the mysterious source of the infection on board the *Ocean Quest*.

He met the porter outside the crew mess below deck early that morning, and had made his way down through the many storage areas to one of the cargo holds of the cruise ship.

The duo would probably have made a strange sight as they descended one deck, and then another, he in his official whites of the ship's doctor carrying his doctor's emergency case and wearing exam gloves, to avoid cross contamination. Down below decks it was always a hive of activity as loaders and engineers constantly hurried from one place to another to check the internal working of the vessel and to prepare it for each port and departure.

Entering into a large hold, which was sectioned off with wire container areas to prevent luggage shifting and to make it easier to sort on arrival and departure, the crewmember led the doctor past various bays, all numbered and coded until he found the bay that he had been working in. Using his electronic key card to open the luggage cage, he invited the doctor to begin his examination of whatever he needed to do.

This luggage bay was reserved for the heaviest and bulkiest of the passengers' luggage, boxes and crates that were occasionally brought on as a part of the goods that they bought whilst on their trips, or if they were on long and extended voyages. White plastic tubs, the size of small tables, and reinforced wood crates were stacked up against the walls in a human sized 3D jigsaw puzzle.

The porter indicated one particular part of the bay where he had been stowing and strapping down with heavy canvas baggage straps a series of plastic tubs and one, very large wooden crate.

"It was that one, I think," the porter said. "Yeah, that bugger caught me something awful on my foot when I had to shift her. That's the one for sure."

"Is it possible to remove it from the stack?" Alan enquired as he examined the outside of the crate. The porter agreed and went off to get a few of the other porters to help him shift it out into the open area of the luggage cage.

The crate itself was a simple, large wooden box. It was well sealed with heavy nails bolted into its frame, but with no special markings on it. The only other thing that he noticed were areas of what looked like dried mud on the outside edges, as if the crate had been packed in wet, earthy conditions before drying when it was transported.

When the team of luggage porters had come back and shifted it out, the doctor asked, "Isn't this thing supposed to have tags on it, or a code?"

"Yes sir, all items should have the electronic print out that we use to discern whose is whose. It's a bit of a mystery why this one doesn't..." He scratched his chin as he nudged it with his boot.

"No, don't do that!" Alan suddenly reached forward to pull the crewmember back. "I want to get this crate quarantined immediately. If it is responsible for your infection, then it could be that mud on the side that you have just disturbed which carries an infective agent."

The assembled porters suddenly took long, repulsive steps backwards. Alan had to grin at the disgusted chorus of movement.

"It should be quite safe as long as you don't get the dust onto your skin, or into any wounds or cuts. If we can carefully move it to an empty luggage cage with orders for no one to touch it, then we should be safe. We'll get some anti-bacterial detergents we keep up in the medical center to wash this whole area down with the assistance of the housekeeping team."

The porters looked grateful, and gingerly moved the thing to an adjacent cage, which was still to be filled. Cruise ships often had extra space in their holds, as a part of their safety precautions for the long sea voyages ahead and to rearrange cargo when needed.

"Now how can we find out who it belongs to and what's inside it?" he wondered aloud, before he called Vince. A thought popped into his head; how he had first met Ernesto and had unintentionally started off the flowering romance between him and Nurse Watkins.

"Tell me; is there a Stefano working down here today?" he asked the men. The one whom he had recently treated the night before spoke up, saying; "Yeah, he's just over there on the short term luggage, I'll call him over."

Stefano, Ernesto's 'friend', who worked as a luggage handler, sidled up and looked apprehensively at the ship's doctor.

"Good morning, Stefano, I am Doctor Mayhew and this matter is of vital importance. Did you help stow this crate on the first day of the cruise, in Rome? And did you get a cleaner named Ernesto to help you?"

Stefano looked as though he would lie for a second, but under the disapproving glances of his fellow workmen hung his head and admitted that he had.

*   *   *

"And so you see, Vince"—Alan was speaking animatedly to the security chief—"the container was rushed through the security checks because it came in as a very last minute arrival. The department manager had already clocked off his shift, leaving Stefano to oversee the last of the loading of the cargo from Rome."

"But how do we find out who it belongs to, or what is *in* it?" Vince asked dubiously. "We can't just go around cracking open clients' luggage here and there. And this crate did not even have the usual identifying marks on it. Then, of course, if it is a hazardous material, it should not have been boarded in the first place."

To which point the doctor nodded vigorously. While Vince had been trying to figure how it got on board without the usual procedure, Alan had taken a small sample of the dust back to the medical center and had tried his best to analyze it. Microbiology and virology were not his fields of expertise, but he could definitely say that there was a pathogen of some sort in the manner in which it reacted under the microscope, in the mini lab on board. The mixture only appeared to need some organic matter and water to be reactivated from its dried, inert state.

Vince postulated, "Well, as it is hazardous material we need to know who is to be held responsible. I will also have to have a talk with the baggage handling manager and this young Stefano chap."

Alan agreed. "Yes, it will be all too easy for whoever is responsible for bringing this hazardous item on board the ship to deny any ownership of it, and it appears to be a very dangerous item. Just by merely handling it, two crewmembers have become infected, Ernesto for trying to 'help' his friend out, and this other porter for having the thing fall on his foot."

"Shame it wasn't Stefano who got ill," Vince grumbled. The doctor could see that he, too, was annoyed that he didn't get to go ashore, or to the beach today.

A thought came into the doctor's head. "I think I have a plan," he said, and quickly left the disgruntled security chief in his office to further ponder the injustices of life on a cruise ship.

That afternoon the passengers started to arrive back on the *Ocean Quest*, tired and refreshed and ready for their Atlantic crossing to Bermuda. That evening would prove itself to be a fun one, starting with the next installment of Babette's play followed by a dance performance in the main theatre.

Babette herself was always pleased to have her plays included in the main attractions of the cruise ship entertainment. As she made her way back on deck, arm in arm with the assistant cruise director, she greeted the doctor warmly where he was waiting for Tiffany.

"I have been wondering where you've been hiding today," Babette said to Alan accusingly. "You do know that this young lady here has got a killer serve on the volleyball courts." She pointed to Tiffany by her side. She was resplendent in a white see through shirt and white shorts over an all-in-one swimsuit. To Alan's eyes she looked every bit the sun bunny, glowing with promises of vitality and adventure.

"I hope you enjoyed yourselves, ladies," Alan replied, a broad grin crossing his lips.

"I would have, Doc, if I hadn't had to coach young Stefan his lines the entire time that we were there," Babette said, laughing. "The boy's a great character actor, and looks stunning in a dress, but really, he has the memory of a frog." She referred to the fact that Stefan was comically playing the part of the maid in her play, 'Up the down Elevator'. "But now, you two will have to excuse me – I've got lots to do before tonight…." And in a moment, Babette disappeared below deck.

Alan peered down at his lovely lady, his grin still pasted on his face. They couldn't openly embrace on the open deck for all the passengers to see, but the long looks that they gave each other must have said it all. His gaze noticed every brush of sand that clung to her body in an almost sensuous way.

"Nice time aboard ship, Doctor Mayhew?" she asked coquettishly.

"Oh, you would not believe the turn of events this afternoon."

Alan then whispered the bare details to Tiffany as they walked the deck.

"That is great news." Tiffany replied. "You don't have to worry about the infection any more now that you have isolated and contained it at the source."

"Well, I wouldn't go that far just yet. There is still no firm diagnosis and we only suspect that the crate is the culprit. If it is, I would really like to throw the thing overboard no matter what's in it to be on the safe side and close off the cargo bay, but procedure must be followed. Vince will be on that as will the captain." He shrugged. "Did Diane Seinz come down to the beach with you? I was going to ask her to look at the samples of material I have, and see if she can recognize them."

"Yes. Besides, what's the point of having a microbiologist on board if you can't use her expertise? That's what I say." Tiffany laughed. "But no, I didn't see her down on the beach, neither she nor her husband. They might have gone out for a walk in town or on the beach. I didn't notice them on the way back either." She looked concerned, "I'll check their cabin and make sure that they are all right, in case they have gotten lost or something."

Alan knew that, by now, as the Assistant Cruise Director – however temporary the position might be – Tiffany took her job very seriously. She always wanted to make sure, on a personal level, that each of her clients was well and safe.

"Thank you, Cruise Director." Alan gave her a grateful smile. "Can you ask her to see if she could help me identify some toxins that I have uncovered? I will be down in the medical center shortly."

Tiffany returned the smile saying, "Yes. But now if you will excuse me, I have to get changed and hope that I don't look too out of place tonight after getting so much sun today."

As soon as Tiffany left, Alan hurried to the Medical Center, where, once again, he was met by the less than enthusiastic nurse Petra.

"More puking children," she announced, dumping another set of overalls in the laundry bin provided in the infirmary. Alan was amazed at her ability to seemingly attract the sick children. He rarely saw any ill kids – they seemed to come in always for minor requests of the nurse for seasick pills or Band-Aids. He did, of course, see the really sick ones that needed real medical attention.

Only shaking his head in reply, Alan set to work isolating a station and keeping it clear of contamination, when he was interrupted by a phone call through internal ship's phone network.

"Afternoon, Doctor"—it was Tiffany's voice—"I am afraid that Diane won't be able to come down and help you today with your investigation, Doctor Seinz says that she is feeling rather ill – he thinks it is the sea sickness again."

"Blast it. I was hoping she could help me work out what sort of infective agent this was and where it came from." Alan paused and exhaled a sigh of frustration. "Never mind, I will have to muddle along the best I can – has Diane taken the medication I gave her? If she had, I would have thought that she would have found her sea legs by now."

"Her husband didn't mention it I'm afraid, still, what can you do if patients don't want to be helped?" Tiffany understood the complexities of trying to encourage some passengers to do anything, through her own work.

"Yes, I suppose you are right. In that case I shall move on to Plan B, and, my dear, I look forward to seeing you later this evening for the next installment of the play."

"I'm glad you have remembered about our date, even if I couldn't entice you to a game of beach volleyball."

Alan smiled and clicked off the phone. He turned to find a disapproving Petra eyeing him over her medical reports and said, "Why don't you take that laundry down to the service department, and see if they have a new batch ready for us yet? We seem to be going over the allotted daily amount so maybe you can smile sweetly to your friend in the laundry and get us what we need."

When the disagreeable nurse had left the medical center, he felt instantly better at seeing her retreating form.

He then set out to work at an unprecedented speed, trying to get ahead on the search before the evening. He often checked some of the online databases and archives to which he subscribed, to ascertain the actual nature of the infective process that he was studying under the microscope. He gradually reduced the number of potential candidates for the infection. The deduction eliminated a few solvents that it did not like (inactivating it) and certain temperatures that slowed it down.

As the evening drew closer, Alan was busy posting several queries on private medical forums on the Internet. He paused and looked up as he felt the characteristic tug of the *Ocean Quest* leaving the safety of the harbor of the Canary Islands. It was almost a subconscious feeling of movement and gravity that pulled slightly at the edges of his stomach and he knew they were heading out to the open waters of the Atlantic – next stop Bermuda.

CHAPTER NINETEEN

***

Open Waters
The difficulty of finding a husband

AT LAST THEY WERE back out on the open waters where the air smelled fresh and pure. Everyone was beginning to relax, and get back into their groove from the prior stop at the Canary Islands. Alan had been exceptionally busy – it seemed he had much more on his plate than usual.

He was excited about the evening coming up. He and Tiffany were going to enjoy a delicious dinner and theater production where all the actors were crew and passengers. He knew it was going to be a lot of fun, and couldn't wait to spend some time with Tiffany. Even though they were both on the same ship it seemed like the demands of their careers kept them apart more than together. Alan let out a sigh; knowing things would come to an end soon with the investigation.

As he rapidly dressed for the evening he wondered what knock out dress Tiffany would be wearing. She always looked good and smelled even better. Her scent would draw you in as if in a trance forgetting everything around you.

Of course, he was not to be disappointed. When he knocked on Tiffany's door he was greeted with her big smile and her stunning attire – the low cut dress seamed to accent her in all the right places. It seemed that every bone in Tiffany's body screamed sexy. Alan thought, *maybe we should just forget the dinner and theater and stay in for the evening.* It had been quite a while since they had had time to themselves. But he knew that Tiffany had spent a great deal of time preparing herself for the evening and he wasn't about to disappoint her. So they headed off deep in conversation.

*   *   *

ACT II

PAPA: (*Looking out of window*) I don't see the car. They should be here by now.

MAMA: They? I didn't count on any "they."

PAPA: I mean the car driver and the doctor.

GITA: I think Raja doesn't want to be early or on time. I don't blame him. (Door bell and knock off stage) He's here. (Maid crosses to door)

RAJA: Dr. (*Voice trails off*) Yoshoda.

MAID: (*Quickly*) Come in please. They are expecting you.

RAJA: (*Looks at self in mirror. Runs hand through hair*) (*To self*) Good Evening Mr. (Shakes head) How are you, Mrs.?

PAPA: (*Enters with Gita*) This is Gita, my lovely daughter.

GITA: I'm glad that you came.

RAJA: Thank you.

PAPA: We will go in the dining room. (*Papa quickly leads the way.*) Doctor, please sit here. (*Everyone else sits where they usually sit*) Now tell us all about yourself and your work.

RAJA: There is little to tell. I passed my boards and I want to be a general practitioner.

PAPA: Why not a surgeon? (*Maid is serving guest first*)

RAJA: Too much like being a butcher (*adds quickly*) except that the doctor is trying to heal the patient by removing the infected or troublesome parts.

PAPA: How do you feel about eating meat?

RAJA: I don't. It's not religious with me. I can't bring pain or suffering to animals. If I did eat animals, birds or fish, I would feel like I was a cannibal.

PAPA: (*Clears his throat*) We are vegetarians – by religion.

RAJA: (*Smiles. Every time he tries to eat, there is a question for him*)

PAPA: All religions – well, almost all religions have certain groups within their religions that do not eat flesh. What city do you come from?

RAJA: A very small village. I'm a real country boy.

PAPA: Your family? Are they business or professional people? Or are they politicians?

RAJA: (*Swallows hard*) They're none of those.

PAPA: I'm glad that you don't come from some of those small town politicians. Most of them are grafters but there are some I respect very much.

MAMA: (*Quickly*) I should like to hear about your mother.

RAJA: She was a very brave and good woman. She had seven children, five are girls. She was an inspiration to us. She encouraged us to study to better ourselves.

PAPA: It is my generation that made it possible for the poor to have an education.

MAMA: We always had to pay (*Papa clears throat, gives Mama a dirty look*) (*Maid keeps serving*)

PAPA: There are examinations now the Americans call it scholarships.

RAJA: I went through on scholarships. Now two of my sisters are already studying to be doctors.

GITA: These days there are a lot of women studying medicine.

PAPA: You haven't told me what sort of work your father does.

RAJA: Are you asking me if I am from a high cast? (*Under breath*) I am not of a high cast.

PAPA: We are the merchant cast.

GITA: Papa knows that in this generation casts don't mean anything anymore. (*Papa gives Gita a dirty look*)

RAJA: Unfortunately they do. I know, I've met people's opinions at work, also in small villages and among my acquaintances . . .

PAPA: Yes, yes the educated man is more liberal.

RAJA: Yes, even them. One becomes the brunt of their jokes. (*There is a loud bang off stage*)

PAPA: (*Jumps. Stands up.*) What was that? (*Starts moving*) Women, go under the table. (Women go under the table) Excuse me while I investigate. (*Claps his hands, crossing to door left*) All men come quickly. Women take shelter. (*Mother reaches up to table and rings bell*)

RAJA: I'll go with you.

PAPA: This is my home. I am the first defence. My servants will help me. You are my guest, as a man you will be second in defence. You stay with the women and protect them if the enemy gets past me; it's up to you. (*Papa*

GITA: (*Comes out from under the table*) What do you think that bang was all about?

(*Mama exits to the UC – up center stage*)

RAJA: I hate to tell you.

GITA: (*To mama*) Where are you going?

MAMA: To see how Papa is doing. I'll be back. (*Exits UC*)

GITA: As you were saying – you hate to tell me (*short pause*) what do you hate to tell me? Maybe that you are married?

RAJA: Nothing like that.

GITA: That my nose is too big.

RAJA: Nothing like that. I might as well tell you – you'd get it out of me sooner or later. That noise was my friend shooting off a firecracker.

GITA: Why would he want to do that?

RAJA: (*Shakes and hangs head*) If I needed to get out of here, that is, if your father was asking me embarrassing questions – and you were a dried up . . .

GITA: (*Laughs*) Old maid. (*Laughs*) You were prepared.

RAJA: (*Laughs*) I always do.

GITA: That's cool. You have a sense of humour. I like that.

RAJA: Your father was getting pretty intimate, but that's a father's privilege. Now tell me about you.

GITA: I'm sure my father has already thoroughly briefed you.

RAJA: On what I'd rather not hear.

GITA: Fair enough. After I tell you what you want to hear, then you answer my questions about you. I have so many things I really would like to know about you. As far as about me, ask what you want and I'll answer you if I can.

RAJA: You went to college. What did you major in?

GITA: Mostly how to get a husband.

RAJA: (*Laughs*) You are honest.

GITA: Most of the time.

RAJA: If that was your major, why didn't you graduate with a husband?

GITA: None of them were worth having.

RAJA: (*Laugh, shakes head*) You mean that there never was a special man?

GITA: No.

RAJA: All those years, there must have been someone?

GITA: Are you asking if I lived with a man? (*Sighs, giggles*) There has never been a first.

RAJA: So you are a good girl – just like your father said.

GITA: All fathers say that about their daughters. They like to brag on the virtues of their child. Some may or may not believe it (*Laughs*) Young man beware – did I kiss? If I did I, I won't tell. Like you said, I'm honest – I'm not a prevaricator.

RAJA: Do you want children?

GITA: Now? No, I don't want to be an unwed mother.

RAJA: Do you like kids?

GITA: Yes, but I've had no experience with them around the clock.

RAJA: Will you be willing to honor and obey me?

GITA: (*Turns toward him and giggles*) I'm not a Christian. My turn now.

RAJA: I haven't finished questioning.

GITA: One more question – only you'd better make it a good one because it's your last one.

RAJA: Why would you want to marry me?

GITA: I haven't said I'd marry you – yet. We'll see.

RAJA: Meaning what?

GITA: Meaning I'll ask you questions now. When did you have your last affair?

RAJA: You get right to the point.

GITA: Was she like the run of the crowd? – Gentile, pretty, never been touched? But, oh how deceptive. But you were smart – you gave her up.

RAJA: I want to talk about you.

GITA: If my parents would not give their blessing to our marriage – would you marry me?

RAJA: My mother would go from her grave cursing me. Then the gods would not approve of me – you know that.

GITA: Some modern educated men feel differently about that.

RAJA: Maybe some but some very few men. You know that without a family, you're the walking dead.

GITA: What if I didn't have a big dowry? What then?

RAJA: (*Shakes head*) My older brother would urge, even so far as to somehow force you for a healthy dowry. What's wrong?

GITA: (*Shrugs*) I just feel like I'm a sheep or a goat that's being sold to the highest bidder.

RAJA: I wouldn't go that far. (*Shakes head*) Poor animals. They bring much money into today's market. (*aside*) We won't think about those things. If we do what our parents want, we'll be blessed by the gods. Besides I'm starting to like you. How do you feel about me?

GITA: It's my turn to ask questions. Would you consider marrying . . . (*Mama enters UC*)

MAMA: I wouldn't want your father to think I left the two of you alone. Go on, what were you talking about? (*Papa enters*) (*Rings bell as she talks*)

PAPA: It was just a firecracker. Now you may all relax. Children are so undisciplined these days. Firecrackers! (*Papa takes tea*) (*To mama*) The tea is cold.

MAMA: I'll ring for some hot tea. You'll have it right away. (Rings bell) (Maid appears) Some hot tea right away. (*Maid exits, taking cold tea out, which Mama handed to her*)

PAPA: Everyone sit down and we'll drink chai and go on with supper. (*Maid appears with tea, mama pours, maid brings in hot food*) Raja, you were about to tell me – what is your family cast? Wait, I must write all these good things down. As you know all this goes toward benefits for you in a bigger and bigger dowry. Yes, yes, I am ready to write all of this down. Now, your cast is?

RAJA: (*Spills tea, starts to wipe it up with his napkin*)

MAMA: (*Rings bell, maid appears with dish. Mama motions toward spill*) Help our guest.

RAJA: I need to leave now. Thank you for dinner and everything. (Exits upstage)

PAPA: This is the second time he has hesitated to tell me his cast. I wonder what it is? It can't be a good one but I have ways of finding out. (*Exits left*)

GITA: Don't let Papa find out.

MAMA: How can I stop him?

GITA: It will ruin anything that could go on between us.

MAMA: What is going on between the two of you?

GITA: Nothing and if there would be any possibility, Papa would spoil everything. (*Papa enters*)

PAPA: Computers and FAX machines are wonderful inventions. (*Laughs*) So are private eyes. This is what I have on Raja. He was born in a tiny village.

GITA: Parents are farmers?

PAPA: Don't I wish? He never had a pair of shoes until he graduated from school and entered medical school. (*Mama pulls her breath in loudly*) No, Mama, he did not go to dancing school. He never saw the inside of a museum or had any other cultural advantages. He ate the simplest foods, like rice and dal, day after day. He studied hard. I know now why he didn't want to talk about his cast. Ladies be prepared for this. Are you ready? His cast is the lowest cast. Imagine this, his people clean toilets or worse. His father was known for taking off his clothes and going down in sewers to unclog them when they were stopped up. (*Shudders*)

GITA: All of his siblings are in college or they are college graduates.

PAPA: (*Overriding Gita's words*) The family has no connections – no money.

GITA: He's a doctor.

MAMA: (*Mumbles*) What do I tell the family? Our friends and the neighbors?

GITA: The truth. Come on, there are no casts anymore.

PAPA: I'll find you another young man.

GITA: I don't want (*Imitating Papa*) "another young man."

PAPA: What could you possibly see in that – that son of a toilet cleaner?

GITA: Doctor. This man, with a sense of humour, is a man of values. There is chemistry between us.

Mama/Papa: Chemistry?

GITA: Do you want to ride the elevator up and down and maybe get stuck in it again? Think of the danger of an elevator. It could fall – even between floors.

PAPA: Enough. Enough. Leave me now – I must think this out.

GITA: (*Cries and runs off stage left.*)

PAPA: Was I too hard on her?

MAMA: (*Nods head yes*) Knowing you as I do, you must have another man that would be better.

PAPA: I went into a 5 star hotel because my office phones were in trouble. There was a good-looking blond man, obviously a European, who was also waiting for the phone. During that time we made small conversation about this and that. However, when I heard him say that he had a white Mercedes, I listened. Business and dollar signs were floating in front of my eyes. (*Clears throat*) I learned that he too is a doctor, a Dutchman who has interests in India and that he lives here. Now there's a person to receive an inheritance and support from his father. What do you think?

MAMA: If he is European, he has no cast at all.

PAPA: Forget the cast.

MAMA: Isn't that what is bothering you?

PAPA: We will not talk about cast now. What do you think of him for Gita?

MAMA: If he has so much money, why would he consider your daughter's dowry?

PAPA: Don't you know that the rich always want more money? That's why they are so rich. What else?

MAMA: He's white. Do you want half and half grandchildren?

PAPA: Lots of Dutch in the Orient have intermarried. Yes, there might even be some black in them. Wheat-like for sure. Look at us here at home with many Indians who are also very black.

MAMA: With slanted eyes?

PAPA: Must you be such a racist?

MAMA: Sorry, I didn't mean to be such a racist.

PAPA: That's where racism starts. People don't mean to be a racist, but they spread the word and look the other way when racists act out their atrocities. (Maid brings tea) Did you order the chai? I didn't. Here, save it for later. (Stands) I am going to call Raja and tell him all bets are off.

MAMA: Over the phone? He'll be crushed.

PAPA: Creatures from his cast bounce back quickly. They have nothing to lose. (*Papa exits left. Mama shakes head, yes and no*)

MAMA: (*Sighs*) This is too much for me.

GITA: (*Enters*) Where is Papa going?

MAMA: Papa is not going. He's calling Raja to tell him it's all off between the two of you.

GITA: But I love Raja.

MAMA: Don't worry. Papa's pride will make him find you another doctor.

GITA: I don't want just anybody. I want Raja.

MAMA: I think you'd like to have him now because you can't have him.

GITA: (*Mumbles*) You don't understand. (*Papa enters*)

PAPA: I told that young man a thing or two.

GITA: (*Crying*) What did he say?

PAPA: Nothing.

GITA: Of course, you told him to get lost and he was speechless.

PAPA: I spoke to his answering machine.

GITA: Right now, I should go see him.

PAPA: No, I forbid you to call him or to go and see him.

GITA: Papa, how can you? (*Cries*)

PAPA: No more discussions.

MAMA: Do you want to change your suit before we go to the Manchandas? Or have you forgotten that we are having dinner with them tonight?

PAPA: Woman, why don't you remind me of these things?

MAMA: Sorry. (*Under breath*) I just did.

PAPA: What time are we expected there?

MAMA: We should have been there now.

PAPA: No problem then – we have plenty of time. We'll only be 45 minutes or an hour late. (*Exits left*)

MAMA: (*Rings bell. Maid appears*) Have the drivers ready to go immediately. (to daughter) Never mind Gita, it hurts now but you'll get over it. We all do. (*Exits left*)

GITA: You don't understand. (*Under breath*) You never do. Tell me why I'm completely cut off from Raja? (*Door bell. Maid hurries to answer door*)

RAJA: Dr. Shandra to see Miss Gita. She is expecting me.

MAID: I don't know. Nobody told me.

GITA: It's all right. I'll see him. (*Raja enters.*) (*To maid*) Leave us now. (*Maid starts to exit*) I'll ring if I need you.

MAID: Thank you Miss Gita. (*Exits*) (*Raja pulls off nose, glasses and wig*)

GITA: So, Dr. Shandra. What can I do for you?

RAJA: (*Still taking off disguise*) I fooled you.

GITA: Yes, until you sat down without being invited. What is going to happen to us? Now I'm forbidden to go see you and I'm never to phone you.

RAJA: I'll call you.

GITA: Papa won't let me talk to you.

RAJA: What have I done to be so ostracized?

GITA: It's nothing that you have done. It's all so stupid and old-fashioned. It's your cast. I don't care about casts, but my parents do and I need my parents' blessings.

RAJA: Your dowry and your family's contacts. It's a real dilemma. I can't change their minds nor can I change my cast.

GITA: (*Cries*) I want to see you.

RAJA: And I want to see you. (*He puts his arms around her*)

GITA: (*Laughs through tears*) You touched me and if this hadn't happened, you wouldn't have dared to touch me. (*Raja drops his arms. They both laugh. He puts his arms back around her. They look at each other.*)

RAJA: Let's not think of your father's orders and enjoy the stolen time we have together.

GITA: (Pulls away.) We've used up enough time for now.

RAJA: I'm sorry. Did I frighten you?

GITA: I'm not afraid. It's just that we are going too fast. Would it help if my father spoke to your father? That's the usual way.

RAJA: It could never happen. Because of his work, he smells badly. He's not used to such a big grand home like this one. In fact, all his life he's probably never seen a dining room or even used a phone.

GITA: No dining room? Where does he eat?

RAJA: On a dirt floor with a banana leaf for a dish. He would be so clumsy that he would break something. No, that wouldn't help our cause.

GITA: Has anyone in your family married into a high (*Looks at him*) higher cast?

RAJA: We don't worry about cast. Usually they are all the same – (*Motions with hand*) – low.

GITA: Starting with uncles (*Raja puts his hand low*) Cousins? (*Raja puts hand down*)

RAJA: Sorry. No one.

GITA: When you were growing up, someone that inspired you and your brothers and sisters to study?

RAJA: Of course, my mother.

GITA: (*Holding her breath*) What cast did she come from?

RAJA: I always thought it was the same as my father's but I can't remember anybody ever talking about it.

GITA: What were your grandparents like? The ones on your mother's side?

RAJA: I never met them.

GITA: Your mother's next to kin?

RAJA: I never met any of them.

GITA: That's it. Your mother married without her parents blessings and she was dead to all of them.

RAJA: You must be right. Nobody from my mother's family came to her funeral. I have an idea. I'll ask about it and try to find out more about them.

GITA: I could hire a private detective. Now you must go before the maid gets suspicious and talks. (*They kiss several times*) I'll contact you as soon as I know anything, only when my parents go out. (*Raja exits right*) Where do I find a private detective? (*Yawns. Falls asleep*)

PAPA: (*Enter Mama and Papa upstage*) That was a dull party. All the men bragged about their sons-in-law. I've made up my mind – I'm going to find the richest man from the best cast and Gita will have to be satisfied with any choice.

MAMA: It's late. If you don't mind, I think I'll go to bed.

PAPA: That Raja had some nerve imagining, yes daring to come here – a man from his cast. Woman, I want you to explain to your daughter that I have no cast prejudice, but that there are still many people who do. I want only the best for her. You must start preparing her to marry a man from a high cast. It shouldn't be difficult. Think of the position she'll have and the money. (*Mama has been nodding her head, yawning*) Woman, can't you pay attention to what I am saying? You know that you are getting old. Perhaps you should see a doctor. (*Yawns*) I am going to bed now and so should you. Come on. (*Exits left*)

LIGHTS DIM AND UP RIGHT AWAY

RAJA: (*With disguise at door, U stage*)

GITA: (*X to run to door, whispers*) Don't ring the bell. Just come in quietly. It's best the servants don't know about our meetings. (*They kiss*) What have you found out?

RAJA: Nothing. Nobody's talking.

GITA: There must be someone who knows something about it. I did get a little information from a private detective. He said that your mother came from a very high cast. Mother's father was negotiating a marriage dowry for her with an influential widower of sixty who wanted to remarry and father some children. All was going well until your mother met your father who came to, to . . .

RAJA: Clean the toilets?

GITA: They fell in love.

RAJA: How romantic it must have been. Father was tall and handsome. I guess he could turn on the charm.

GITA: They did everything the right way. Your father's older brother asked your mother's father for permission to marry her. But he said no immediately. Your mother was sent far away to relatives. Somehow, nobody seems to know how your mother managed it but she was able to contact your father. He walked and walked miles and miles in the typhoons in the heat of the barren country. Whatever, he just kept walking. Finally they were reunited and so they ran off and got married. Now her family has totally disowned her and cursed her from their graves.

RAJA: What good will this tragic story do for us?

GITA: Don't you see? You come from one of the high, high casts (*drops voice*) on your mother's side.

RAJA: If it's true, it is still only on my mother's side. The female doesn't count for much.

GITA: Female doesn't count? What do you mean by that?

RAJA: Your father appears to be so cast conscious, he wouldn't consider the female side.

GITA: I thought you would be thrilled with this information.

RAJA: I'm just trying to figure out how best we can use it.

GITA: (*Looks at her watch*) You've got to go now Papa should be here any moment.

PAPA: (*Papa off stage*) Just leave the car on the driveway. I might be going out again tonight.

RAJA: I feel like a thief.

GITA: (*Whispers*) You are. You are stealing his daughter. Put on your disguise. (*Pushes Raja out of U stage door*)

PAPA: (*Mama enters*) Who was that? (*Gita exits left*)

MAMA: Probably a delivery person. I ordered some things to be delivered.

PAPA: Have Gita come here right away. I have something to tell the both of you. (*Mama exits left. Mama and Gita enter*) ((*Papa pauses, see some food on the table, eats*) I have good news for you. (*Both women sit*) The perfect man. In fact, I have been negotiating with his grandfather and grandpa is a rich old man. A politician, way up there in the big government. I am one smart man (*Laughs*). His grandson is well educated of course. He is asking for a big dowry. Never mind, I am willing to pay. Yes, yes now all there is to do is have me sign and the old politician sign and woman, we'll have ourselves a wedding feast. Come, come – where are all the bravos and thank you Papa?

GITA: (*Runs from the room crying*)

PAPA: Woman, what is the matter with your daughter?

MAMA: You surprised her.

PAPA: Any other girl than your daughter would be thrilled.

MAMA: She's not just any other girl. What are your plans?

PAPA: I'm a man of the twentieth and the twenty-first century, so the thing to do is to have the young people meet, that is, if the grandpapa goes along with that. I showed the old gentleman Gita's graduation picture. He seemed impressed with it. Now, this young man can take you to dinner, the theater. I guess that you will have to be a chaperone all over again.

MAMA: Gita is not going to take this easily.

PAPA: What I say goes.

MAMA: When are you going to have the grandfather over for dinner?

PAPA: I told him to come over tomorrow night.

MAMA: Oh, dear me – so soon?

PAPA: It is to be an elaborate dinner with many courses and the finest of service. If we need to put on extra help for service and in the kitchen, be sure to do it. (*Maid enters and whispers to Mama*) Maybe I myself should go into politics. You know, I've often thought about it but something always came up and it wasn't the right time to do it. Now, with this old man who would be a member of our family, the road would be paved for me. I want you to wear a sari to dinner, an expensive one. I would like you to wear the white silk one with all the beads on it. That would look nice on you. Be sure to put on much jewelry. Get Gita to dress up so that she looks her best. Red would be good for her. Now, about the menu – when you have worked it out, let me look it over. (*Telephone rings. Papa exits left*)

MAMA: (*Mumbles*) I always do. (*Papa enters*) Yes Papa. Who was that?

PAPA: Sis had her baby and it's a boy. Think of it – at last I have a boy. He's the first boy in this family.

MAMA: They need us. We must go right away. You'll want to see your boy as soon as possible, won't you?

PAPA: Hurry woman. What are you waiting for?

MAMA: (*Calls out at door*) Gita's big sis just had a baby boy. Papa and I are going to the hospital. This is a special time for Papa. Do you want to come with us?

GITA: I can't come now. I'll drop by later.

PAPA: I'll send the car back for you. But with traffic at this time of day, it might take awhile. We can't wait for you now. (*To Mama*) Come on woman, I want to go now. (*Mama and Papa X US*)

GITA: (*Enters left, X to door up stage. Calls.*) Raja, Raja are you still there? Guess not. (Starts to close door) I wonder where you went?

RAJA: (*Enters*) Under the car.

GITA: Just like a cat. Do you know that you could have been killed?

RAJA: There was no other place to go. (*Kisses Gita. She pulls away. Raja follows her & tries to turn her to him*) I can do better than that.

GITA: Don't you understand? He's dealing with the old man, arranging a marriage for me.

RAJA: I thought he liked me.

GITA: He does, it's only your cast that stands between us.

RAJA: What does this fellow have that I don't have? Whatever he does, I'll do better.

GITA: (*Shakes head*) He likes you all right, but not your cast. I've though and thought and I just can't find the answer.

RAJA: Your father might change his mind when and if he'd try to know me better.

GITA: Be realistic. It doesn't work that way. How much money do you have? (*Raja takes out his wallet, opens it*) A few rubies? That won't do. It's not enough. I thought that if we had much money, we could buy off the old politician.

RAJA: (*Sits*) I am very depressed. And very disappointed. (*Gita goes over to him. Sits on his lap and kisses him*)

GITA: Doesn't that feel good?

RAJA: (*Kisses her*) Unfortunately, our love has many stumbling blocks and I can't think where we can go with it. (*Knock on door off stage*)

GITA: (*Jumps off Raja's lap. Maid opens the door. Man enters. Maid motions him to sit down.*) (*Gita to Raja. Whispers.*) Out, out don't do anything foolish. I'll think of something and I promise you – I'll find a way.

POLITICIAN: I am Raja. (*hands Gita his card*) the governor. And you must be the daughter, Gita.

RAJA: I'm a doctor, also a Raja.

GITA: He's visiting me.

POLITICIAN: I'm sorry that you are ill. You're father didn't tell me.

GITA: He didn't know. Maybe it will pass.

POLITICIAN: Really? I didn't get your name.

RAJA: Dr Raja Kermar with a K. I must go now.

POLITICIAN: That name Kermar. I've heard it before. Of course, now I remember. Please don't go Dr. Raja Kermar. I am related to you. You are my nephew. Your mother was my older sister.

RAJA: Sorry Sir, but I'm afraid that you must be mistaken. I only come from a village.

POLITICIAN: Never mind. Were you never told the story of how my father, your grandfather, disowned your mother because she married against his will? I was not the oldest brother and could do nothing. Bit I did not accept what happened. Still, later, I tried to find your mother and could not. What could I do? I could not disobey my father. You have become a doctor? I am very proud of you.

GITA: Perhaps you can help us.

POLITICIAN: I am a politician. People are always asking me to help them.

GITA: My father chose Raja for me and we both want to get married to each other.

POLITICIAN: Then what is the problem? Dowry can be negotiated.

GITA: It's nothing like that. It is only because Raja's cast is not good enough for my family.

POLITICIAN: (*Explodes*) Not good enough?

RAJA: (*Aside to Gita*) Now you've done it. (*To politician*) It's not your cast, sir. It's my father's cast.

POLITICIAN: History repeating itself. (*Off stage Papa talks*)

PAPA: I sent the car back for her. She didn't come. The car is still waiting here for Gita. Her sister had a boy. She is a new aunt. Family comes first. What is this car in our driveway? Oh, may the gods forgive me. I totally forgot about the Governor and our appointment.

GITA: (*Whispers to Raja*) Go! Go!

RAJA: If you need me, I'll be under one of the cars.

POLITICIAN: Stay here! No family of mine has to go under any car. (*Raja turns back to Papa. Papa enters upstage.*)

PAPA: Sir, I am so sorry that I am so late for our appointment, but my eldest daughter just gave birth to a son and I went to see my first grandson. I just couldn't get my wife to leave. You know how a grandmother is. I see you brought your grandson with you. Young man, I am happy to meet you. (*Raja turns to Papa*) Oh, it's you. (*Loudly*) Get out of my house and never come back.

POLITICIAN: Gladly. (*Turns to go*)

PAPA: No, not you sir. It's that scum standing next to you.

POLITICIAN: This fine young man is my flesh and blood. He is my nephew – my sister's son.

PAPA: Sir, I apologize and beg for your forgiveness. This is all a big mistake.

POLITICIAN: I agree with you. . . a great mistake and I regret having come here. Raja, come along with me. We are leaving.

PAPA: What about the details of the dowry?

POLITICIAN AND RAJA: (*Exits upstage*)

PAPA: (*Follows them*) Can we make another appointment? When could you come to dinner? (*Door closes*) I am a desperate man. Woman, where are you?

GITA: Could I say something? (*Mama enters*)

PAPA: Only if you have a simple solution to the problem.

GITA: Do you want me to appease the politician? And do you really want to make me happy?

PAPA: Yes, yes what is your simple solution?

GITA: Raja is from this politician's cast – it is the highest of casts.

PAPA: No, no you don't understand. I was working out the dowry for his grandson.

GITA: It's simple. Replace his grandson with his nephew.

PAPA: The cast is on the female side. He does not even have the politician's name. Try and fix that. Yes, yes.

GITA: I think I can do that too.

PAPA: That's the trouble. It's always your thinking, your wanting, your ideas – when will it all end?

GITA: In peace Papa.

PAPA: Peace is when I die. I want some peace now. Why have the gods forsaken me? I am a good man, a splendid father and a good grandfather and husband. Woman, aren't I all of these things?

MAMA: Certainly. (*Aside*) If you say so.

PAPA: You see, your Mama agrees with me.

GITA: She always does.

PAPA: I am a ruined man. I can never show my face again. If you don't care about me, what about your poor mother? You marry a nobody and your mother will be disgraced in front of her friends and all the women.

GITA: The politician could adopt Raja. That way, Raja would have the politician's famous name. (*Slight pause*) Your daughter would be the honored wife in a leading family of the highest cast.

MAMA: Papa, only you could make it work.

PAPA: Yes, yes. I've been thinking about that very same thing. If all this hadn't been brought to a head today, I might have worked it out. Now, I have this problem (*paces*) of getting on the man's good side. It could be that he will never want to see me again.

GITA: Just phone him. You don't have to see him right away.

PAPA: I'll never get through to him on the phone.

GITA: You've always told me to think positive. What if?

PAPA: Did you hear that? Another what if? Stop all that "what ifs?" Without your what ifs, you have nothing – zero.

GITA: With your permission, I could call Raja and have him talk to the old gentleman.

PAPA: What if? (*Stops, looks at Mama, looks at Gita*) I can say what if, if I want to. You two women may not. (*Softens*) If it pleases you, you may try to ask Raja to call his uncle.

GITA: Thank you Papa. You are wonderful. (*Hugs Papa*) I'll just go and use the phone in the den. (*Exits left*)

PAPA: (*To Mama*) What are you going to do?

MAMA: (*Looks flustered*) I'm going to tell the servant to call us whenever Raja calls. (*X to exit left*)

PAPA: When he comes here, tell them to be very polite and let him in right away. And let us know the minute he comes. (Sighs) What would I do if I were that old man? I wouldn't have anything to do with a man who insulted my family like I did. (*Pausing*) Would I want to adopt a person whose father's cast stunk, who himself stinks? Adopting a grown man? The only good thing is he'd have free medical advice. (*Slams fist on table*) I wouldn't want anything to do with that slummy family.

MAMA: (*Mama enters pushing maid towards UC door*)

PAPA: Where are you going in such a hurry?

MAMA: I heard a knock at the door.

PAPA: There's a doorbell.

MAMA: His cast may not know . . . about doorbells.

PAPA: Sit, sit down. See, the maid is opening the door. The doctor may be a small town boy, but he is not an idiot. For god's sake, he's a doctor. Did you happen to overhear anything?

MAMA: When? Where? What are you talking about?

PAPA: You passed right in front of Gita, who is talking on the phone. What is she saying?

MAMA: I wasn't listening.

PAPA: Why not? Never mind. Would you say that the doctor likes Gita? (*Mama shrugs her shoulders and her head*) Did you find him to be a stubborn young man? Certainly a mother and daughter talk. Talk woman talk.

MAMA: What do you think about him?

PAPA: He is lazy, gets along with people but has a cold temper.

MAMA: Have you found out if he has had many girlfriends?

PAPA: He had one or two romantic episodes.

MAMA: Did they last a long time? How did they end?

PAPA: I didn't ask.

MAMA: It's something a mother wants to know – like father, like son.

PAPA: I will find out for you before we sign any papers. That is, if we ever get to signing. (*Sighs*) I was just thinking this is our last daughter we have to marry off and (*laughs*) I hope Gita's husband has many, many female children. From the grave my spirit will be laughing at him finding husbands for all of them. Can you hear me laughing? (*Laughs loudly*) (*Mama sort of snickers*)

LIGHTS DIM OUT. MUSIC UP QUICKLY. CURTAIN UP FOR BOWS.

*   *   *

As the lights went up there was a thunderous general applause, completely drowning out the sound of the piped in sitar music that emerged from the speakers under the stage.

Alan was not surprised to see a standing ovation slowly erupting, and he was quick to join them. With Tiffany on his arm, they watched the actors come forward and take a bow. Last to arrive, of course, was Babette, wearing a stunning purple ball gown with a glittering butterfly brooch. The only slightly unfortunate aspect to the whole night was the way she blushed deeply to match the shade of her dress.

CHAPTER TWENTY

The North Atlantic
A question of soil

THE NEXT MORNING AT SEA, Alan was woken up by a phone call from the security center, and the voice of an excited Vince on the other end.

"I have some interesting news, Doc, something that might be interesting for you to hear!"

Alan rolled himself out of bed, over the mumbling form of Tiffany, and stepped out to get himself ready. Her dress was draped over the chair, where it had been thrown last evening, and her shoes lay tossed in the corner. Alan washed up and began putting on his shirt, but he couldn't resist looking back to see the beautiful form of his lover lying there in his bed – the strong curve of her spine, the white flesh of one breast peeking out from where it was pressed against the covers. He breathed deeply, taking it all in, and wondering how on earth he ever came to deserve a woman like her. He bent down to kiss her lightly on the cheek, before quietly making his way out of his cabin. It was a wilder day today; the wind was strong, forcing the ship to power over the huge oceans swells and waves. If Nurse Petra was fed up with her famous 'puking children' a few days ago, then she certainly wouldn't be looking forward to today, because it was going to be a lot worse. Alan knew this weather was going to send people to the medical center in greater numbers.

By the time Alan reached the security center he found Vince overseeing a shift change, and busy barking orders at his staff.

"Doctor?" Vince said, throwing him a broad smile. "Take a seat, I have made some progress on our friend Mr. Montague, or at least, I have found out some things about his associates."

Alan raised his eyebrows at the sheaf of paper that Vince held out. They were some collected sheets of company background, website and news clippings about Secure Holdings PLC; the company Mr. Keriakis owned. The very same Keriakis who had wanted access to the cruise ship back at port, and whose company bank account number came into the possession of Gillais Montague.

Secure Holdings was a shipping firm, but a very specialized one. Its reach was trans-global in nature, with offices in New York, Mumbai and Barcelona, offering its clients the removals and the moving of rare artifacts.

"An art dealer?" Alan enquired.

"Almost, although I suspect that many art dealers use them. These are the people who can come in, secure your painting, your statue, your book or whatever, and keep it in its original condition while it is transported across the world," Vince explained. "Apparently a lot of paintings don't do too well at higher altitude; especially books. Secure Holdings PLC will transport these items as sea-freight to any destination in the world. Apparently they are in the business of outfitting whole galleries, museums and private collections."

Alan read down to the news clippings, a couple of CEO changes, some business news concerning the company maintaining profitability even in the midst of the recession, and one last clipping relating to a museum gallery that had been closed down due to the ensuing scandal that had been cast over its names and that of its suppliers – Secure Holdings PLC.

"Ah, you've got to that bit too?" Vince grinned. "Interesting, isn't it?"

"So it looks like Secure Holdings could be quite a disreputable company; they can provide rare artifacts for your establishment, but the provenance of the items might be questionable...?"

"They might be stolen, counterfeit, found on the black market, that kind of thing I expect. There is probably also a question of customs duty and how much they are actually paying on it, given that it is easy to change the ownership of an item as it moves across the world so often."

"Right, wow!" Alan felt as if he had walked into the middle of a movie. "So the owner of this firm came to our vessel and pretended to me and to the front desk that he was a passenger on board this cruise liner – I wonder what for?"

"And why did Gillais Montague have Keriakis's bank account details in his notebook?"

"Perhaps Montague was investigating them; after all, he did work for Interpol. Perhaps that is why he was killed, because he was onto something?"

"Perhaps," Vince said, "but what about our Cinderella theory, the knickers, and the complementary bottle of poisoned wine?"

"Either Keriakis was working with someone on board this ship, or there is another person responsible... Can you pull the logs on the standard communications going to and from this ship that day?" Alan asked. "Maybe we can find someone phoning Secure Holding's offices twice a day, or another clue that will tell us exactly *why* he was killed."

Vince shook his head. "It would take us weeks to analyze all of that data – all of the phone calls, mobile phone messages, emails, and Internet websites visited over the cruise so far. But we can isolate certain people's records; we can start with Gillais's records and see where that gets us. But we haven't exactly got a lot of time to play with – the vessel had barely left port before the transmitters went off line during that storm."

Alan nodded. "Thanks, Vince. Let me know as soon as you find out something," he said, getting up and walking out of security office.

Coming back to the Medical Centre, Alan found Kelly already at her post, completing the review of medicines that they would have available for the final leg of their journey.

"How is your Ernesto doing today?" Alan asked cheerily, knowing the response it would provoke in the color of Kelly's cheeks.

"Much better – the antibiotics really worked. I was scared there for a while, from what you were saying about this agent, that it would be a resistant strain."

Alan nodded, understanding the danger that the young nurse was talking about. As all infective agents are organic creatures, they replicate and evolve to match their environment at an astonishing rate. For example, every year a 'new generation' of certain bacteria appears and must be treated with stronger and stronger antibiotics. The difficulty comes, however, when the bacteria adapt to the latest antibiotic medication. So there is effectively a race between the development of antibiotic medicines and the bacterial infective agents.

"Yes, surprisingly it seems that this infective agent, although very potent, is not very resistant to modern antibiotics."

"Really? That is quite strange – how does something get so strong without developing resistance to modern antibiotics?"

"Aha – that is a very interesting question." Alan moved over to his workstation where there was a sheaf of printouts with complicated medical diagrams and blown up pictures of the infective cells. "I asked my fellow physicians, on some of the online medical forums yesterday, and we have come up with this rather nasty character as the most likely candidate.

"This infective agent seems to be in a family of organisms that live in a highly specialized environment..." He paused for effect. "The soil generally found close to the coffins of certain graves."

Kelly scrunched up her face. "Yuck! That is gross."

Alan nodded and smiled. "Quite, although not very dangerous, they are highly infectious, living on the peculiar mix of compounds that often surround the soil of crypts. Because they only live in such a highly specialized environment, the general population is rarely exposed to them, and so rarely have time to adapt to antibiotics."

Kelly shivered at the morbidity of the findings. "Well, I guess that is good news for us – anyone infected can most likely be treated easily by one of our ordinary antibiotics."

While agreeing with Kelly's statement, Alan was already questioning the fact that such an organism had introduced itself into the mud on the side of the mysterious crate and how it had survived the dry environment.

"Yes," he muttered to himself. "We may just have to request that the crate be opened in a controlled environment, so that we could see what we are dealing with."

Having said that, Alan sat down again and began working on a plan of attack – this 'bug' would not have the opportunity to see him beaten anytime soon.

*   *   *

Later that night, a party was in full swing in one of the ship's bars where officers and passengers were already mingling freely by the time Alan arrived. His experience had demonstrated that on the longer sea journeys, the officer crew always seemed to party harder. It was as if their 'isolation' on the waves made everyone a little more party minded. Of course, a cruise liner was never really isolated – not with the current modern communication technology. There was always a constant stream of reports and checks with the nearest port, and the home base of that particular cruise company when any cruise liner was on a long sea voyage. The navigators and captains kept each other abreast of weather fronts, sea conditions and the like.

Earlier that day, the *Ocean Quest* had passed very close to another cruise liner of the same company, making the journey in the opposite direction toward Africa and the Canaries.

Alan knew that there was a lot of traffic on the seas these days, and it was fairly usual to see trawlers or oil tankers steaming their way into the horizon as they went about their business. Sometimes, one would see a particular tanker or cruise ship for many hours off the bow of your own ship, if they were traveling at approximately the same speed and direction. There was often an unspoken competition among the passengers as to which vessel was going to overtake which. In the openness of the great oceans, it obviously had more to do with the sea lanes and many ships traveling at approximately the same speed and direction.

Today, the *Ocean Quest* and the *Dolphin Spray* crossed each other's paths at a close distance – less than a quarter of a mile to be exact. Alan was sure that the navigators had subtly adjusted their course so they could 'swipe' each other.

Using the general announcement system, Captain Halvorsen had informed the passengers and crew that, if they wanted to, they could join him on the front deck to wish a safe voyage to their sister vessel, the *Dolphin Spray.*

As the cruise ships neared each other, each captain sounded their foghorns, and the crew and passengers of each vessel could be seen waving.

"Yes, a most agreeable chap," Captain Halvorsen said to the doctor. "I had quite a long chat with the captain of the '*Spray* as we passed and he wished us all the best on our voyage."

Alan knew that captains loved meeting each other out at sea, each sharing bits of gossip and the latest news from their own vessels, before promising to catch up in the drinking establishments of the world's ports, if they ever had shore leave at the same time in the same port.

"You didn't mention our – ugh – recent complications then?" the doctor teased, "…about our French-Belgian?"

The captain looked aghast. "My God no! That would have those old sea dogs talking about my ship for years." He laughed. "But I did tell him to prepare for the norovirus when they reached the Mediterranean, as it seems that a number of ships have had to call a 'Code Brown' in the med over the last few weeks."

Alan chuckled, still surprised how this could make him laugh this many years into his industry.

The bar was busy tonight, but not in the way that Alan would have thought. There were fewer passengers in attendance tonight, and more of the ship's officers – a fact that he found mildly interesting. Usually the passengers such as the Hemmingsworth's and the Seinz's would take every opportunity on the longer sea voyages to avail themselves of every activity, such as those that the entertainment staff had arranged here tonight. This evening, a rather talented jazz pianist was hard at work, his instrument trying to overpower the human voices. Alan was not particularly a jazz enthusiast, so he was more than willing to chat, rather than listen.

One of the reasons for the absence of passengers quickly became apparent. Ralph, the barman, called the doctor over to answer a shipboard phone call. It was Frankie, the casino operator.

"Doc?" said his rather worried voice. "I have a bit of a situation down here – and I think I had better warn you in advance..."

"What is it?" Alan asked, immediately worried.

"Um, it's a Lady Hemmingsworth related incident. She has been causing some issues again down in the casino, demanding that she win every game, and now she won't leave me alone. I'm escorting her up there, it's the only thing I can think to do."

"Really? Can't you keep her down there?" Alan pleaded.

"No can do – uh-uh, here she comes – Lady Hemmingsworth. What a delight, shall we make a move?" Alan heard over the line. "Sorry, Doc," was the whispered reply. "gotta go...."

The line clicked off, leaving the doctor to sigh heavily. It sounded like Lady Hemmingsworth was in full swing tonight.

The duo arrived at the doors to the club where the security doormen allowed Lady Hemmingsworth to come in, but questioned Frankie's access in his telltale casino uniform – a white shirt with sleeve ties, black bow tie, gold trimmed waistcoat, black trousers and a small black hat. He flashed a wink and a thumb's up behind the Lady's back and happily made his way back to his preferred environment.

The Lady's beehive hairdo weaved its way through the crowd as Alan saw that she had already 'enjoyed' the bar in the casino to quite a considerable extent. He watched her tottering hairdo from afar as someone might watch a singular flamingo on a lagoon. It weaved its way towards the nearest affluent man, and then, upon finding a higher ranking officer would turn and weave towards the next on the hierarchical food chain. Seeing Lady Hemmingsworth always made Alan wish that her father had had a vasectomy *before* she had been conceived.

It was only a matter of time before she..., yes..., Alan saw her spot the form of Captain Halvorsen, surely the highest of all the ranking officers in the club tonight. Unerringly, she moved like a warship, all assets forward, throwing aside lesser suitors in her wake as she steamed towards captain.

Alan watched in horror, as she forcefully intersected with the captain. After a brief moment of panic, he seemed to respond predictably. Captain Anders Halvorsen was many things, and one of his qualities was very predictable. When facing a fine specimen of a woman with many sparkling... *attributes, (after all* she was wearing a sparkling bodice and dress), he was totally helpless.

Their conversation and action caused a ripple of amusement surrounding them, and while thinking about the mysterious Lord Hemmingsworth somewhere below decks, probably holding court in his rooms, Alan came up with a plan.

He made his way to the couple and tried – smoothly – to introduce himself into the conversation.

"Captain?"—he sidled up to his elbows—"Lady Hemmingsworth. What a welcome sight you are tonight, but I am afraid that I really must have a chat with the captain about a rather serious issue."

"Oh don't be a bore doctor," Lady Hemmingsworth uttered dismissively as she would a bothersome servant. "But do tell what could be so important as to interrupt our conversation…?"

"Code Brown order, milady."

"Code Brown? My word that sounds intriguing – what is it, a theft? Oncoming storms? Pirates at sea?" she queried, a mocking smile coming across her pouting lips.

"No, a ship-wide outbreak of diarrhea, milady." Alan tried to keep a straight face as he said it.

Lady Hemmingsworth's whole demeanor changed like a cloud before the sun. "Oh, I see. Ship-wide you say?"

The doctor could see her looking at the doctor's hands and the cleanliness of the people around her.

"Ship-wide, I'm afraid, yes. Nowhere is safe from these little bugs, especially anywhere where there is food and drink."

Lady Hemmingsworth's eyes were instantly drawn, to the bar with its accompanying little bowls of peanuts and bar snacks.

"I see." She swallowed. "You know, it has been a pure delight, Captain, Doctor"—she nodded to each in turn—"but you really must stop keeping me from my adoring husband." At that, she turned in her tottering way, and politely asked one of the security doormen to escort her to her room. After she had left, there was an audible sigh of relief throughout the whole club.

"Another Code Brown, Doctor? Do you think we maybe

overdid it?" The captain grinned, looked slightly concerned, but was visibly grateful. "You know, those two help support your salary and mine…, so be nice."

"Thankfully not, Captain, there is no Code Brown at this point, I just wanted to discuss a plan I have to determine the owner of this crate down in the hold."

"Oh, good show. I was thinking we should just chuck the thing into the sea, but, my petty officers told me that would be bad form."

"Yes, well if I am not mistaken, dumping toxic material into the Atlantic is actually a criminal matter."

Alan then outlined the nature of the infectious agent and the strange soil that must be present on the crate.

"My, I see what you mean. Okay, well done, Doctor. We'll give your plan a go tomorrow."

"Thank you, Captain. I hope we won't be disappointed."

Feeling much more at ease, Alan considered that they might just have enough time to clear up this one mystery before Bermuda.

CHAPTER TWENTY-ONE

Bermuda
A pile of bones

"ATTENTION – TO THE CARGO DEPARTMENT chief – would you come to the holding cargo bay and oversee the sea disposal of a large wooden crate in the holding bay immediately please?"

The message was repeated three times over the course of an hour after the midday meal, about two in the afternoon. The passengers, by this time in the journey, were well used to the PA system announcing various ship–wide events, such as islands they had passed, the crossing with the *Dolphin Spray*, the daily weather report and the list of upcoming entertainment.

Alan was sitting in the Control Center while the captain read out the message over the general communications microphone, and wondered just what would happen next, since it was most unusual to hear this type of message. Normally, the internal communication phones would have been used for this type of announcement.

They had chosen the 'quietest' time of the day to make the announcement, to ensure that the maximum number of passengers would have an opportunity to hear it.

The chief of the cargo department was already in the security chief's bad books. He had agreed to spend the day in his quarters not to arouse any suspicion over their plan. With any luck, the doctor hoped that whoever owned the crate would immediately make a complaint or would race to attend to their muddy luggage.

Brrrring! The phone rang, and the captain flashed a grin at the doctor, anticipating an imminent success.

They were both disappointed however, since the person on the other end of the phone was not an irate passenger or a clue as to the crate's owner, but Vince, the security chief.

"Good day, Doctor," Vince said over the speaker phone, "I have some pretty important news – not about your crate, but about the Montague case itself."

The doctor's ears perked up. "Yes, what is it?"

"We've run the analysis of all of Montague's communications, and there were only a handful, but once we had received the permission from the phone companies and the ISP's – the Internet service providers – we managed to get the reports and were surprised at what we found."

"Well don't keep us in suspense – what are your findings, man?" the captain demanded, sitting on the edge of his seat in anticipation.

The security chief told them, and the captain swore.

"I should have known." Alan thumped the desk. "It was obvious – staring at me in the face."

"The benefit of hindsight...," the security chief's tiny voice said over the internal communicator's speaker.

"Have we sent a security detail to the cabin?" the captain asked, getting up from his seat.

"Yes, sir. On their way now."

"It's not just the calls..., it is all connected," Alan said, realizing the impact and implication of what they had just learned.

"What on earth do you mean?" asked the captain, capturing the doctor with his eagle-like stare.

"Vince – can you meet me in the cargo hold?" said Alan rapidly. "Captain, bear with me. If you would accompany me, I think I know exactly what is going on here."

"Will you please explain yourself, Doctor," the captain barked as Alan led the way, at a trot, down the deck and to the crew access elevators in the center of the ship.

"No time, sir. Trust me, if my instincts are right, then Vince's security detail will not find anyone in the cabin, they will be down in the cargo bay trying to get in and trying to get rid of the evidence. It was so obvious now that I think about it."

A few breathless seconds later another phone call from the security officer confirmed that the cabin was empty, and that no one had seen the occupants.

The ship's doctor and the captain raced to the cargo bay, which was relatively quiet at this time of the day during the usual crew break time, only made more so by the fact that Vince had asked for some of the crew to take the whole afternoon off while they conducted their 'operation' to discover the owner of the infected crate. At the doors to the main cargo bay, the captain smoothly assumed command, ordering the guard to accompany them as they opened the door and descended into the bowels of *Ocean Quest* via the metal ladder.

It wasn't long before they were walking in front of the main hold, in front of the wire luggage cages. Then Alan rapidly led them to the wooden crate that was believed to be the source of the infection.

They heard a thump and hushed voices in the darkness. The captain motioned for the doctor to hold back while he took the guard's long and heavy flash light and walked forward, with the security guard flanking him.

Where is Vince? Alan thought wildly. *He would know how to handle this.* No one on board the *Ocean Quest* carried any sort of weapon, it being a civilian vessel run by a cruise line company. So, if they were faced with anything like a gun, then they would have to find some other way to negotiate the capture of the criminals. What the doctor had seen in the past was that the heavy-set security guards' size was usually enough to overpower any drunk, disorderly or rowdy passenger. But against professional criminals…?

There was another muffled sound and a creak as Captain Halvorsen stepped out into the circle of light with the security guard at his side, and turned on the flash light at full beam towards the barely visible crouched figures.

"You! Stop by order of the captain!" he shouted, as the torchlight caught the suspects squarely in the eyes, blinding them temporarily. They looked like a couple of raccoons caught in the act of dispersing the contents of a garbage can. The guard jogged forward.

There was a thump as the side of the crate they had been wrestling with to open. By now, the broken joints of the crate gave way and into the circle of the captain's torch, tumbled its macabre contents – a pile of disintegrating bones.

"Careful! Don't touch the bones!" Alan called out, to warn the security guard, as he moved forward to take a rough hold of Doctor and Diane Seinz.

The academic duo had been opening the now spilt crate, and by the two large duffel bags at their feet, they were obviously planning to remove their contents and spirit them away, fearing that the whole crate would be disposed of as the PA announcement had declared.

Within moments their party was joined by the hurrying form of Vince and his team of other security guards to take the Seinz's into custody.

"Doctor, Diane," the security chief growled, "I am taking you into custody according to Maritime Law, on behalf of the Order of the Captain of this vessel, you will be held until such a time as we reach a court of law, where you will be charged for the transportation and smuggling of hazardous materials. You have also been implicated in the murder of one Gillais Montague. Do you understand what I am telling you?"

The Seinz's blinked, and the doctor, worriedly, shook his head as the security chief continued, "You have all the common rights as described by Maritime Law, of which you will be briefed when you are secured in your cabin."

"Montague?" Diane suddenly burst out, her usual astute features twisted with fear and shock. "Why on earth would we want to kill Montague – he was our dealer."

"Perhaps the doctor can explain that?" Vince turned to Dr. Seinz, who was hanging his head in guilt. "Is it not true that you had grown suspicious of your wife's affair with Montague? That you used her skills and laboratory supplies to find a way to remove Gillais from the picture? What better way to do it but out on a cruise where no one could trace you?"

Doctor Seinz said nothing, just looked guiltier as Vince nodded to the guards. "Confine them to their cabins, remove all luggage and personal belongings, and isolate their communications until we get to Bermuda tomorrow."

The pair was marched off and the three leading officers aboard the ship looked at each other in surprise.

"You know one thing, Doc," the captain said.

"What's that, Captain?"

Anders indicated the pile of infected bones at their feet. "If I only knew they were going to bring this poor soul on board I would have charged them an extra ticket!"

*   *   *

The next day the *Ocean Quest* docked at Bermuda, a British Protectorate. They had already informed the port authorities ahead of their arrival and so the Royal Bermudan Constabulary at the docks met their party, and the Seinz's were taken into custody ready for transport back to Athens.

"Although, it turns out that there are many multiple charges to be levied against them, it will be a nightmare trying to sort out the jurisdiction powers, and I imagine that the Seinz's will be transported from one port of the world to another for the next six months as different crimes are heard in each prosecuting country," Alan explained to Tiffany while sitting on the veranda of a restaurant in Bermuda.

They had each been given an extra twenty-four shore leave as Captain Halvorsen thought the cruise could do with an extra day on this paradise island. Alan knew that one of the reasons – aside from frayed nerves and many papers to be signed at Bermuda's Customs and Constabulary Offices – was the extensive cleaning of the hold that the captain had ordered, and the proper storage of the relics that the Seinz had been trying to smuggle to America.

"So, they were relics that the Seinz couple was transporting illegally then?"

"Yes, and that will only be one of the charges against them – a few well-placed phone calls from the Captain deduced that at Vatican City, where Doctor Seinz had been working, there was a whole different set of questions. There was indeed a whole area of the vaults, underneath the Vatican, that had been cleaned out. The Vatican City authorities did not realize that there had been a theft, because Dr. Seinz was the only archaeologist on the scene. When one of the Fathers was making a regular check of those vaults, he discovered that Seinz had stolen the relics. There was evidence that he and his wife were definitely planning to skip town and transport the stolen relics to America. The value of some of the smuggled items would garner a great financial lotto. And if they would sell them to the Secure Holdings PLC Company associated with the mysterious Mr. Keriakis, their take would still be very sizeable. No need to worry about not having retirement funds for that couple. Secure Holdings would sell them on the black market, or even ransom them back to the Vatican."

"Oh my word! So they are responsible for theft, smuggling, and transport of hazardous materials?" Tiffany sounded baffled.

"Yes, quite. As soon as I discovered that the organism came from the soil that surrounds coffins, I grew suspicious, there were alarm bells ringing in my head. I couldn't fit all the final pieces together."

"Well, thank God that no one was seriously hurt in the process – a grave bug indeed." Tiffany shivered in horror, pulling her cotton shirt over her shoulders, and hiding the 'strappy' thin top that she was wearing underneath it. "But how does Montague fit into this? We do know that he was in contact with Mr. Keriakis. We also know that Mr. Keriakis tried to come on board this vessel in Barcelona...?"

"I presume that he was trying to gain access to either the crate or the Seinz's. At that point, you see, Montague was already dead. Therefore, he couldn't secure the contact between Secure Holdings and Seinz. I imagine that Mr. Keriakis was growing suspicious or angry and was trying to close the deal early, and get the crate before it made the long trip across the Atlantic.

"What clinched the case against the Seinz couple were the transcripts of the communications between Diane Seinz and Montague. It appears that they had fallen in love, or at least, in lust. Gillais Montague, being an undercover Interpol officer knew Secure Holdings well and knew all the international networks that the Seinz's would need, to pull a job like this one off, and so he offered his services – he was a corrupt Interpol agent."

Tiffany shook her head in amazement and sipped her cocktail.

"Little did either side know that Diane would fall in love with Montague, and it appears from the transcripts that Diane was leading a passionate affair right under her husband's nose. It was she who suggested that Gillais Montague ask to get posted to this cruise while he brokered their deal with Mr. Keriakis, just so they could get the opportunity to be together."

"So," Tiffany cut in, "Obviously Dr. Seinz was livid. He must have been enraged at their carrying on."

"Absolutely," Alan said, nodding emphatically. "He must have planned the murder before he even came on board the cruise. As they had planned their boarding very carefully – moving their crate and themselves at the very last possible minutes, meant that Dr. Seinz could secure some of his wife's supplies from her microbiology laboratory. I guess he carried his supplies of syringes and the *Digitalis* on his person, and subsequently brought a bottle of wine as a 'gift' for Montague during the voyage."

"And here comes the *very* chilling thought – that he must have had help with his operation," Tiffany filled in. "You told me about the communications that were tampered with the night of the storm?"

A dark shadow passed over the doctor's face. "Yes, I have no proof, and only the testimony of Dr. Seinz will prove me right or wrong. I strongly suspect that the sudden appearance of Rick Hammer, just before the cruise set sail in Rome, to be highly suspicious."

"Really? It does sound odd that he would show up then, especially considering what you told me about the navigation engineer's character..." Tiffany pondered, taking Alan's hand and squeezing it affectionately.

He nodded. "Yes. There are just too many coincidences and questions." he looked out towards the pastel colored beaches of Bermuda and to the ocean beyond. "Rick Hammer turns up in Rome just before we set sail, asking for a job at the same time that Dr. Seinz was planning the French-Belgian's murder and his smuggling operation.

"Rick knew my cruise work schedule, and was enraged when I disrupted his plans, as if he wanted me kept at sea in Alaska. Was he pumping me for information about the cruise particulars? Yes. What electronics was he building and what else was he doing with the radio antenna while we were traveling the waters of Alaska? Was he figuring out how to dismantle a transmitter to stop the news of Montague's death getting ashore?" Alan shrugged helplessly. "Also, how did Seinz know when and how to board at the very moment that there would probably be the least security checks? How did the Seinz's get down into the cargo hold when we caught them, without meeting the guard Vince had posted – they must have had some inside information as to the internal layout of the *Ocean Quest*."

"We will find out," Tiffany assured her companion. "Just wait until the Seinz's are questioned, I am sure the truth will come out then."

Alan nodded, feeling better already.

"And the bones – whose do you think they were?" Tiffany asked. "It sounds like an action film doesn't it – the relics of some mysterious figure in an unknown part of the Vatican's Vaults."

"Aha, that is the question." Alan's eyes twinkled. "Who could have been so important to risk everything, your career and your marriage, to smuggle across the Mediterranean?"

"A saint?" Tiffany guessed.

The doctor shrugged. "Who knows, hopefully the truth will come out, as you say, but for now the information will be held classified by the police investigation and the Vatican. An important Saint? One of the Disciples? Someone so important that the Vatican cannot reveal whom they suspect it is?"

Tiffany's face lit up with the adventure. "Well, apparently Saints' bones have miraculous properties, so tell me now, Doctor Mayhew, any miraculous events happening to you recently?"

Alan Mayhew peered into her eyes, thinking of a number of things that he couldn't even begin to say. For a wild moment his heart jumped and he wanted to tell this lovely, intelligent woman that he was already blessed, and that every day with her was a miraculous event. Smiling at his schoolboy romanticism, Alan took her hands in his own and, leaned over to kiss her cheek.

"Well, I am not sure I feel very Holy right at the moment, but I would say that I *am* quite blessed." He stood up and, taking the assistant cruise director by the hand, he led her off the veranda to the beach where they would walk along the surf.

EPILOGUE

A five-hundred year old bacterium
The flesh now earth, and here my bones,
Bereft of handsome eyes, and jaunty air,
Still loyal are to him I joyed in bed,
Whom I embraced, in whom my soul now lives.

The death of Cecchino dei Bracci – epigram by Michael Angelo

THESE WERE MICHAEL ANGELO'S own descriptive words of what would become of the bones of his very dear friend, Cecchino dei Bracci.

The poem had been found together with Cecchino's remains in one of the Vatican's crypts when Doctor Seinz had worked in the subterranean dig underneath the Holy City.

Since this discovery had not been catalogued or recognized as saintly relics, but were nonetheless of immense value to any museum in the States when it came accompanied of the parchment written by Michael Angelo's hand, the archeologist thought – and rightly so – that the entire relic would fetch a handsome price.

The doctor and his wife had managed, as Alan had deduced, to crate the bones and, with Gillais Montague's help, load them aboard the *Ocean Quest* at the right moment. Gillais had apparently flashed his Interpol badge at the porter – Stefano – and had menaced him of severe reprisals, if he would breathe of word of the presence of the crate aboard the vessel.

Although an informed microbiologist herself, Diane Seinz had not taken into account the fact that the bacteria, which surrounded her husband's find would be re-activated once exposed to water and a renewed supply of oxygen. The bacteria had lain dormant since Cecchino's interment around 1543.

"Extraordinary," Alan mumbled to himself when he finished reading the forensic archeological report that had been issued by the Smithsonian Institute. One of the sentences contained in the report had also attracted his particular attention: "*However, the number of possible distinct prion strains is likely far smaller than the number of possible DNA sequences, so evolution takes place within a limited space..."* such as in the confines of a coffin, Alan had surmised.

The Smithsonian had offered their able assistance – at the Vatican's request – whence their scientists had heard of the strange toxicity of the bacterium.

The report was lengthy to say the least, but Alan's insatiable thirst for knowledge had seen him reading it hours after hours – not noticing the time, which was, in fact, "extraordinary" for him.

In the intervening weeks since the Seinz's arrest, the authorities had finally tracked Rick Hammer down all the way to Tunis where he had been hoping to find a boat that would take him to the Middle East. He had tampered with the transmission and communication systems on board the *Ocean Quest* in the hope that Montague's death wouldn't have been the subject of immediate reporting. However, Diane's clumsiness and recklessness, while in total ignorance of her husband's intention to murder her lover, had forced the issue and, upon Vince's further investigation, the plot had been uncovered.

Months later, as he was writing this part of his memoirs, Alan was reading Michael Angelo's poem and was, once again, amazed at the foresight of the man.

~ End ~

Paul Davis MD

Cruise Ship Crime Mysteries

The Curious Cargo of Bones

Paul Davis MD is the author of *Cruise Ship Crime Mysteries: A Medical Murder Mystery; The Curious Cargo of Bones and the upcoming novel, The German Intrigue.* He was trained in Family Practice and Emergency Medicine in Canada, the United Kingdom and the United States. Dr. Davis uses his insider knowledge, as his novels are based on his ten-year career as a cruise ship doctor. He currently lives in Canada and is the director of a medical specialty group.

Visit his websites at:

http://www.cruiseshipcrimesite.com

http://cruiseshipcrime.wordpress.com

Dr. Paul Davis is available for lectures and readings. For information regarding his availability, please contact Skye Wentworth, Publicist, at 978-462-4453 or email skyewentworth@gmail.com.